GUTTING
THE MONKEY

(Searching for Enlightenment The Hard Way)

This is the incredible story of Billy Halverson. Follow his strange journeys; thru dark jungles, across sun scorched deserts, and along dangerous streets, as he attempts to find a way out from the abyss.

As told by: James Iverson
and
P. Farcy
Revisions by J.W Iverson

Argus Enterprises International
New Jersey***North Carolina

Gutting the Monkey© 2011 All rights reserved by John Iverson

A-Argus Better Book Publishers, LLC

For information:
A-Argus Better Book Publishers, LLC
9001 Ridge Hill Street
Kernersville, North Carolina 27285
www.a-argusbooks.com

ISBN: 978-0-6155503-2-9
ISBN: 0-6155503-2-0

Book Cover designed by Dubya

Printed in the United States of America

"Monkey on Your Back"—a phrase meant to describe the voices (Monkey) that seem to come from somewhere just over the shoulder. The Monkey pushes us to release our worst inner demons, such as: drugs, violence, and deception. The Monkey can only be destroyed by attacking with ferocity equal to the primate's feral nature – usually a "Gutting" will suffice.

TABLE OF CONTENTS

<u>Overture/Forward</u>

Author's note—The majority of this book has been taken from the Diary of Billy Halverson.

This is a book about pop culture, redemption, danger, and the darker side of adventure. However, in some respects it is equally about music and how songs can conjure memories, both good and bad. In order to adhere to the theme, please cue the song "Marque Moon" by Television, before you begin reading this book. If you do not have the song on Vinyl, I Pod, tape, CD, or can sing....then by all means "*go get it.*" I'll wait until you get ready.

waiting.......

still waiting.........

Okay. Push play.

First off, I would like to get the "*Dedication"* out of the way. This novel is to honor my friends and family, many of which you will find listed in the acknowledgements. But, more than anything it has been written to provide a lesson for my nephews and nieces. I regret that a better example was not set by me, and while you were growing up, I was gone, lost, and bound for places off the map.

It has been my greatest of pleasures to have been the "the crazy uncle", much more than being "just plain crazy." However, at this stage of my life, I am a wiser (if not better looking) version of the man you knew as children. And so, I am sorry for not have been a better teacher and example. For...although it is certain that all of you got some good attributes from me, there were many more qualities that I failed to properly demonstrate.

It gives me some comfort to think that you all may have got a heightened sense of adventure from me. However, I failed to also teach the most important thing; *"nothing outside is of any value, without virtue and honestly on the inside."*

So...take this offering—my second novel, as an apology of sorts. Here are words to remember: *Strive hard to be what I am, strive harder to be... not as I was.*

And

Now

You

May

Begin

<u>Overture continues – Words from the Authors</u>

A long time ago Billy Halverson did more acid (except for Syd Barnett and Peter Green) than was humanly possible. He then sought out perilous adventures. Some of this story is from that trip...maybe all of it.....maybe none of it.

Introduction—Search and Destroy

To state that I was not born with a Monkey on my back would be an accurate declaration. That type of birth would have made for a very difficult delivery. The Monkey did not come into my life until well after my own conception; to claim otherwise would be the ramblings of an insane man. Maybe I am and maybe I'm not ... of that others can render judgment. I came from a good family, attended catechism on weeknights and went to Church on Sundays. My five brothers and sister were very close, with the kind of relationship that would remain supportive as long as we lived. Having a big family meant that there was always someone to play sports with, take fishing, or do any of the other activates kids do. We may not have had much money but it didn't cost much to have a dirt clod fight, collect bugs, or play hide and seek. There were no video games or internet in those days to rot our blank slate minds, so most of our hobbies and games involved playing outside. The absence of gamer technology, cable T.V, multipurpose phones made indoor playtime a complete waste of time, thereby increasing the lure of the outdoors, contributing greatly to my love of nature. It was fortunate that I was not exposed to graphically violent computer entertainment, for if that had happened, there is no telling the kind of miscreant that might emerged from my youth. There was already a violent seed germinating in my brain that promised dark times. All it needed to sprout was fertilizer made with nightmare compost. A predisposition to seek out danger and violence boiled deep inside me, just waiting for the right catalyst to make it grow, which made being victimized by bullies, or video games like "Call of Duty," or "Grand theft Auto" unnecessary. I already was hard-wired to seek out bloody confrontations.

I was somewhat of a rarity among my peers as throughout high school there was no real drug use. Except for smoking a little weed on weekends while listening to "Space Ritual" by Hawkwind, my partying was limited to a six-pack and a few shots of tequila. By that time my friends had already began experimenting with cocaine, hash, and acid.

I completed high school as the country was leaving behind the idealistic hippie culture, exchanging John Lennon for John Delorean, opting for a lifestyle on the opposite end of the spectrum—the materialistic narcissism of yuppie-dom. In the blink of an eye, American Universities went from "Black-lights and Dreamers" to "Black-Operations and Beamers". The accepted usage of pot—among youthful cool people considered to be culturally relevant—evolved, making cocaine the drug of choice for students and jet-setters alike. The American aspiration went from "a day's pay for a day's work", to "everything now for everybody." It was a perfect marriage between drugs that insisted on total devotion with an American public devoted to nothing but extravagance. Everybody wanted to kiss the bride and throw rice ... or better yet ... dice.

It became obvious after high school that I was not immune to the lure of hard drugs and took them as others tilted back cocktails. But, as bad as my addiction became with the passage of time, I never stooped so low as to call it a disease. It was very clear to me that comparing drug use to an unfortunate malady diminished the plight of those unfortunate individuals contending with an illness beyond their control. Nobody ever went to the store to buy a bottle of cancer, or visited a midnight crack house to smoke-up some polio. At some point there is always a voluntary choice when it comes to alcohol or drugs. I traveled around the world, but have yet to hear a story about someone being kidnapped at gunpoint, duct-taped to a chair, forced to drink some Jack Daniels, and snort some free railers (lines of coke). So whatever reasons given to explain my descent into drug-hell, they are only meant to be lessons for others that might ignore their gifts, in favor of (as the "Allman Brothers" wrote of) *Midnight Ramblings*.

There are no excuses, nor would I choose to give any, because there aren't any to speak of without coming across like a pathetic "*woe is me*" cry-baby.

I enlisted in the Marines after graduating hoping to be sent to Viet Nam. The war had ended a few years earlier. But there were still rumors that it was only a temporary lull in the fighting, as the instability of Asia and our own country (following Nixon's resignation) made it clear that things were going to flare up again. The "new and improved" counterinsurgency might not be located in Viet Nam. Quelling the chaos in the region might require troops to be sent to Laos, Cambodia, or maybe a direct confrontation with the Chi-Coms before they amassed too many nuclear devices. It didn't matter where they sent me because either way I was 'good to go!'

At that point in my life, I foolishly considered the opportunity to fight for the red, white, and blue a patriotic honor, well worth dying for. If the situation escalated, resulting in our government calling up the military again, I wanted to be among the first to saddle up. However, it is doubtful that the eagerness to ship out would have been so pronounced if I had experienced the aggressive foreign policy of future decades. That kind of misplaced bravado would have caused me to have second thoughts about having even a spitball fight, as long as those kinds of assholes were leading the charge.

The transition into becoming a Recon Marine Team Leader was a relatively smooth one. I went into boot camp in freakish physical shape. Since my goal was to eventually get accepted into a Recon detachment, the previous year had been devoted to running, doing countless sit-ups, pull-ups, and boxing. After scoring the high score on the physical fitness test— for the entire series (out of nearly 400 Marines) at the end of boot camp, I was promoted and became very confident that soon there would be an invitation to test for entry into a Recon or Scout/Sniper unit. There was no direct transition from boot camp into Recon. All candidates had to first complete an M.O.S school for a primary specialty, before getting the chance to go through Recon Indoctrination and hopefully get accepted into the elite unit. Field Radio and Wire Communications was my primary job description, which involved cross-training as a forward observer. The ability to navigate, plot mission routes, and correct Naval Gun fire, Artillery, Air-strikes was instrumental in getting into Recon. It certainly didn't hurt that I possessed the stamina of a wolverine. Although some would say that it was actually the same amount of brains and caution of a wolverine.

After attending numerous schools; including Jump, Jungle Warfare, Combat Swimmer, and Amphibious Recon at Little Creek, my platoon got sent to West Africa. Our orders were to act as special advisers to friendly African nations, instructing foreign troops on how to conduct elite insertion/extraction techniques, insert demolition, and how to correctly setup ambushes. It often seemed like a waste of time. The African military seemed more intent on learning various ways to cut off heads, pillage, and torture, rather than learn how to observe the enemy without giving away your position.

We started in Morocco at the Northwest tip of the continent. Once there, we stopped briefly to pick up some UDT guys, spend a few days on shore-leave, then continue on a southerly heading, down through Senegal, Ivory Coast, Sierra Leone, and Gabon.

The mission required us to set up shop in or near the embassy for an undetermined amount of time in each country, instructing their military along the way. Morocco was a beehive of commercial activity, every citizen buying or selling something. Other than that, it was a relatively boring shore-leave. In fact, the only thing that really stood out about the country was the amount of times bearded merchants tried to convince us to buy a carpet or a tapestry. The Moroccans were the most aggressive salesman on earth. It was not enough to say "no" to their sales pitches. The only way to declare there was no intention of buying cheap rugs usually involved a few hard shoves. When the shoves failed to stop the harassment, another form of persuasion was used to get the merchants away; by touching them on the face with the left hand, each seller returned to their individual stalls lining the road. The Moroccans believed that the left hand was dirty and was only used for ass-wiping; apparently they did not know how to use soap and water.

As we traveled further south along the western coast the training began. The days were mostly spent teaching IBS (rubber boat) silent beach entry, high speed cast and recovery, rappelling out of helicopters, Spie-Rig operations, and inland bush recon. At night we demonstrated the proper way to set up an ambush using claymores, how to place trip wires across trails, the concealment of booby traps, the proper way to assemble death snares using trees, and creating L-shaped kill zones. It was a third world environment, wrapped in a forth-world shit-hole, inside a fifth world continent. Africa was a county where disease and death could be seen just about everywhere you looked. Senegal wasn't much different.

Occasionally, our team caught glimpses of Nile Monitors, Warthogs, and Oryx. However, that occurred only if we went deep enough into the bush, far away from the stench of humans and garbage. When on a mission, we bivouacked in the shrubs, a small distance outside the slums. It was not the most pleasant environment. No matter what direction we looked, all that could be seen was a depressing ensemble of poverty-stricken children, lepers, and paramilitary warlords. Outside of the base camp or town, every adult male we came across was armed with Russian surplus AK's, hatchets, or rusty blades removed from tilling tools. The AKs were in such poor shape, the chance of a misfire, or jam, was much more likely than the successful emptying of a clip. Still ... it was better to treat any weapon as if it had the potential to put holes in the intended target Regardless of whether the Africans had industrialized rifles or makeshift edged weapons, each man had one thing in common—the yearning to steal anything not secured to our bodies.

This was the real African wildlife, not the exotic animals on T.V shows like Wild Kingdom or Disney. The Warlords, forgotten wretches, slaves populating the poor nations we visited were the real predators and prey of the African landscape. It was during my travels through Africa that two events transpired. Each changed my life forever, thereby giving birth to the sinister beast; a beast that before the deployment overseas merely existed as a spark, an itch, maybe even a sneaking suspicion.

The first thing that influenced me in a detrimental way was somewhat mundane when compared to the dangers of the African bush. We had been waiting for several hours for the helo's to show up so we could begin the "Cast and Kill" instruction. While we waited a sound reached us, familiar, conjuring pictures of home.

From a Navy Seabee's cassette player, somewhere off in the distance over a dune, I heard the familiar words and chords of Iggy Pop's "Search and Destroy" off the album Raw Power. It was situational music for situational ops.

While preparing to instruct on the shoreline, one of the Senegalese infantryman produced a small amount of cocaine laced with heroin, purchased from a local tribesman. No matter what swamp, jungle, or dune concealed my team, tribesmen ingeniously found ways to appear out of thin rancid air with drugs. The tribesman had many characteristics in common; yellow teeth, fake gold jewelry, slavery branding—the most obvious being disfigured toes and fingers resulting from numerous breaks. They spoke in a dialect that sounded like an offshoot of Bantu, garbled with a variety of French and English cusswords. As we ingested the drug, the tribesman stood off to the side watching intently, hate in his face; which caused me wonder if the shit had been whacked with strychnine. *Fuck it ... sink or swim,* I thought.

The concoction of powder was known as a Speedball. But Cannonball would have been a better name. When snorted it would produce a feeling like being shot out of a cannon and staying airborne until morning, but once the sun came up, the inevitable headache would feel like being struck by a cannon ball. I did a blast into each nostril. Within seconds every essence of my body took notice and decided that this was the thing that I had to have in my veins from that moment on. It felt like an epiphany, finding a true God, a brand new deity's whose sphere of influence insisted all converts must seek solace on bended knee. It was as if the speedball was saying to my brain *"you incomplete me!"*

The collision of my brain and cocaine created an addiction that would take over two decades to beat. The lure of drugs for someone with my chemical imbalance instantly became as important as oxygen to the lungs, or blood to the heart. My curse, or luck as it may be, was having the ability to never physically show any signs whatsoever of being an addict.

Throughout my usage, the only appearance that I gave off was that of a high-caliber athlete, so hiding my problem was not difficult at all. However, with every lie told came another stab into the soul.

Since I showed no outward characteristics of being a coke fiend, it was relatively easy to deceive others about my condition, almost as easy as deceiving my own instincts.

Lying comes natural to an addict and it has been said (quite accurately) that..... *"there is no better liar then a drughead"* but maybe it is more accurate to state *"there is no better drughead than a liar."*

Solving such a paradox is nearly impossible. It was like attempting to determine which came first; the chicken or the egg, an unanswerable inquiry demanding lateral thinking beyond normal thinking, or at least beyond my own. Thereby, to ask questions such as: which came first the drughead or the liar or which came first good Billy or bad Billy leaves only one answer – Yes. Some riddles should remain riddles.

My second life-altering occurrence (after being exposed to cocaine) happened coincidentally that same night, while hanging out with some arty guys previously met at Camp Zuckeran. They invited me on one of their nightly excursions to a village several miles outside of Senegal Proper; located roughly between the Sine-Saloum Delta and Brikama. The reason for their trek was to trade C-rats—mission food packs—for oral sex with a couple of native prostitutes. After seeing the condition of the village and of the woman themselves, I wisely passed, not wanting to get one of the multitudes of high-bred high-octane, super-resistant venereal diseases. In the same regard, being a peeper was as unacceptable as hanging around when the arty guys shot their loads. I plotted a course back to the Navy dock on the map and headed back to base camp. Probably, under the circumstances an unwise decision, but getting out of the area fast was a priority, as an intense feeling of shame was creeping up my spine for accompanying these assholes and risking a case of the clap.

I had a .45 automatic that was capable of making an exit hole the size of a fist, and fired a round that would knock down just about anything wishing to eat me—be it human or animal. Most guys I worked with preferred a .45 sidearm, believing that firing a smaller caliber bullet was much the same as shooting from the ladies tee. I had the right weapon and could navigate the route with ease, so the danger of something dire happening seemed remote.

That was the cocaine talking. In truth, being an American alone in the African bush was incredibly stupid, even with a .45 Penetrator. I was only few miles from the village when a wrong turn was taken, a mistake resulting from out- of- date reference points, not incompetent maps reading. The only way to correct my route and get back on track was to get on a narrow deserted gravel street that passed through a decaying mass of ramshackle tin huts. All of the structures appeared to have been thrown together without much planning, surely an attempt to make the heap of tin and plywood pass for a small city. However the site failed miserably, if the goal was to impress, as the tin, planks, tires, and scrap wire created just another abandoned and decrepit relocation project, rather than a growing metropolis.

At the end of the alley there was a tangle of very small human limbs protruding from underneath the flattened cardboard boxes. I pulled out my weapon, glanced around to make sure nobody was watching, and then flipped the cardboard off the bodies. The image forever changed my worldview, and destroyed whatever commitment to any type of higher power.

There was no rational way to accept the mutual existence of a higher power and the five or six dead children under sheets of cardboard and plywood. Some of the dead were tiny as babies, and were strewn about like garbage, among fruit peelings, and rusty cans. I stumbled back, while reminding myself that any sound would draw attention to the gruesome discovery. I held back the vomit undulating up my throat like a thick wave of putrid jelly and took several deep breaths.

This was not the time to be careless; warlords roamed throughout the countryside, and none of them would be too pleased to find me at their obvious dumping ground. I examined the bodies for any clue of life. However, upon closer inspection it was plain to see from the advanced decomposition that these poor wretches were long dead.

I thought about notifying the local authorities, but my deliberations were cut short by the appearance of a local thug holding a blood-stained machete in one hand and another dead child in the other. There was a moment of shared disbelief between an American at the right place at the right time and an evil savage with disregard for life beyond description.

His position blocked my retreat. There was only one path out from the deserted series of huts and he was standing in the way. There was no fear or any other emotion distracting me from what had to be done. My mind flashed, planning an alibi and getaway after shooting the asshole.

The desire to kill the Senegalese piece-of-shit was based more on rage than a sense of justice. Shooting an African citizen was not an act to be taken lightly, even a baby-killer, as it would certainly cause an incident, or if nothing else, bring more of the Machete Brigade into the alley to learn what the commotion was about.

"Fuck it! I said partly out loud. If there is no justice in putting a few rounds in a baby-killer, then there is no justice.

He raised his primitive human-slicing weapon and I raised my modern 'Colt Automatic Asshole Stopper' and gave him one to the chest and one to the head. He was dead before the second slug entered his brain. I secretly hoped he felt intense pain before dying. Felt every twinge as the gray matter left his skull from the back of the head. He dropped on top of the tiny bodies. If there was ever a case of universal karma, well, then this had to be it. Neither of us ever spoke of what had happened that night to another person, but for far different reasons. I pledged that night to remain silent to avoid trouble. Somewhere—from down below—I heard the devil pledge to torture him and vow to get to me later. *Get in line,* I thought. Even if the guy I shot were able to speak from the dead carrion, beetles and maggots aren't interested in what a Bantu fuck-head had to say. The noise of gunshots woke his clan from sleeping off the effects of booze and opium. Within seconds two men stepped into view, glanced down at their friend, then started down the alley to get revenge.

I pointed my weapon at their faces, so they would not misunderstand how badly I wanted out of the alley, and then walked purposely towards them. Part of me wanted to double tap each of the guys blocking my hasty exit.

Why not, I'd be doing the world a favor, save a few kids from potential harm. That option was eliminated by the sound of several other unfriendly voices fast approaching. It was time to start running, and save the ammunition, especially since I had neglected to bring an extra clip, as the night out was not supposed to include any unauthorized weapon discharge.

Luckily, both Africans blocking the exit backed out and gave me plenty of room to run out of the village.

My thoughts churned as I sprinted back to a safe zone. Behind me outraged people yelled threats and obscenities in my wake, making it unquestionably clear that more savages were chasing me to get some Senegalese-style payback. I thought about finding a place to set a trap so I could surprise my pursuers before they caught up and did their worst to me. And in Senegal "doing your worst" fucking meant something.

The beast inside me opened a yellow slit feral eye, woke to the carnage, and wanted more blood, but I ignored the temptation to get more revenge for the innocents, instead kept running, kept alive. My imagination gave the beast that cried for blood a face and a name—The Monkey.

Funny, I thought. *Monkeys are nothing but comical little circus performers.* That assessment was dead wrong. Only the flesh and bone kind of primate are humorous, the rest are evil bastards. Running to the ship did not prevent my mind from re-evaluating existence. I instantly recognized the folly of believing in a merciful God, certain there was nothing above that cared for earthy inhabitants. Christianity, Islam, Judaism, it didn't matter much, the names may have been different but to me it was all the same bullshit.

My consciousness had been opened to a new reality. From then on, the combination of drugs combined with the memory of the lifeless forms in the alley haunted me, so that upon my return stateside I was a changed man. After returning home, communion was taken from a new form of religion, dogma with no Gods, no servitude, and no deities that promised salvation. No, my creed was one of hedonism and denial ... denial of everything.

In what (for most people) should have taken years, I traversed a string of beliefs, accomplishing the feat in mere seconds. Spiritualism, Existentialism, Nihilism, all took seed and wilted so quickly, I had no time to embrace any of them, thereby creating my own brand of recognizing the world. I don't know what to call it, but it was several degrees on the below the south side of Nihilism. There was no meaning to life and to even think that there was truly absurd. The events in Africa gave me a new irresistible Higher Power to accompany me stateside, offering relief that only he could give, all I had to do was invite him into my life. As soon as my feet touched the airport tarmac, The Monkey was already waiting, I held out my arms, and gave The Monkey all the invitation he needed.

This primate was the kind of animal that needed doors to be slightly cracked to gain admittance, but that did not mean he would ever pass up on a door flung open. Just as cocaine had whispered alluringly *"you incomplete me"* The Monkey also whispered his own words ***"I incomplete you"***. And true to his words, The Monkey did incomplete me … cell by cell … he took me apart. If I were the type of guy who presented excuses, it would not be farfetched to lay the blame of my metamorphosis on Saharan Winds, or maybe the Beast/Monkey came from the radiation issuing from an errant Meteorite streaking across the night sky.

Maybe it was the fact that Mars was governing the Zodiac at the moment of my conception and foretold an omen of fury, anger and hate. However, it was not the Saharan Winds, there was no meteorite, and astrology is all a bunch of crap. The blame is mine and mine alone.   Better yet, maybe it was the dead children that destroyed my soul. A destructive life is not a complicated process; you just have to *"show up!"* I hope my novel will cause other people to rethink their lives and not just *"show up."*

Before my first snort or my glimpse of dead children I believed that there was an angel standing on my shoulder, providing guidance, forgiveness, hope. When I woke the next morning the angel had vanished. Only the beast remained in the guise of The Monkey.

Blitzkrieg Bop—1979

With my tour of duty over I returned stateside. The North Shore of Chicago had not changed in my absence and it felt good to be home. However, it was even better to be a civilian, able to think and function as an individual instead of a collective. After years of mandatory grooming requirements, as crazy as it sounds, growing my hair long and living the relaxed and unsupervised life of a gypsy was a priority. Punk rock was still all the rage, so my previous military-style haircut probably would have fit in better than the hippie look. I really didn't care what type of hairdo was in fashion, because after being told for so long how to dress, look, and speak, long hair went better with the hippie ideal of rebellion, which was the new way for me. My confrontational, aggressive nature secretly hoped some jackass would crack wise about the hair, beads, and surfing shorts, just so I could have at him. The look might have been slacker surf-dude, but inside there was still the heart of a warrior. Pooka shells, peace symbols, geometric cubes, and colored crystals were strung on necklaces of anger, and complimented perfectly my misplaced sense of coolness.

I left the service with all kinds of gear in my possession. Two months before rotating out, my company commander put me in charge of the Scuba locker. This made it simple to leave with as much military equipment as possible, especially since the A –Team Leader from my previous unit was in charge of the Supply Hut, which was located just a couple hundred yards away. The only space separating our corrugated buildings was a narrow stretch of sand, inhabited by fiddler crabs, sand grass, and green tiger beetles. On a bright afternoon the beetle's hard translucent wing covers made them shine like tiny emeralds.

The Recon Detachment was separated from the rest of Camp Lejeune by the New River Inlet, so for much of the time NCOs operated on their own, far from the prying eyes of butter-bar marine officers. With my billet as Scuba NCO approaching an end, going back and forth between buildings—to trade Scuba supplies for mission gear, filled up most of the day.

I made sure to leave with as much gear as possible. Rappelling ropes, packs, sleeping bags, scuba gear, bush shoes, holsters would all be put to good use in the civilian world. The rappelling tackle was used extensively around the steep cliffs overlooking the old McCormick Mansion section of Lake Michigan. The area was very secluded, therefore a perfect location to teach friends and family the art of fast descent, smoke some weed, fry a few mushrooms, then sneak off into the night to skinny dip with some babe. Hallucigens were my drug of choice, preferring color ripples, void diamonds, and optic vibrations, to a speeding pulse or barbiturate slumber, on any day of the interstellar calendar.

The Scuba gear was used in the same region, but of course, in the water. I also left with an assortment of colored smoke grenades and even a couple C.S tear-gas canisters. Each outing, regardless of whether the morning's activity was undertaken in the water or high above it, was an all-day affair. Coolers of beer were consumed, and lots of dope smoked, in order to emphasis the surreal aspect and danger quotient of whatever crazy stunts were scheduled by yours untruly. Before every outing, each new participant was told that the ultimate high was being dropped to the ground at break-neck speed by rope, or by chute, while being whacked on grass. However, nothing imitated the unique experience of Scuba diving under water, while high on skunk-weed or mushrooms. When the drugs kicked in, the next phase of the dive was to find schools of fish, then have staring contests with individual perch and bass, when the fish swam closer to investigate the unusual human creature in their waters.

My personal belief held that when the Great Spirit put psychotropic plants on earth, he did so to give mankind the chance to reap a wild buzz while being submerged in water. Even the water took on a personality, reflective, open to wonder, womb-like in the wet embrace. The fish were reserved, seldom offering wisdom, or revealing the closely-guarded secrets given to all sea creatures by the Water-God Poseidon before the time of the air-breathers or fire-people.

The plants were far more gregarious. On several underwater excursions, the sea lilies and tube-grass waved me deep into their mass of kelp-like stalks. It was a comfortable darkness broken by pencils of sunlight. Once, as I got into the thickest section of seaweed, a sunken stump raised a root and bid me welcome. "Come closer, and I will tell you the secret of the seas." The Stump said in a voice, so powerful, it actually hurt.

The mushrooms were screwing with my perception and recognition of time. Maybe I'd been down too long. Maybe the Stump was lying. Maybe I'd done too much mind-altering shit. But I had to know the mystery. I swam next the Stump and placed a hand on where I assumed the shoulder was. "Tell me." I bubbled. "Please, I need to understand."

"Here it is, the Secret of the Seas." The Stump said and continued. "When you go in the water don't drown and stay out of dark alleys in darker continents."

The Stump's reluctance to share or possess any significant knowledge was a tip that I'd done too many mushrooms and should surface. "Fucking stump, the advice on the alley is a little late and not drowning is not exactly a new concept. Maybe he should take his own advice, I'm not the one stuck underwater, never to see sunlight again. Besides, those assholes in Senegal deserved far worse than a bullet." I left the water, vowing to visit the Stump again, maybe have a better conversation next time—on a better batch of 'shrooms.

On these adventures, I neglected telling my friends the real reason for these little field trips, as the morbidity factor might give them pause. I wanted adventures that brought me closer to death, so as to obtain more adrenaline satisfaction, even if the end result might be crocking or choking. I wonder how many friends would have joined me on my activities if they had known my inner thoughts and the uncontrolled way I lived since that night in Senegal. My bothers would have insisted on going, for in some ways they were as nuts as I was. Deep within my clan was the DNA memory of Vikings, explorers, and going back into history maybe even a scoundrel or two. However, I suppose that if anyone searches their own family tree, beginning with the lowest branch; before the renaissance and subsequent illumination, all would most assuredly find scoundrels.

But as far as my friends were concerned, if they knew of my longing to count coup on death, nobody would have been

"On Belay" and there would have certainly been no "Swim Buddy." except for my brothers, stumps, and globe faced fish.

On the second day home as a civilian, I announced my return (to my brother Tim), by hurling a smoke grenade on to his second-story apartment balcony. It was unseasonably warm for November, so his sliding glass door was open just enough to suck in the thick cloud of red smoke. I thought about giving him a dose of teargas, but reconsidered, thinking that might be too extreme of a way to let him know his older brother was back in town.

Teargas would have been one hell of a surprise. But even without the use of C.S, it was a still funny to see him and his roommate Perry dancing on the balcony in the middle of the night, coughing and fanning smoke. They displayed a mixture of anger and panic while trying to figure out what the fuck was going on. As the smoke billowed, it occurred to me that Tim might get a gun from the apartment and begin shooting, so as to fight off the invasion. A not too unrealistic possibility, as Tim was the kind of person that would rather confront an assault than wave the white flag and make nice with the enemy.

The Halverson family motto was that strangers were automatically enemies, to be evaluated as some variant of asshole, unworthy of friendship, until they proved worthy by demonstrating (through actions not words) that they were above the slash-mark on the asshole barometer. It was the only way to be sure a new acquaintance was A-okay.

As Tim said, "Taking it for granted that a person isn't a conniving moron is how you find yourself in trouble, or worse, surrounded by conniving morons." Harsh but true, as most people have not been screwed by many believed to be close friends. If King Tut or Jesus were around, they might say the same thing as Tim.

When the smoke finally cleared, Perry and Tim saw me down below, leaning against my car, and laughing like a nitrous hyena. Luckily, the loud guffaws eased the tension, making it instantly clear to the other residents that there was no fire, just an ill-conceived joke by an ill-defined person that lacked a sense of self.

So the fire department and police were never called. Little to their knowledge, a fire WAS narrowly averted by Tim's quick thinking, as he tossed the sparking canister away from the apartment. That was the beginning of a series of bad judgments on my part that often turned unfunny.

A few days later Tim got me a job working the door and bouncing at a local music venue called The Alley—aptly named, because in its previous incarnation it had been a ten-lane bowling alley. It was the hottest club in a fifty-mile radius and consistently got the best bands; more importantly, the club attracted the best-looking women. It had everything for me; great music, easy access to drugs and alcohol, and the nightly occurrence of a good dust up—most likely resulting from showing some loudmouths the door. And ... at The Alley, nobody getting tossed ever went easy. It was like an unspoken code, maybe a tradition among drunks, or I guess it could have been something else entirely (like pride). If a person was asked to leave, punches must be thrown, or he was a pussy. The massive interior was always filled to capacity; wall-to-wall people energized by cocaine, newly acquired courage, wallflower nerds becoming barbarians, bolstered by massive consumption of cheap bar drinks. Add the loud and angry backbeat of bands like The Ramones, Tu Tu and the Pirates, Cheap Trick, and Off Broadway into the mix and that was The Alley.

Friday and Saturday nights were especially tremulous affairs. On those nights it was so confrontational we thought that the manager must be running "Loudmouths Drink For Free" specials without telling us. The biggest draw was a group called "The Ramones" from New York. They had already proved themselves at CBGB's, and thereby were considered one of the most interesting bands to spring forth out of the punk movement.

When The Ramones took stage, blasting two-minute tunes—done as fast as humanly possible—the club was packed. The band always came prepared to deliver a sonic assault, beginning each set with an unmatched level of decibels and fury (except for maybe the Clash or the Sex Pistols).

Leading the Ramones in their machine-gun pace was Johnny Ramone; legs spread wide, guitar slung low, hair covering his face, playing faster than humanly possible, no emotion, no concern, and as The Pistols said...*"no future."*

With titles like "Blitzkrieg Bop" and lyrics like "Beat on the Brat with a Baseball Bat," the band wasted no time in making every member of the audience into one of the converted. Each concert began with a crowd of unemotional listeners; gradually the throng of people were hypnotized by whiplash guitars, and soon rapidly morphed into riotous mob, caught up in wave after wave of violent pogo and slam dancing.

Those were the nights when the biggest fights would break out. Shoves became tackles, and tackles became beatdowns. Tim, I, and the other doormen would wade into the undulating swamp of bodies, drag the instigators out of the pile, head butt when applicable, return punches when feasible, and nut-kick if necessary—sometimes (if the guy was a real prick) even when not necessary. After the brawlers were moved away from the stage, we propelled them in the direction of the door where other doorman waited to add more force to the offending party's momentum, finishing the assholes' involuntary exit by tossing them out into the streets. Tim and I invented the world's first asshole conveyer belt, but regretfully we never bothered to get a patent. We did however file for a copyright on the "hip-toss table smash," surely a concept that is still pending litigation.

The level of violence escalated whenever the fights got close to the door. Anybody getting thrown out usually had friends waiting by the double doors, ready to jump into the fray, anxious to get in a few cheap-shots. At these moments, we were usually outnumbered, but luckily, our own buddies were in the crowd ready to jump in so as to even the odds a bit.

Those were some bloody scraps. As the fights raged on, we had to be alert for flying beer pitchers, chairs, and avoid tripping and get stomped while on the ground. I managed to maintain vicinity control when things got ugly, stayed on my feet and only rarely ended up on the floor, which was amazing considering the many large-scale fights I participated in. I was well- schooled in the number one rule of unarmed combat; avoid the ground or prepare to get kicked in the face by some coward. There was always some asshole outside the action perimeter, not willing to scrap, but perfectly willing to sneak into the melee, and land a shot to the face or balls. Once the strike was delivered, the coward ran back to the crowd, mingled in the mix of people, and hid until another cheap-shot opportunity arrived,

Sooner or later we eventually regained control. The customers never minded the violence and The Ramones definitely didn't appear to mind. The Alley was tough, but nothing resembling the movie "Roadhouse." We didn't carry our medical records with us, rip anybodies throat out, or stitch up our wounds in the bathroom ... but it was still a club that gave us plenty of black eyes and bleeding mouths. We joked with the other bouncers that "working the door at The Alley should earn a person a few college credits since it was like attending "Gladiator Preparation."

Two flights up from the bar, located in the same building, was a three-room apartment. As it happened, the occupant – Jimmy Bolini—was also the landlord. Jimmy was as thin as a skeleton, barely maintaining flesh on bones—this was probably the reason his nickname was "the cadaver." He had strange features, emphasized by a snapping turtle nose, a cone-shaped chin defying normal growth, adorned with a cappuccino sipper's soul-patch beard. His bizarre appearance made it very easy to distinguish him, but when facial characteristics weren't enough, his attire was. Jimmy wore the color black, Black tie, on black shirt, black pants, black shoes. The combination of dark clothes and Sicilian features gave Jimmy a look usually reserved for actors in a Mafia movie. It was difficult not to smile whenever I had the opportunity to speak with Jimmy— usually about drugs, never about the weather.

Jimmy's nasally high-pitched voice seemed truly miscast to go along with such a disturbing and psychotic appearance. Whenever Jimmy got ready to talk, listeners expected his voice to be deep, something like Bogart, but what they heard was Don Knotts.

Jimmy collected the rent, while dealing grams of coke from his residence only meters above the stage. Jimmy was a good guy and could make anyone laugh. When things down below (in the bar) got slow, he welcomed visits throughout the night from the doorman. So everybody working the door took turns running up the stars, making small talk with nasally Jimmy, and snorting a few lines. In my case, never a few, unless the white trails were railroad ties.

The manager did not care what we did as long as we broke up the fights and threw out the garbage—both living and non-living trash, that is. For most of the music acts, the manager was "half in the bag" or "all in the box," so he rarely knew what was going on in his club. This made bouncing at The Alley a real good gig, as it meant that Tim and I were really running the place, not to mention that it allowed us to catch some of the best acts around for free. In many cases, we got signed albums and memorabilia from the groups we did special favors for. When it came to the other most important thing about club life—scoring with women—my brothers and I put up numbers that came close to rivaling Ted William's baseball record. I could be counted to swing for the fence and hit the long ball. Women loved being close to danger and I loved being close to women. I exited the club with a new girl almost every Saturday night. During my tenure at the Alley, I met many of the biggest drug dealers, eventually forming relationships with them and gaining their trust, showing no Rat Qualities. The offers for collections and protection started coming in and it was hard to resist the lure of easy money and drugs.

The Monkey had not completely materialized to the point where he was a constant companion. I knew he was near, aching to influence my actions, but he was not a fully realized entity. He popped in and out of existence at his choosing, exerting control over my actions, crushing my conscience, only when it entertained him to do so. But things were beginning to change. The Monkey made his intentions clear as he got stronger. He wanted to destroy my will to be a better person and destroy my will to resist him. Slowly, certainly he escalated my drug use and increased my love of danger. It was a potent mix, just the thing that a lost spirit like myself, could never refuse.

While working the door at the alley it was hard to pinpoint any particular event as something to be really proud of. However, right before quitting there were a few heart- pounding moments that produced an end result, as righteous a deed as could be found anywhere.

My brother Sven and I prevented the rape of a helpless young woman by three Latino gang members. We came out the back door and heard the girl screaming and struggling to get out from under the two guys holding her down. The third cretin was filling the role as a lookout, or maybe he was a eunuch, and sexual assaults were beyond his flaccid capabilities. Sven and I ran down the steps and beat the shit out of the two guys that were actively involved in the assault. The lookout split once he saw they had been caught in the act. We held the other two gang-banger pussies on the ground, driving fists and elbows into chins, lips, and noses, until the cops arrived. The cops cuffed them and put them into the squad car.

But not before I kicked one of the gang-banger in the nuts, so hard, that I think his gonads are still orbiting Uranus, or maybe just his anus. It would be a long time before that guy used his dick again for anything again, except for measuring the thickness of drywall.

The other deed happened about a year later. The antagonists were also a couple gang members. This time the event involved a different brother: James, to be exact. The gang-bangers stabbed two of the other doorman multiple times, leaving puncture wounds all over their stomach and chest area, and sending each of them to the hospital. James and I gave chase, finally catching the assailants in a maze of back service drives that ended at a ten-foot high brick wall. It is no exaggeration to say "we gave those assholes the beating of their lives." James and I used stomp heel thrusts to the sternums and reverse donkey kicks to disable each Mexican as they tried to stick us with their Tijuana pen-knifes. Most of the stabbing attempts missed, except for a single slash that cut into the palm of my hand. While I took a second to examine the wound, James interceded, by using with a solid hammer blow to the knife-fighter's solar plexus which drove all the wind from his lungs and caused bone-shattering pain. I wiped the bleeding palm on my shirt and then got to work on the other guy that had regained his feet. By swimming in with both arms, I won an over/under hold and then hip-tossed him to the ground, where a cross-side position was secured, taking away any chances for him to initiate any further attacks.

During the fight, The Monkey flickered into existence, then as fast as he took shape, he disappeared, sporadically fading in and out. When he was fully materialized, he prodded me to do some real damage, maybe even kill one of the Mexicans.

"It is self-defense. Their prints are all over the knives, plus back at the bar are a couple bouncers with holes in their chests. Come on...at least break one of their wrists." The Monkey said. I looked over at James to see if he heard the command, however it appeared The Monkey was nothing to anyone but me.

"Well if you're not going to bust up an arm or two, then crack the nose of the guy you got pinned on the ground."

That Monkey idea was something I could live with. Wouldn't be the first nose I'd made crooked, so I smashed the nose, and then broke the fucker's ankle on my own volition just so that the Monkey knew I was the boss. It was a decidedly bad lesson. Much as hitting the ground after jumping off a building proves that gravity is not the boss. Thankfully James pulled me off the guy and we took off, exiting the area so quickly it left the Monkey speechless—the resulting silent monkey would never be experienced by me again or any other druggie, not for a very long time. James and I went our separate ways. He went across town to go fishing with Tim; I on the other hand went back to my place to do the last remaining half-gram seal of cocaine left over from the night before, and see what I had left in the hallucinogenic department. Coke was good, but acid was my thing. It took away memories of dead babies, alleys, Africa, and the desire to do harm. "It's kind of problematical seek out violence while tripping your ass off, well it is much more difficult anyway" That was my system, knowing I had no self control, when it came to fights, I chose color trails over doling out arbitrary beating.

When I arrived at my apartment, I put on "Wait for the Blackout" by The Damn, knocked back a drink, letting the blow do the rest of the job. Luckily on tab of acid left, it taunted me from the package, so I did what must be done – swallowed the son of a bitch. Unfortunately I was not alone. The Monkey followed me home, probably by using synaptic bread crumbs, dropped along the way from my cerebellum. The creature took shape, entering my world from somewhere deep within the ether, Once merely a zygote composed of guilt and shame, he changed into a fully fleshed-out idea, which collected quarks, then gathered building material from the invisible, all giving forth to strangeness, and from dimensions unseen found the final ingredient—charm.

He looked straight into my eyes and said, *"I could take the appearance of just about anything, but for you and those of your ilk, my shape is that of a full grown Monkey. This embodiment of a common animal should serve my purposes well, for if it is to be known, there is nothing viler, yet more innocent looking than a chimp, except for maybe puppets and clowns. I considered emerging in the guise of an especially creepy puppet. However, I just want to torture you Billy, not scare you to death ... at least not right away. So for now, it is Monkey over clown or puppet."*

What could I say? How do you respond to what you suspect is a drug induced phantom or a vision from crazy town. I had questions ... so asking them seemed logical.

"Why pick me? Why not haunt somebody else. Besides you don't frighten me at all. You'd be better off going after somebody weaker and more susceptible to your bullshit."

"Why you? Because you're already chemically addicted to narcotics and mind altering substances. You're just not fully aware of how bad the problem is. You're a junkie, hardwired at birth, pre-programmed with the necessary receptor sites so the addiction will be unbreakable, requiring just the occasional gentle shove from me." The Monkey swayed from side to side, excited, seemingly happy to be speaking. He continued in a more somber tone.

"Billy...may I call you Billy?" He said. I shrugged. *"Behind your back, even your best friends say that you have a huge ego. It has been said that if anyone took a hundred pictures of you to sell ... .you would buy them all. And, Billy, all of us know nobody hits the ground harder than the proud."*

"Go fuck yourself." I said tossing back another shot of Jim Beam. "I'm not some idiot. Anytime I get tired of listening to your shit, I'll stop with the drugs and violence and that will be the end of you."

"What you fail to realize, is there is a distinct advantage of being an imaginary Monkey. I live outside the normal physical restraints, which gives me limitless power to warp those I wish to destroy. The laws of gods or and men hold no sway over my somewhat questionable existence, so there is no readily definable strategy to rid me from riding your back. In fact, most removals are merely temporary, as lapsing back into alcohol and drug use is—in most cases, nothing but a foregone conclusion."

Man, this is one intelligent sounding delusion. I thought to myself. I had to reply with something profound, a rebuttal that would really cut deep, the right adjectives that would hurt the Monkey—in such a way that he would never want to do battle with the likes of me again. The worst thing you can do in a situation like this is to let the Monkey continue with his rant without giving him as good as he gives. "Come on at least give him an insult or two." I told myself. However, before I could say something; about his decaying brown teeth and lice infested nappy fur, he interrupted my prepared speech.

"Billy, listen to me! I will assume complete control by becoming equated with all the things you likes best; music, adventure, danger, and women. Once I'm part of all your little innocuous pleasures, each previously sterile hobby will be converted into something unclean; clouded by lines of cocaine, tab of acid, and spikes of heroin." The Monkey smiled in the most evil way imaginable.

And imagine I did, voluntarily, hungrily.

"Let me put it into military terms, Billy. Whenever your defenses are down, I will slip into the mental perimeter, low-crawl past synaptic observation posts, choke out gray matter sentries, and silently slip my way into The Billy Halverson Cerebrum H.Q. There I will wait. There I will hide, safe within the Gray Matter Command Post. I will stay close to the shadows – otherwise your higher brain function might kick on and alert you to the fact that there is a Monkey in the bunker."

"Why single me out? Everyone else does drugs, so why shouldn't I? I only do it to sharpen my wits and bring the night into clearer focus. Hallucinogens take me to places that dreams cannot. Besides I'm not weak like other people and can quit anytime."

"Keep telling yourself that crap. But you should know this Billy. As intangible Monkey's go, I am one of the strongest. I have already brought down Poe, Sid Vicious, Jim Morrison, Mark Anthony, and many other people far more celebrated and talented then you."

Styx and Stoners The 80's

It was the early 80's. I was spending less and less time working at The Alley. Skinny ties and loose-fitting pleats were in, wide burlesque ties, and skin-tight blue-jeans were out. My new occupation—of collecting and protecting, provided plenty of action, which caused me to be invariantly found in bad rooms, and often in critically worse situations. This job was no different. The collection was to be made at a singles complex, complete with the standard allure two swimming pools, a communal clubhouse, patio barbecues, tiny flower beds, and many, many, upwardly mobile pricks and prickettes.

The apartment door was unlocked, which made entry a simple affair. I was immediately struck by the unusual smell in the room, aptly described as a smoky combination of pine incense and strawberry candles, both of which assaulted my gag reflex in such a way, I feared giving myself away by coughing. Swallowing hard, and breathing through my mouth, eventually alleviated the sensation. This job had been a rushed assignment, so I had not brought any weapons. The room had nothing that might be of any use, unless of course you count the ragged broom leaning against the obscenely high mahogany stereo speaker.

These guys must have been sold on the marketing concept claiming Quad-Sound systems were the future of audio technology. I laughed silently. Each corner of the living room had one of the giant reddish-brown rectangles. The speakers stood like sentinels, watching over whatever mischief the owners involved themselves in, while still operating according to factory specs by providing the appropriate soundtrack for their twisted lifestyle. The large green ferns scattered around the speakers caused the room resemble an Irish countryside.

Look at this shit, five foot speaker totems, ferns, incense, candles. The place looks like fucking Stonehenge and smells like a Wicca coven. Great I've been sent to collect money from

Druids. I thought, while memorizing the room and mentally filing away anything of value, in case grabbing some collateral became critical. I shifted my attention back to the broom and mentally compared the wooden handle to a person's skull. *No help there! Broom would lose, even though these guys are equipped with skulls as soft as grapefruits...the wood looks softer.*

In most cases, I would have been much better prepared for this type of confrontation. However, in my haste to complete the job, and get back to partying, I failed to pick up ballistic persuasion, or the always handy concussion-inducing leather-bound sap

It probably won't matter. They will assume I have some sort of weapon with me, I continued thinking while analyzing the situation. The word on the street was that I never go anywhere without a piece tucked away under my trench-coat, in all reality an exaggeration, but a useful one. Even without coming in braced, I felt safe. I knew something about these guys. My boss, Bitsy informed me what these guys were like before sending me off and before I accepted the job.

"There would be no problem going in soft, since the targets are all hippie wimps and it would be shocking if they were any trouble." He told me.

Yeah..... Bitsy will be shocked, but if he's wrong, I'll be dead! I thought to myself while promising not to get too relaxed—no matter what my boss said.

But then again, not bringing artillery into the mix was also wise council. Most encounters of this type were better handled with brains and not with bullets. I told myself to end the mental debate.

It did not hurt that I was six feet tall, 220 lbs, with a fighters frame carved from the hardest granite ... well maybe not granite, but at least oak—alright, no oak, but hard enough to handle most guys. However, the most imposing thing about my appearance was the absence of life in my eyes. My irises were as lifeless a boiled lobster, showing as much connection to the real world as the black pellets at the end of ocean crawler's eye-stalk. Yeah, that was a fair comparison, a lobster ready to be eaten, by bibbed dolts that were incapable of understanding that cooking an animal alive is obscene by any measurement. My lobster eyes stared outward much in the same way, but said something completely. "Try and boil me mother-fucker and you'll get your teeth knocked out."

Eyes were an important thing in expressing dominance, in fact, the right stare is the best tool in the box, when it comes time to make prey understand who the predator is, or who is the Alpha and who is the Omega.

"So...with or without a weapon, in this situation, every-thing should come out roses." I said aloud while geometrically scanning the room. The act of learning the decor was much shorter than usual, time was short. The sundial located in my spine had already spun, telling me that it was five seconds till violence. I took in the rest of the sights.... cheap wicker furni-ture, bean bag chairs, crappy plastic magazine table—with an even crappier assortment of porn magazines. A two level book-shelf held the entire collection of Mack Bolin, "The Execution-er" paperbacks. On the far wall was the only redeeming feature, a dog-eared poster of "The Cure". The sight of "The Cure" caused me to think that (despite outward appearances) maybe these cretins had some class after all. Robert Smith, of The Cure was on the poster. He was one of my music heroes; representing everything good in music and everything bad—in guys wearing makeup. Except for "The Cure" poster, it ap-peared the residents of this shitty apartment had no taste in lite-rature (unless "Hustler" was Hemmingway and "Penthouse" was Plato), no taste in music, and worse taste in living accom-modations. It was easy to tell where the cocaine profits had been going; into their noses, instead of into some halfway des-cent furniture, or at least an assortment of air fresheners.

My observations rode along the faded tan wallpaper, stop-ping only when I saw an old friend sitting on top of a book-shelf—The Monkey, now fully materialized and still with a belly of guts.

I got the first real good look at him. When I saw him dur-ing the last fight, my mind was still under the effects of some Peyote, and there wasn't time to fully examine him while breaking the gang bangers ankle. The Monkey had aged slightly since our meeting in Africa. However, although the added years went only skin deep, it was certain his desire to do harm others went all the way to his Simian bones, without age and without accumulated loss of power. "Furry Demon", "Seething Beast", "Eater of intent", "Digester of Neglect", nothing but names. The Monkey was my tormentor now, and somehow I felt that he was going to accompany me over the next several years. Although every derelict had his own Monkey, my banana-eating companion was real only to me. Therefore, only I was able to hear his chattering insults, feel the unrelenting pressure placed upon my limbic region, urging me into the seedy side of existence.

Since The Monkey was a creation of my drug addled brain, I had given him characteristics and peccadilloes that resembled a nightmarish caricature of my inner abandon. He was like a primate version of Mr. Hyde. My imaginary Monkey was easily distinguished from those of other coke fiends and heroin addicts. My mind had given him slate-blue eyes to match my own. My imagination dressed him to reflect the times. Sometimes he came to me wearing garish Hawaiian shirts, which imitated the loud apparel worn by Tom Selleck—in the role Magnum P.I. Other times he dressed as different pop culture personalities or historical figures. The Monkey shared almost nothing with me concerning his own behavior. However, he did let me know that looking stylish was very important while prowling the streets with me. He had a strange sort of vanity embedded in viciousness. His ego was inflated by my own subconscious asylum, bound together in drug-fantasy, which made us up to the task of masking our wish to inflict injury, while wearing Armani and Gucci, or cloaked in rage. Seeing The Monkey brought forth a saying I had heard many times before. "Dress for the position you want, not the position you have." I wanted death, but could never seem to find attire matching that of a funeral director.

My personal Monkey also had his own collection of battle scars. His abrasive nature caused him to have problems, even with other imaginary primates. Strange...his accumulated injuries seemed to mirror my own. I guess it would have been much stranger if they hadn't.

"I should have done you back in that alley fuckhead!" I told the Monkey while at the same time mentally cursing him for his taunts and insulting jibes.

The Monkey laughed, fidgeted, and waved me forward, daring a fight. I did not take the bait, as any altercation would only serve to alert the Stoners to my presence, but I sure as shit wanted to beat some simian ass.

The Monkey wiggled his fingers and toes in obvious anticipation for what he knew was bound to be a jungle confrontation between me and The Stoners. He rocked back and forth, plucked bugs from his hide, inserting each crawling ambiguity in his mouth. I could hear an audible pop as his teeth connected with anthropoid shell.

"I hope you choke." I told him in a whisper. "All you need is a couple of cymbals to smash together and you'd be just another little annoying toy." I examined the Monkey closely, hoping that my insult hurt and might cause him to leave me alone and fade away. I was pissed off that the Monkey had a front row seat, privileged to view whatever unfortunate circumstances awaited me, or my victims.

I felt the Monkey's tug on my spine and his unrelenting push on the reptilian part of my character to do the deed.

"Quickly now...better fuck these assholes up first. Then while their all on "queer street", look for drugs. Give Bitsy his money, but keep everything else you find. Think of it as a well earned tip," The Monkey said.

I did not argue. At this point in my life the Monkey was often correct, plus I never met a drug I didn't like. The Monkey did not do drugs. He vampired all the benefits of narcotics by simply feeding off my pain. But I knew deep down it my heart, that one day after kicking my habit, the Monkey's ass would be next. I allowed the leering primate go back to doing what he did best, which was being an demon and convincing me to do harsh things to low-tide people

"Come on...wake up....get back to business.... stay alert, ignore the Monkey. He would like nothing better than for you to get your head bashed in." I reminded myself. "Just collect the money and don't start any unnecessary shit. If the druggies can't produce all the money, only hurt them a little bit, maintain control, but absolutely scare the living shit out of them." I said, while forcing myself focus and stay Zen-like—in the microsecond. However, it was doubtful that Buddha or Lao Tzu ever encouraged their followers to become tranquil as water, unbound as the wind, peaceful as a flower, then head-butt some-one's skull in. Regardless of the drug use, somehow I had dis-covered a technique, which funneled heightened Taoist aware-ness and energy with the brutality of a Viking Berserker. So, as a Berserker, I grabbed one of the ferns and threw it on the floor. Then I hid in the shadows as a Taoist for the Stoners to stumble into the room. However, it should be noted; unlike a Berserker, I did not dress in wolf pelts or consume fire.

The Stoners filed into the room, rubbed their eyes, and tried valiantly to push away the pot induced cobwebs from their five senses—six senses if you count being a moron as a sense. The fat doughy one paused, pulled out a bottle of Visine, and squeezed out a few drops into his semi-closed lids. They came from a well-lit room; this made their night vision ex-tremely fucked up, so the advantage of sight was mine. If things did not go the way I wanted them to there would be punches coming. And in the dark, in their dazed condition the Stoners would think the fists were coming from ghosts—disadvantage Stoners.

"Gets the red out ... right, asshole? I said, while stepping into the dim light, waking them to a new reality of bumping night-things. It was time to get the pendulum swinging, no rea-son to waste too much time with these guys. It was easy to see that I was in the company of dimwits. They all looked confused and unable to recognize the potential harm that awaited them. Fatty, and his waif-like stoner friends, had no clue to the trouble they were in if the money owed to my boss wasn't pro-duced, and quick.

They saw me, but not their dilemma! They only wanted to get back to the lines of coke on the mirror. Two inch slender trails of white powder, which incidentally did not belong to them, until they gave me the cash that belonged to my prin-ciple.

Theirs was a borrowed high and I had been sent to collect the interest. A bank might have charged 4% on a loan, but fail-ure to pay my Bitsy got you 100% of a brutal pummeling. From a business standpoint, it was a lose/lose proposition.

The Stoners sputtered out unintelligible words. Everything they said was a major annoyance, as I had heard the same tired song and dance many times before. "We don't have the money right now but we will have it tomorrow ... how about a railer," The heavyset one said, and then presented me with a rolled up bill. The twenty-dollar bill was guaranteed to be coated with herpes, dog-flu, or some other currency sticking disease. I passed.

"You fuckheads think you can to buy me off. This is not a good way to start our conversation and it won't get you anywhere... because if you don't have what I came for ... then all the shit belongs to me anyway." That scared them! Not because they realized I was looking for a reason to dole out fists, but because they thought the drugs might be taken. However, since they owed money to an evil bastard like Bitsy, losing a high should not have been the biggest worry. This was a going to involve a beating.

The Monkey nodded his head in agreement with my strategy. What the fuck else was he going to do. ***"Kick their asses!"*** He screeched. As he worked himself up, a Simian spit projectile shot from his peeled back purple lips, spraying my sleeve. The Stoners were unable to hear the imaginary primate or feel the spray of saliva. *Lucky fucks,* I thought.

I decided to get physical on the Fat Dipshit. He was unable to stop grinning. Maybe he was under the false impression that I was standing in front of him to only issue a verbal plea for the money, or maybe he was just too fucking high to understand the predicament. But, to smile at me, that was the act of an idiot and therefore confirmed that I was in the presence of morons. Trying to provide mood lighting with a goofy smile was a very unwise move and would earn a very bleak answer to having such blissful ignorance to impending doom. Fatty also happened to be the most viable target. His seated position was unstable, so as he put the end of a straw to the beginning of white lines, the chair began to tip over. I took advantage of the lack of balance and made him the first recipient of a couple hard slaps. The chair flipped over and he went sprawling to the floor. He righted the chair and sat back down. Large red welts were already forming on his cheek, but the smile remained glued to his face, which demonstrated without a doubt that he was not taking my presence serious, or that he was in fact retarded.

I was getting an adrenaline spike; soon I would red line, cobalt orange, pillaging dial turned all the way up to number 13. If Spinal Tap's guitar volume controls went to 11, my punch-o-meter went all the way up to 13.

But, going 13 was not good for them or me. "Don't escalate things until you know where the money is," I told myself, knowing that my rage sometimes clouded decisions. So setting the dial to 13 was out of line for these dope-fiends. *Give then number 9. Number nine—less Viking more Taoist ... but not nearly enough Taoist.*

I did what a setting of 9 demanded (and also what action came naturally) and kicked the leader in the face. That got the desired attention, setting the storyboard, getting things moving in the right direction.

I watched as a couple things exploded from his mouth, and bounced against the wall. *Was it teeth or part of his tongue?* I wondered. It was hard to tell ... probably teeth, because bits of tongue could not possibly make a pinging noise when striking a solid object. The mood of the room changed drastically. Everyone in the room became rigid. I made an overly dramatic show of going for something tucked into my loose fitting parachute pants. There was no weapon, but staying true to method acting required the display, in order to get them to imagine a bazooka, not a big mental leap in their buzzed condition. The pantomime of reaching for a non-existent weapon, settled them down, making them think about what kind of object might be tucked away, instead of jumping me all at once. Now they were on the defensive, no more secret looks, impetus for an all-at-once-attack was gone. I began the well-rehearsed speech, given on many occasions, to other behind-on-payment-shitheads that resided all over the Northshore.

"Don't make one fucking move, except for you (pointing to the recipient of my boot). You go turn on the rest of the lights, and then go pick up your teeth." He sheepishly flipped on the remainder of the track-mounted lights, stopping only to occasionally blot his mouth with one of the shirt collars. With the lights on, he then picked up whatever used to be in his mouth. "Sit down, you moron. I was just kidding about getting your teeth."

The next thing that had to go was the music. Not because it was too loud. That would have been fine because the volume helped drown out the noise. No ... I shut off the stereo because the band that played thru the tweeters and woofers was in a big way responsible for bringing about the apocalypse of fine art. It was a type of music that eliminated Mozart's generational dare to seek greatness by risking the alienation the masses.

"Is that Styx? I fucking hate Styx." I said. The absurdity of having a poster of "The Cure," yet still being able to listen to crap like arena rock, shocked me, and worse still, impinged on my eardrums. Once the music got past the inner ear, each instrument registered on my built in shit-detector. The sounds made me cringe; tremble, much as fingernails on a chalkboard evoke a wish for silence or death. *Might as well listen to Journey,* I thought. The objects in the room mirrored my own paradox. I may have been here to lay down a beating, but when not on the job my character reflected that of a relatively peaceful person, Taoist, painter, avid reader of great literature, student of nature, a far different cat, than when in the warm embrace of drugs. Under the influence I became something else; werewolf, enforcer, con-man, and an odd Zookeeper with only one animal to feed ... The Monkey; who grew stronger every day from my abhorrent behavior. The Monkey was never satisfied, always wanting more carnage, unrelenting, pushing for greater amounts of pain. He had an appetite like a two-ton-teddy at a pie-eating contest.

I was uncertain which was more visually and acoustically repulsive, The Monkey or the Hair-Band Styx. It took some deliberating to get it right. The Monkey was certainly an asshole because he brought forth my dark side, but he never gave the world Mr. Roboto. So at that moment, the Monkey was off the hook, which meant that Styx and The Stoners got the majority of my wrath.

"How dare you fuckheads force me listen to this crap? It's bad enough that I have to drive here in the middle of the night, just to get the money you should have paid last week. "

My life may have been embroiled in drug use, self-destruction, and inner turmoil, but there was always music to ease the feeling of despair.

While waiting for the Stoners to come out of their daze, I thought about the importance of music throughout the years. The convergence of new wave's artistic ingenuity with Punk's angry disregard for rules created the emergence of bands that had their own unique identity and sound. Music therefore scored the most memorable events in my life, a catalyst that lets me picture the past in Technicolor—without the aid of acid. To think back on my youth, an appropriate tune filed in memory, existed to bring forth visions, sounds, and smells otherwise lost to the march of days.

Leaving for the Marines—"Free Bird" ... Ambib Recon School— "Just what I Needed" by the Cars ... First Parachute Jump—"Sonic Reducer" by the Dead boys ... First acid trip— "Friction by Television ... spending some time County Jail— "Dead Man's Party" by Oingo Boingo. I was lucky, as for each chapter of my life there was a track playing in the somewhere in the background. Music got me through moments when all seemed lost, and of those, there were many, too many.

I stopped thinking about music. It was unwise to daydream in a crisis and I had a bad habit of drifting away into surreal meanderings, amusing myself, even it the most dangerous of situations. This collection was already taking much too long. I needed to accelerate the payment process because my brothers and my most recent girlfriend were waiting for me at a late night bar called *"Scornovicians"* Neither my five brothers, sister, parents, nor even any of my girlfriends knew what my sideline was. Although, rumors reaching their ears, and the assortment of scars on my mug, revealed that my part-time job was not cashier, bank teller or accountant, unless you were a Samurai Accountant that is.

The reality of the job and the ticking clock came surging back into focus. After feeling my stingray-skin boot on his left cheek, the recipient was very anxious to go get the money—the same money that prior to the rather crude dental work was supposedly unavailable. He retrieved it out of a crumbled Crown Royal bag which was tapped to the back of a dresser drawer.

"Fuck, can't you guys do better? All you drug-heads do the same thing, stashing dope in the same places, while congratulating each other on the ingenuity."

He handed me the bag and nervously sat down with his Droogs. Blood had splashed his cheeks, and trickled down his puffy face. I tore off a paper towel from a roll and tossed it to him. "Wipe your face off ... you look like a Sid Vicious after a razor lashing."

Then I saw something that shook me at the very core. I began to shake with a mixture of revulsion and nausea. I involuntarily jumped back in fear.

Next to the towel rack, there it was; the worst album of a notably bad series of records by Styx. I picked the album cover up and called out to one of the idiots to bring me the disc that belonged inside the empty sleeve.

He gave me the vinyl record. I slid it back into the album packaging and proceeded with the only act heroic enough to save the world from bad taste, repair my soul, and give peace to Mozart. I put my lighter to record, sleeve, and cardboard, letting it burn, until it was a charred mass of Rubbish. I looked at the poster of the Cure. In my slightly high state I believed for an instant that Robert Smith (Goth make-up and all), smiled at me and said *"Domo Arigoto"*. For a few seconds music from Cure's "The Forest" played in my head and I thought Mozart and Smith would have gotten along.

I turned my attention to the Stoners, warning them about what would happen next time they did not pay on time. "If you assholes ever hold out again, I will come back here with some friends and 'stomp the stupid' from you guys. Nod your heads, or should I kick a few more of you guys in the face?"

The three scumbags paid tribute, enthusiastically demonstrating there would be no more delinquent payments. If they were dogs (and who is to say they weren't), they would have rolled over to show the pale tint of their soft underbellies, so as to convince me that there was no more threat. The term Dogs was an unproven moniker, but that did not mean they were not Curs. I went to their fridge and stuffed a beer in each pocket of my trench coat. I was not practically thirsty; however I wanted them to know of my contempt. On my way out of the house, I also did their lines, since I really lacked the time to scrape the white power back into the seal for later.

"Now you can pick up your teeth, asshole. I better never have to come here and talk to you trolls again. If I do you better have all the money and you better NOT have replaced that Styx record." I made an abrupt movement as if to strike the closest one to me. He bounded a few steps backwards. I chuckled, it was funny, the expression of fear on his face. My distain gave him courage. He looked at his friends and signaled his intent to jump me, newfound boldness catching me slightly off-guard.

"End it fast, before he gets his strength back." I told myself in order to initiate quick and final action. I drove my fist, thumb flattened over the layer of fingers to form a spike, into his Adam's Apple.

Both of his hands clutched the area of the throat where my thumb made contact. The impact made his lungs push out rasping gulps of air; as his body curled into a fetal ball and every muscle struggled get some air. The other Stoners saw their buddy's pain and decided to curtail the attack.

Before exiting the shithole, I glanced back into the room, and stretched out my arms—as I had done in Senegal so many years ago. The Monkey sprang from the bookcase and gladly jumped aboard. As he clung to my neck, I heard his thoughts, echoing my own expectations of night, darkness thrills, bright lights, beckoning chills, drugs and mind fucks, getting laid, getting messed. It was a laundry list of vices. *"So many urges, so little time."* The Monkey whispered.

"Shut up. This was the last time I do the bidding of small-town kingpins or imaginary Monkeys!" I lied to myself and to him. It was my usual lie. I was not the Organ Grinder—I was the bastard holding the tin cup. The odds were that a bad end was coming before I managed to change direction and Gut the Monkey. Deep down, I wanted to turn everything around, quit doing drugs, and working for people I despised. There was some comfort in the knowledge that anybody who got a beating from me probably deserved it. And if not delivered from someone like me, sooner or later it would be from the cops. At least, after getting punched out by me, there was no jail sentence to deal with. Well, that is not exactly true. There was always the possibility of jail, but only for me. For the first time, I began to feel like my luck was running out, drug overdose, jail, violence, living by the sword, all that shit, was catching up to me. It seemed like the earth was trembling at my feet and something huge and unrelenting was about to crush me. While as high on grass, I pictured a Karmic Tank rolling over bodies of derelicts, and I was the next asshole to be flattened.

I left the Stoners place, walked a block down the street to my motorcycle parked clandestinely between a couple pickup trucks. The ES 1100 was the fastest production bike made—up to that year. It had black paint with thin red stripes, aftermarket Carbs, Kerker Header, Dunlop Elite Tires, Oil cooler, and racing handlebars. A motorcycle meant for trouble.

The bike was plenty fast and I always rode fast. Maybe because I realized the Monkey would never be silenced, unless we were both turned into skin-streaks on some dark highway...but not on that day. I had drugs, my bosses money, and friends ready to order me a round. Tally ho. Speeding along the road, I leaned into curves so sharp my knees almost touched pavement.

Colored lights of green and red flash by. The Monkey held on tight, put is black lips inches from the side of my head, and with no helmet to interfere with his speech (helmets were for pussies) began to tell of plans and future escapades. I downshifted, so the engine noise might drown out his voice, forgetting, no ignoring, that he was in my head.

"Billy, you have potential. You could possibly go on to live out a fairly bright future. I mean after all you do have a certain amount of charisma. And your appetite for creativity is without question, even managing an artistically surreal method to your fights. But a happy life you will never have."
The Monkey yelled over the ogre -throated engine noise.

"Fuck off; can't you see I'm trying to drive here?" It was not an easy job to ignore his insults, while he was so holding on that close. He leaned awkwardly as if he's never been on a motorcycle before.

"I will cause you to seek out violence rather than a painters brush, the open road of a drifter instead of hearth and home, the sword rather than the pen, and soon I will cause you to give up the race, so that your only finish line will be a ribbon tape of death."

The last comment got me very angry, almost to the point of purposely laying down the bike, and making a Monkey Smear on Lake Cook Road, even if it killed me in the process. "Shut up or we're both going to die. I'm not kidding around."

"No. You need to know what is coming for you. Each time you see me, I will appear dressed in bizarre costumes; causing you to wonder if it an acid flashback or if you're going insane. Music will be equated with dark deeds; fertile hopes will wither on the vine, creating a garden of thorns, weeds, and mushrooms. There will be no need for the face tearing and genital biting my material counterparts do in the real world to fuck you up."

"I'm telling you for the last time. Dying is nothing to me, shut up or we'll both end up a bloody splotch." I warned The Monkey, but thought, *genital biting; that is really fucked up.*

"So…Billy, on this day my mission to destroy you begins in earnest. Of course, much as my earlier victims, you will struggle valiantly to shake me from your spine. I'll bet you've already began to tell friends about the gutting I have in store. Gut me…indeed. The nerve!"

This was the longest, most unpleasant ride of my life, more like a dream. Dream or not, either way, I let the motorcycle dip precariously towards asphalt, hoping to stop the dialog. The Monkey was not impressed, although my sphincter was, warning me colonially of any further disregard for intestinal safety.

"You're really scaring me now, Billy. Drop the fucking bike. This is a fight you can't win. It will take more than toughness to gut me. Come on, put the bike on the pavement, I fucking dare you." He said, while securing a better position on me and the bike, in case I really had the balls kill both of us. Once he had a better grip he continued with his simian rant.

"Soon, your own family will get tired of the game and refuse to provide shelter from the storms raging inside your head. Enveloped in shame, your only escape will come from "blood on knuckles" and "drugs in veins." Like Alice, you'll drop in to Rabbit Hole and become Mad as a Hatter. Since music is so important, maybe you should have listened to Grace Slick from The Jefferson Airplane, when she sang "Go Ask Alice." Alice would have told you to; "Never leave the boat for Mangos" and "Never go down the fucking Rabbit hole."

And then with that last parting barrage of threats, the Monkey was gone, leaving me uncertain if the whole thing was in my head.

Was the passage of time, length of ride, primate passenger...all an illusion? I thought, trying to shake the weirdness from my mind.

I arrived at the bar, parked, sauntered in, and was greeted by three things: A Doorman who knew better than to get in my way, A Centipede video Game beeping urgently, and the last verse of "I Did You Know Wrong" by the Sex Pistols. The Pistols were a good omen and Steve Jones' chords crackled with provocative energy, hinting of untold possibilities for adventure and a substantial degree of mayhem close behind.

I briefly glanced at all the patrons, checking for anyone that was staring at me a little longer than normal, like a lone stalker, a stranger gave off revenge vibes, or if a face glaring out of the dark was trying to Mad-Dog me. In my line of work there was always somebody lurking in the shadows, waiting for the right payback opportunity and cold-cock you, steal from your boss, or snitch you out to save their sorry ass. Giving me 'The Pearl Harbor Treatment' was going to be a tough chore, as I never let my guard down.

I was not in some drug-house on a collecting errand, so my Zen mind returned, allowing acute senses to provide advance warning of any looming threat. But even if the Zen/Taoist state failed, there was always the Berserker to fall back on. As I often told my brothers, "It will take more than one punch to put me down boys, 'cause, I like getting hit, gets me in the mood."

I saw nobody that might have had a reason to seek retribution. However, I saw the person the collection errand had been for; one my principle employers—named Bitsy Moroni. Looking at him made me grin. Bitsy's appearance was so cartoonish that nobody could take a gander at his unusual face and not secretly chuckle. He was lumpishly heavyset, had sunken eyes, and a Sumo-like thick neck. He was wearing a 'Member Only' jacket. The jacket was so tight over his portly frame that it resembled a sausage casing, rather than any type of normal overcoat. *Any club that would allow Bitsy to become a member must hand out plungers at the door,* I thought.

A close examination of Bitsy would make any civilized person picture a caveman. Although Bitsy may not have looked too bright, he was clever in a way that only the streets can teach. So I never underestimated him. Even his Italian name—Bitsy Moroni, sounded like something out of a James Cagney movie. Maybe "White Heat"… Cagney's words drifted by "Top of the World Ma!"

Bitsy was drinking "Jagermiester" and shoehorning the drink down his gullet with another shot of cheap bar gin. I wretched inside; which was an unavoidable consequence, of trying to imagine what the combination tasted like.

I silently asked my ancestors to spare me from getting hit with a blast of Bitsy's face-melting breath. Any air rushing out from that human-bellow could not possibly be pleasant.

I laid my hand on his shoulder as if to say hello and casually stuck a wad of bills in his jacket pocket. He pulled the stack of cash out and flipped through the bills, apparently glad to see the remaining $5,000—from a $20,000 deal the Stoners made with Bitsy. I was glad the job was an easy one, not big, but easy. And Easy was always better then big.

"All there," I said.

"Any problems?" Bitsy asked

"Nothing that should concern you except for the fact they live like cockroaches. You shouldn't front those guys coke anymore. I don't think they're selling product anymore … it looked like they had been doing it a shitload of it."

"I ain't worried. That is what you get paid for. That brings me to another job. I need you to go with me to the burbs and drop something off. Tomorrow, at 7:00. I don't completely trust the guys coming to the meeting. Better bring a couple friends with you."

"No problem. Let's talk tomorrow about it … right now I need a drink." Bitsy nodded and shook my hand. He pulled his hand away. But not before leaving a couple hundred and a gram of coke behind in my grip. Payment made and job done.

With business over, the sounds came to rushing back in … clinking glasses, bad pick-up lines, clacking foosball handles, "He's a Whore" by Cheap Trick played, and best of all the sound of my brothers calling out join them at the bar. The sound of my brothers' voices temporarily loosened the Monkey's grip, so I threw him off my back and onto the floor, kicked at him and missed. He glanced up from the floor, scrambled to all fours, preparing to leap on to my back. But his power over me was lost while in the presence of my family. It was like kryptonite to him.

I accepted a drink and watched the Monkey retreat into a corner, merging into the shadows, beneath a "Terminator" themed pinball machine. Empowered by family it was my turn to give out a few insults.

"Go back to throwing feces and playing with your sack" I said under my breath to the Monkey. However, the insulting command I gave to the Monkey, could have probably applied to many of rouges drinking at that dive during the witching hour.

My brothers and I shot some pool. But not before I gave my girlfriend of the week a proper greeting with just the right amount of affection, demonstrating the right amount of care, while holding real emotion back, so as to give the message that she wasn't currently with some kind of dishrag to disrespect or cheat on—even if our tenure was short-lived.

My girlfriends all knew to never interfere with the personal aspects of my business and never ask questions. Prying into affairs that did not concern them was inexcusable because I was not the type of person that believed everyone deserved answers, especially from soon-to-be ex-girlfriends. Part of me was sure that each girl liked living on the edge as much as I did.

When my turn to line up a pocket came I did my best to sink a ball, missed, and resolved myself to another loss at the hands of my youngest brother, who like the rest of my clan was a Ringer, not above taking money from the other players, including me. It was all in good fun. My brothers and I were so close that any money lost would more than likely go back into drinks, golf, or a fishing trip anyway. So nobody really gave a shit. Besides I was making plenty of money from dealers, so what the hell.

Everything in our family was shared. If there was ever a group that epitomizes the phrase "*close your inner circle and everything stays in the circle"*...it was my family. I had many friends, but enjoyed the company of my brothers over most others. Each one was tough as nails and very intelligent. All of us would lay down our lives anyone of us....anytime and any-place.

Our relationship was rare, when the majority of people were only in it for themselves, turning into chicken-shit if things get dicey. However, as great as it was to see everybody, I decided to split and spend some un-quality time with the girl.

We exited the bar and she jumped on my 1100. Nice having her on the backseat, instead of The Monkey. I turned the key, the Kerker coughed twice, and then eased into the deep rumble that is the standard of all headers. Knowing what awaited when we get to the apartment, I made it a point to find out just how fast the bike can go on the straightaway that leads to our destination.

We hit 150 miles an hour, with not even a tremor or squeal from the girl on back. The Monkey is still not to be seen. *I may not have the spine to gut you right now, but that doesn't mean I can't outrun you.*

Money for Nothing

The motorcycle was a great way to escape. It couldn't lose the Monkey, but whenever there was a need for solitude, or to put my latest troubles behind, the two wheeled hot rod never failed. My brother Tim had the same Suzuki model, bought on almost the same day, from the same outlet. When we made the purchase, both of us thought the owner at the Suzuki Dealership was going to call the cops, as the payment was made with 10K in cash that smelled like mold. Thankfully, he wanted the sale more than he wanted justice. The only difference between the two motorcycles was the colors and aftermarket hardware. Tim's was blue with black stripes and was not tricked out as much as mine. The bikes were special to us because of their unmatched performance, high level chick appeal, and the fact that we had managed to get them for free. In order to explain, I need to go back in history, but only a few months into the past.

The incident occurred in spring, three months before one of my earlier collection tasks, the same job that had forced me to listen to Styx and throw a scare into the three Stoners. I was working for another dealer at the time named Jumbo. He was in the process of building a new multi-million dollar home, financed solely from his ability to move large amounts of coke, at a ridiculous profit margin. The construction project was a monster, which according to the blueprint (when the last hinge was finally secured into place); would become a garishly ornamental structure of turquoise and gray hues. Like most dealers, Jumbo was caught up in the romance of 'Miami Vice', believing his own press, convinced he was a colorful drug trafficker, larger than life—which physically he was, hence the name 'Jumbo'. The home was already beginning to resemble a movie-set piece, interior outlined with neon lights, gold inlays, and ornamental railing for multiple stairways that stretched around the structure.

The risers running up the three stairways were spacious enough to accommodate Jumbo and a girl on each arm. Jumbo may not have been Prince Charming, but with no shortage of Coke Whores looking for free drugs, he got laid on a nightly basis. On many occasions, there would be too many girls for Jumbo to handle, even with his legendary cocaine fueled stamina, so Tim and I were glad to handle the overflow. We were in effect, the dam that plugged Jumbo's flood of girls, complete with fingers in dykes.

There was even a clamshell-shaped fountain that had winged cherubs frolicking in the water-catch. I had the distinct feeling that if the cherubs knew of the depravity going on inside, they would have found a way to tear away from the concrete base and take a bath elsewhere. It would have taken many baths for the cherubs to scrub away Jumbo's bad mojo. The fountain provided great entertainment, whenever things were slow at Jumbo's late night palace. When darkness enveloped the grounds, Jumbo flipped on multi-colored lights aimed at the jets of water spraying the air. That was a fine time to drop acid, lean over the balcony, take in the red, green, and blue lights, and then watch the Cherub's change from rigid statues, into kinetic little elves, that danced in a festival of mischief. The sight was so captivating that on one occasion I watched the display till the following morning. The lone member of a rapt audience dosed with so much acid that when the cherubs turned into elves I considered asking the pointy-eared revelers if they still baked cookies in a hollow trees and made shoes while people slept.

I eventually ceased using the fountain to escalate my hallucinations when the cherubs began to criticize my failure to kill all the baby-killing warlords in Africa, as they were obviously upset at the death of their innocent brethren. That particular viewing was so startling that it caused me to edge out the window, slip, and began to slide off the roof, only to be saved by Tim's outstretched hand. Good thing Tim took smoke breaks on the roof.

Much as Jumbo's home violated all architectural normality, Jumbo was also a violation human construction. This made it impossible to describe Jumbo without using lame clichés to emphasis his freakish facial characteristics. Sometimes clichés are the only way when the person defies normal adjectives. The best way to envision what Jumbo looked like would be to imagine a Zombie with close set ball-bearing eyes, shiny, but devoid of mercy. Add a mass of tangled dark hair, a fanatical stare, a bloated beer belly, and you got Jumbo. Tim and I occasionally felt bad secretly calling Jumbo a Zombie; often feeling we should apologize to Zombies for disparaging them.

After a few coke -bumps mixed in with a few pills, Jumbo even stumbled around like a Zombie. But as far as Tim and I knew; Jumbo never ate human brains. Tim had a way of explaining Jumbo's strange habits by saying "I guess it is true what people say, that in some cases ignorance is bliss, and when it come to Jumbo's bizarre hobbies, well.....ignorance is just plain smart."

Jumbo wanted me on the job site everyday during the construction, so as to prevent any of the laborers and contractors from trying to rip off his drugs, or try to take advantage of him on the "time and material agreement"

I brought Tim and a friend named Marco along on the job. Providing security would have been impossible without some extra backup, because even though the house was still without locking doors, or an elaborate security system. There were too many places without actual doors and windows. Tim was tough, a good guy to have watching your back, hands like stone, jaw like iron. As with the rest of my family Tim had very pronounced Nordic features, a mortal version of Thor. When not throwing overhand rights, his brawling style was fairly simple, pick them up and slam them on the ground, repeat as necessary.

Marco had the build of a typical Italian Bricklayer, giant torso, short, stubby legs, overly-large hands, close-cropped bowl haircut. When it came to absorbing punishment he was in a class all by himself. He was the only guy I ever knew to survive getting hit with baseball bats by three guys. Even after getting hit multiple times in the chest and legs, he still found the jam to kick the shit out of them. The story was of mythical proportions; three guys, three bats, three concussions. In a city where everybody was a rowdy, fight-ready fuckstick, Marco was a legend. Riding with Marco in his truck, on the way to a job, was without question a heart pumping affair. He carried a .25 Auto handgun under a cut-out section of molding over the driver side door and he was not afraid to use it. In the event another driver had the audacity to cut him off, tailgate, or flip him off, the other vehicle received rolling body work, in the form of a couple bullets. I can't say for sure how many times he fired slugs into traffic, at least two times with me, and a few times with friends. How Marco was not in jail for his temper or on city weapon discharge violations was an ongoing mystery to all who knew him. Then again, I suppose many thought the same of me.

His family life was no "day at the beach" either. One brother died of aids in jail, but not before taking out an eye of another brother with a broken bottle, in a fight over some girl.

Needless to say it was a good crew. Counting Tim, Marco and myself, The Monkey made four. However, unlike Marco and Tim, The Monkey was a worthless, ball-biting, piece of shit, not the type of non-humanoid creature that you wanted on any caper. If the primate was of flesh and blood, and not a creation of my tortured mind, he would have been the kind of asshole to rat out friends, and drop dimes, like Tim dropped girlfriends. But the Monkey did have one good trait—some might say bad, able to come up with great money-making schemes, since it was his constant greed for violence, drugs and money often spurred me into action.

The creature pulling my strings is a fucking shit-tosser. I wonder if all addictions come with this kind of companion. Sure would have made me think twice before doing any kind of fucking drug if I'd known that The Monkey went with the package. "I'm still in charge; there are plenty of cocaine users in much worse shape than me." I told myself each before embarking on one of the countless nefarious escapades he coerced me into doing.

Jumbo's home was a long way from being completed. With that many entries and exits into the construction site, having a couple other guys around, made things far less stressful. Jumbo was doing so much coke while the home was being built, he was getting increasingly paranoid that somebody was watching him, or trying to sneak into his new party digs. In most cases, the days passed without too much excitement, so occasionally boredom would set in. The only real confrontation happened when I had to throw a drunken carpenter down the steps for being a smart ass. Once in a while a few shots would be fired nearby, but the rounds never hit anything except trees on the undeveloped lot next door. Which probably meant the shooter was a jealous husband, not a drug rival. On the days were there was no action, we offset the tedium by helping with the drywall construction.

We did not do this purely to pass the time or out of generosity. We knew that Jumbo often hid stacks of money in the back section of the house behind the old drywall. He had been living in the finished part of the house for about six months. This meant that there was sure to be plenty of cash somewhere in the web of wood and metal.

I also knew that Jumbo stashed whole ounces of coke in sweat socks, then also forgot about those stashes, which meant that once in a while it was laundry day for the boys. Thank god that as far as clothing goes, it was only Jumbo's socks that he hid stuff in.

After the money was stashed, he usually forgot where several bundles were. That was how much cash he had, so much that he would forget where he was piling it away. Each day we made sure that we worked on the rooms where we believed the money was stashed, or where he might have passed out the previous night.

Two of us took turns walking the perimeter of the house while the other replaced sheetrock, and searched for the loot. It wasn't hard to fool Jumbo, since he never failed to be high on Valium, Coke and liquor. In that condition, he was lucky to have us around, or he would have been an easy target for any Homestormers or druggies looking to roll him.

I was on drywall-detail when we found one the bundles, squirreled away in the rafters, wedged tight between triangle frame supports. As I ripped away a chuck of plaster it fell to the ground with a thud. I repositioned myself and looked down.

There it is ... shit ... better grab it before Jumbo or one of the workers comes in, I thought, while jumping down from the ladder, and stuffing the cash into a big pouch on my tool belt.

Plenty of room in the belt pockets for cash, several were completely empty since I geared up differently than most other tradesman. One hammer, and one .38 was generally all I carried. The Hammer was to pound in nails, and the .38 to pound skulls or maybe it was it the other way around.

Finding Jumbo's $50k matched perfectly with the song we played before starting work each morning; "Money" by Pink Floyd from "Dark Side of the Moon".

Appropriate music scored every event in my jaded past, sometimes from coincidence, and sometimes from a little too much acid. It seemed on good days that I could even manipulate fate itself, and stand outside of what might be considered the firmly established boundaries of the material world. I was an example of a guy caught up in doing too much fucking acid. Doing that much LSD altered to way I viewed the universe, the most ridiculous premise being that—while under the effects, that I was quite possibly the smartest man within three galaxies. The most dangerous thought I had about the universe was that it was trying to kill me. During those acid trips, I just chalked it up to the universe being jealous of me *Fucking universe just can't leave well enough alone.*

After finding the money, I immediately headed for the bathroom, a good spot to count the hundred-dollar bills. *Fifty thousand dollars...not a bad take*, I thought. It was clear to me that the wad of cash had been up in the frame for a long time, throughout most of the construction process, so rain must have had gotten to it. Each of the bills was spotted with dark gray mold, mildly wet and smelled like decomposing meat.

"That can be handled ... we'll figure something out." I muttered. Before leaving the bathroom, The Monkey rose out of nowhere, taking form on the sink, sitting cross-legged scratching his balls, leering, unashamed.

"You're fucking disgusting" I said, while regarding him with hateful eyes.

The Monkey held out his human-like hand. "**What about my cut of the take? Don't be greedy, Billy**"

"Even though you're most likely not real, I'm not touching your fingers; you just had your hands on your balls asshole. But I'll tell you what; since you're a figment of my mind, here is a figment of money." I said to him while flashing a sliver of invisible bills.

I was high, as mixing acid and coke had become a daily ritual, digging the trip and distortion they provided. The Monkey swatted the imaginary bills away. "**Okay, nothing for me. Fine, screw me over just because I'm a monkey. You're a si-**

mian bigot, Billy. Well, at least take more of the money for yourself. Tell Marco and Tim you only found ten thousand."

The Monkey pleaded with me to double-cross Tim and Marco, and thankfully stopped scratching his nuts.

"I'll never rip off my friends ... unless they're Zombies. There is no way I'm going to screw my partners. Why don't you leave me alone and go mess with somebody else." I told the Monkey.

"Kill anybody or seen any dead babies lately, Billy? How would you like to?" The Monkey said, while holding up hands that were all of a sudden covered with blood. In a flash my mind saw mutilated tiny corpses, worms seeking out organs, entrails, among more entrails. I felt the hot desert wind blow through my hair. The cherubs were right; I should have killed all those African pricks. Then as if by magic The Monkey was gone, off to torment another, leaving behind nothing but skin-flakes of evil.

Get yourself together, it is all an illusion. I wiped away the sweat, controlled the shaking, and put everything back into the pouch. Exiting the bathroom, I went to find Tim and Marco so I could share the news of my discovery.

But, before that could be done I had to talk to Jumbo. I found him dozing in and out while watching T.V. He was "railed up" and "blinkin and stinkin," but amazingly he still managed to mumble some coherent sentences. As was the case most times with Jumbo, if there was no idea what he was trying to say, smiling and nodding was the appropriate response. I rarely refused a request from Jumbo, being careful not to aggravate him; otherwise he would have emotional outbursts and mood swings that might last for days. Regardless of his instability, it often became necessary to warn Jumbo to be careful how he talked to me.

He was a screamer and sometimes the only way to shut him up was to threaten him with violence. The downside to attitude adjusting Jumbo was that after cooling down he would want to hug. Hugging was just not my thing, preferring to keep a bit of distance between Jumbo and me, as there was something (call it a black aura or an undeniable freakish presence) that Jeebied me out ... sometimes even predicating it with a dose of the Heebees.

Jumbo woke up, confused, groggy, and saw me standing next to his favorite crashing couch. "Jumbo, I got to go. I must have caught a case of the flu or something. Don't want to puke all over your new house. I'm going home … but Marco and Tim will stick around" I said quickly. I was impatient to get out of there, get to my place, and start cleaning the loot, so I pantomimed the vestige of a sick dude ready to empty his stomach all over the new house.

"Want a bump before you go?" Jumbo said voice raspy from cigarettes. He held out a tray with two massive lines of coke on it. "Come on, Billy ... it will make you feel better."

"Yeah, right, Jumbo. Only you would insist that someone does blow to get rid of a fever. Listen, man. If it is okay I'll pass, go home to get some sleep, and be back tomorrow." I reminded myself never to seek Jumbo's medical advice if a limb got chopped off. He would probably tell me to do a bump to stop the bleeding."

"Come on, one line won't kill you. When did you turn Amish? Jumbo joked, and then blew his nose in a wad of tissue. A truly revolting amount of mucus came out. Now I really was getting sick.

So I did a line anyway. Otherwise he might have gotten suspicious. Everyone knew that (as Marco put it) *"priests will stop molesting kids before Billy ever turns down a bump."* I was glad to leave; Jumbo had a weird way of knowing things. Not 'physic', 'psycho', but he seemed to have the ability to read minds, a trait that made most people feel nervous around him … even me!

While moving through the house I thought about the worst case scenario if Jumbo caught on to the rip-offs. *He may be the Boss, but he better not accuse me, or I will fuck him up, let the chips fall where they may. He'll send other goons after me... but his other guys were mostly big bodybuilder type, all show and no go.* My mind drew a mental sketch of the slow and clumsy fighters sent to teach us a lesson—the kind that have never been hit hard in the nose and are really nothing better than Puffer Fish in a scrap.

Shit! I'll take any of my brothers and Marco over an army of assholes like that. I thought to myself as I went outside the house.

I stepped through the baroque front entrance and I waved Marco and Tim over. They followed me to a secluded corner of the torn-up backyard, stopping behind a pile of wood and metal scraps.

"Dude ... you found it didn't you? How much? Let's see." Tim said, using a vernacular and rhythm that slipped in and out of surf lingo. Marco and Tim moved closer to inspect the stack of cash. They smelled it before they saw it.

"Fifty thousand ... split three ways. But ... as you can see, and smell, we going to have to clean it up before we spend it". They leaned and got a closer look at the mold-covered bills.

"Does Jumbo suspect anything?" Tim asked.

"No way, Tim! He's so fucking high right now he doesn't even know what day it is. I'm going to my place, clean each bill off in the sink, and then hang them up to dry on a clothes line. I'll rig everything up around the apartment and have it set by the time you guys arrive." I said to keep them patient and see that everything was under control.

Of course it took all their will power to remain at Jumbo's and watch over him while I split with fifty grand. But they knew me and knew their cut was in good hands. Besides, if we all left at once then Jumbo's weird brain antenna might have noticed something unusual and made him more paranoid then he already was.

"I agree ... we have to function as if someday he will notice the money missing. In his condition it is a long shot ... but it pays to be careful." Tim said.

When I got to my apartment I began the process of scrubbing each bill in detergent. After rinsing the bills I hung every one up to dry as fast as possible so it could be spent on the lavish celebration that was already floating through my brain. Before long there were five hundred one-hundred dollar bills attached to every conceivable location throughout the entire apartment. We had decided that whenever the money was found, we would all buy motorcycles. But it would look strange if we plopped down wet bills that still smelled like soap.

So I gave it all another dip in the sink. "What a time for one of my friends to stop by...or worse yet my landlord," I jokingly said.

We all ran in the same illegitimate circles, so we agreed that nobody must find out about our self-produced good fortune. If that happened it would eventually get back to Jumbo that we came into some money. Then we would really have some explaining to do.

For the first couple weeks we all stayed true to the promise of not going on a spending spree. But eventually we could not help ourselves; buying motorcycles, stereo, VCRs. As expected, somebody with a big mouth drew attention to our unexplained windfall. Jumbo wasn't certain that we stole from him, but he sent a couple guys to put a little pressure on us anyway, just to see how we reacted. Jumbo was aware that he was missing money. It was a bad break! Of all the stacks of hidden cash and coke Jumbo had forgotten over the years, he remembered the one we got.

The confrontation occurred at an after-hours bar called Craig's Annex, which was a local hangout for late-night partiers, dealers, and coke heads. Tim and I were out drinking with Jumbo on Halloween, and were not aware that he had any suspicions about the theft. Tim and I excused ourselves from Jumbo's table, and walked outside to get away from the smoke-filled atmosphere, and get some weed from our car. When we got halfway to our vehicle, four guys approached Tim and me.

The tallest guy went by the biker name Bumper. He was a real specimen; with a frizzy dervish haircut, ink-covered forearms, ring clips on both ear-lobes, and (according to the smell that assaulted our noses) way too much Brut cologne. He twisted his face into a tough look, gritted teeth, made crazy eyes, and then said "Jumbo's missing some dough. We better not find out who took it or they're dead"

Tim and I looked at each other, knowing full well that neither of us was going to let some asshole invade our space with that kind of tone. We let them step a little closer until their leader was standing right in front of me.

"I am a black belt in karate ... just thought you should know." He exclaimed while doing some kind of complicated Kata in the air. His exaggerated sweeping hand gestures and static stance showed he practiced the fake martial arts. Probably attended the kind of school that taught "Dragon begets

Swan to seek out Crane" instead of the much more useful "Right hook meets left cheekbone."

"I'm going to put you all to sleep, Bumper. Just thought you should know" I said directly to the group, still mildly amused at the display of bullshit. The guy continued with his Kata.

"Very graceful, he's just like a kung fu ballerina, isn't he Tim? Hey, dickhead, did you earn your black belt for punching air? I said and Tim laughed out loud.

"Please don't hurt us, Bruce Lee." Tim said, and then we went to work.

Bumper had both hands close to his ribs, focused into some kind of chi-filled horse stance. I filled my lungs to capacity and looked for an opening. His height and misguided stance (no space between each leg) made a wrestling takedown the easiest attack. I hit him low, right where he bends—at the knees, with a double leg scoop, and then picked him up over my shoulder.

When I had him high enough in the air to produce a crushing impact, I slammed him on the hood of a nearby BMW. The elevated power-drop was a bonus strike. As Tim and I hated yuppie's cars almost as much as we hated the guys driving them"

The impact drove wind and courage from Bumper at the same time. Tim gave the other guys each a hard shove. When one of them angled forward, he exposed his lower back. Tim stepped to the side and threw a liver punch that was so hard it made the other guy piss his pants. Bumper slid off the BMW, shook off the cobwebs, and squared off with me. This time he shifted his initial fight posture into a variation of "Passing Cloud Tai Chi Chih." While his arms and hands "passed the clouds" in a very esoteric striking sequence, I shin-kicked his jaw, grabbed his hair, and then bent him over so I could sink a guillotine choke. Instead of going for the choking arm, he reached for my legs, allowing me to tighten the stranglehold and close off blood to his acorn-sized brain and stop oxygen to his lungs. After about 30 seconds, Bumper sagged, collapsing on the ground.

His friends came forward and helped Bumper up back to his feet. The other guy—that got the blast from Tim, apologized for the misunderstanding.

Yeah, you're sorry all right; for the misunderstanding your liver had with Tim's fist, I thought. I hoped Bumper learned a lesson about being careful who he accuses of stealing from Jumbo.

"Fucking Jumbo, sending these morons to feel us out." Tim said as we brushed off our shirts. "I knew we should have waited longer before spending the money."

"Too late now, Tim. We'd better go back in and straighten this shit out." I responded.

We went back into the bar and rejoined Jumbo at his table. He denied being any part of the fight that happened outside.

"Must be some kind of mistake ... you guys know that I would never think it was you. I only wanted them to ask you what your opinion was," he said to Tim and me.

"Jumbo, we've known each other a long time, but if anyone else mentions this shit to us, ever again, you're going to regret it. You probably lost the money just like you lose everything else."

Things were still very tense, so to break the mood and make us laugh, Jumbo placed a bag filled with coke under his nose and blew into it. The light powder exploded from the bag and stuck to his sweaty face turning it white. "Boo! I'm a ghost!"

I have to admit it was pretty funny. However, that foolish display—in a public place—began the baby-sitting part of the job. Tim insisted Jumbo put the shit away and wipe off his face while I shielded the table from the rest of the late night partiers. Everyone in the bar did coke, but covering your face with blow was going a little too far.

Controlling Jumbo's impulses to do stupid things was always a big part of watching over him. He had a tendency to think he was invincible. This applied to the law and to most other things when he was tooted up. That night at the bar was like a bad omen of things to come for Jumbo. He left the bar, so fucked up that he passed out at a red light—only a few blocks from his house.

Jumbo sat there—in the car for about ten minutes before the police found him and took him away. During the following court proceedings the judge also took his house for being ill-gotten gains. We felt bad for him, but it was bound to happen to him. Better Jumbo in jail then kill some innocent person on the way home.

It was five in the morning when I got home. Birds were already outside the window singing.   I called a cokehead named Jill and told her to come over. Within minutes after she arrived we were high as a lightning storm. I put on "All the Way from Memphis" by "Mott the Hoople." and together we watched the Sun came up.   While we sat there in silence, I swore that this was the last time doing drugs, it was out of control, a habit, screwing up my mind.

"Next collection goes towards setting up a legitimate business or maybe even to help with college." I said after Jill passed out.

Looking down at her prone body across my lap, coke residue under her nostrils, saliva oozing from her mouth, told me all I needed to know about my life.

But I had said this pledge many times before after each night of debauchery, so this promise was nothing new. This time there was a feeling of certainty that I was going to die in some gutter, or get shot in the back of the head.

My hangover caused an impressive head throb and morning pain. But it was nothing compared to the knowledge that I was wasting my intellect and that my dream of being a writer and geologist were fading fast. The unrelenting pull of drugs was overpowering me. It was if I was becoming an imagined phantom and the Monkey was becoming the real entity. Maybe he was dreaming me. Seppuku beckoned from a distant future knowing of the shame that waited for me on black streets.

Turning Japanese

I went back to my apartment later in the afternoon. I opened the door and flipped on the radio. Outstanding! The song surging across the airwaves was a favorite of mine *"Turning Japanese"* by the Australian New Wave group *"The Vapors."* I mouthed the chorus to myself and tossed my faded bomber jacket on the couch. The taste of the nights activates was still on my lips, so I tore open the fridge, and chugged down a bottle of Perrier. The Monkey had arrived at my place before me and was seated at the kitchen table. He was smoking a filter-less cigarette, flicking the ashes on the tile floor, even though an ashtray was within reach.

"Hey, fuckhead ... there's an ashtray right in front of you. Do you have to drop that crap on the floor?" I said while reminding myself to clean up the pretend mess with a pretend vacuum. His foul smell assaulted my nostrils, rising above the smoke rings. I flung open a window and fanned the room with my shirtsleeve. He ignored me, blew another smoke ring, then put the cigarette out in his hairy palm.

"Aren't you the tough guy, huh?" I said, more of an accusation than question. The increase of unconfirmed Monkey sightings caused me to question the large quantities of acid I'd been consuming.

As of yet, there are no goblins, unicorns, or aliens following me around. Nor are there genies steaming from magic lamps.... so maybe I'm being too paranoid. Shit....after all, even Sir Arthur Conon Doyle, the writer of Sherlock Holmes, believed he had pixies and fairies living in his garden, I thought. Then while looking directly at The Monkey I said "Fairies— shit how bad can you be?"

The Monkey seemed as if he was about to open his mouth, but apparently thought better of it.

He must be using his finely-tuned emotion receptors to decode my current level of patience, thereby instantly determining that I'm not in the mood for any of his banter, I thought.

I slipped into a peaceful, contemplative state. Seeing no opportunity to push me into anything destructive, The Monkey climbed up the wall like a crab, and jumped out the open window. "No doubt on his way to locate a suitable strip club or bowery where he could cause some trouble." I whispered, while glancing out the window at my own garden.

Still no fairies or pixies.....good. I was relieved.

The Monkey was gone but his return was inevitable as he was undoubtedly waiting for the coming of night to create mischief. It was an easy thing for him to bide time, and put off the next strike, until the rise of the killing moon. Only then could he be positive of regaining control over my appetites.

"Turning Japanese" ended but the music's influence on my imagination did not. The title made me think of the time I spent in Japan. I pictured Mt Fuji. In my mind, I saw the snow-capped upper layer that rose high above the spring blossoms of pink and white down below at the foot of the mountain. Ever since my travels in Asia I had become enamored with the Chinese and Japanese philosophers. Once I set foot back in the States, I considered myself no longer shackled to Western values, or misguided beliefs in American Exceptionalism. I reduced myself to having the same value as dirt or dust, and practiced non-interference by closing my inner circle. I could hear spiders and feel light....I was a Taoist, firmly entrenched with the belief that man was of no significance with no impact on the universe what so ever. I walked as a ghost and spoke as a man. But the ghost part of me was gradually overtaking the flesh part of me. I had only disdain for the weakness of the flesh part.

"If anything holds a hope of defeating the Monkey and guiding me back towards a more fulfilling life and peaceful existence.... it will be by delving deeper into "The Way of the Taoist." I affirmed, as a preamble into *"The Way."* My nights may have been saturated with drug-fueled misadventures and irresponsible decisions but the morning belonged to me.

This was the part of the day where habitually I practiced Tai Chi, meditated, and visualized a life without drugs. I promised the Sun I would someday shatter my subservience to white powder, rid myself of demons; be the devils Monkeys or any other animal from the zoo menagerie. In a Zen state, living as nothing, that was when I was at my strongest. At times I believed that casting out my devils was close at hand.... but then the night would come, and my strength ebbed. And the Werewolf once again sought the killing-moon, howling, over city sounds, and Monkey screams.

I pushed the negative thoughts away and considered the positive. I had become extremely well versed in the works of Sun Tzu, Myamoto Mysashi, and Lao Tzu. Going so far as to occasionally read the "I Ching"—but did so only for entertainment value, for I knew full well that it had as much ability to predict the future... as Nostradamus's ramblings. It held the same logic to me as "Burning Witches" saying "The Rosary", or carrying a rabbit's foot did.

"You had to be a moron not to understand that given a long enough timeline, combined with enough predictions ... anything would begin to resemble accuracy. The human brain learns by recognizing patterns and looks to find them even where there aren't any." I said such things at parties from my soapbox during highlights of keen intellect infused with stentorian oratory skills ... and too much Mexican skunk-weed.

But I had earned the privilege to make such bold statements because of a special insight into human nature. All druggies thought they had such a power. But it was a skill that did not really exist, demonstrating how misplaced my understanding of what was happening to me was.

Granted, I was a fuck-up, but not your everyday brain-dead thug. Ignorance bothered me a great deal, especially after pounding a few cocktails. After a few stiff drinks, I often searched out the most bigoted and intolerant person to argue with...another bad habit of mine to be sure. Normally, the people spouting the most nonsense were the same blowhards who claimed a unique education, the type of intellect gotten from the regular act of paging through scripture (but only after a day full of cheating, lying, and coveting).

How could anyone choose to use the religious doctrine as a source of information about the world over the writings of Sagan, Kierkegaard or Thoreau? I thought, whenever confronted by Bible Freaks and their ridiculous claims of their intimate relationship with morals and truth. Sometimes The Monkey's witnessed my statements, sharp round ears locking in on my assertions, or seeing my obvious intentions to convince others of my cleverness. He would shriek the same rebuttal in order to reintroduce me to the reality of my own existence as a pathetic drug user. *"Stop pretending to be Plato and go beat someone up, you asshole."* When the Monkey was right he was right!

However, (Monkey insults and taunts aside) the philosopher that I identified most with was Nietzsche. When he spoke of good, evil and described how *"the abyss stares back at all men if they gaze into it long enough."*... well it seemed that he was talking directly to me.

But pondering Nieztche did not assist my daily attempts to create a feeling of balance and harmony in the chaos of my tortured mind. So my heart went out to the Eastern Sages. Tia Chi and Gi Gong were not disciplines I fell back on when things got ugly. They were far too esoteric and passive to be of any use in a bone-breaking altercation.

"Do they allow you to breathe better? Yes! Do they allow you to move better and regain your footing when forced into an awkward position far quicker than a non-adept? Yes," I told most of the guys I trained with. Then explained to them how it works in the real world.

"In the event you ever find yourself facing down a charging 250lb maniac, there is no substitute for Mauy Thai or Pankration. You do not need breathing exercises that bring forth visions of swans on silver lakes when fists and kicks are flying. What you need are the elbows, knees, and the brutal chin strikes of Thai boxing, backed up with the throws, chokes and pain submissions of a grappling art like Pankration. Since I was an expert in these skills—way before UFC—I was ahead of the fighting curve as it applied to unarmed combat.

Having such abilities also meant avoiding random altercations at all costs...which I did. I can honestly pronounce that I never started a fight. In fact, I wanted to stay clear of delivering series injuries—for the other guy that is, and therefore steer clear of the cops. But for all my knowledge and experience in unarmed combat, I was still easy prey for The Monkey. His jabs counters (strengthened by years of climbing imaginary trees) always seemed to penetrate my defenses. He was undefeated as the reigning champion. He was a hairy Jedi Warrior with an uncanny talent to find a hole in my armor and bring forth my most predatorily instincts.

It was also his great mental game that made the Monkey such a dangerous opponent. He also had impeccable timing, bobbing and weaving from the outside, until the moment was at hand to strike, when his victim was at his weakest. Then—and only then, could The Monkey be sure of penetrating all noble defenses.

"That is what makes me the Champ and what makes it impossible for you to remove me from your back." The Monkey reminded me whenever he felt I was getting a mite too cocky.

There were several occasions where I believed I had the Monkey on the ropes. At those times I threw my hardest shots at him, and my most secure (and impossible to escape from) joint breaks. He withstood them all. But there were some rare occurrences when I got a reprieve from his malevolent urgings. The short, yet long-awaited, advantage over the antagonist resulted in the simplest of occurrences. It was the look in the eyes of my family and the twinge of guilt that came from the seeing the glimmer of disappointment that I was gradually slipping deeper into the void and losing the best parts of a fading self.

If I had tried harder—maybe by moving away, and out of the reach of my so-called friends, there might have been a chance to cast aside temptation—not the Christian kind, but the feral kind of temptation. I did not move fast enough, and so when regret finally eclipsed my ill-conceived fondness for infamy.... it was too late.

The Monkey had already fed off my pain to the extent that although he might have exhibited the size of an average chimp; he had the strength King Kong and the fleetness of a gibbon. However, I was not going to just drop my hands just because internal shame tossed a few wimpy punches my way. It would take much more to put my ego on the mat and put an end to my belief that doing drugs was an event that could be ceased whenever I felt like it.

Since my addiction started at seventeen, shortly after I entered the marines, it would not go away easy. How much judgment does anyone have at seventeen, especially during a cultural time which basically stated to all; a person could not be more cool or hip, then by snorting blow? To be clear, making excuses has never been my method of getting by, so I'll end my sob story right here. I can see the writing on the wall, it says "much as age brings wisdom it also brings the sadness of realizing there are no *"do overs"* ... *only do betters."*

My normal workout lasted several hours. It was the only way to stay sharp in so many disciplines. Can't let yourself turn into a sugar-cookie when you're in a line of work where you never know if you're about to take or give one on the chin. Wobbly legs just won't do in my occupation. Or, as my old drill instructor used to say, "fail to operate at the highest degree of excellence and you will face failure at the lowest level of incompetence."

I finished my workout right as my brother got home from work. It was Friday! So as night came we were all going to meet at Bennigans, which back then was not a yuppie breeding ground, but instead a pretty cool hangout that played eclectic music. On a good evening you could hear everything from popular bands like "The Doors" to obscure Power-pop musicians like "The Shoes" or "Pezband". This particular Bennigans attracted some of the best looking girls on the north shore. It wasn't even necessary to partake in small talk, be sensitive, or laugh at fem-jokes to get laid. All you needed was a gram of coke and a boner ... and most of the time my friends and I had both. There were still a few hours to kill before we went out, so we cracked couple more beers and watched a Clockwork Orange. Six o clock and we were already tilting back a few cold ones, while intently observing the movie's anti-hero – Alex, as he planned some "Ultra Violence" and played "Hogs of the Road."

My other brothers arrived and took a seat to watch the conclusion of the movie. The ending was a sad conclusion to Alex's life of rage. His life of crime is cut short, after being captured by the authorities, and to makes things even worse, during lockup Alex is brainwashed into becoming a pacifist and incapable of violence. While helpless, and unable to defend himself, he meets all his previous victims. Each person he previously harmed, during his numerous crime sprees, takes a turn in fucking him up – including the old gang. It was a great ending to a great movie. However, it made me wonder. What sort of beating have I accumulated for all my past transgressions? At least, my LSD use, would save anyone the trouble of brainwashing me. Hallucinogenic chemicals had already started to scrub my gray matter clean—of everything, and fill the empty brain cells up, with extraordinary and preposterous notions.

To ensure we got the best movies at a time when availability was severely limited we had both Betas and VHS. The bookshelves were lined with cassettes bought with Jumbo's stolen money and collection cuts I earned. We had Elephant Man, The Kinks—One for The Road, Phantasm, Bootlegs of Ice Station Zebra, Mad Max, and Jeremiah Johnson. All were standards of viewing at our stumble-abode. As years passed, the collection went on to include all the classics like; The Deerhunter, Apocalypse Now, Mean Streets and Platoon, violence being the central theme. We gathered together in the center of the room and initiated the *"going out ritual"* to draw forth the Viking gods. We each held up a shot of tequila as my brother Tim placed the diamond stylus on a spinning vinyl disc and played the song *"Chained"* by Van Halen.

Some were beginning to shrug off Van Halen as Rock Jokes and David Lee Roth as the Clown Prince of Crapola.... but we still thought that V.H shook the heavens much as the Viking Gods themselves. But for all his finger flash, and fret tapping, Eddie was unable to match the ethereal brilliance of Bill Nelson, Tom Verlaine, or Jeff Beck.

Sometimes the Monkey would appear and try to make a music selection. However, his choice was the same every time, "George of the Jungle" or "GuitarZan" by Ray Stevens, so it was easily vetoed. The Monkey could make me take drugs, but chimps will never select my music, especially when there is the need to "Go Congo". That was the right time to listen to "The New York Dolls" and "Johnny Thunders." The Dolls were one of my favorite bands and there was never a bad time to blast the sound of "Babylon" or "Showdown."

Yeah...you can gather the inner strength to prevent the Monkey from bending your will when it comes to music, but you can't resist his push to stare into the abyss, I thought as I prepared for the night.

Since it was Friday night it was not the appropriate time for technical subtlety on musical instruments. Instead, it was the time for searing guitar and Bonham-like stomping.... so Van Halen would do just fine. With one 80 proof shot down our down our throats, and since it rapidly approaching 8:00, the boys were all antsy to hit the road. The only person missing was the habitually unpunctual Andy Benjamin. He joined us every Friday night. Andy was a very rare kind of cat who dressed like no other guy I knew. The attire he wore was between Outlaw Biker and Wall Street Banker. It was as if his mother found him at Sturgis and insisted he throw on a good Armani shirt over his torn blue-jeans, chaps and cowboy boots in order to go the Granny's for "Sunday Brunch after Church."

Andy was also the only person in our group that rode a Harley. He considered Jap Bikes to be yuppie rickshaws and often exclaimed, "Anyone who rides a rice burner is a fag...except for you guys that is! Nobody gets more chicks then a Harley rider."

"That might be true, Andy, but you've never seen our bikes broke down on the side of the road, blowing oil fumes, or our clothes covered in grease just from riding. And that's why you and that slow Buffalo piece of shit are always the last to show up."

In most cases, Tim fell for the bait, and engaged in the timeless argument of 'Hog' over 'Crotch Rocket', while everyone else was forced to listen to the two of them insult each other's bikes. If not broken up, the debate could quite possibly rage for hours. Luckily someone always interceded during most of the passionate conversations and an uncomfortable truce was arranged.

The ceasefire was a good thing for Andy because if it ever came to blows, Tim would wipe the floor with him. That is not to say Andy was not tough...he was...Tim was tougher. We doubted that Andy would ever let it get that far. He was a merciless bully, but only if you showed any sign of weakness ... of which Tim never does.

For all his aggressive bullshit, Andy had a quality that made him an asset in any situation. His humor could liven up even the most mundane events. Like most of my friends he was a dealer. In fact, the demand for coke was so great during the 80's, almost everyone we knew dabbled in the supply side at one time or another. This fact often caused Tim to ask "if everyone we know is dealing drugs, who the fuck is buying them?

Andy died shortly after our last get-together from a shotgun blast to his head during an obviously successful attempt at suicide. He had everything to live for but his heavy use of steroids and reliance on massive amounts of Coke warped his brain. One day he got depressed over a girl and decided to put his brains on the wall. A guy who could get any woman he wanted kills himself over a chick because drugs made him irrational.

Andy's death was another one of life's lessons that I should have taken to heart, but failed to do so. Like all users I answered my grief with the self determination. "Man, he had everything going for him. That will never happen to me."

Andy was the first of my friends to die at such a young age, outside of the military that is. Each day was rapidly sinking into a quicksand thick with drugs and violence. He would not be the last! The Monkey joined me at the wake as he never met a funeral he didn't enjoy. He hopped from chair to chair until his last jump landed him on top of the closed casket. He did a jig, dancing for several seconds, and then opened his mouth to ridicule my dead friend.

I turned and walked out. No way was I going to give the Monkey more of an opportunity to say bad things about Andy. Even though I stopped the primate from further disparaging my friend he still managed to convince me to go have a drink and take my anger out on the first asshole to put his hands on me and push me the wrong way.

That tragedy (Andy's Suicide) as well as my own attempts, was still in the future, and for right now there were more pressing matters to consider like putting down one more shot and enjoying Andy's amazingly sharp humor while it lasted.

Shark Attack

With all the pre-party rituals in order, we got on our bikes and roared to our next destination. Andy rode his chopped Sportster, Tim and I sat atop on our ES 1000s, James and Sven on their Suzuki 750s. Emil and Mike chose a four-wheel method of travel instead of fighting gravity on a two-wheel mode of transportation, probably as their common sense was significantly greater than ours. Each time we rode, my eldest brother Emil reminded, "There are two types of motorcycle riders: those who have already dropped their bikes and lost layers of skin, and those who are about to." He turned out to be quite the oracle, a few years later both Sven and I suffered some pretty serious injuries that resulted from motorcycle accidents.

But that night, for those of us utilizing the two-wheel mode, it turned into a race to see who could pull up to the front doors first. We flew in and out of traffic with little or no regard for the laws of centrifugal force, making the journey not without risks, but so much the better … for me that is! Winning the checked flag was more important than a possible road rash. Success was determined by which of us got to the bar first and had a round waiting for the snails. The privilege of lining up drinks usually belonged to me. My bike had superior horsepower, and I rode fearless, taking exit ramps at a 25 degree angle, while passing cars with reckless abandon.

Once all of us were inside, beers were downed, and all of us immediately begun to review the female talent. Each of us had their own system of attracting women, some strategies very successful, others producing nothing but the Large-Boned-Good- Personality types—or as James used to say "fatties." Andy relied on his machete-sharp wit to get the attention of his quarry, whereas Tim and I preferred a more direct approach: offering rides on the Motorcycles, or when that failed, quoting obscure philosophers.

Emil introduced women to his finely-honed intellectual gift of gab. Sven used a variation of the ambush approach. He used his rare ability to act interested in anything that came from perfect lips, no matter how boring or stupid. I make no boast that all of these tricks were of our invention, I'm sure Neanderthals used much the same approach, in the event that hitting their potential mates over the head with a club didn't work. Time tested and percentage of wins proven, the cons we used to bag big-game, were nothing more than standard operating procedure for guys on the prowl.

However, James and Mike employed the most terrifying technique to get their fair share of potential One-Nighters. They actually danced!

Well ... strictly speaking, James danced, and Mike swam around like a Great White Shark, just waiting for the opportunity to bite down with his dagger sharp charm. Mike liked to call it his "Charm as Chum" method. It was an interesting approach, something I would have never attempted, being as how I was usually too high to "Cut a Rug."

But watching James dance was kind of cathartic, due to the fact that his spastic movements cast some demons from me. Tim and I called James dance steps "The Exorcism Boogie" for that very reason.

It did, however, draw many females out of the crowd to watch him move. Mike singled out women that were the most gullible, but still conceited and obnoxious enough to be his victims. He often explained; the strange combination of characteristics he sought in women by saying; "Any girl who is that abrasive and yet still not bright enough to see I'm just feeding her lines ... deserves a date with me." I thought of Mike's explanation as some sort of strange Natural Selection, except Nature favored the strongest and Mike favored the Dumbest.

Fortunately, there was always plenty of chicks (that fit his specifications) to choose from, as they drew nearby to view James quirky jerky rumba steps.

One time; while watching James' moves, a drug-induced vision of the flame-scorched Hindenburg popped into my brain, the dirigible cried out "Oh ... the humanity!" There is no way to be certain where the ghostly cry resonated from, but I always assumed it came from somewhere deep within the void. Can burning blimps observe people like James dance? Nobody can know for sure. However, I hoped the Hindenburg Blimp somehow felt better about its own fiery demise after viewing the carnage of James' rhythmic pulsations.

So, when "Shark Attack" by the "Spilt Enz" came over the speakers, James hit the floor, and Mike became a Mako. I must admit James could really make the dance floor his own. So finding a partner and holding court was a foregone conclusion. In a family of 'Brickfoots', James was the only Halverson with the fabled magic legs. And he had them way before Forest Gump. "Dance Forest Dance!" mystical voices cried from the ether.

My first stop—before casting my own babe-net—was to hit the restroom and either do my own coke (or if the Monkey had his wish), "take it from somebody else." The act of taking drugs from people (we didn't know) was accomplished by watching for any idiots unable to control the impulse to sniff. Once we picked someone out that seemed to be too high to know what was going on around him, we followed them into the bathroom. One of us watched the door, as the others flipped open fake badges. After we had their drugs, we let them sweat for a minute or two, and then informed them that we were cutting them a break, so the best thing for them was to beat it and not to ever come back ... we kept the drugs of course. Either way, whether it was my coke or someone else's didn't much make a difference to me! I only cared about finding a way to "rail up" and take in the surge of adrenaline.

After fueling my receptor sites, I searched out Tim and found him speaking to a group of enthralled girls. He was explaining the scientific method called "Occam's Razor", which was helpful in formulating the correct solution to just about any problem. The three girls listening to him were wide-eyed and marveled at his apparent genius.

"Shit ... he is using Occam ... that's my opening." I thought. I prepared to launch into a second choice—Aristotle, when my attention was pulled to a commotion around an Asteroids game. A bloated sailor was pushing a skinny guy and calling his girlfriend names. From what I was able to ascertain, the Fatass and his squid buddies had been caught in the act of goosing the girl.

The skinny guy was doing his very best to stand up and defend her honor, but being outnumbered, he was now a human pinball, pushed back and forth between the sea-going assholes who chortled with agro-glee. My brothers and I held bullies and loud mouths to the greatest distain. We considered it a matter of honor to stick up for the little guy or anyone else who was unable to fend for themselves against the tyranny of ignorant toads. In my opinion, there was nothing better in life than taking the wind out of a windbag. Or maybe in was not chivalry, maybe I just wanted to fight.

I took a few quick strides and positioned myself inbetween the Squids (navy personal). I could tell by their appearance that these were not Seals or UDT ... only rust scrappers. I wanted to try and calmly talk them out picking on someone so much smaller. It was not going to be an easy task, because they were all still itching for a fight—or maybe it was just a form dermatitis that made them itch—after all, the Squids had probably been together on ship a long time.

When the two groups separated, I spoke directly to the biggest of the Squids, obviously their leader.

"Come on....there is three of you and this guy is half your size. You can see he does not want to fight so leave him alone!" I said rather forcefully, while at the same time guiding the guy and his girl out of range.

"Why don't you mind your own business, Homo?" The biggest Squid (who henceforth will be referred to as Fatboy— due to his ration of blubber to muscle) replied. It wasn't much of a clever insult, but it was probably all he could muster using such a feeble brain. Then he glanced at my marine tattoo, on my forearm, and his face lit up. It was obvious that he felt delighted to have stumbled upon the words on my arm; it gave him the ultimate insult to a former Recon Marine.

"Marine, huh? Yeah ... I know a lot of marines. I met them after leaving their barracks after fucking their mothers. Marines are all a bunch of pussies."

I responded by pointing out his disfigured cleft above his upper lip. "Nice hair-lip ... borrowed that from Stacy Keach, did you?"

He apparently harbored embarrassment over the lip mutation. His face turned the color of a tomato, most likely from embarrassment, but maybe from a small amount of suppressed and misplaced anger, bad childhood or something like that. He followed the verbal assault with a hard shove that sent me slamming into the video game. I bounced off the game and prepared to give Fatboy a new mutation to tell the emergency room doctors about. In my mind, I heard an imaginary bell ring. Fatboy stood with his legs spread wide, fists up, ready to trade punches. The Monkey popped into view. He swung from a fake street sign located behind Fatboy, who saw me gazing over his shoulder, probably wondering what the fuck I was looking at. On this occasion, The Monkey was dressed as both coach and cut-man. He punctuated every swing by calling out combinations. ***"Double jab, right hook, high knee, and step under suplex."***

"Shut up, I got this." I told the Monkey, causing even more confusion on Fatboy's face. Round one was under way. The lesson for today was that untested—out of shape— rednecks should mind their manners when in the presence of women. Especially when faced with the inherent danger of running into the wrong guy while playing Badass.

"Welcome to the world of wrong guys" I told my oppo- nent, while ducking under a haymaker, then grabbing his col- lar, crossing each lapel, so that the pressure slowed his breath- ing.

To the Monkey's disappointment, I did not increase the pressure. Instead I got a few inches from his face so only he could hear what I was saying.

"Listen closely to what I'm about to tell you. You do not want to fight inside this bar and trust me; I'm the last guy you want to put your hands on. I'm going to go across to the other side of the bar and if I were you I would stay here and brag to your friends that you "put me in my place. If you approach me again or say one more word to me I'm going to break both your arms." I paused to let it sink in and then continued with anoth- er warning. "I want you to ask the people that work here, and anyone else in the crowd, if you should fuck with me. They all know me here you should listen to what they have to say."

If he had taken my advice, the issue wouldn't have gone any further, the bar staff and most of the regulars had watched me stomp a couple of rednecks a couple weeks ago. The bar- tender in particular was in a position to speak of my fighting prowess, since he got his coke from Bitsy, and therefore knew well of my reputation.

I did not wait for a reply because at this point conversation had no value so none was needed. It was time to move on....if I stayed in the circle of Squids, it would encourage them to do something as stupid, like charge me all at once. I moved away from what was surely turning into a rumble. I joined my brothers and friends near the end of the bar, hoping the sailors would not mistake my desire to avoid trouble for a lack of fighting ability. My brothers did their best to help me to stay calm.

But ... a more persistent voice chimed in over my brother's advice. The Monkey would not be ignored. He fully materialized by the bar (still dressed as a corner-man) and spoke right on cue.

"When did you turn into a pussy? The sailors are all laughing at you right now. Come on, go Jap Slap them.....do you want the word on the streets to be that you're a pushover?"

"Shut up...Can't you leave me anyone for once?" I mentally implored him.

"Can't you quit drugs? I'll tell you what. You quit drugs and I'll disappear forever. What .... no deal?" He said laughing.

I ignored the rest of what the Monkey was saying and turned my attention to my brothers. The last thing I ever wanted to do was fight. If it didn't involve doing The Protection/Collection Gig, then risking injury, or dealing with cops was not worth it. To me these guys were harmless drunks and completely unaware of the potential danger they were in. I hoped that common sense would prevail, but it was not to be so. Fatboy neglected to heed my advice and was fast approaching with his deck -swabs in tow.

I glanced around to make sure my brothers were aware of the impending crisis and were ready to handle the other Squids. Which of course they would do at the drop of a hat. Fatboy got right in front of me and stopped only a few feet away. One again, he brought his fists up, inflated his chest, then gave me his best line. "I'm going to rip off your balls and feed them to you!"

"Scary stuff!" I said, rolling my eyes and then continuing with the only remark that came to mind. "Now you really got me frightened. You should grit your teeth when you talk like that...it will work better for you! I do not want to fight you."

The Monkey drew more impatient *"What more do you need? I'm embarrassed to be your incubus!"* After the Monkey's tirade, was over, I recall thinking. *Incubus.... that's a big word for a primate.*

Fatboy, or as my brother Tim called him "Giant Squid", took my refusal to fight as the sign of a coward. He jumped within range to hurt me and threw a right hook. I slapped it out of the way, and head-butted his nose. I struck him so hard the crack could be heard over the signature Rickenbacker bass notes of *"The Stranglers"* playing in the background.

The Giant Squid stumbled down a series of steps lined with colored lights and flattened out on the floor. He wiped his mouth, and to his credit, was still game for more.

He started to regain his feet. I could not allow that to happen. I blasted him with a knee, mounted his prone body, and then landed four fast punches to his mouth, sending him blissfully to see the Sandman. Blood splattered everywhere, several drops even hitting the people closest to the beat-down. Girls shrieked, guy's moaned, drunk assholes laughed.

My brothers kept all the other Squids at bay (no pun), which was no easy task, since everyone from their ship seemed to come out of the woodwork. The crowd was totally on our side. I knew most of them, so was certain they would appear in court later, in order to inform the judge that "I got hit first and was only trying to break up a fight."

The Monkey was the first to hear the sirens and signaled me that it was time to go. His appetite for carnage was well sated. He rubbed his belly while giving me a sinister smile. My brothers could not see the Monkeys pantomiming, but they also heard the sirens, so they steered me outside the bar and around back before the cops arrived. My brother James told me later that he saw an entire squad of police raid the bar, with a team of paramedics close behind holding a stretcher. It was not the last confrontation that I was to have with this group of sailors. They never forgot me, and unbeknownst to me watched for the right moment to get their revenge.

The bartender called my apartment and told me that the injured sailor's face was scarred and swollen like a ripe melon. Knowing the cops were on the way to arrest me, I convinced my roommate, Claudio to belt me in the face a couple times, so it would look like I got blasted first. We both knew that it was jail-time, unless I had injuries of my own to show the cops. The first punch hit me square on the chin, the second landed with so mucn force behind it, that it caused me to flip over a coffee table. "That should do it." I said Claudio.

But, internally I thought. *He sure seemed to enjoy that.* However, Claudio's punch was nothing compared to the pain and disappointment that coursed through my body, a result of knowing the Berserker won out again over the Taoist. And lately the Taoist seeped to be losing out more and more.

The cops arrived and took me into custody. But everything turned out okay. Thanks to a swollen eye, a cracked tooth, and the help of the bar regulars, I got off with probation. The skinny guy's girlfriend even showed up in court so she could thank me again.

I ran into the Navy boys in the hallway, grinned at the sailor that got the beating, and then gave the entire group the finger and a warning for their bandaged friend. "You assholes better tell Gilligan to stay on the boat next time."

However, the incident was not without a penalty. Within 48 hours I ended up in the hospital because of blood poisoning. The infection was so bad that the Doc told me that it would take a week in bed to get better. I got the germs from the sailor's mouth, as during the beat down, my knuckles collided with his front teeth so many times, my fist got split open. My entire hand was filled with so much fluid that it was the size of a small football. The illness made me wonder what the Sailor had been eating. I'm sure a guy like that had been told to eat shit by many others. Who would have thought he'd take them literally?

I did not stay in the hospital for the required week the doctor had ordered. Temptation to leave early came from the visitations of demons in human and primate form, each arriving to check on my condition. They came forth, bringing with them a bouquet of bad judgment, pleading to my dark nature.

Bitsy (demon in human form) showed up on the third night, during visiting hours, and invited me to a party, crushing my refusal to exit the hospital by waving a few grams in front of me, while urging me out of bed and into his black 'Vette.

"I'm going outside for a smoke, meet you by my car, south exit. We got work to do." He said, while moving his eyebrows up and down repeatedly—John Belusi style.

The Monkey came to see at visiting hours shortly after Bitsy left. He also pleaded for me to leave the hospital.

"Pull out the I.V's and sneak past the nurse. You'll be fine. You don't want to miss a good party do you ... just because of a few cuts on your hand."

I sat up higher in bed and considered the order. Drugs kicked in. the Monkey came closer. He was dressed in a physician. He had it all: white coat, stethoscope, tiny flashlight, fake concern, real greed.

Leaning very close he spoke. *"Turn your head and cough."* I complied. *"You'll be just fine. Get some exercise, cut down on the smoking, and next time you punch somebody, aim for their nose not their mouth."* And with that he was gone.

I did as the Monkey instructed and went to the party with Bitsy. The merriment did not last long. Within hours of leaving, I collapsed with a 105 fever, almost beating Andy into an early grave. Bitsy drove me back to the hospital. The doctor came to my room when I had regained consciousness, lecturing me about the foolishness of leaving the hospital in my seriously weakened condition—without his approval.

"You won't be so lucky if you ever pull a stunt like that again." He said, peering over a clipboard, so that only the top half of his angry scowl was in view.

The Monkey appeared after the physician left and then gave me his own view of the future; *"This will not be the last time you lay near death and survive. You will come to wish you were dead and curse the inability to find a way to make it so!"*

Then he followed the predication with a prescription *"Take two of these and call me in the morning."* In his hand he held two syringes filled with heroin. He opened up both hands and showed me my choices of his diabolical medication. I shook my head.

    "No? Then how about one of these?" He said.

    In one palm was a rusty straight razor...in the other was a bottle of sleeping pills. The relief of death over addiction seemed like the right idea. I reached for the razor. He snatched it away, obviously not ready to let me die quite yet. ***"You cannot take your life until we have had all our fun."***

There's Someone Looking at You

My swollen hand was totally useless! If there was a situation that required the thumping of some asshole, using my favorite punch—an overhand right—the fist would explode like a pus grenade. I called Bitsy and told him to put off his big exchange for a couple days, prolonging the meeting for a few days, until I was confident any unexpected complications could be handled, without making my condition worse than it already was. My decision was a smart one, as there was always somebody lurking nearby to rip Bitsy off. Without action, it was a difficult task to stay inside the apartment since I had become used to going out practically every night, either on a job, or on nocturnal explorations realms inhabited by Bottom Feeders. Being stuck indoors, away from the limelight, drove me crazy, which made finding something to ease the recovery period crucial. I really needed some R&R. My friends and brothers had gone to an INXS concert at Poplar Creek. Since they would all be gone most of the night, and therefore out of the party equation, as far as entertainment, or comradeship was concerned, I was on my own. Joining them at the concert was not an option, mainly because unruly crowds bothered me, and sooner or later some idiot would show disrespect. This would inevitably lead to unnecessary conflict—something I had enough of. What was needed was an adventure that could be done alone, and without setting foot outside my apartment.

"There has to be a way to prevent the evening from being a total waste." I intoned. "Wait a minute. You still have a couple tabs of Windowpane and a few mushrooms that you were saving for a rainy day. Well ... it looks like a storm is on the horizon; a downpour of hallucinations is coming." I forecasted and prepared for the worst and for the best.

I retrieved the acid and 'shrooms stored in a flashlight next to the fuse-box. Not a great hiding place, but still better than the usual junkie hiding place; in a fucking Crown Royal bag taped under a drawer.

I was relieved to find that all my drugs were all still there...still waiting for a rainy day. *Better get an umbrella...looks to be a monsoon,* I thought, laughing at the joke.

That night was going to be a science experiment, conducted to determine the mind-altering possibilities produced by combining a concoction of one hit of Acid boosted with three blues-stemmed Psilocybin 'shrooms. The plan required a thirty minute pause between ingesting each tab, in order to get the biggest peak, without going nuts and overstaying my welcome in Wonderland.

After swallowing the mind-altering brew, I briefly considered calling up an old girlfriend to come over to hang out. But then the first rule of the LSD handbook popped into my head, and reminded me that of: "Chicks and Acid don't mix." It was a rule that deserved further pondering because it was illogical to state, "Chicks and acid don't mix, but then allow Monkeys to join the fun."

The tryptamines kicked in fast and hard, creating multiple ripples of nausea, each wave jolted my abdominal muscles, while resonating throughout my entire body. The temporary stomach distress didn't matter because it was part of using mushrooms, and was the calling card of the pre-trip deliveryman. *"Here it comes!"* I clutched the armrests so as to prepare for launch. The signs were all there; body heat, bug hair, dilated pupils and sack mouth ... the ignition had started, and lift off was just seconds away. A new world was on the verge of discovery, as Prism Pupils, contacted Crystal Receptors. *Columbus be damned, this is the New World,* I thought.

The linier, dark grain on the wooden desk started to move in oscillations, flowing down the frame, and even further down the Cedar legs. There, what had once been wood grains pooled in fine watery filaments. Lights got brighter, spectrums intensified; the room took on an organic quality, much like I was in the belly of a whale.

"You can call me Jonah," I whispered to my brother's autographed photo of Eric Clapton, propped up on a nearby coffee table. Eric didn't act as if he heard, but somehow, I still sensed that he wished me well on my journey—since Eric had no shortage of bizarre drug-induced trips of his own.

Crossing and uncrossing my thighs left blurry trails of motion that reminded me huge caterpillars. Caterpillars were a certainty that the real psychedelic effects were beginning to take hold. Nobody has the exact same trip, but most people usually have experienced a vision that probably included caterpillars. Caterpillars were like strange international ambassadors from another world, entering the acid trip so as to create an uninhibited entry to a place without passports or baggage-checkers. A good thing, as my mind had a great deal of baggage.

"Nice! This was going to be a trip to go down in the encyclopedia of cellular distortion." I told the clock, in response to the carefree ticking.

"I forgot music. Shit ... this requires the precise album to really make this a good surreal encounter." I said to the clock again, taking the timepiece's silence as I had with Clapton, a firm agreement to whatever nonsense I spouted. "You've always been a good friend." I told the clock. My brain was so muddled by drugs, the ability to distinguish between inanimate objects and living things was gone, and replaced by a happiness to know them all.

I had to hurry and see to the music, because until the perfect vinyl disc was spinning, the grooves could not boost the LSD peak and work in sync with the acid. Doing hallucinogens was not the same as swallowing pills, spiking a vein, or snorting power. A trip would only be pleasant if the mind was at peace and the surroundings were comfortable. Dropping acid required that several rituals be completed, rituals such as: no people in the same room that you disliked, no bad vibes, nothing to cause anger, and no stressful or shocking interruptions. However, most important ingredient was playing the right music. I went to the stack of albums, and took great care in respecting the ritual, so as to choose the beat that would help the surge of chemicals to my brain.

I sounded out the titles in my mind while scrolling. "**The Ramones**—no, too fast ... **Hawkwind**—no, too scary for an acid trip, unless you want to see space monsters … **Roxy Music**—no, too esoteric and high-brow ... **Boomtown Rats**—perfect, that is the one!"

The Boomtown Rats had two albums that perfectly fitted the occasion—"Tonic for the Troops" and "The Fine Art of Surfacing." TFAOS "was the Boomtown Rat's best, because it had an operatic texture. I placed it on the turntable and flopped into a lazy boy chair centrally located in order to make best use of ears.

I remembered the eight P's that form the 'Shroomer's Bible; proper – prior – planning – prevents – piss – poor – psilocybin – projects. I wanted a purple haze event to beat all others. I got my wish ... in the worse way imaginable.

As the album began to play I dropped the rest of the acid. Leaning back into the cushioned backrest, I took in the sights of a chemically-enhanced universe without ever leaving the room. Bob Geldorf—the Singer, was my tour guide. His band took me on a journey of melting walls, liquid floors, and crying colors from the synesthesia galaxy. There was no method to measure the duration of individual spikes within successive waves of light-syrup, especially since the clock had changed into a time machine.

"'I think I'll steer clear of trying to assess space and time, and leave those distinctions to Einstein." I mumbled. This time Eric Clapton acknowledged my presence. He looked out from the photograph, concurring with my opinions in a series of verbal chords from his Cream days. The guitar spoke in the language of Layla and I answered by humming "Sunshine of your Life". It was not an exaggeration, to say that while chemically enhanced; men and guitars could talk to each other. LSD was my Rosetta-Stone. I listened, using the vibrating guitar strings to decode the space/time continuum that I had planned to leave to Einstein. Someday, maybe my next trip, I would learn secrets from the Woodwind and Brass Horn Clan, seeking out clarinets, piccolos, and oboes, but never a Tuba, because he was a Bassoon, sorry I'm a bit high— I meant to say Buffoon.

The album — "Fine Art of Surfacing" had a cover which displayed a swimmer bursting out of foamy water. But when the acid hit my brain, the swimmer ceased being an artist's rendition of just a normal man stroking thru the ocean. It changed from an intimate object decorating the cover of an album into a living thing. Floating in the air, hovering, and occasionally stroking harder and in order to surge forward, and perform circles—directly over my head. Things turned slightly menacing, as he seemed to be waiting for the right moment to pounce, and choke me. The swimmer's circle of freestyle-strokes got smaller, and the artistic human form gradually morphed into a water-demon.

The demons multiplied, becoming two, then three, and then four aquatic entities, eventually all imaginary creatures, switched from using freestyle arm movements to an Olympic caliber breaststroke. After a few minutes, they drew closer and smothered my fleeting sanity. As each demon passed directly over my head they whispered a word I'd never heard before.

"Horm," the first one said, and each additional demon whispered the same word when his turn came, "Horm." I had no fucking idea what a "Horm" was, but it still scared the shit out of me.

Are these demons warning me of another repulsive beast that is about to enter my nightmare, or are they predicting that I will meet 'The Horm' in the future? Whatever the message, I must scan through the Junkie-Hallucinogenic-Dictionary and find out what the fuck a Horm is. It would be a difficult book to locate, because the 'Junkie Hallucinogenic Dictionary' was not a typical reference book, unavailable at Amazon or Barnes and Noble. I'll have to go to the Shroom library and purview The Worst Seller List, I thought, while attempting to rationalize the trip and relax. Then internally, I made a more forceful plea: "Demon Swimmers, Shroom Libraries, Horms … wake the fuck up."

The trip deteriorated further and became the most terrifying night I'd ever experienced—from doing drugs that is! I was very close to ending up as a permanent passenger on the kaleidoscope train. On that train the tickets could only be punched by an insect conductor. Losing control or dropping one more tab of Pane would have taken me to the Horror Hotel, a place located in the aforementioned ghost-town of Weirdsville. Nobody ever made it back to reality after visiting Weirdsville. It was a town that had a population requirement of … One acid-trip town ... One nutjob … one mayor—Syd Barrnet

Thankfully my brother Sven stopped by after the concert. He helped me cling to the real world and to my fast retreating sanity. Sven immediately saw the fragility of my composure.

In a split second, he ascertained that my grasp of reality was fast approaching the point of no return. He took immediate action, doing the only thing that someone could do—in that type of circumstance, talk me down, even if it took several hours.

After an unknown amount of time, relief finally came. Three of the swimming demons faded from view, leaving only one demon remaining. The last form was no longer a demon; he had become my arch nemesis—The Monkey. My old enemy grunted a simian greeting, swam over to the couch, and sat down. It was the only night that seeing the bastard made me happy. It wasn't some sort of paradoxical change of heart that stirred this emotion within me. Anything would have seemed better than being surrounded by demons, so even an asshole like The Monkey was a welcome sight to behold. Sven checked to make sure there was not going to be a relapse and left. With Sven gone, The Monkey and I were all alone. We stared each other down, neither of us wanting to break the silence. Eventually I could not take it anymore, for what I saw in his eyes, was much too disturbing.

The next day I woke up with no ill effects or residual drug hangover. Mushrooms are organic, so they never made me feel like shit in the morning. Acid was far from organic, but it was a drug abnormality, in that it did not seem to cause a type of morning sickness, except of light and noise sensitivity. However, acid did have risks. Down the road (if you did enough) your brain would occasionally misfire and give you flashbacks during the most inconvenient moments. My use of drugs was making it hard to separate dreams from what should have been reality. It was a good thing there weren't any after effects from the night before, as today was the day my brothers and I were supposed to set off on a Devonian Fossil Hunt, hopefully to collect long dead creatures for our future geology business. The Geology business was an idea that we talked about often. For me, it meant a possible salvation, as there were no drugs to be found under layers of sedimentary rock.

Bitsy called earlier to say he would not need me until the following day. This meant that science was in and violence was out ... at least for now.

The Tale of the Giant Stone Eater

My brothers started to arrive around 5.00 AM. Nobody ever missed our monthly fossil collecting expedition. After parking their cars, each came into my kitchen, and then grabbed a cup of black coffee. In some cases many cups were downed, so as to wake up quicker. Sugar and cream was never added, except for Tim, who drank his brew under the "equal amounts of sugar to water system."

Tim had a reason for drinking the unusual blend "If anyone drinks coffee solely for the caffeine buzz, then why not load it up with sugar and get a double energy rush." It was hard to argue with that kind of logic; as long as the enamel of your teeth wasn't a big priority, and you had immunity to nervous tension. Tim finished three or four cups, then fell into uncontrolled hyperactive pacing, followed by small-talk chatter. It seemed foolish for a person to drink so much coffee, especially since anxiety and agitation were usually the end result. But, who was I to question his habit of sugar and caffeine, as I had a much bigger problem to deal with.

"He who lives in houses made of mirrors shouldn't throw cocaine rocks." I told myself, not quite sure if the phrase was correct. I knew it went something like that; maybe it was glass houses and stones.

After everybody had "coffeed up", including the last brother to arrive, we went outside loaded our packs and gear into the back of Tim's Chevy Tahoe. Once the equipment was stored properly, everyone stood outside the truck for several minutes, debating the proper way to call Shotgun—therefore settling the issue of whose claim of the front seat had the most validity.

We couldn't leave right away because my youngest brother, Mike, needed to finish 20 minutes of primping, and hair combing, before setting off for the outback.

He had an unorthodox view when it came to picking up chicks, believing that a good chance of scoring existed everywhere he went, regardless of the environment.

That morning was no exception to the rule. It didn't matter to Mike that we were going to spend the next 48 hours at the bottom of a granite quarry, isolated, and surrounded by pig and cattle farms. He had faith that his quest to locate woman in the middle of nowhere would be fulfilled. In some ways I respected his wishful thinking. It takes a special kind of guy to believe there is always a possibility of hitting on women, even when the most attractive female around those parts would most likely be a big boned Swedish girl. Not that a BBSG was such a bad thing, except when considering that since she lived in the middle of farm country it was probably a safe bet that she only had two things on her mind—"State-fair pie-eating contests" and "pork rinds." So unless Mike was edible and made of fat or grease, his prospects of getting a date were about a million to one.

But according to Mike, "Those weren't bad odds."

The Iowa fossil site was eight hours due north, a short distance outside the town of Rockford, near the Lime Creek formation. It was going to take six hours of highway driving, followed by a jaunt along gravel farm roads, before we got to the deep pit, which was three miles in diameter. We did not expect to find anything valuable, only perfectly preserved shells, horn corals, and maybe an ammonite or two. The site was at one time a Devonian Sea so everything we dug up was going to be an invertebrate. However, considering the variety and excellent condition of specimens from that area, it would make for a successful gathering outing.

Besides, for us, half the fun was the road trip itself because if you were with the right group of people it could be as entertaining as any activity outside the confines of an automobile. But it was the nighttime that we favored the most, as camping and exploring in the dark was as exciting as unearthing a new discovery. That is not to say that the daytime adventures were not exciting; they were, but it is in the blackness in the middle of nowhere that you really discover what a man is made of.

Mike finally decided he was attractive enough to leave the apartment and crawl around in the mud searching for Precambrian sea-dwellers. He went out to join the others. They were still arguing over which one of them had called the front seat first. Being last out the door and locking up was my responsibility. After securing everything, I grabbed my tools, took a last look around and made sure nothing incriminating or of value had been left out.

I stopped for a brief instant by the door, waiting, wondering if the Monkey was going join us with his own make-believe pick and shovel. Realistically (talk about the wrong word to use), there was little chance of him showing up, as there was not much he could do to me on outdoor exploits when in the company of my "Monkey Hating Family" and in broad daylight. Thinking of the primate caused me speculate on just what a Monkey would look for on a fossil dig anyway.

"Would he hope to find one of his prehistoric proto-simian relatives attached to an Austiolopithicus Humanoid, or maybe a clinging to a Neanderthal? Did Caveman have their own versions of the Monkey that drove them to embrace their primordial instincts? Could he make caveman do prehistoric pot, thereby causing them to forget the spark that led them to the invention the wheel?" I asked myself.

"All interesting questions, Billy, all best answered on your next mushroom binge. Science is for scientists, not junkies." The Monkey's said, using a voice deceptively soft, and able to enter my mind. It amused him to ridicule my attempts to solve universal mysteries while high.

"Fuck, I can't see you ... but I can hear you. There is never going to be more mushrooms for me, asshole." I said to the Monkey even though he was not fully tangible and was only a voice in my mind. The Monkey was wrong, my drug use was a phase, a bad one no doubt, but one I could fight my way out of. *My dream of being a writer or a geologist will be fulfilled one day,* I thought, firmly entrenching the idea in my head, in order to mentally vomit out the monkey's words.

Shit…… I better get in the truck with my brothers before he convinces me to take some blow with me, I thought, while running to the truck to join the others.

Once we got outside of Chicago and crossed the Mississippi, the terrain changed drastically, becoming perfectly square geometric farm fields, antique bridges, Hooterville-Towns, and vast acreage of green woodlands composed of old growth Oak and Maple.

The flat forests and cornfields were joined occasionally by rolling hills that sprung up every ten miles or so. If the road cuts were steep enough, horizontal lines of strata would be seen, increasing the probability of finding long Cephalopods cones embedded in the exposed sedimentary layers. The Cephalopod fossils had magnificent spirals running along white shells, which made them pretty easy to spot against the light - brown backdrop of strata. When the Cephalopods were sighted, the result was a mad dash to the formation, followed by quick pickax-assisted climbs to the upper layer. When everyone reached the top, a battle for the area with a level shelf began, as each brother wanted good footing while in the process of digging.

That was the enjoyable part of the hunt because it became a contest about not only who found the biggest specimen, but also who got knocked off the embankment and hit the ground below with the hardest thump. Daylight adventures had nothing in common with my nighttime prowls. So ... throughout my journey to become something better, outings with my brothers were important elements, helping to convince my brain that there was still hope of changing the destructive path I was on.

Trips with my family caused me to never lose sight of the fact that I was not all bad. In the presence of my family, I still had talent to someday to become a writer, painter, geologist, or even if all else failed ... a far better person. So needless to say, if there was ever going to be a time when the Monkey would be 'gutted', such an event would only be accomplished by embracing the spiritual side of nature, and more importantly staying close to my family

Sven was an avid rock-hound and took as much pride as any of us in finding good fossil, but on many of our trips he actually prized sending one of us to the bottom of a steep hill much more than adding a new specimen to his collection.

I guess it would be fair to say that Sven collected bruised egos and butt-cheeks as much as fossilized plants and animals. That was all well and good, as the former was immaterial and could never be showed off in a display case.

To get through the doldrums (that began six hours into any kind of road-trip) we played the well-known (among wayward travelers) "radio game."

Any person that has driven long distances—across country, knows the game and the rules well. The passenger in the front seat scrolls through the stations and the entire group tries to guess the song and band. The game got us through the last couple hours, and since we were getting close to our destination, it was agreed that the game was over and Mike was declared winner. So, for the remaining miles Emil scrolled down the dial, looking for the station that had consistently played the best tunes so as to stay on that frequency.

Emil's searching led him up and down the spectrum, producing bursts of music mingled with static from the speakers. "Johnny Cash"... great but too depressing, "Wings" .... too bubblegum, "Bee Gees"... too Glib—or maybe too much Gibb. It was the kind of morning; when nothing but crap was on the radio, and we doubted the right music was going to be heard, before getting to the dig site.

Then all of a sudden, when musical salvation seemed lost, the opening guitar salvo for "The Tale of the Giant Stone Eater" by the Sensational Alex Harvey Band saved the day. The virtuoso fret work of Zel Cleminson and the howling vocals of Alex Harvey were just what the first-stage of the fossil adventure required. The song told of how technology and the mass consumption of natural recourses had destroyed the Earth. The lyrics about a bulldozer crushing trees and unearthing a Brontosaurus that *"lay wrong way up"* put everyone in the correct frame of mind to enter the huge pit and go back hundreds of millions of years.

We got to our destination shortly before 3:00 PM. After pulling into the dig site, we continued driving down a narrow road so bumpy that our heads rebounded off the truck roof. We drove until we found an area to park that was close to the quarry entrance.

After filing out of the vehicle, we took a narrow, unmaintained footpath that traversed along the rough terrain. We walked carefully, moving from shallow gully to shallow gully, pausing when we got to the deepest section of the gorge. The steepest face was layered with loose clay and football-sized rocks. From where we all stood, it was easy to determine, this was the specific formation where the greatest abundance of suitable fossils could be found.

We climbed up the slippery side and instantly regretted that nobody brought rappelling gear so as to rope down and tie in. The difficulty of gaining traction on the precariously wet layers of sediment could have been avoided if we had prepared properly and brought enough rope and ranger seats. If any of us fell, it would not be a normal spill, because beneath our feet (maybe ten stories down), was a two-meter shelf that circled the pit.

That little section of land was the only thing that could stop a tumbling body from dropping into a pond of putrid water and sludge. If anybody lost their balance and began to slide down the embankment towards the pond, there would only be couple chances to sink his ax into the quarry face. If the ax failed to slow the descent, there would be nothing left to stop the person from hitting the shelf, then rolling further into the ooze.

This was not an ordinary mill swamp that was at the bottom of gravel or marble pits. This waterhole was far more disgusting as it was filled with seeping compost and bubbling gas that released methane upon bursting. The slime that wallowed on the surface of the pond was a concoction all to its own. This was the "Emperor of Stinky Waterholes." As years passed, the runoff from the nearby pig farms sought out the lowest level, dripped and dripped, then eventually drained to the bottom of the quarry. This was the substance that formed the pond at the bottom of the dig site, a pool of shit to be feared and avoided at all costs.

Knowing that pig excrement amid a microcosm of bacteria was directly under our feet made the game far more dangerous and disgusting.

As James put it, "This is the Superbowl of King of the Hill."

"I believe you meant to say Shitbowl, not Superbowl." I replied.

In the beginning, we concentrated mainly on the act of collecting, so each of us got some really fine specimens. Every once in a while we paused to take pictures and enjoy the view from high above the depression.

But after a couple hours dusk began setting in. It was time for someone to take a fall into the slop. We side-stepped carefully to get closer to each other, while pretending to inspect an outcropping, making it appear that each person was looking for a possible discovery. Everyone acted as if they did not notice the gap between us getting smaller and smaller. Each person acted nonchalant as they searched for more brachiopods. But we all knew what the real intent was—get within range to shove somebody into the quagmire first. We all had the greatest respect for each other, however, sometimes you have to put brotherly love aside and go for bragging rights.

It was not hard to rationalize our strange behavior. We believed that all families had siblings wanting to push each other into pig shit. Sven and Tim attacked first. James and I took the brunt of the impact, which caused our safe positions on the cragged edges to give way. The battle against gravity had begun! There were several wobbly attempts to regain a firm hold on the face of the wall; pickaxes were driven into any solid looking mound, legs scrambled for solid purchase against loose rocks. As James and I fell, we tried to stay flat, rolling onto our stomachs, so we might prevent somersaulting like a human avalanche.

But no matter how many times our picks sunk into the side of the pit, we could not slow our speed. Each of us fell towards the pond. We both hit at the same time; luckily we landed on all fours in only about two feet of water, so our heads and upper torso remained out of the brown water. We looked at each other and laughed.

To an outsider our fun might have seemed brutish or the result of misplaced humor. But our laughter was grounded in the knowledge, that as usual on these trips, we made it a habit to bring extra clothes, since dirt and mud was always on the menu. James got to his feet first and began his jog to the truck so he could wash off the stink and get into cleaner stuff.

I was crawling out of the sludge, when something in my peripheral vision made me freeze. I strained my eyes to get a better look. Amazingly, a dark shape swam towards me and stopped only a yard away. We looked at each other. My initial thought (considering the foaming liquid that surrounded my body) was that the shadowy figure was a type of giant bacteria or maybe a pus-paramecium. I got a better view when the creature swam forward into the fleeting light and immediately determined it was a strange-looking fish.

"How could anything (fish or mammal) live in this putrid mud-hole, much less find oxygen to breath." I wondered.

A closer inspection proved the fish to be some kind of mutant carp or catfish. The color was of a tint not found in nature, and the bulbous head violated any preconceived notion of streamlining.

"How the hell did you get into such a bad situation? I asked the fish.

"How the hell did you get into yours? The fish replied.

How dare a fish—living in a cesspool, question the direction my life has taken? Although, then again, who better to make the best observation of how things seemed to be turning to shit for me? I thought.

The fish remained, fluttering tail and dorsal fins in order to stay where he could watch me. It starred at me, focusing deep into my soul, using a quzi-prophetic vision reserved for aquatic harbingers of impending tragedy.

"Can this be another acid flashback? Maybe I'm reliving a weird memory of my days diving on mushrooms." I asked, while slightly worried. Up until this moment only imaginary Primates had the ability to speak—outside of acid trips.

And where does that creature get the nerve to question my place in the world? Is that scaly asshole comparing a life in a cesspool to my addictions? Can't be ... no fish is that smart, even fantastical specimens that have figured out how to bathe in my guilt.

The whole mess was very disconcerting. I considered asking if he wanted me to help him out of the pond so he could live in a better place, but decided against asking the question. It scared me that the mystery fish might ask if I wanted help out of my own hole. The condition of my mind was bad, but I refused assistance from a fish, even if it was a genetically unheard of mutant creation.

That was more than enough fish and human interaction for a single day. Tim and Mike were waiting for me on the ridge to give me a hand up, while James (the clean version), Emil, and Mike, had started the process of erecting the tents, placing them between strands of trees on beds of dead leaves. The tents were well away from the stench of the quarry and the far-off squeal of pigs. The trip had been a good one. Our satchels were full of fossils and many interesting pictures. As the sun went down, coyotes emerged from their dens, and then in canine fashion, began to call to each other. Deer came from out from concealment, Owls hooted, and the peaceful envelope of night settled in.

It was the time of campfire tales, cigars, and Canadian Club Whiskey. James regaled us with exciting stories about our Grandfather's explorations into the Canadian wilderness and his subsequent discovery of a lost tribe of Ojibwa people. James' descriptions of the past fired up new conversations, and the rest of the night was spent recounting our Viking heritage, earlier road trips, strange encounters, and debating which of us had experienced the most astonishing adventure. As I lived on an astral plane which tittered on absurd angles, when it came to incredible stories, I had everyone beat my miles.

Part of me reconsidered my joy that there was no Monkey to be seen. If The Monkey had followed my tracks, and was watching from me the trees, it would mean that he was also miles from civilization. If the Monkey was in the area of the dig, there was a good chance he would get lost in the dense undergrowth, stumble around, and end up in the pond.

My last thought before falling asleep was, *I sure hope the fish is hungry. What a fitting curtain call it would be for the Monkey to get eaten, and then swallowed by a creature as repulsive and mysterious as he is. Maybe in another couple hundred years someone would dig him up.*

I thought more about the end of the Monkey. My enjoyment was hard to contain while considering the many ways to kill my invisible enemy. *Maybe even give the fossilized simian remains a scientific name in Latin. I could hear the Nobel Prize winners speak as their words echoes off hallowed halls. "Ladies and Gentleman I give you 'Assholicus Monkeylosis Scumsuckinus'."*

Shock the Monkey – The 80's

We got back from Iowa the next morning around 9:00. The first thing we did was divide the fossils up. James claimed the most notable unearthing; a chunk of coral resembling cauliflower the size of a hardhat. The fossil had taken a good deal of work to remove from a crest of clay near the uppermost layer. The octagon configuration with tiny interconnecting lines was as beautiful as it was ancient. Several of the other well-preserved specimens were intentionally put aside for schools and nature centers, so as to be displayed and used as teaching aids. Over the years, we had developed the habit of donating fossils to educational organizations, as many institutions had budget restraints which made it problematic to afford a large assortment of rocks and fossils. Helping schools teach science and the value of nature might create future conversationalists, so that one day, they might assist in protecting the wilderness. Therefore, our motives were not purely humanitarian, and there might have been a certain degree of selfishness attached to our goal of protecting the wilderness. Maybe by exposing the ancient creatures, millions years old, I was really trying to expose something in myself to the light, an entity not as old but certainly as primitive.

"The Earth only gives when you give something back. Otherwise you're nothing but a poacher," Tim said while polishing the last of his shells.

After we finished and everyone went home, I checked my missed phone calls by pressing a few buttons on a "Sports Illustrated Football Phone" that was attached to a beeping message machine.

Leaning against the machine was a Peter Frampton tape. These were two things everybody from that decade just had to have.... a "S.I Phone" and "Frampton comes Alive".

As expected, six urgent calls—from a panicky Bitsy, were already on the machine.

Each message repeated the same demand, tone showing panic, insisting on a return call right away because he needed me for the meeting that was to take place that night. Aside from panic, the voice that came through the device was hoarse, tired, and scratchy, which left no doubt that Bitsy was smack dab in the middle of a three or four-day coke binge. I decided to make something to eat and then do a couple railers before calling him back. Bitsy was occasionally arrogant; but all times pushy, so pissing him off was a secret pleasure of mine.

Do him good to wait. I thought. *Wouldn't want him to get the idea I'm on a leash....besides he'll offer more money if he feels desperate.*

I pounded down a few eggs, took some vitamins, railed up, and then, and only then, did I call him back. He was glad to hear from me and gradually began to relax over the phone. He knew he would be safe and would not be the victim of a rip-off, with me on the job to oversee the exchange. He had other guys to protect him while meeting with buyers. There was never a shortage of rented muscle because everybody in town was eager to score free blow. But if the deal went south, or if one of the other assholes tried to pull some shit, I was the person Bitsy had complete faith in, with a past record of handling circumstances in the appropriate manner without losing composure. Over time I had gotten a well-known reputation (in the right circles for the wrong reasons) for my acute ability to in size up potential dangers or rip-offs before they happened. The Buyer we were scheduled to meet was a new referral, and had no real history with any of the people we associated with, so tonight was going to be an especially tricky affair. However, it was too good of a deal to pass up, and Bitsy's contacts with the police told him the Buyer wasn't a snitch and not a cop.

It came as no surprise that Bitsy had connections on the force. All big dealers had somebody inside the department to tip them off; otherwise your tenure as a drug dealer was going to be remarkably short, although your sentence in jail would be remarkably long. To remain on the streets and not end up behind bars, dealers needed two things; someone like me to keep the riffraff at bay and make collections, and also somebody connected enough to issue warnings of impending busts or investigations. Both cost money. Although I came much cheaper than the cops.

The meeting was still a few hours away, so to sharpen my senses, and get into the correct frame of mind, I drove to the gym near my apartment. I began the workout by striking the 200 lb. Muay Thai heavy-bag with Thai clinch-elbow-knee combinations, moved on to jab-shin counters, then finished with stomp kick-uppercut-knee blows. After warming up with the bag, and stretching, I was ready for a moving target, preferably one that threw some punches back at me, so a few upright rounds were fought against a regular training partner. That took about an hour, then for the last hour we switched to rolling on the mat, cycling through trying to obtain dominate ground positions, and once in control, setting-up submissions. I also went through a series of throws that did as well on street as on the mat. We did not practice anything that would not function on some slippery, dirty, barroom floor. Sometimes fights got real nasty, and when that happened, chokes and bone breaks were my ace in the hole. Because fights started on the feet and not on the ground, Judo and Greco throws were practiced during the beginning of each ground workout. Next came grappling drills, concentrating on the most practical chokes and arm bars, finishing with the most neglected submissions—the leg-locks. Many of my fight buddies refused to perform leg-locks. They did not see the value in leg-locks; mainly because they applied the hold wrong and therefore failed get the desired pain effect from their opponent. Most missed leg submissions were a result of poor figure-four joint manipulations or from dropping into the ankle and knee locking position too soon, ahead of knee or hip control. It also might have been that the fighter neglected weight training and lacked the strength needed to immobilize the limb. Thinking that leg-locks were useless in a fight was a big mistake.

Training a variety of leg-locks and body take-downs was a crucial element to my fighting style. In my line of work you had to be good with escapes, because there was always the risk of being mounted by your opponent, getting both shoulders pinned to the ground, and then being on the wrong end of a major beat-down.

I considered it more important (that if I went to the ground) to hurt the other guy's leg first. Injured legs meant he would find it near impossible to stand back up or run from me. Or if he was a 300 pound monster ... not run after me. The workout concluded at 5:00. I felt good, my edge was back and my lungs were pumping. It was time to put Bitsy's negotiations into play.

Bitsy had already given The Buyer permission to bring along only one other person (his protector) and nobody else. If there was any sign of another person, then the meeting was over. Since we decided what time the meeting was to take place, he got to choose where the deal would go down. He picked a vacant lot behind a Ford dealership that had long ago closed up. It was shielded on all sides by the thickly forested border of a nature preserve. This was as good as any spot. The old building with its broken windows and crumbling parking lot was surrounded in every direction by tall oak trees. This cover would ensure the right amount of privacy. The parking lot was big enough to give an unobstructed field of vision for one hundred yards on all sides.

A series of lights ran around the perimeter of the dealership, but as most were broken, they provide no real illumination, except for the flickering of a single filament atop the centermost pole. The poor lighting was probably the result of melted wiring, or cracked bulbs; I did not care why they did not work... only that they did not. The darker the better! I functioned very well in the in the absence of light, and the two guys with me did too! I doubted that the Buyer and his Goon would have night vision as good as we possessed. The section of land around the preserve was an area that I knew very well. My brothers and I had fished the lake located in the middle of the forest many times. As a result the whereabouts of every dirt trail, barbed-wire fence, and thorn patch that existed in and around the preserve were known to us. My hiking experience in the region made it easy to select the best spots to strategically position my guys, giving us the high ground and best line of fire ... just in case.

These types of meetings can't be described without sounding like a movie because there is only one way to accomplish the exchange and everyone knows how the deal works, even

Hollywood. However, here goes the description anyway. I was going to stay alongside Bitsy, standing slightly to the right, and only a few feet behind him. My guys would be concealed on opposite sides of the forest, establishing flank superiority. They would each have an unobstructed view of the parking lot while being able to observe the forest on all sides. My guy on the left flank had a three-mile view of the old entrance road that ended at the Ford Dealership. That meant he would be able to have an advance view of anyone driving down the road in plenty of time to alert us. After analyzing the plan and looking for chinks in our armor I was unable to find any. It seemed like we had a distinct advantage if the Buyer stepped out of line or tried to steal from Bitsy.

Before the meeting, I told my flankers to park a mile from the dealership, so as to hide their vehicle from anyone inspecting the terrain. The place where they were ordered to stash their ride was a pot-holed service street, overgrown with hanging willows, blacktop almost non-existent under the mud and leaves.

The plan required my guys to get to the meeting a couple hours before everyone else, immediately get into position, and not to move or make any noise, just watch and listen—as if in an observation/listening post. Each of my guys had been in the military, so they had been well-schooled in noise discipline, and taught that in an area with branches and twigs covering the ground, an approaching threat would be heard way before they would be seen. They each had the necessary tools of the trade, but were not to take any action unless Bitsy or I were in danger.

Bitsy picked me up in his silver S500 and together we drove to the Ford Dealership. He was nervous so I told him to be cool.

"Take it easy man, everything was under control, trust me ... I don't want you looking all jittery. It might make them get all nervous, and we don't need that. Right?

"Yeah ... okay, if you say so, Billy. I brought this along just in case." He said lifting his shirt and showing me his Berretta.

"Bitsy, take that thing out of your waistband. It sticks out like a hard-on. Put in the small of your back, tucked under your shirt, and don't you dare take it out unless I tell you to. Got it? He nodded, but with Bitsy you could never be sure. Bitsy was like Jumbo. Both always did what they wanted, not what was the smart thing to do. Bitsy and Jumbo, like most dealers, believed in a false security, had enormous egos, boosted even bigger from habitual cocaine use. I was kind of on the same program, but at the time, even though my denial probably matched their own, I was under a worse delusion. My folly was thinking that I could walk away from the drugs and my disappointing lifestyle at the moment of my choosing. I was dead wrong on both counts.

Bitsy and I arrived at the Ford Dealership and took in the sights. The building had sale stickers, announcing savings, still in place—where the glass wasn't broken. The crumbling cinder block walls and dilapidated showroom, regardless of being closed for years, promised lowest prices in town, $1000.00 off sticker, and 3.9 financing. The pavement was littered with broken glass, pieces of broken grille, old tires and shredded wiring.

I was surprised to find that the Monkey had beaten me there. But ... I didn't notice him right off. The primate had chosen the centermost light-pole to climb and was scuttling up the steel membrane. He climbed effortlessly by using a Kung Fu grip that only a primate, lemur, or sloth possessed. He stopped about halfway to the top, and only then—in the sporadic light, did I get a good look at him. The strobe effect of the flickering bulb caused him to appear even more disturbing than usual. He smiled, pleased to see me back in his preferred element— separated from my family, 'coked up', and ready to rock and roll. He may have tried to con me by romanticizing the destructive path that drugs predicated, but deep down I believed that my end was going to a very bad one. I hoped the people close to me would be unscathed by my transgressions. That was my hope even though I was aware that in real life things never happen that way. Bring a reptile into your home and somebody will always get bitten by the snake.

Bitsy got out of the car. He took a wide and forceful stance that displayed too much aggression, which was not exactly the right pose to present when everybody is loaded for bear. While Bitsy pretended to be a tough guy, the Monkey was making aggressive moves of his own. He shinnied down the pole and then bounded across the pavement until he got within range to leap into the air so as to land on the hood. After regaining his footing he then scrambled across the car until he was close enough to grab my collar and swung onto my back...his favorite position.

"Home sweet home! Miss me? How was your fossil trip loser?" The Monkey said, attempting to get my temper going and create drama.

"How does it feel to know that your mother had sex with me?" I said, and then instantly regretted that my insult made me a 'Monkey Fucker'. I never should have swallowed the bait. Pushing the thoughts away I got my mind back where it should be, on protecting Bitsy.

The Buyer and his guy had arrived before Bitsy and myself, just as I suspected they would. It was a good thing that my men got there even earlier than they did. The Buyer had come to the meeting in a Black BMW 5-Series with tinted windows and black rims. They were parked at the far end of the empty lot, adjacent to the body shop section of the building. The BMWs headlights were on high-beam in order to screw up our vision. It was an old trick, but an effective one. Bitsy and I saw two silhouettes standing next to the vehicle. They were barely visible in the glare of the headlights, but we could see they were motionless, waiting, and constantly scanning the area for anything out of the ordinary. "Out of the ordinary"— there is an interesting phrase, as if exchanging money for drugs in the dark with people you don't know and probably can't trust even remotely resembles anything ordinary.

After a thorough examination, it became obvious which of the two shapes was in charge—the actual Buyer, and who was the Goon. The difference in stature said it all. The Goon was at least six foot four or five and probably crushed the scale around 290 lbs. The other guy was maybe five-foot tops and probably weighed 130 soaking wet. No threat there!

So, unless the Buyer was the bigger of the two, and liked to employ midgets to protect him ... it was clear which of the two men was Master and which Blaster was.

"Big Bastard, better keep your distance, and no matter what, don't take your eyes off the money man. I'll handle his protection." I said to Bitsy and then thought. *Let Bitsy worry about the shrimp.*

Sizing up the Goon made me glad (for the first time in my life) that The Monkey was with me. If I had to take on a guy that big, my fighting skills might not be up to the challenge ... so Monkey-induced rage might come in handy. When the Goon got close enough, recognition set in and I was able to put a name with the imposing presence. His last name was Cooper. I'd seen him around before, somewhere downtown, couldn't remember exactly where I'd bumped into him, but I knew his reputation as a guy who liked the sight of blood, a real sadist. Cooper stood out in a crowd, as he no ear on his left side. His appearance reminded me of a line from the movie "Cat Balou" starring Lee Marvin. Marvin playing a notorious gunfighter that wore a fake metal nose, which was held in place by an elastic cord, tied around his head.

The scene begins like this: Two Cowboys watch Marvin ride into town.

The first Cowboy says "That guy had his nose bitten off in a barroom brawl. I sure would hate to meet him (indicating Marvin) in fight.

The second Cowboy responds with this very memorable line "Yeah, well ... I'd hate to have to fight the guy that bit the nose off."

I felt the exact same way as the second Cowboy. Somewhere out there was a guy that had bitten off Cooper's ear. He was the guy I'd hate to have to fight ... not Cooper.

Never in my life had I ever thought about the possibility of the chance of losing a fight. I always approached a conflict with the same resolution; concentrate on finding a way to win, not whether I could take my opponent.

But regardless of losing an ear, Cooper was a whole other "kettle of fists", impossibly huge, definitely capable of landing some hard shots, and maybe putting the hurt on me. "In the event things turn to shit, and survival comes down to knuckles and knees, hit him first with a throat shot." I told myself, to activate the reptilian part of my brain, alerting it to the heighten potential for violence—now that I knew that Cooper was involved.

Maybe for once it is a good thing The Monkey is here. With him jolting me with Opiods and Adrenaline, on top of the half-gram I just snorted, I'll have even more of an edge against Cooper. I thought, while getting into the role.

If they made a hostile move against Bitsy my first concern was going to be bullets. The word on the streets was; Cooper was a shoot-first kind of guy, and had already planted more than one adversary in the ground. I had no intention ending up as another one of Cooper's victims. Making sure I had backup in the woods might have been the smartest act I've ever done. You could never be too careful with a sadistic fuck like Cooper.

The Buyer must have lost his fucking mind bringing someone like Cooper to a negotiation that required some modicum of self-control and discretion. It was like bringing a pocket full of blasting caps into an explosive factory. Not a bad comparison when taking into account Cooper's famous short fuse.

This was not the first meeting in a vacant lot for any of us. I only hoped that Cooper didn't have anyone in the woods with rifles, waiting in the shadows, ready to pay for the coke with cartridges.

Bitsy and I walked towards the Buyer with our hands at our sides, palms open, in plain sight at our sides. They did the same. Both parties halted when there was 20 feet between us.

"About twenty feet … good, well within range of my 45." I whispered to Bitsy.

Cooper shifted his weight, and nervously looked at the forest, then shifted his gaze to the building. Cooper was not the trusting sort, his eyes should have been on us, and the fact that they weren't was not a good sign.

The jerky little movements of Cooper's head reminded me of an Ostrich. It would have been pretty amusing, the way he moved, if it not for the fact that in the real world large birds were not known for carrying weapons—other than spiked claws. Cooper was sure as shit braced; I could see the telltale handgun bulge in the waistband of his trousers.

"What a dumbass. He's too stupid to hide his weapon! Fuck, this better not turn into a gunfight." I said to myself, while preparing for the worst.

Bitsy waved the other men forward and began working the deal. Bitsy showed them the product; the Buyer picked out a random batch, tried it, and then signaled all was good. We asked to see the money and I immediately sensed something was wrong.

They should have instantly shown us the cash; that was how things were done—see the goods then show the money.

Delaying any part of the transaction would create distrust and that is how people got shot. All it took was for someone to mistake a minor movement for a threatening gesture, then all hell would break loose and before you knew what was happening, you were playing dodge-ball with bullets. To aggravate matters further, the Buyer began making small talk, chatting up Bitsy in a way that was completely out of place in this kind of atmosphere.

Get in... get out.... don't say more than you have to, that is how it was supposed to be done. You weren't supposed to stand around sharing cooking recipes, or glad-handing each other. In fact, unless you are some kind of moron, don't say shit except hello and goodbye. All these ideas flashed through my head in less time than it takes for a hummingbird to complete a single wing-beat.

"Is there something else? You've seen the goods and said you were happy with the quality. So why is it that you have not brought out the money? Bring it out now and give it to him (indicating Bitsy) or we're out of here." I told the Buyer, while angling my position to get a better look at the shadows surrounding the old showroom. I wasn't worried about the forest because that is what my guys were in place for. With my guys in the woods, trouble wasn't going to come from that direction, it would come from the darkened corners of the building. It was unlikely Cooper would try anything first because he could see that my attention was not going to waver from his direction.

"Okay ... okay ... relax you're going to get your money. What's the rush? I'm just trying to be friendly, we may want to do this again, you know?" The Buyer said as he too started to glance around.

"What is the rush? Is this your first circus or something? If you want to make friends, go to the ball-cage at Chucky

Cheese. But right now ... get the money and stop talking. And you, (I said pointing to the Cooper) better quit fidgeting and looking at that building, or were going to have a big problem."

They still made no move towards their car. I could see that they were waiting on something. Then it came. Two shots from the north side of the building. Both rounds missed. I grabbed Bitsy and shoved him towards the Mercedes. The Buyer had already made it back to the BMW and was getting into the front seat. He put the car in reverse and backed up to where the bullets came from. Cooper went for his piece. I went for mine but in my haste to bring it out before he did I made a rookie mistake and snagged the hammer on my shirt flap. The .45 dropped directly at our feet.

"What a fucking dumbass!" The Monkey screeched from his position above the fray. Or maybe it was Copper that called me a dumbass. Either way, whoever said it was right.

Cooper's face contorted with a mixture of emotions; anger because the plan was going array, and shock at his good fortune that I had dropped my piece.

"Stupid fuck. Can't even hold on to your weapon." That time it was Cooper for sure talking.

He had his pistol almost all the way out and was already pulling on the trigger. I stepped in close, gripped his hand, goose-necking his wrist so that the hand holding the weapon was immobilized. I continued to bend his hand, until his wrist and finger bones were at such severe angle, the barrel pointed vertically at Coopers head. I kept the pressure on, so as to prevent getting swept by killing part, and accidentally eating a bullet. The pressure on his arm forced Cooper's entire body backwards. Once his balance was broken, I tripped him to the cement. A couple of his fingers remained in my grasp, so I broke them,

Cooper's head bounced off the hard surface, and before he could shake off the impact, I knee-dropped his chest. Several ribs cracked, and could be heard over the commotion. I finished him off with a couple elbows to the bridge of the nose. I got to my feet quick and assessed the situation.

My battle with Cooper took only a few seconds. But in that short span of time, the Buyer had already driven to the corner of the building, and picked up his other man, previously hiding behind a thick column supporting a rusty garage door.

The Buyer threw the transmission into drive, then stomped the accelerator, aiming the BMW in my direction—no doubt intending to run me over. The vehicle came upon me so fast there was no opportunity to completely dodge the front bumper. The two-ton hunk of German Engineering, switched from Luxury Sedan, to Battering Ram, striking me just below the hip.

I was able to deflect most of the energy, by twisting to the left side, and thereby avoiding a straight thump, which easily could have broken my back. But the clumsy pirouette did not save my body from being damaged. I still absorbed enough force to knock me to the ground, temporarily dazed, with plenty of pain traveling up my spine. Cooper got his shit together, leaped to his feet and searched for the dropped weapons... but came up empty. The loud gunshots and yelling had all the neighborhood dogs barking. Soon phones would most certainly be ringing at the precinct and units dispatched to the scene. With the clandestine part of the meeting shot to shit (literally), Cooper wisely decided not to hang around looking for his gun. Instead, he ran to where I was laying, still trying to recover from getting hit by the car.

Without breaking stride, he punted me in the face. It hurt like a bitch and must have been karma for the kick I gave the Stoners. The impact split nose cartilage and sent a front tooth racing towards to the moon. He was setting up for another kick, but reconsidered, when he saw my guys running out of the forest in our direction.

As they ran from the woods, Bitsy sent a few rounds into the air. A crazed Bitsy waving a gun was all that was needed to scare Cooper, thereby ending his assault on my face, in favor of getting into the BMW with the rest of his crew. Once the Buyer had all his guys loaded into the vehicle, he gave the tires all the horsepower the engine could muster, and flew out of the parking lot.

The wheels lost control on a pile of gravel and smacked into a strand of trees growing near the exit (should have bought an Audi I would think later), where it got caught up on several large limbs bent under the front wheels and stalled.

The Buyer attempted to restart the car, cranking it over and over. In the meantime, his guys got out and looked things over, then tried to yank out whatever was impeding their hasty retreat. I watched all of this, while on all fours, still on the cement, still struggling to get the wind back, squeezed from my lungs by the impact with the car.

The Monkey figured this was an appropriate moment to tempt me into rash action.

"Get up, you pussy. Come on ... find your gun and chase those fuckers down. You still have time to teach them a real lesson."

The Monkey had worked himself into frenzy that was almost comical.

"Remember the kick that asshole gave you...they even tried to run you over." The Monkey said as he scampered halfway up another light-pole so as to lecture me from a better position.

I said the cleverest thing I could think of under the circumstances. "Shut the fuck up." Not the brightest comment, but it's not easy to be clever, with no air in your lungs, and a mouthful of blood.

The Monkey began shaking the pole like a gibbon trying to dislodge ripe fruit from a jungle branch. **"Come on, do something. Shoot that guy."** He said pointing to Cooper, outside the BMW, pulling the last big branch out of the grille.

I'd never shot anybody before (outside of the military) and was not about to start now. It was time to go. I found my weapon by crawling on my hands and knees. My guys got to me and helped me to my feet, then carried me to Bitsy's car, where not a second was wasted getting inside.

I got in the backseat and glanced at Bitsy to see why we weren't moving. He was behind the steering wheel snorting blow. Sweat dripped from his face and he was shaking like a Jackhammer. His face was red, and maybe it was the way the shadows danced across his face, but I could swear he was digging the turmoil. *God Damn thrill junkie!*

"Dude .... what the fuck are you doing? Not enough excitement for you? Are you trying to have a heart attack ... put that shit away! Come on let's get out of here." I yelled at him.

The other vehicle was already gone. There was nothing left to do except drive through the exit, put the whole affair behind us as quick as possible, and mend our wounds.

"This was really fucked up! This was my last job for you, Bitsy." I said out loud, in the hope that by hearing the words come out of my bloody mouth the decision would be set in stone, and somehow magically make it so.

"Yeah, sure, whatever you say. I'll call you when I need you." Bitsy replied, as if he knew my statement was far weaker than my habit. I couldn't really blame him as he'd heard it all before.

As we left the area I took a last look behind me to see what the Monkey was doing. He had climbed higher up the pole and was within reaching distance of the light itself. My imagination, aided my chemical residue, took his existence to a new level, a level that made me think for the first time, that I had some control over how the Monkey acted. So I let my imagination run wild and envision dreadful illustrations involving the Monkey ... things that would hurt him.

What I saw was real enough. The Monkey reached a finger into the socket like he was trying to grab a fig or something. Or maybe my mind made him reach into the socket. I'm not certain what caused him to do it but the result was the same.

His finger made contact with the exposed wiring, dangling in a knot from a cup, where a bulb used to be. A connection was made between voltage and primate flesh. The wind picked up and I thought the smell of cooked Monkey permeated thru the air. It made me think of the line by Col. Kurtz in *"Apocalypse Now"*. The one difference being that I didn't think the burning Monkey smelled like victory ... too early for that ... it smelled more like revenge.

Bitsy's car moved further down the road, but not before I observed the Monkey taking in about 10,000 volts. I smiled and let myself once again think of something that also gave me comfort.... music! A song that seemed very correct for situation began to play in my mind, I listened to the lyrics and thought of the title...... "Shock the Monkey", by Peter Gabriel.

Fucking right.....shock the Monkey!

Monkeys On Flame

I spat some blood, which had seeped from my cracked tooth, into the sink; it landed on lumps of mint-green Crest splotches, probably left there by Tim's morning brushing. Now it had hardened and was stuck to the porcelain like a tick. Tim was known for having many good qualities; however, cleaning up—after producing a mess, wasn't one of them. I thought about wiping the sink out, in the event I got lucky, and a girl stopped by, and then thought better of it, and instead went with the "Fuck it" option. There was still plenty of time before I had to link-up with Bitsy. He had to be going out of his fucking mind, while attempting to sort out the disturbing episode from the night before. Bitsy had a hard enough time dressing himself, so there was little chance of reaching any earth-shaking conclusions on his own.

So, with a lull in the action, I craved the release of a more cerebral endeavor, such as improving on my writing skills. "Watch out Stephen King" I commented to my Id (the part of the brain responsible for instinctual actions). "Watch out Penthouse Letters", my Id commented back, using an internal voice full of doubt as it pertained to the relative merits of my writing style, especially when my drug use and questionable behavior was factored in. Shakespeare wasn't known for beating the snot out of people for a living when not touching quill to ink. But then again, both Poe and Nietzsche were both junkies, so I had that going for me.

Maybe this pursuit, even if it is a pipe dream, will be the ingredient that has been missing, in order to find a new direction in my life, and make up for all the wasted years, I thought, while attempting to organize the words jumbled in my head. It was no coincidence that I had chosen writing as my way out of the gutter. Putting pen to paper might just be the only career that would make up for all the lost years.

Besides, what better punishment for past deeds was there, other than to seek out the most humbling task—creative writing

—a pastime that absolutely promised the greatest amount of criticism and rejection?

"It just won't do if my scribbles appear ridiculous and merely the wishful endeavor of an untalented hack. Shit ... even if I am a fucking retard and have an entire brain destroyed by drugs, who wants the whole world to know that kind of thing." I said with no small amount of trepidation. The mental deliberations were not beneficial to the process, so I pushed everything aside, and went back to the keyboard. I was not ignorant of the paradox that existed in my pursuit of writing, as destroying brain cells isn't the general method used in creation. However, as I was an arrogant sod living in denial, I was remarkably unfazed by the opinions of others. Okay, it was a lofty dream to have, becoming a writer that is, but questionable lifestyle aside, my resolve to succeed was stronger than ever.

There was a string of thoughts that refused to go quietly. *How can I be certain that "my reality" is anything like what other people perceive? How much of what I write are really artistic flourishes, and how much is the result of consuming too much acid and mushrooms.* It seemed that more and more that the division, separating my acid trips from "the actual" was becoming very tenuous. Therefore, it would be reasonable to extrapolate this very disturbing idea; that whatever I come up with, fiction, non-fiction, and horror of horrors—poetry, will be the kind of stuff an average person will not relate to, maybe even find distasteful, or worse yet, merely the words of a madman. I considered the term—'Madman'—even to the point of allowing the title to roll over my tongue a few times. Well, at the end of the day Madman still beats the hell out of asshole. Madman it is.

I began writing again ...

As Bitsy's Mercedes drove from the Ford Dealership I stared out the rear window, wanting nothing more except for watching the Monkey suffer. The electricity coursing through his body, heated his furry hide, so that his entire body was smoking.

Tiny glowing cinders floated up from his shoulders and rode the summer breeze into the night sky. Panic stricken and in obvious pain, The Monkey scrambled down the pole as fast as friction and gravity would allow. His speedy descent fed oxygen to the smoldering fur, and caused the flames to grow twice as high, making it seem as if he was a fire-afterbirth, maybe resulting from the copulation of A Mexican Jumping Bean and A Tiki Torch. His feet touched the pavement around the foundation of the pole, and he began to hop around as if performing an Irish jig, jumping from leg to leg and waving both arms in the air.

His screeching was mostly comprised of primate obscenities. His screams merged with the sound of barking dogs and gave the impression that a "Monkey Hunt" was underway somewhere in the Forest Preserve. The pain from the electric shock and resulting fire caused the Monkey to realize that his dancing was not helping in dousing the flames, and in fact was probably only aggravating the situation. He stopped fanning the fire and searched his brain for the best survival instinct, one his ancestors had used in similar circumstances, and also involved putting out flames. The Monkey vowed to his miserable simian god, ***"I'm not going to turn into a charcoal briquette ... because I'm not thru with Billy yet."***

Try as he might, The Monkey was unable to find the best way to put out the flames. His mental vault contained nothing about burning monkeys, so he switched to a new tactic, and began to roll over and over on the surface of the parking lot.

Unfortunately—for me, the rolling action worked, quenching both fire and my hope to see him spontaneously combust. There would be no giant fireball, as his smothering solution extinguished the flames. Only wisps of smoke from scorched Monkey hair remained in the air. The cloud slowly spiraled up and around the light-pole. The sight made me think of a children's book I read as a kid, something about a maypole as I recall.

The last thing I saw before we left the vacant lot was the Monkey brushing himself off and giving me his version of the finger. Crazy ... but I dug it.

I took a break from typing and read back what I had just written. *"Crazy"* turned to *"Crap"*. For crap was the only term that applied to my first attempt at becoming a writer. But imagining voltage coursing through The Monkey had an unintended reward. In that as I wrote about the Monkey's fiery boogie, another of my favorite songs *"Cities on Flame"* by Blue Oyster Cult popped into my cerebral cortex. Change the title to the track, add the right words to ring out over Buck Durama's stun chords, and you would end up with *"Monkeys On Flame."* I made a mental note to call Buck for soundtrack contributions ... if my story was ever was made into a movie.

Perhaps I was putting "the cart before horse", as my creative talent was at a stage that made it pretty much a certainty that I was not quite ready for a new career. More importantly, I was certainly not ready to cast off the Monkey. Not exactly a good feeling, but nothing a couple lines of blow and a beer couldn't cure. I got the right blend of alcohol and chemicals flowing to my brain and began to unpack, and clean my most recent mineral acquisitions from Iowa. The restoration procedure was an arduous job but a satisfying one.

The exacting task of using an etcher to refine the original patterns (each millions of years old), was not unlike a Japanese Tea Ceremony. The fossil was important. However, the real prize was the methodical process of renewal, involving every stroke of the vibrating tool, followed by the slow, deliberate application of clear enamel. The time consuming, exacting procedure was my favorite method to clear my head, therefore renewing my state of mind—aside from Tai Chi that is.

This confirmed the ritual as being the next best thing to meditation, very relaxing, and a reminder of what the future might hold—if I changed my ways. The internal voice, which demanded change, came from deep within my conscience, and spoke to me each time I picked up a different specimen to work on. Once each specimen was finished, each one was aligned adjacent to other previous finds on a special bookshelf that had been made specifically for displaying my collection.

Each tier represented groupings from a certain age and location. Devonian Trilobites from Antelope Springs Utah, Eocene Fish from the Green River Formation in Wyoming, Cretaceous Ammonites from the Apache Mountains, and brachiopods from Kansas.

All were part of the personal museum that my brothers and I had put together. We shared the responsibilities of curator, director, but I held two other titles that they did not have;

'enforcer' and 'lead asshole' for other shady organizations. Our little museum was not open to the public, unless of course you count; Andy, Jumbo, Bitsy, an assortment of loose women, and additional derelicts of the night. Most of which would not know a fossil if it bit them on the ass. And come to think of it ... probably didn't know paleontology from astrology. Earlier that year I had tried to get Bitsy to understand the allure that fossils and ancient treasures had for my family. It was like trying to explain evolution to an evangelical ... a total waste of time and resources.

Bitsy often patronized me by pretending to be interested in the fish plates from Green River and staring intently at the specimen. He would follow every examination with a random assortment of stupid questions.

"Hey do you think caveman ate sushi? Shit ... I'll bet all they had to do was hop on a dinosaur and ride to a lake, spear a big tuna, and put the flesh on a bed of rice."

I never made the mistake of responding to Bitsy's stupid questions, to do so would automatically insert me into a conversation with an idiot, and thereby obliterate every bit of gray matter in my thick skull. Bitsy's knowledge of science was wrong on so many levels that addressing such a comment would be like entering the fight ring and not keeping your hands up.

Lay down with dogs wake up with fleas, isn't that what they say. I thought as I placed the last mollusk shell on the small wooden stand that had been designed for such a purpose.

Shit ... I lay down with fleas and then wake up with more fleas.

Don't think like that...you have time to change...so shut the fuck up. I pushed away the negative thoughts about Bitsy, Fleas and derelicts. Laughing, I twisted the words in my mind so that the sentence emerged as: 'Bitsy's Fleas are derelicts' ... a phrase which was much closer to the truth.

A measure of pride crept in as I admired the fossil exhibition. It had developed into a fairly impressive collection that was suitable for "pleasing the educated", or if necessary, "confounding the idiots." I wondered if the phrase "confounding idiots" was some kind of oxymoron. I promised look to up oxymoron in the dictionary so as not to misuse it. However, when it came to idiots....the last two syllables of the word (moron) sure seemed to apply. I broke up the word play, going on in my mind, by looking at my fossil collection, while comparing it to Tim and James displays.

It almost rivals the collection that James and Tim started a few years ahead of me. I'm catching up, I thought.

Whereas James had the best collection of Sharks' teeth, Tim had a very impressive assortment of large Ammonites.

Most of the ammonites were found around the Permian Basin—in Texas, when a few years back we had taken a road trip and spent a week prying loose shells and casts from the small mountains located just off Route 10. It was at one of those sites that he almost got attacked by a mountain lion.

The animal had stalked him from above while he explored a narrow canyon cut into the rocks by the pelting rain and flooding. The depression also happened to be the location of the lion's den. But unlike the story of Daniel, Tim did not need God to save him; instead he relied on fast feet and keen eyes for his salvation. It was as Tim said, "If you wait for God to save you, you're going to be in for a long wait. I'd rather rely on my own skills to get out of a jam."

It was getting late, so the time had come to stop my paleontology hobby, and get back to the business of knocking heads. If I did not leave right away, there was a good chance my meeting with Bitsy—at to Scornovicians would be missed. Talking with Bitsy and sorting things out in regards to the attempted rip-off was more important than working on fossils. We had to get together and develop our next move to rectify the situation. There had to be a fitting response to the foiled rip-off attempt, or Bitsy's reputation (which really meant my reputation) was as dead as Nero. Earlier that night, after leaving the Ford Dealership, I immediately got on the phone with everyone I knew, pushing for information, calling in markers, anything that might help us find the Buyer and Cooper. Unfortunately—as of that moment, the Buyer, Cooper and their crew had disappeared. We knew enough from talking to our friends the guy that had referred the deal to Bitsy, an act that put the recommendation square on his double-crossing shoulders, was also long gone.

Better he never shows his face again, I thought, while grabbing my jacket and making a hurried exit from the apartment. Since it was a nice day, and it wasn't far to the meeting place, I decided to walk. Maybe even stop along the way and say hello to several of the tavern owners on the strip. I could smell the pasta cooking from the Italian restaurants that were nestled between each block of bars. All the restaurants were in the process of quickly feeding hungry customers, giving the check, and herding in the next wave of paying customers. The drinking establishments were also busy, as there was much to prepare before night came, along with the onslaught of thirsty regulars anxious watch "The Bulls" on the big screens. There was activity everywhere you looked. Over the last several years I had assisted many of the owners in numerous ways, so there was no shortage of friendly smiles and invitations for a free meal or a drink or two.

Sadly, I had to pass up all the offers. My conversation with Bitsy could not wait. I was about a half a mile from Scornovicians when a white van pulled up alongside of me. I had been taking a shortcut through a wide delivery alley that led to the receiving bay of the restaurant.

A scruffy looking fellow, wearing coke-bottle glasses, leaned out of the open van window and waved me over, in a way that wasn't the least bit friendly. It was an unforgettable face, covered with acne and pock marks.

I deliberated on why his face seemed so familiar. Then I remembered that he was one of the Navy guys from the fight that gave me blood poisoning. I considered advising him to ease up on the sweets, just to cut through the bullshit; since there was no doubt that this was a precursor to big trouble.

Might as well get them angry and throw them off their game plan, I thought. But I settled on a more peaceful approach, since being extra careful was a much smarter move. All the bad shit that had happened recently gave me serious misgiving about being too close to strangers...... especially those wearing phony grins while acting angry. Something weird was happening. There were too many people reappearing from my past. Adversaries that should have been nothing but unpleasant memories defied all odds, and were returning into my life at the most inopportune moments. It was if my consciousness was vibrating on some crazy cosmic frequency, the kind only people I'd harmed could sense, telling them where to find me to get revenge. So, instead of instigating anything, I played along and see what developed.

"Hey, man....how're doing buddy? Want to get a great deal on a T.V ... "32" inches for only 200.00?" The Window Leaner said as the van continued to parallel my path down the alley.

"Yeah ... that's a good deal, but I'm late for an appointment." I responded. Not knowing how many other assholes were in the van I prepared to run.

The van angled across the alley, and then parked, leaving only a few inches between the front bumper and the brick wall. The Van was positioned to cut off my intended route of escape.

"What's a matter, man? You afraid the stuff is stolen? Where are your balls?" Scruffy boy said. And in the light; his complexion was far worse than anything I had ever seen. It was time to cease the fake pleasantries and force their hand.

"My balls are right where they should be. Remember ... I took them out of your mouth last night. Oh yeah, some prepubescent teenager at the other end of the alley wanted me to tell you that he wants his zits back. "

It had the effect I wanted. They were plenty mad now, caught up in their anger, ready to jump me—before getting into position. If they came at me one by one I stood a good chance of not getting Gorilla Piled.

"Okay ... Shit is about to go down. Do something fast." I told myself while considering several different getaway scenarios.

I turned to my right and strode purposely towards the rear of the van. I still did not move too fast, as looking calm, and showing no fear was a key component to any survival strategy. I wanted the assholes to think there was a fight brewing, not that I getting ready to bolt.

If they thought my plan was to run and get my friends, all of them would exit the van together. I did not want them all out of the van and set to give chase before I had a gotten big enough lead. For a second or two, my plan seemed to be working as it looked as if there was plenty of space to maneuver and then sprint down the alley so I could leap over a wall.

I never made it. The rear door of the van swung open and two assholes jumped out. They were on me in an instant, each grabbing an arm, while another watched for the cops from inside the van. When the two guys holding me had a tight enough grip, they began to drag me towards the open cargo hold. I almost broke free by jerking violently backwards and at the same time, head-butting the nearest guy. The impact sent him careening into a trash can. While he tried to recover from the head butt, I spun to face the guy still holding my left arm. He had pretty good reflexes and went for a chicken-wing on my arm, pushing it up my back.

Using my free hand, I pushed his chin at a painful angle, and then tore my other arm free, at the same time driving the elbow across his exposed temple. The fucking guy's eyes crossed and drool spilled from his open mouth. It actually looked as if I was going to make it out of the alley in one piece until the scraggy asshole exited the van, joined the fray and pinned both my arms to my sides.

From that moment it all became a blur. I remember getting hit with three, maybe four (but whose counting) punches in the head. I felt myself go to Queer Street ... legs wobbly ... balance off ... sight filled with tiny stars ... loud buzzing in my ears.

I forced myself to stay awake, or the boots were going to be put to me. I kept on fighting, not stopping, even while three of them pulled me completely into the van. Using my bent knees to generate thrust I drove my head back again and hit one of them right on the mouth.

After my last experience of striking somebody's teeth, there was a brief vision of blood-poisoning in my head. I was unable to ascertain if the guy got knocked out from the blow to his mouth, but his grip on my neck loosened, allowing me to brace myself on the edge of the inside wheel-well.

The hub-cover gave the support needed to cycle my legs and kick the other two assholes in the neck and face, multiple times, each with surprising force. They fell out of the van and lay in a heap on the greasy, oil stained assault. I got my hands under me and crab-crawled out towards the rear hatch to freedom. I stomped on the torsos of the two attackers that had fallen outside the van with each step.

Since it is impossible to get away without crossing over the bodies, why not break a few ribs. I thought.

I fucking won ... who will believe it? Get out of here ... wait a second, stomp that fat bastard again ... kick that other asshole one more time. The thoughts came so fast; there was no way to physically react to all of them. But the one that told me to "stomp the fat bastard" was heard and answered. So before I got "the fuck out of there" Fatboy received a well-placed kick in stomach. I shouldn't have paused and should have left the alley when I had the chance. I was bringing my leg back from the kick, when something hit me just above the ear. I figured out what was happened right off; the guy that received the head-butt (inside the van) had followed me out, waited for the right moment, and then stuck a sharp object into my head.

"This is for calling us squids and breaking our friends jaw. Next time we meet you're a dead man," the attacker yelled, with nothing else left to do, as his after his tool struck the intended target ... my scalp.

I turned, grabbed him in a body-lock and tripped him to the ground. While he was rolling to his feet, I yanked the object out of my head. It was a long, thin flat head screwdriver that had luckily glanced off my skull, and only pierced the flesh between bone and hair. I thought about returning the favor and injecting the screwdriver into the attacker's eye, but the pain was starting to set in, and a weak, dizzy, feeling surged through me from head to toe. It seemed smarter to get the fuck out of there before I collapsed.

I ran down the alley towards the restaurant, along the way, and flinging the screwdriver over a wrought iron fence, so as not to be seen running with a bloody metal object, certainly not exactly the image I wanted to portray at the time. I felt like hours and thousands of steps before I got to the rear entry doors of Scornovicians. Blood was streaming from my head. I made my way to the closest waitress alcove, the place where table settings and condiments were stored, and grabbed a handful of napkins. Something was needed to act as an antiseptic, so I slipped behind the busback bar, snagged a vodka bottle, and poured on to the cloth. Holding the napkins against my head, I made a beeline for the nearest restroom. Luckily nobody else was in there, except the attendant, frozen in fear.

"Get out!" I told him, while handing him a couple ten dollar bills. Having the restroom to myself did nothing to alleviate the sensation of passing out. I braced myself on the sink, splashed water on my face, and took a deep breath. I was almost afraid to examine the damage in the mirror, because if it looked as bad as it hurt ... then it was back to the hospital for me. I was quickly becoming a regular there, having been treated five other times for serious injuries—besides the fight with the squids. Most of the treatments involved stitches in the face so it was not a stretch in thinking the hospital staff had figured out that I was an asshole—the kind that liked to fight. One more visit and the nurses were surely going to call the cops.

When I finally got the courage to check out my reflection in the mirror, the bruised and swollen face that stared back was a true horror show. Two black eyes, puffy lips, missing tooth—thanks to one-eared Cooper—and a narrow channel carved violently into the side of my head.

"Good thing you started off as such a handsome fucker, or you would scare the shit out of the people eating next door...or at least make em' puke." I told my reflection, as injecting a little levity always got me through any to the situation. "Can't cry over spilled blood."

The was nothing left to do except clean up as best as possible, which I did after grabbing a few bandages from the first aid kit stashed in the supply room adjacent to the restroom. To take away some of the pain, a couple of Percocet capsules were swallowed, followed by a tab of purple-microdot LSD. The acid was not for pain, but for brain.

"Beaten up by a bunch of sailors ... if I was you ... I would get a bunch of friends together, go to Great lakes Naval Base, and find the bastards—and then kill them," said an all too familiar voice.

My first thought was ... *I sure hope there is another person talking to me; otherwise the fucking Monkey has found me again.* It was foolish to think, that in a crisis, the voice came from anything or anybody except for The Monkey. And then I saw him, sitting on a trash canister, slapping the little swinging door – on top if the can, back and forth, using hard slaps from his wrinkled brown palm.

"Hey, Billy! Screwdriver in the head, that has to be a new low ... even for you. Yeah, yeah, I know about the fight with the sailors in the alley. You must really be ashamed, getting your ass kicked by a bunch of sailors." The Monkey said, while tearing up bits of paper, sticking them in his mouth and spitting them on the mirror.

"Any reason you like to make an appearance in restrooms so much? I guess you really are like Curious George. Now beat it ... I got things to do." I told him while blotting up blood from my head wound. *There is definitely some link I'm missing that connects The Monkey and my Acid trips.* I thought.

He read my mind and responded *"Yeah there is a link ... a missing link. Get it ... I'm a Monkey ... you said link ... then the word missing."* He saw I wasn't amused.

"Missing link, that's funny, even if you don't think so." He came closer peering at my wound. *"Hey, Billy ... I have to install some kitchen cabinets; know where I can find a screwdriver ... one that hasn't been inside your head?"* He laughed. The Monkey grew impatient, bored with the trashcan, the mirror, and jokes at my expense. He craved violence and in my present condition there would not be any.

"Yeah, I'll leave for now ... but I'll be back tonight just in time for your revenge ... don't you worry about that." The Monkey faded from view, but not before I threw a haymaker at him. The punch passed right thru him and broke the mirror.

But before the mirror shattered, there was no mistaking the fact that it was my reflection, and only mine, filling the mirror. The Monkey slowed his disappearing act just long enough to say, *"Look at you ... so fucked up, that now you've taken to punching mirrors."* He shook his head mimicking regret then released the most hideous wail he'd ever made. Glad he was gone I started for the door.

"Can't walk out there with napkins on my head, people will think there's something wrong with me. I murmured and then thought, *You just tried to punch a talking Monkey, a hallucination that can only be seen by you ... yeah there is something wrong with you.*

Think about that shit later, get cleaned up, Bitsy is waiting. I went back to the attempt at mummifying my head with strips of gauze, and covering the other cuts with Band-Aids and then walked through the swinging kitchen doors. I found Bitsy at a corner booth, checking his watch, and with his free hand reaching for a pitcher of beer he had ordered.

"Little early for cocktails isn't it, Bitsy? I said while sliding into the opposite side of the booth.

Bitsy took a good look at my face and cringed. "Yeah ... but apparently not too early for getting the shit kicked out of you!" Bitsy said, while looking at my black and blue eye sockets. "Jesus ... who made you a raccoon? I sure hope the girl looks worse then you."

"That's hilarious; Bitsy ... black eyes ... raccoon ... and a girl beat me up ... real funny. The Monkey already made fun of me ... and now you?"

"What fucking monkey?" Bitsy said.

It dawned on me that Bitsy had no idea what I was talking about.

"Never mind."

"Alright ... seriously was it those assholes from last night ... everybody says they left the state."

"No it had nothing to do with the rip-off attempt." I replied.

"Shit ... that's a relief. Marco and I went by to see the guy that vouched for them. His door was wide open, place was empty, looks like he packed up and split."

"You don't say?" I replied sarcastically. "Imagine that. The guy that tried to set us up and get us killed left town. Who would have thought? Maybe next time you'll listen to me when I tell you something isn't right about a deal. And the next you decide to sell shit to people we don't know, count me out. In fact this may have been my last job for you. Bitsy, you're getting way too careless. I've told you that a hundred times." I paused to let all sink in. "Oh yeah, one other thing, as to who punched me out ... it wasn't one girl ... it was four of them".

Bitsy downed his beer. I could see he was getting worked up to ask a bunch of stupid questions about Monkeys, sailors, and girls. But I interrupted him.

"Don't worry about it, Bitsy. I got in a fight with four sailors. They were after me because I kicked the shit out of their buddy. It had nothing to do with last night, or anything else I've done for you."

Bitsy tried to give me the impression that he was heeding my council. But I could see it was all an act. As soon as we left the restaurant he would forget all about our conversation and go back to winging it and flying by the seat of my (his protector) pants.

Better to have him fly by the seat of my pants, then try to be in them, I thought. It was rumored that Bitsy played for both teams. Bitsy poured some white powder on a menu and pushed it in my direction.

Fuck it ... I'll quit tomorrow, I thought. Then snorted everything he put out. But as I 'hoovered' up the coke, another idea struck me.

"Tomorrow is turning out to be everyday of the week ... stop thinking you'll quit tomorrow ... walk away from the mess you made of your life and start over." After mulling how ridiculous my own words sounded, I asked myself the question that haunted me every waking hour. "Will it take an overdose before you grasp the point of your sermon?"

But at the time there was no use in trying to change, Adrenaline and chemical fueled excitement were consumed like breakfast cereal; a warped version of Madison Avenue commercial brainwashing. My craving for a rush was like Trix to a Rabbit. Better yet, I had become Coo Coo for Cocaine puffs. It should have been comical—my relationship with an invisible Monkey. How could anyone not laugh at such a ridiculous playmate? But there was nothing funny about the bond between the Monkey and I, it was a 'lose—lose' kind of relationship. Defined by me losing my fucking mind and the Monkey losing his current victim—once I gave him the overdose he so desired.

There were certainly other questions that deserved attention. But it was a sensitive issue when arguing with oneself. How does one go about asking if they are becoming an idiot pawn in an imaginary game—without offending said idiot pawn?

The whole time I was lost in my own thoughts, Bitsy had kept on rambling, going on and on in the background. Primarily about the deal that went south and how we had to get the fuckers before they got us. I was sick of him and was equally sick of debating myself. I figured it might be a good idea to get some sleep and throw some ice on my injuries, so I got up to leave.

I was supposed to go out with my brothers later that night, and missing a night out, regardless of my facial injuries, was not even remotely possible. "I'm ready for my close-up, Mr. Demille." Besides who doesn't like a good screwdriver in the head story?

Dream On

It was an amazingly realistic and feverish dream, unusual in that The Monkey had never before spoke to me in a dream. The change might have occurred because I had fallen asleep to Aerosmith. Dreams had always been a safe haven, but with the invasion of the Monkey into nocturnal pastures, there would no longer be any escape. His appearance was very disappointing for another, less dangerous reason; he had interrupted a pretty good dream, of girls on the beach—all wanting me ... big time!

"Hello, Billy ... sorry to put an end to your "King of the Beach" fantasy, but we have things to talk about." The Monkey said.

I sadly watched as the dream faded. Beach, girls, summer breeze, ocean, gulls and terns all disappeared, only to be replaced with the image of my arch enemy. The Monkey's entrance into the dream made it frightfully realistic. I felt his desire to do evil, absorbed the terrible glee, and smelled the jungle essence of Chimp. I was really able to feel the hate he had for me. To adhere to the occasion, be it dream or not, he was wearing board shorts, Quiksilver-T, and sandals. Revelation hit, and it finally dawned on me why The Monkey sometimes dressed in outfits deemed as comical; cloaking unimaginably horror in festival customary made the horror that much more disturbing. I thought again of my childhood nightmares of Punch and Judy. Now it all made sense.

"What the fuck are you doing here? I'm sleeping. Couldn't you at least have waited until my dream was over?" I asked, pissed that girls had been forcibly ejected from my dream in favor of the negative allure of a primate

"I could have waited till you woke, but where is the fun in that? Dreams, fantasies, LSD trips and wishes, I'll be joining you in all of them now. We're forever attached at the hip, Billy."

"Okay, say what it is you have to say. Fuck, you're just like Marley visiting Scrooge. I presume there will be two other Monkeys that enter this dream, in order to teach me the error of my ways. Scrooge used to be one of my favorite films, no more. I'll bet the first can be expected when the clock strikes one, and the last will haunt me at the sound of 2 bells. Being the plagiarist that you are, there is no doubt that the last Monkey Ghost is supposed to scare the shit out of me. Am I right? I asked.

"I don't need any additional phantoms to scare the shit out of you Billy." The Monkey said as he moved within a few feet of me ... still no beach ... still all jungle. *"Here try this on for size."*

My gaze was drawn to the image of the Monkey, try as I might to look away. The Monkey grew in size, until his image was three times that of his previous stature. His face became all the things I feared most. He morphed into a weird combination of a Clown (resembling the one that hid under the bed in "Poltergeist"), and a Puppet with a mouthful of teeth. Then shifted to the image of Regen from the "Exorcist" and then back into The Monkey. The vestige went back and forth between childhood memories, flew towards me, and stopped only when it was inches from my eyes, then screamed—much like Marley had done to Scrooge. I screamed back, partly because I really was scared shitless, and partly because a scream was all I could muster, while staring at the demon. After I finally calmed down, a single thought floated in through my mind and sought out some semblance of amusement. "Fuck, not only is that Monkey a good dresser, but he also really knows his movies," I said, to ward off the evil.

The Monkey got the screams he desired, so he returned to his regular shape, complete with beach attire, obviously wanting an honest discourse, without the distraction of me acting like a hysterical little girl.

"We have lots to talk about, Billy. Forget about the writing. There is no chance of a loser like you becoming anything but a sociopath. The drugs must be doing a shitload of damage to your brain, much more I'd hoped for. Somehow, the chemicals have affected your inner filter, and separated what is possible, from what is a goal beyond your level of education and discipline.

"Really Billy, of all possible endeavors to consider, you choose the one profession that has least likelihood of ever

being attained. For a guy that is drinking, fighting, and fucking his way through life, you sure have big dreams, Billy."

The Monkey paused to take a deep simian breath and continued. *"Hemingway was a boozer too, but he produced some great literature, before I melted his liver by driving him to excess. However, Billy ... you are no Hemingway, more like an infant with a new box of crayons, scribbling away, fake contentment locked in colors, but meaningless to the astute. Your family should tell you the truth—that there is no nuance, or poetry, in punching teeth out, or breaking ribs. Your writings are best suited for bathroom stalls."*

As the Monkey spoke, I tried to pull away, end the dream, but there was no way to ignore him. He just kept going on and on. But I was thankful that there were no more clowns or puppets.

"Go ahead, Billy, pursue being an author, so much the sweeter the remorse after failure comes at the result of your own hand. You romantically see yourself as a tragic poet warrior, shrugging off defeat, battling inner demons, splintering the barricades, obstacles that would halt a man of less resolve.

"Time is short, Billy, I have better men to break, so listen. Your life will be one of taking risks, unable to settle down, a drifter that writes nothing but crap. What possible words can you find to put to paper that can defy the damage already done to your brain cells?"

The Monkey scratched, yawned and continued. *"We both know that you did acid every Friday for an entire year. Your mind must be so fucked up that there is no plausible way to tell reality from flashbacks."*

I stirred restlessly, caught in the seemingly endless maelstrom of Monkey and Dream.

The Monkey stood up on just two feet, looking as a biped, tall, more of a man than I. He went on with his well prepared nocturnal speech. *"I've been privy to many of your late night conversations, while surrounded by the usual gathering of stooges. If they weren't so scared of telling you what a pompous ass you have become, one of them would have questioned your sanity.... Or at least mention that it was time to cut down on Purple Microdot and Windowpane.*

"I know well of your initial attempt at writing. "Monkey's on Flame"—not a bad title! But to describe my body on fire and then tell perspective readers, 'The pain was so intense that I danced around with sparks trailing from my hair' is pure speculation and unoriginal pulp. Okay ... yeah, I admit the electric current coursing thru my nervous system hurt like a motherfucker ... but not as bad as a screwdriver being wedged into your scalp by a couple of Squids. Besides, I'm a Monkey; so dancing is nothing to be ashamed of."

The Monkey yawned again, wider, conveying that even the act of appearing to me in a dream was boring beyond description. He continued with his rant.

"Dancing is nothing to be ashamed of, Billy, unless were talking about your brother James. When I'm not sniffing myself, screeching, or tormenting you, Billy, I often entertain myself by dancing in the privacy of the Void. Doing so warms me up before popping into your pathetic life in order to cause trouble. I have to stay loose, got to stay energized, or I might get Gutted. Isn't that what you have planned for me ...a Gutting?" The Monkey rubbed his belly then went on with the lecture.

"Being sliced open isn't a very comforting picture! Instead of ripping out your self-respect, it would be my belly cut open, monkey intestines coiled up on some dirty street, drawing wispy spectral flies, and insects as unreal but as bothersome as I myself am." The Monkey's features momentarily contorted into a worried frown, but it quickly faded, as confidence returned and his insults proceeded.

"No! That will not happen. So far my plan to bring about your corruption and eventual death is going very well. There is no running from your habit, Billy. I'll use all my influence to keep dealers around you ...always ...no matter where you go. I will cause you to unintentionally seek out those in need of some protection or cheaply-bought muscle. Then you can go to work, get free drugs, and sink further into addiction. I'll get my own high from your downward spiral into hell. That is the sort of buzz that I crave, the kind that makes the high from drugs, pale in comparison. Billy, you ever seen a Monkey with his load on, high as a kite from snorting lines of sadness, trembling with amphetamine ener-

gy gleamed from the broken promise of 'what could have been'. That is a trip that no combination of ordinary earthy concoctions can match.

"You probably think that I have an addiction of my own that needs to be addressed. That is a foolish assertion, Billy. "Monkeys of the Mind" cannot possibly have their own "Monkey on their back". It is absurd to consider that one such as I should try a twelve step simian program to kick the habit of tormenting you." He moved even closer, almost as if he had passed through me. His voice changed to a whisper.

"How does the "twelve step Monkey program" affirmation go? Help me God because I am powerless to break the addiction of watching Billy's destruction. Snorting his misery has warped my Monkey brain. Fuck you, Billy …never happen. Rehab is for spineless humans.

"But it does bring up an interesting point; if I was to pray to a god, would the deity take the form of Orangutan or Gorilla? No matter. If I had the weakness of humans—and needed to find comfort in false religions, then Wicca would probably suit me best. Worshiping in jungles is a better place for Monkeys to question the universe. Jungles have trees, and trees have limbs, and limbs mean swinging. Swinging leads to grooving, and grooving leads to dancing. Fuck … dancing there I go again. I have to stop talking about my desire to dance, and stay with what I know best, causing the pain of others.

"However, I need to get back to the job of torturing you in the real world, not while you slumber. I prefer your waking mental and alert condition. In that state, a slight push could bring about something very dark. Darkness … the very thought gets me excited."

Pretty Vacant

I headed north down route 41; it was a nice day for a drive, slightly cloudy, although no rain, and almost no traffic. The Sex Pistol's song "Pretty Vacant" pounded thru dash speakers. The fast pace of the music invigorated me so I pressed down on the accelerator as there didn't seem to be any highway patrol monitoring speeds.

"Vacant", a word that best described the feeling of being lost and empty, a word that I could easily identify with, however indentifying with the message, provided very little comfort, as knowing that my attitude most closely resembled that of Johnny Rotten, was not something to crow about.

I hoped to change the emptiness inside by moving to a new environment shortly after the summer. I was headed to the V.A at Great Lakes Naval Base to fill out the forms, speak with a benefits advocate, and complete all the requirements to facilitate attending college for free. Being under the Vietnam Era G.I Bill, meant that books, tuition, and a college education were all free. The V.A even paid $450.00 a month for expenses, each month, as long as a passing grade was maintained. This was a deal too good to pass up. It also presented a chance to try and kick my habit, while at the same time giving me the opportunity to disassociate from the cretins and thugs that I worked for. I chose Southern Illinois University for two reasons; my brother Sven had already moved there and was on his second year, and it was known as the premier party college in the Central USA, a fact that in all honestly probably meant I was not really all that serious about getting off drugs. Sven was a far better student then I could ever hope to be, but because he excelled at being an overachiever, I figured maybe.....just maybe, some of his diligence and scholastic discipline would rub off. I wanted more than anything to make college work and start over.

Anyway, what can it hurt to change the scenery and ease into a new kind of life? Go to school. That is the answer. Maybe I'll learn a new career, make new friends, and end the involvement with nefarious street-hustlers? I thought, and then declared to my bad side. "Don't blow this chance."

I was surprised how easy it was to get into college as a veteran. My grades in high school were shit so there was an expectation of having problems with my admission especially as I was kicked out of graduation. The expulsion resulted from being a known trouble-maker and because I happened to be in the vicinity when a friend of mine cornered a science teacher, and threatened him with bodily harm—if a passing grade was not given out. The teacher nearly had a heart attack on the spot, an ambulance was called, and panic ensued. Since I was part of a crowd of hooligans, consistently in and out of fights, the School Disciplinarian decided the graduation ceremony would be better off without my presence. I concurred by egging his house and vandalizing his garage.

With the low grades, an unflattering student file, and low attendance, I thought even the V.A would turn me down, and reenlisting was going to be the only choice. That was not the case at all, as my admittance was so easy that you'd think my last name was Sagan, Marconi, or Tesla. I guess they liked the fact that the government was flipping the bill, so there wasn't a problem getting the bills paid that accumulated each semester for tuition or books.

I still had my ES 1100, Sonny Crocket clothes, and sharp (if not sometimes cruel) wit, so getting chicks should be no hard shakes. My last few jobs for Jumbo and Bitsy had produced a great amount of extra money, so when I got to school, the apartment would have the best Nakamishi sound system, a big screen T.V, and an impressive grill and barbeque deck appliance, which were the furnishing necessary for indoor or outdoor parties.

I hadn't even officially started college, yet the struggle to reorganize my priorities was much harder than expected. My goals were honorable, but there was a mountain of obstacles in my way. I had much to overcome before achieving such lofty goals of someday becoming a writer or geologist. I spent every waking moment fighting the desire to get high and reprogram my school check list, so that getting laid did not take precedence over getting passing grades. I decided to occupy all my spare time when not hitting the books by playing Rugby and writing short stories, leaving no time for bar hopping. My academic goals were in line with my chosen professions, but there was always The Monkey to contend with, and he was a powerful adversary.

My brother Sven was very popular with the right crowd. The previous year he had proved to be an integral part of the A-Side Rugby Team, already knew lots of attractive coeds, and knew his way around the campus, so for me, making the transition from "Stupid to Student" would be fun. We planned on rooming together when school started at Carbondale's notorious Lewis Park apartments, taking over the exact same unit (27E) our friends from Chicago had moved out of, having gotten their diplomas. The reputation for wild parties at 27E was so bad, the landlord made us swear we didn't know the tenants that had moved out.

"Those guys sound like they were real assholes. All my brother and I plan on doing is studying," Sven said with a straight face as he signed the lease.

Of course, that was not exactly the truth, as we knew the former residents very well. Unfortunately, it was going to take more than good intentions to stop me from falling back into old habits. Sven's studious regiment would help keep him out of trouble. But for me it would take a lot of discipline to avoid keeping the tradition of 27E intact. Sven and I made a pledge that our apartment would not become the most rowdy unit within the whole complex. He maintained his promise, but I found it difficult to ignore The Monkey and we eventually got kicked out of the unit. The people that moved in our old unit had previously resided across the street in a trailer park. They were continually complaining about the noise and parties at the Lewis Park Complex. We knew them from the student center, Jesus Freak Assholes, the kind always preaching to others. Every afternoon they could be found at the sports complex, speaking to anyone stupid enough to listen, that all men are sinners—except for those who found salvation through Christ. That type of idiocy really offended me and usually had the same effect of getting me worked up, maybe enough to do something a bad Samaritan might act out. I had my own scripture; it started with these words; "The Prodigal Son returns from Africa and seeks to cause havoc."

One day, after failing on my sobriety, The Monkey won out and to give the bible-skinners something earthy to wonder about—before we moved, we cut a hole in the drywall, filled the space with garbage and old red meat, and then sealed it back up in a very professional way. You didn't have to be a genius to imagine the conversation between the nutjobs as the stink set in.

"Gee Whiz, Caleb, what do you think smells like the devil in here?"

"I don't know Mortici, maybe you're possessed by the beast."

If there was a Jesus, he never seemed to get pissed off about the way I treated the religious hypocrites. I never got plagued with boils, cast into a sea of flames, or bound into slavery. Although he did give The Monkey power over me, so come to think of it, I suppose that whatever God that existed might have been a touch peeved after all."

But I am getting ahead of myself. There was an entire summer to be enjoyed before Sven and I left for school. I did my best to prepare for an education. However, the lure of drugs proved impossible to ignore, promises and pledges fell apart, and soon I was focusing my attention in bars, instead of books. I ended the humid month of July by returning to old habits; doing collection rounds, or by watching over Bitsy or Jumbo. And babysitting those two morons never got any easier over the years! With their ill-acquired wealth, huge egos fueled by cocaine, and rude, self absorbed behavior, protecting them had become increasingly difficult. Every night out with those two was full of tense situations, more often than not ending up with me having to throw down, or at least cool down the heated moments to a bearable scorcher. During that summer there were so many scraps that each night I expected a bottle, pool cue, two by four, or a bat broken over my head. But over the years, experience had made me extremely adept at spotting the assholes waiting for the chance to beat the shit out of Bitsy or Jumbo, or the ones that planned on not paying-up. I never pushed people to violence, much rather preferring to complete a collection, or win a fight with words.

But when voices got loud with profanities, or if the guy stepped too close, getting sucker-punched by some asshole was never an option. So when hands came up, I moved fast and ended it faster, being always careful to never let it get to the ground unless absolutely necessary.

There was no disputing that a barroom floor was the worst possible place to end up in a fight—even if you were winning, as rolling on a slippery beer soaked floor was probably going to get you kicked to jelly by unknown enemies in the crowd. For me, that rule was more important than for most people. Maybe the people doing the kicking were a past collection job, held a grudge for personal reasons (I'd made plenty of enemies), wanted to dethrone the current title holder and have bragging rights. It didn't matter ... staying on your feet was always the best strategy. Staying on your feet meant you always had the option to run. That's right, run. There is no shame in running. If I'm in a fight and the other guy picks up a chair, then I'm going to start RUNNING, making a beeline for the nearest location where something heavier and bigger (than a chair) can be found and then brought back into the fight. There have been times when it was necessary to go outside the bar and come back in with a branch off a tree. Branch, bat, hockey stick.... what's the fucking difference? Reminds me of the line from movie, "The Untouchables", with a minor change to the saying "He brings a knife, you bring a gun." I preferred, "He brings a gun, you bring a bigger gun;" "He brings a bigger gun, you get the fuck out of there and don't go back until you have a few fragmentation grenades."

In some cases relying on Asian wisdom is the smartest move, such as Sun Tzu's "Art of War", a masterful book that recommends many strategies including: "Take the high ground, take the enemy by surprise, and take their resources. Beat your enemy not only in a material or physically way, but within the fortress of his mind. Break their spirit and break their will to continue the fight. Many times when backed into a corner, I wished to have Sun Tzu at my side. But since I was several centuries too late, my brothers were a welcome alternative.

Throughout my struggle to escape my violent nature and drugs, I took part in many a saloon slug-feast, most occurred while collecting, quite a few that made the bar-fight in "Shane" seem tame in comparison. But, as fate would have it, the worse altercation for me was not while on the job. It happened in a Brunswick pool hall located in Deerfield behind a Jewel Food Store.

It was only a couple weeks before college was to begin. Tim and I were shooting eight ball with a couple of buxom dates. Our dates were reputed to have sex with anyone who had few lines of coke and a few dollars in their pocket. We had both so it would be good trade. The girls Tim and I dug were the type usually only seen in a Russ Meyer film. Mine was sluttish as the day is long, with long hair that was fire-engine-on-fire red, and freckles, lots of them, kind of like a porno Raggedy Anne. I guess that made me kind of sociopath Raggedy Andy. Tim's girl was a "horse face of a different color (Wizard of Oz reference not a racial one, not that I was above the latter.) There isn't any kidding around when I say horse face. Saying she had teeth like a horse (to go with the face) was an understatement. Everyone has heard the statement "teeth so big she can eat an apple through a picket fence." Well Tim's date had teeth so big she could eat the picket fence. Sure, she had a great body, for an Equis, but greatness of body notwithstanding, an important question had to be asked.

"Tim … I have to know … if you plan on getting between her hooves—don't you have to stop feeding her carrots and kiss her?

His reply was as abstract as the question. "Yeah, but carrots don't cost much, and I can ride her home after the date."

The bowling alley also had a bar, which made it an okay place to hang out on a weeknight. We knew the bartender (one of Jumbo's coke heads), so the Miller Lite was "on the house."

We were finishing up the last game when two large truckers entered the table area. Both were typical long haulers; of a character defined by usually drinking too much and thinking too little, and wearing attire defined by too much flannel in the shirts, too much Sears in the Boots, and too much John Deer in their grease-covered baseball caps.

Add in rust-colored Cajun-style beards, and Tim and I knew all there was to know about those guys, and what was on their "Hee-Haw/Monster Truck minds. They came to brawl. Tim put down his stick and took a place at the corner of the table, so as to be between them and me. That way he could intercept them, should they decide to throw a punch, while my attention was focused on the act of lining up the next shot.

"Combination, 2 to the 4, cross-side." I announced. "Followed by a combination of horse's head to a human body". I whispered just loud enough for Tim to hear, but not so loud as to offend horses, or women with elongated cranial structures.

"In your dreams," Tim said holding out the Ladies Aid (the brace for lining up shots considered by most to be a chick-tool), while acting as nonchalant as possible. I pushed Tim's remark and the handicap stick away with a confident smirk.

As I stroked the two-piece cue stick, the bigger of the two guys ran his hand over the table, knocking all the remaining balls into the nearest pocket. Not satisfied with simply fucking up our game, he followed the intrusion with an obscene comment directed the girls.

He was drunk, so every second or third word came out slurred and hard to understand. However, it sounded like he was trying to say something about their jugs. It was difficult to ignore the size of the girl's giant breasts, so although the trucker was an asshole, he possessed a refined eye for tits, even if he did have very horrible judgment.

I straightened up and shifted my attention from the table to the biggest of the truckers. He swung a right haymaker at my jaw. The punch arced so wide, it might have grazed Neptune. He continued throwing looping punches, which I blocked with my forearms, while stepping inside and hitting him with several short hooks and elbows. He stumbled backwards, giving me enough space to grab his neck and sweep out both legs out from under him. He fell hard and I thought that was the end of it.

He got up surprisingly quick for such a big guy. He slapped my hands away and managed to wrap both arms around my torso. I broke free and grabbed him by the hair, pulling his head so that it was exposed, and then striking with several knees to his face. He should have gone down, but didn't. Five knees to the face and he still wanted to fight on. It was at that exact moment, that for the first time, I thought that I'd met somebody tougher.

Tim was busy with the other trucker on the opposite side of the room. He seemed to be getting the best of Bubba, by using a nine ball to pound on the guy's ribs. But there was no clear winner in either fight because at that moment the cops came in.

The cops assembled the witnesses and demanded to know who started the brawl. The patrons explained that it was the truckers who had initiated the whole altercation, and that Tim and I were just trying to defend ourselves … which was exactly the truth.

While the cops took the story from the asshole that I'd been fighting, I got behind the cop out of his vision, and made fun of the trucker's broken nose, pointing at him, and imitating someone crying, which was solely intended to insinuate that he was a baby. My plan was to piss him off so much all control would be lost and he would behave like an unstable jagoff in front of the cops. It worked. He lunged at me and threw a punch in front of the officers. Bad move. They took him away in cuffs while I made sure that the last thing the trucker saw was me laughing my ass off.

Have fun in jail, pal, I thought.

"A sleepless night, full of unwelcome corn-holing awaits that dickhead." Tim said loudly after the place calmed down.

"I don't know, Tim. He looks like the kind of guy that might welcome a corn-holing." I replied. Both of us shared a chuckle at the comment and the fact that dickhead was going to jail.

Tim and I bought the witnesses a couple round, to say thanks, then ended the evening. But, as I left, a disturbing thought lingered in my mind that I almost got my ass kicked by some guy that was able take five knees to the head and still have fight left in him. As Tim and I got on our bikes, I made a mental note to watch out for that asshole in the future, reminding Tim to do the same. The trucker wasn't going to forget the incident and it would be smart for us not to, either. It should have been a good feeling that nobody (including the truckers) got hurt in the fight. But all I could think about was that two weeks before college was to start The Monkey had won again, I was fighting, drinking and playing the fool. The sensation of being totally and hopelessly lost was overwhelming.

Twentieth Century Schizoid Man

I had one last job to do before leaving for Carbondale. At first I refused; having promised my family that my days of working for Bitsy (or other cretins) were over. But this collection errand was of an entirely different variety then the previous missions. Somebody had broken into Bitsy's home and ripped off all his loot. Most of the stolen money was owed to a Chicago connection that treated late payments very harshly, sometimes very permanently. I guess turnabout really is fair play, for without my intervention, Bitsy was going to get his legs broken or possibly worse. Funny, he was at risk to receive a punishment without mercy just as he had ordered to be done to so many others. Unlike previous collection jobs, this one did not require the residents to be home, in fact, it would be much better if they weren't. If things went according to plan, there wouldn't be an encounter—of any kind. I only had to find the money stolen from Bitsy. This was just a B and E errand, not the type of non-confrontational errand that was not really up my talents, but still, the job resembled the kind I had swore to never do again. However, like it or not, I could not leave a man behind, even if that man was Bitsy.

"Just go in, search the house, and get the fuck out of there. If you don't find the money, Bitsy's going to have to leave town for awhile, because I'm not going to hang around and protect him." I said under my breath. The occupants of this first floor condo were out to dinner, probably stuffing their gullets with sushi, or some other equally trendy food such as: oysters, caviar, and calamari. I only hoped they hadn't already blown Bitsy's money on something other than dinners—as Tim, Marco and I had done to Jumbo. Buying motorcycles, boats, and cars would really eat into the stash that needed to be returned to Bitsy.

The job required me to break into their condo while they were out to dinner, search all the rooms, and take whatever money was found. Then Bitsy could hand it over to his Chicago connection—minus my 20% of course.

If I didn't find the money, Bitsy wanted a phone call, so that he could go to plan B. The alternative plan was to send several goons to the restaurant and forcibly drag the assholes out of their chairs, and into a waiting van; something I wanted no part of.

There was no way to know how much cash and valuables that might be in the condo and it really didn't matter; my task was to seize it all.

Back to the job, everything appeared normal, quiet, no activity, and even better—no sign of The Monkey. *Good! Maybe this caper can be completed without him showing up.*

I entered the residence by using an industrial glass cutter and creating two hand-size holes thru the sliding glass door. The doors appeared to be very costly, with scrolls and wavy designs, bordering the glass section of the partition. The extravagant patio was decorated with a flagstone deck, a narrow garden adorned with snapdragons, and ceramic figurines resembling Olympic goddesses—or some other tasteless crap that rich assholes love. *I live in the lamest decade. Imagine what kind of fucking asshole spends money on this kind of shit.* I thought, while failing to see the irony of spending all of my money on drugs.

There was a good reason for cutting out two sections of glass. One hole enabled me to push away the wooden stick off the track so it no longer held the door closed. The other hole was cut so I could reach in and flip the lever into the open position. I made sure there were no hidden wires or other security devices, so as to make the clandestine entry as uncomplicated as possible. College was on the horizon, which made violence—of any kind. a non-starter for me.

But, it was a rarity for coke fiends and rip off artists to have alarms. Druggies and criminals were the last people that wanted cops answering alarms. I searched the whole condo, room by room, and was down to the last section—the entertainment space. So far nothing of value had been found. If no cash, jewelry, or drugs were hidden in this room, then Bitsy was fucked.

If anyone unexpectedly returned, then the severity of the beating would be directly related to the occupant's musical taste. I did not want to fight, but that desire did not eliminate the survival mode of "fighting my way out." Analyzing musical taste (during collections) was my own barbaric version of a cultural appreciation night. The system of determining the level of possible violence in relation to what music was found—at any location, could never be ignored or violated. This meant that discovering eardrum dissolving music—such as Jimmy Buffet, usually involved a kind of special beating if the money was not produced. Parrot-Heads were like mice! If Jimmy Buffett enthusiasts were fed and/or offered friendship, his loyal listeners would breed fast, mice-like, and never so away. Then the huge population of Parrot-Heads would swarm cities in droves and swallow up talent, like so much cheddar. Thinking of Parrot-Heads caused a tune by Buffet to (regrettably) flow through my mind, an unfortunate result of my ability to call forth any type of music, lyric by lyric, chord by chord, beat by beat. The song was "Cheeseburger in Paradise," Buffet had to be a real asshole, how else could any respectable singer, or artist—with any semblance of compassion, force his audience to endure such sonic drudgery. While searching the room, I amused myself by coming up with a better song title. "No Fucking Jimmy Buffet Music Makes Anywhere a Paradise." Now that was closer to the truth, probably be a Billboard top-ten…. maybe even a gold record. It was s good thought, and somewhere in the imaginary world I'd created; Eric Clapton, Robert Smith, and Jeff Beck rejoiced.

I went to the section of the entertainment room that stored the resident's musical essentials. Little wooden shelves were stacked four high, each filled with cassettes that were arranged alphabetically. As I was an aficionado of music, reading the titles of every tape, was as important as stealing their stuff. They seemed to know their shit when it came to bands. Of all the places I went for Bitsy; this condo was only location, where the music represented somewhat of a refined taste, mirroring my own.

It would be shame if these guys had to be seriously injured by Bitsy. But finding the money or not, down the road Bitsy would demand more than a few slaps or a broken thumb for retribution. After all, they did steal from him.

I should have concentrated on the job, but the hash I'd smoked earlier made the concept of examining the music overly important. I silently mouthed the labels with growing respect. Midnight Oil—"Diesels and Dust" ... Richard Hell and the Voidoids—"Blank Generation" ... Mick Ronson—"Slaughter on Fifth Avenue" ... A live bootleg of a King Crimson concert that included the song Twentieth Century Schizoid Man—and my to my pleasant surprise—three Ry Cooder tapes.

I took a deep breath and considered the situation carefully, hoping that due to their knowledge of music these shitheads might get some sort of pardon from Bitsy and avoid really nasty physical punishment. The world needed people like these guys. They had a refined musical collection. I read the titles of more cassettes, row by row, shelf by shelf, nodding my head in approval to the overall selection. Then my mouth dropped open and my gag reflex went into overload. I came across a musical title encountered before, on another job, a title that had always driven me to the edge of tears, if not insanity.

This changed everything. It was that horrible. It instantly killed any compassion I felt towards these assholes. I'm ashamed to say it, but it even made me hope Bitsy would make them pay for this travesty. Not for ripping him off; for bad for musical taste. What I saw should never have happened within the confines of a balanced and fair universe.

"Fuck! There it is again, mocking me, maybe sent to torment me from Dante's most terrible of levels. I could not be, but it was ... Styx ... Mr. Fucking Roboto ... again!"

"How could such a thing be possible? Is there no celestial mercy? Why me again?" I asked, to the God of Thunder—Jimmy Page, hoping for intercession. There was no response, but I understood the lack of an answer, as Page must have enough to do, as taking a violin bow to a guitar was no small matter. I was confused, caught within a maelstrom of various, no-compatible drugs, flowing through my veins. And then, from within an LSD flashback relief and counsel came to me from what normal people would undoubtedly consider the unlikeliest of sources—an autographed concert poster board of the band Mountain. The center of the poster was focused on

Leslie West. The image of West was no longer three dimensional and he was in the midst of tearing his guitar to smithereens, probably thrashing chords to the song "Mississippi Queen." He paused halfway through a dead-string barrage, poked his massive head from the photo and said, "Billy. You better get ready to fight, because there is somebody else is in the house." Then Leslie added, "By the way what did you think of Nantucket Sleigh ride?"

"Dude, loved it!" I answered. Short, I know, but all I had time to say to my hero.

It was surreal. Leslie West's genius and Mr. Roboto's toxic shock vomit in the same room. "This cassette must to be destroyed", I murmured, but was unable to act; somebody else was in the room. I spun.

A picture frame exploded directly above my head. I was being attacked by some manic swinging a seven iron. I backpedaled away from the metal club-head and sized up the assailant, while looking for an opening.

He sliced the air in front of me with the club. His impossibly fast whirling motions turned his human form into like some kind of windmill. No, that is not quite the appropriate description, as "windmill" is too passive a term to designate his actions. It was more like a Stephen King Windmill; possessed by Cicada eyed Gremlins, milling hacked limbs by utilizing the power of crimson rivers.

Was it another acid flashback from a drug soaked mind … maybe, but the windmill of destruction still surged forward. The violence was very real, but somewhere off in the distance, in a place absent of horror writers, cicadas called rhythmically in the hot months of August, with or without Gremlins, with or without Stephan King. They chirped my name. Then I understood…acid flashback and reality were converging on my senses all at once. However, knowing what magical event was transpiring wasn't going to stop the windmill.

So I kept moving, defending myself, by holding up a footstool to absorb the golf swings. As I jockeyed for a striking position, The Monkey took shape, standing on the T.V. He had on a green and yellow striped Ralph Lauren Polo Shirt, collar up, shirttail out. Below the beltline he wore Jack Nickelson signature Golden Bear Double Knit Pants that were tucked into argyle socks in order to give the impression of 1940 style Knickers. The pants had been pulled up much too high, but then again, what did Monkeys know of fashion ... still he looked good, I mused.

That Monkey really knows how to make an entrance, I thought, while ducking swings at the same time.

"Kill him Billy! Kill him ... kill him," The Monkey screeched. Menagerie Fun was over, here was pure evil, and there was nothing amusing about The Monkey's clothes anymore, as no matter how he looked, fancy duds could not conceal demonic entity hiding in the flesh-garb of Monkey.

I paid the Monkey no mind, bucking up against his torments, while wondering where he got those orange and black socks.

I got back into the fight, caught the shaft in mid arc, and tore it from the hands of the guy seeking to improve his handicap. I swung it up into his nuts and then struck him sharply on each clavicle to immobilize his arms. He hung suspended, bent over, gasping, mumbling incoherent pleas for me to stop trying to make par.

I grabbed a handful of dirty hair, and joining in with the cicadas, lice grunted dissatisfaction that I had the audacity to yank on their hair-home. I shoved my attacker into a lazy boy chair. *Lazy Boy in a Lazy Boy,* I thought and laughed silently. Holding the club like it was a bat gripped by Ted Williams, I asked him where the money was.

He did not immediately answer, so I gave him a good whack in the shins with the heavy end of the club.

"Take a mulligan, Billy, and hit him in the other shin!" The Monkey said, while making Baboon-type golf swings with an invisible sand wedge. Since I was on the clock for Bitsy, I paid no heed to the Monkey's orders.

The lack of attention caused The Monkey to become so animated that he turned a magnificent back flip into the air, landing effortlessly in the exact same spot, with little or no exertion at all. *That Monkey really knows how to make an entrance.* I though again.

The Monkey continued to demand more physical harm be done to the person who had attacked me.

"Break his fingers!" Back flip.

"No!" I answered.

"Cut off his toes!" Back flip.

"No". Again I refused.

"Break one of his legs!" Another back flip, this time a double—an obvious final feat to punctuate his displeasure.

The Monkey landed his last somersault, his form worthy of a ten out of ten. Once again on firm footing, he morphed into something that would really piss me off. He was wearing brand new attire and was so proud of his chosen ensemble he grinned from chimp ear to chimp ear. The gleam in his monkey eyes told me that he was certain that he had formulated the correct way to ignite a spark of rage. On his stubby feet he had on a pair of beachcomber flip flops, a Key-West style button-down shirt, patterned with a tiny flotilla of boats covered his hairy torso. Completing the get-up was a pair of knee length kaki cargo shorts – shorts that no respectable surfer would be found dead in. In his left paw he held a margarita and in his right he clutched a cheeseburger.

"How smart you are!" I said to the Monkey, for he had read my mind and changed into a rabid Jimmy Buffet fan. The Monkeys' image was so perfect that he even wore a tan legionnaire fashioned baseball cap over a human-like straw colored hair snipped into a Jimmy Buffet replica bowl haircut- complete with sparse bangs over high forehead. It might have looked ridiculous but it got under my skin and I felt anger rope-climbing my spine.

"You bastard, you know me so well." I whispered, disappointed that the Monkey had gotten into my mind, dug up another image, got my goat, and brought out the tiger in me. Monkey, goat, tiger ... such thoughts could only mean another drug flashback was coming, a mushroom safari on game trails curving through wasteoid savannahs. Back in Africa....dead babies in Senegal ... my brain flashed back to a tortured past. "Get a grip." I told myself and snapped back to reality.

I took out my rage on the long-haired fuck by hitting him a couple more times on the shins. The pain caused him to give up the location of the money. I retrieved the bag and then relinquished command of my brain to The Monkey. It was time to make a statement, an example of sorts, something to be heralded in the streets. The Monkey knew that fact even if it eluded me.

The example came in the form of my fist breaking the guy's nose and then a few ribs. In a few hours, his nose will resemble a giant red grape and both eyes would be black. Statement made…point gotten across.

The Monkey was still not pleased with the lack of permanent damage I inflicted. He wanted much more. I looked one last time to big Leslie West to tell my how to play my hand.

"Smash that Monkey fuck. Oh yeah, and check the new re-mastered Twin Peaks. Dig your groove, Billy" That was the end of Leslie's contributions to carnage.

I took Leslie's advice and gave The Monkey the violence he so desired. I swung the club—with the power of Thor, at The Monkeys' neck. I aimed to decapitate Monkey Melon from Monkey Stem. The club slashed in crazy, strikes through the air. I was out of control, enraged, wrecking everything in the house, while the occupant cowered in the corner. When there was nothing left to destroy, I tossed the club through the window and got the fuck out of there. Later, I returned Bitsy's money to him and in couple days left for school. I talked of nothing but a new beginning for me for the next several days, and then went out and bought a copy of the re-mastered version of "Twin Peaks."

<u>Schools Out Forever.</u>

School was underway, Sven and I moved in, met our two other roommates, and were feeling excited to be in Carbondale. I did my best to stay away from drugs, the old desperate lifestyle, and follow the benevolent urgings of my better nature. However, in only a few weeks, my association with local dealers was growing as strong as it had been at home. Instead of forging my shield so as to keep the vermin at bay, I began to hang around with the same kind of low company, consisting of a local pot farmer and a townie that was the big Cocaine connection.

At college, regardless of good intentions, I watched helplessly as some of my most virtuous qualities slipped away. I was a street thug and junkie, undeniably, but never rude, thoughtless, and never a bully. But as I had not quite hit rock bottom, the drugs put more effort into warping my brain, producing a totally alien personality. All the adjectives apply; loudmouth, inconsiderate lout, boisterous prick, and all were accurate and well-deserved. My vessel was cracked; but not yet broken. Then, and only then, would salvation come. So, for now, please say hello to impolite jerk Billy, and goodbye to the compassionate poet warrior. The warrior was all that remained. The chink in my armor was self-made, was really just another hole in my defenses—intentionally opened by yours truly, which allowed dealers to get close. By thinking that I was doing everything humanly possible to stay away from the scum yet still leave them an opportunity gave me deniability of fault once they gained access into my life. Anybody that has an addiction problem, or is acquainted someone that does, knows of the little window to an addicts soul, which is left open—a just a crack, so dealers can locate their next sucker. The window is the excuse addicts need give them peace of mind, so that when abstinence is broken with a dirty syringe, or a few lines of coke, they can still assert that " I did everything possible to stop doing drugs, but no matter where I go, or what I do, the assholes out there keep finding me." Ergo—the window; always open—just a crack.

Moving downstate was not enough to remove The Monkey from my back. But deep down, getting rid of him meant kicking the habit, an act that I really hadn't committed to. "Kicking" was all talk, placating friends and family, nothing more. So in no time at all, The Monkey found the window, crawled through, thereby crushing my will power. My plan, to get away, graduate, become responsible, and find a good job, fell apart within about two months. As with Chicago; the remaining time at Carbondale was going a torturous affair spent in the company of my own special primate inquisitor. Even with their medieval chambers housing iron maidens, racks, and incising tables (for organ removal), when it came to giving agony, The Spanish Inquisitors had nothing on The Monkey.

The Monkey arrived at S.I.U ready to blend in. While on campus, he wore blue-jean cutoffs, with the cuffs rolled up (a type of shorts worn only my rural folk and fashion morons), open toed sandals with white socks, a harvest-time checkered shirt, and a ball cap embroidered with a dirt-track racing logo.

It seemed The Monkey had obtained a Credit Card from the land of LSD "Farm and Fleet" outlet stores, how else could my imagination explain how he could have gotten his homestead duds–so quick. That ended the deliberation concerning who had better credit (in the real and fantasy world) between the fucking back-clinging Monkey and me.

The Monkey had even gone so far as to shift his accent, altering his diction, so as to blend perfectly with the Carbondale farmers, so as to avoid standing out at the southerly location. "Standing out", was a ridiculous thought. I was so used to his presence that it was becoming easy to forget that he was a fucking invisible primate. The metamorphosis was so complete (from City-Monkey to Rural Monkey), that in his front shirt pocket was an envelope of Redman chewing tobacco, and below the beltline a wallet was attached to his shorts by a thin length of chain. More amazing was the distinct smell of corn and cowshit whenever he materialized. The same thought entered my brain with the arrival of Monkey, just as it had countless times before, *That Monkey really knows how to make an entrance.*

At Carbondale, I began to question existence, more specifically, which of us was a mirage, and which "was the living breathing embodiment of certainty." Did the Monkey live outside of illusion, or did I? Those were just a few of the puzzles that needed to be solved before real commitment to cleaning up could be made. Whenever I took the time to really scrutinize the Monkey; be it Chicago, Carbondale, flashbacks, or dream, interesting ideas came to mind, ideas that might the way to eventually defeating my enemy once and for all. Reverting back to Sun Tzu, and the concept of "knowing the enemy could", was quite possibly best path to victory" I knew that by gaining a better understanding of the Monkey, victory could be attained, and then the primate would get the richly deserved Gutting.

However, serious considerations and plans aside, when the primate first showed up in Carbondale, his outfit perplexed me. "What do you need a wallet for and when do you leave for Branson, Missouri?" I asked The Monkey, as he had taken the whole hick-thing to far, dressing more for the Vegas of the Ozarks (Branson), than for Carbondale, therefore ready to attend a Box Car Willie, or Oak Ridge Boys show, rather than stroll around the Campus.

Since The Monkey ignored me the first time around, I asked him again, "What do you need a wallet for?"

"What does a human need a Monkey on his back for? This is your hallucination not mine; remember?" Touché, he had outsmarted me again, making it clear it was not the right moment to attempt the Gutting. My time would be better spent thinking of the new environment, instead of Monkeys and their dress code. *Really ... when did you become the "Acid Trip Fashion Police? Fuck the Monkey and Fuck his Wallet.* So switching gears, I thought about college life and Southern Illinois.

"Carbondale," the name says one thing: "Welcome to the land of rednecks and good-ol-boys." The surrounding towns also had the same rural, confederate flag-waving, "Pentecostal-I can speak-in-tongues," kind of names. Murphysboro, Carterville, Harrisburg; the titles of each backwards community suggested two things, "The south will try to rise again" and "Abolishing slavery was a bad thing." The only thing the locals hated more than blacks was city-folk, and being as how my brother and I were both from the Chicago area, there were sure to be many altercations with the townies. Personally, I was just fine with that; as there was nothing I liked better than giving a beating to some loud-mouth "squirrel-roaster".

People that still lived in the past, and reminisced on the "good ol' days" of lynching and segregation, deserved a fucking beat-down. That was the most shocking part of Carbondale; that there were people out there that had no problem acting as if the civil rights movement never happened, or if acceptance of the movement was forthcoming, they were really pissed that did happen and wished for another attempt at success.

My cut of the collections (I did over summer) were big enough that, when combined with the V.A benefits and Sven's student loans, we would be living high on the hog, and trust me, there was no shortage of hogs in Carbondale—of the four-legged and two-legged variety. There was a downside in our living arrangements as we were disappointed to discover one of our new roommates – Paul, was a 'bible nut', and from the first day he proved to be a real pain in the ass. He had his own habit which was; an Angry God, in place of an Angry Monkey. Each night he read the Old Testament, out loud, in his room, then come downstairs promising to cure us of our wicked ways, and worse yet, there was never a shortage of "tisk-tisk" stern condemnations—following each notably shameful night of debauchery. This "kind of shit" got on our nerves real quick, so needless to say, we allowed the Rugby players to piss in his fruit juice.

Allow me go back into the past for brief moment. There was a good reason for desecrating Paul's juice, besides the fact that he was such an asshole. Everybody in the apartment shared their food, except Paul, so although there weren't any issues eating our stuff; anything he had in the fridge was strictly off-limits. So after he took a swig from the bottle of his personal juice a line was drawn on the container enabling him to determine if any of us were drinking his personal groceries. The punishment for acting like such a dipshit; was the addition of Rugby urine into whatever beverage was hidden in the refrigerator, this series of acts, gave new meaning to the term— "Freshly Squeezed."

Sven and I never insisted on the introduction of piss and other human seasonings into his drinks, but on the other hand, we never exactly discouraged it either.

Well…maybe sometimes we did encourage it, but never actually participated in the depravity, that is, until the fateful day of the fabled and feared "Shit Meatloaf." But that is a story for another time, on an empty stomach and on Halloween.

Sven was a much better student than I. He would socialize just as late, attend the same parties, and hang out in the same bars. However, when the next morning came, he was alert and ready for class, whereas I was usually hung over, leaving myself with barely enough time to get dressed and jump on my motorcycle. With so little time to get to class, driving about 80 mph down the narrow little avenues between the University buildings was the only option. Upon arrival, all the parking spots were usually completely filled. Being the last student to arrive, required locking up the motorcycle as close to the entrance as possible; sometimes on the grass, sometimes on the restricted cement section directly in front of the building. In one year, there were roughly fifty or sixty tickets placed on my low-profile racing handlebars. I had no intention of ever paying the citations, occasionally even attaching them to other motorcycles (after rubbing the ink so the writing was hard to read) just to see if they would get paid. Mixing tickets up on other bikes added amusement to the mundane task of going to class, because there was nothing like watching as other riders exited the lecture hall, usually in a good mood, and then turn angry, for getting citations for parking in the assigned location. There was only one ticket that I actually paid. It was for a combination of things while returning home from a bar. My friends dared me to ride all the way home with my pants down, while speeding, and blowing off a couple stop signs.

Due to the sheer stupidity of the offence, a court appearance was necessary. I told the prosecutor my pants fell down as a result of driving so fast; needless to say the judge did not buy the explanation for the nudity and a hefty fine was levied.

The Monkey showed up in court, took an imaginary seat next to me, and whispered in my ear, ***"The best defense is to*** *give the judge the finger. Tell the right honorable pompous A-hole to go fuck himself!"*

It was a good thing I didn't take the Monkey's advice. Shortly after that episode I almost got nailed for going 155 MPH down Route 13 during a race with another rider, with a tricked-out Kawasaki 900—bored way-over stock. The cops were on my tail and I could not lose them on the highway. By slowing down and entering a residential district, I found a way to go through several yards, almost getting decapitated several times by clothes lines, and finally (when the squad cars lost sight) intentionally laying the bike down. Out of sight, soon became out of mind. After about a half hour the cops gave up, and I split. However, there was a reprisal for my actions. With the cops gone, and before I was able to right the bike, the homeowner came out the garage door, holding a shotgun. I got away, but not without several rock-salt pellets in my leg. When I got them out with tweezers, half a bottle of Jim Beam, and clenched teeth.

It wasn't all excitement while attending college. There was the usual boring shit such as making it to class, trying to study, being civil to teachers, which gave me even more pleasure while playing barbarian, or as I liked to call it "responsible thrill seeking." My entrance to all classes went the same way; run in, brush disheveled hair from bloodshot eyes, smile innocently at the teacher, and then search for an empty seat near the best-looking girl. According to my playbook, being late was never an excuse for not hitting on girls, as making the best of a bad situation is the only way to go. Time honored tradition amongst the uncivilized and all.

Punishment for being tardy was rarely handed out. Most of the professors liked me, because participation in discussions and debates was nothing I shied away from; and many times was able to argue my point of view with the best of eggheads. When not arguing with the academic elite, I got laughter from my strange, yet funny quips, while acting as class clown—not the scary mouth full of teeth kind of clown, from King's book "It." I had a phobia for clowns and mimes, as they often came to be in nightmares, painted faces, silent, but malevolent.

The one thing that I had going for me was an uncanny ability to memorize almost everything read or heard, so knowing the material was easy. It was the lack of studying and miss-ing tests ruined my grades, not lack of intellect. The tests that I completed were taken while still under the influence of sleep deprivation, or in some cases, while under the mind-altering effects of acid. The worst trip—during an exam, happened af-ter watching "An American Werewolf in London" the night before while on a massive dose of acid the previous night. The next morning during the test, I was plagued with hallucinations of wolves circling my desk. They snarled and panted eagerly, with the unmistakable intention of biting off a leg. Later my friends asked me "So, did you pass?"

I replied the only sensible way ... "Pass! I was under the influence of drugs. The fucking wolves wouldn't leave me alone." With anyone else talk of wolves and tests would have been alarming, not so with me, just another day.

More so was the disappointment of ignoring appropriate behavior. I could have been an A student, but instead chose drugs over trying to make something of myself. Understanding lessons, retaining information, came so easy for me, that taking those gifts for granted was just as easy.

While I took advantage of owning a high-end motorcycle to get from place to place, Sven drove my white Ford known as the 'Vomit Comet'. We used the vehicle for many late night activities during instances when it was raining or we all wanted to travel together in one group. The name of the car came from the history of the vehicle itself. Every time it was used to go out at night, at least one of the occupants barfed out the win-dow after a night of hard drinking.

The Vomit Comet was just one of several unusually named vehicles driven while Sven and I attended college. There was a light blue station wagon known as the 'Scar Mo-bile'; appropriately named because of the long gash along the length of the left side, plus most of the football and rugby play-ers that rode in it had their own gashes. When the wagon final-ly broke down, we drove a bright orange Volkswagen Rabbit. The Rabbit could only be started by arcing out the ignition with a metal object. As that was hit and miss procedure, it was known as the 'Grateful Pumpkin'—since we were grateful any-time it actually made it to a destination without stalling. Last, but not least, was a maroon Dodge Sedan, which was known affectionately as the 'Potato Bug', because we found a family of potato bugs and cockroaches living under the floor mats. The 'cockroach-mobile' just didn't have the right ring to it.

It seemed that my friends as well as Sven and I had a habit of giving everything a nickname. One of our later roomies looked like Dracula and couldn't hold his booze, so we called him 'Count Puke-ula'. Even our one-night-stands had nicknames. There was: 'Skeleton Head' (for her tiny head), 'Rooster Head' (for the pointed chin and fluffy hairdo), 'Brianiac', named after one of Superman's arch enemies, due to the sheer size and scope of her forehead, added with her special powers of deflating boners – or was that from the coke booze?

'Spamster' (teeth like a Hamster and exhaling the smell of Spam), and 'Sir-Talks-Alot' (named after one of the "Knights of the Round Table"—she never shut up) and 'The Outlaw Nosey Nails' (after the Clint Eastwood movie—she had a long nose and garishly painted equally long nails). These were just a few of the names applied to nightly conquests. The mind-altering mushrooms helped to spark creativity in expressing originality to the monikers given out. It seems that there was a "how the face and head looks" theme to most of the designations, but that is what you notice first and last, while saying hello then goodbye. It was funny then, but as with most things it my life, I would grow to regret the rude and thoughtless ways I treated women. They certainly deserved better and being high all the time was and is no excuse.

But the weirdest thing ever given a nickname; was a large cast-iron cooking pot that chilly was prepared in—before card games. We brought it (loaded with chilly) to football player's trailer homes for card games. We eventually began calling the pot 'Big Ed', treating it as one of the boys, human, and taking it to bars with us (even when empty). We bought him/it drinks and including it in conversations. Big Ed was like a jolly fat friend, always the life of the party and a good ice-breaker to pick up dumb chicks. Big Ed never got laid but that was okay, he attracted girls to us—just like a fat guy with jokes. Every night some bimbo would stroll up and ask why we were talking to a Pot. You could almost hear the thoughts in her tiny brain "cooking utensils can't speak ... or can they?" It was the only phase of my life that I recall talking to a pot, instead of smoking it.

Sven and I both played wing forwards on the Rugby Team—a position specially chosen because it fit our game-day goals, which was to "lunch" (rugby term for tackling with extreme prejudice) as many opponents as possible. Preparation for each practice begun with the song "Schools Out Forever" by Alice Cooper.

Alice did not pack the punch of the Sex Pistols; however, there was no disappointment to be found in Glen Buxton's soaring guitar solos

We played hard and fought often. Fighting was by no means out of bounds in Rugby, quick punches were thrown whenever two opposing team members hit each other—out of sight of the refs. In scrums, well, that was simply an excuse to head-butt people, slip in an accidental elbow, and stomp feet. I enjoyed every moment on the field, it was a good way to release aggression, stay in scrapping shape, and meet good people to share a beer with after the game, and sometimes during.. One game in particular stands out for the knocks delivered and absorbed. It was against the St. Louis Celts, our biggest rivals in the division; well known for the cheap shots and huge hits. Sven had his nose broken in the first few minutes, a real bloody mess, but that did not stop him from staying in the game.

When the Rugby pitch (match) ended, his purple and white striped jersey was covered with blood and sweat.

I suffered one black eye, a deep slice in the right calf, and was unconscious for a few seconds. However, I still managed to give out several swollen lips and bruised cheekbones to a couple guys on the Celts team. They had it coming since they had been especially brutal to our guys after the tackle. In rugby, it is allowed to cleat and kick the player on the ground if the ball is not released quickly after the player is tackled. Our injuries never kept Sven and I from making the post game parties, chugging beers, playing dizzy sticks, and hooting it up with the opposing team; field violence forgotten and forgiven. That was the Rugby Gentleman's Code; be as mean on the rugby pitch as you wanted to be, but when the game was over join your enemy in songs and reverie.

The greatest thing about the Rugby parties was the Rugby Groupies; they loved the players for the grit and outright craziness, so spending the night with a player was the ultimate trophy.

At night Sven and I bounced at two different bars; which were located directly across the street from each other. Sven worked the outside door at the Carbondale yuppie and jock - meathead establishment (The Tap); whereas, I controlled the drunks at a beer and pizza place (Laroma's), which had an extremely rowdy and loud booze garden. When not tossing out stooges, I watched with amusement, as Sven manhandled idiots out the doors—by their head or necks, then pushed them down the steps. Often he persuaded them to leave with a right to the jaw. Sven would look up after the tussle, grin, and wave to me. I rated the throws, using a thumbs-up, a thumbs-down, or by just giving him the finger.

My altercations were not as graceful as Sven's, so henceforth, each bout was graded rather harshly by the judges. I usually forced assholes out by fish-hooking a cheek, pinching an ear, or a clump of hair, when that didn't work, squeezing a hunk of oblique belly fat, always did.

Nothing caused more sharp pain then grabbing a wedge of skin around the mid-section; while clamping down like a pair of pliers on the layer of flab. The crowd at Laroma's was of a more uncivilized type, mostly local hayseeds and wanna-be-bikers. The bikers never went easy, often trying to prolong the fight once we got outside. I was happy to comply, usually putting them on the sidewalk, raining down punches, finishing with a shoulder choke or arm triangle. The slovenly motorcycle outlaw riders were tough, but really had no stamina. Thirty seconds was about as long as the overweight bikers could last.

Bikers usually ran straight at me, while flailing away with quick series of haymaker punches. They quickly got winded; succumbing to the excess baggage of lard protruding from a beer-gut attached to back fat, and dropped their hands. My eventual big showdown with redneck townies came as no surprise to anyone.

It was my own fault, even fair to say I was spoiling for a fight, purposely aggravating the redneck bigots, by dressing as someone that has "read too many GQ magazines" and "has too high opinion of their looks." I had money from collections, an element of conceit from cocaine, so dressing like a yuppie dork didn't bother me too much. Trolling with what is in the bait box is how fish are caught and fights started.

The brawl took place at T.J McFlys, the most popular bar in Carbondale. I was there with my brother and a few of the guys from the wrestling team. We got separated when they went up front in order to watch the wet T-shirt contest. I had on black leather pants, a sure sign of a homo-faggot (in the words of the townies). Wearing attire of that kind of attire was an invitation to locals that "it was time to beat some ass." It was obvious they were laughing and whispering insults about my pants. So I edged closer to the group so as to present a target, way too good to ignore. Sure enough, the leader of the gang (certainly from the bad part of corn and okra fields), started up with me. This threat was not to be taken as lightly as a biker brawl. As a rule; Rednecks were known to have good stamina, would go the distance, and naturally fight dirty. The Hillbilly Rule Book had allowances for all kinds of cheap counters not authorized by the Marcus of Queensberry. So, when scrapping with a redneck, there were a variety of dangerous techniques to watch out for, such as: Fish-Hooking, Biting, Eye Gouging, larynx chops, and my personal favorite; finger breaking. They also used a ground and pound method, which had a foundation in "Rasslin" instead of Wrestling.

Carbondale Townies fought smart, usually taking off their shirts before the fight, so it was hard to get hold of sweaty torsos. This would normally have been a good strategy, except for just one thing; they usually left their wide leather belts on – complete with fancy oversize bumpkin buckles. In the absence of a shirt or coat, there were no better handle to grab then a belt; leather straps around the waist never tore away, which allowed for one hell of a Greco throw. Yeah, nothing is better to grip than a belt when attempting to force an attacker to the ground, except for a pony tail. However, in an instance when someone picks a fight while sporting a long tail of hair, they have to blame themselves for losing. It was their own questionable desire to look like Willie Nelson, which gave an opponent the opening to use the 'pony-tail slam'.

The fight started with the usual insulting salvo. "Hey boy, nice pants you got there. You must be one of them Homo City Boys," he said in a loud voice that was an unmistakable challenge. They all got a good chuckle out of that one. It did not take much for Rednecks to think something was clever.

"Very fucking smart! Did you assholes get a free pair of overalls with that cow manure stink? You guys should get off the farm for awhile and maybe take a shower." I said to them and then stepped even closer. "Look at you assholes, too stupid to go to college and too ugly to get laid."

That fight was one of the few brawls that occurred when I was not drugged up. With a clear head, I was firing on all cylinders, tuned up, with reflexes sharp as a kitchen knife. It happened so fast that it was a blur, but my friends described it to me later. They saw me hit the first four guys in the face with the one-two combo, while bobbing and weaving, slipping punches, running down the entire row of assholes, putting each of them on the floor, one by one.

Each of the first four rednecks dropped like stones. The fifth guy lunged at me, and in return got a "nutshot-headbutt" combo platter, one from column A—the nutshot, and one form column B—the headbutt. No waiting, no tipping ... but I deliver.

My brother was the first to arrive at the scene and landed a classic left hook right—uppercut sequence. The score was six goobers down and out.

The last redneck got blasted by so many of my friends; it is hard to say which one struck the finishing shot. But knowing my brother – my guess would be Sven. The townie got rocked so hard, his mullet got sent into orbit. On a cloudless night, the mullet can still be seen circling around the buck-tooth nebula.

The cops patrolling the streets of Carbondale had been raised on Skoll, tractor pulls, moonshine whiskey, and "Dukes of Hazzard" reruns. Up until the fight at McFlys, they had mostly turned a blind eye to my fisticuffs, as the fights had taken place with students instead of locals, and while bouncing for a bar. After that night however, things changed for the worse, I had beaten up a few of their own—farmers tan, inbred eyes, and all.

School proceeded as expected for Sven and me; he continued to get good grades, while I stayed true to form, making friends with dealers, having unsafe sex, and milking my V.A benefits to the max, until the agency saw my transcripts and got wind of my failing grades. Then the V.A cut off my subsidence allowance for having grades below a C average. My marks were a few notches below that. In fact, there was no measurable scale to determine just how low my grades had sunk. My evaluation was somewhere between mentally disabled and afterbirth; not quite of 'special Olympic caliber' but certainly of 'Food Store Bagger' standards.

But school did have a respectable share of perks. Top on the list were the girls known to be book smart but in most cases street stupid. Women were different than men when it came to the reasons for getting wild during the years spent at college.

Guys behaved badly because since the dawn of time—it was their nature to do so. Dominate and Procreate, that was the mission, pure and simple. Women on the other hand were born with a greater amount of common sense and decorum, which was cast aside as soon as they stepped foot on campus. For them, it was all about rebellion, acting promiscuous to prove maturity, ignoring restraint to show individuality, and seek out bad guys to feel menace. That made me a suitable conquest for many of the newly arrived co-eds, which made surrender the most agreeable option, and surrender I did. There probably has never been a whiter flag waved than the flag I unfurled while in the company of women hunting for the dangerous-kind-of-guy. Funny; how females all end up marrying the 'sensitive yes-dear dishrag type', but randomly fuck the 'I don't give a crap about you type'.

College concluded exactly as expected, diploma for Sven in Aviation Technology, boot in the ass for me—once the benefits ran out. Sven took an offer from a very successful Aerospace company, and moved to California. Every few days he would call me and from what I could gather from the conversations; surfing was good, there was no shortage of good weather, and the beach was a Bohemian mix of good-looking chicks and post-70's era hippies.

I moved back to Chicago; leaving a bread crumb trail of bad grades, bad judgment, and rednecks on their backs counting stars. The amount of failed tests has to be some kind of record. My disregard for exams would have been comical if not for the fact that failing classes sent me back into the violent, pathetic life I so badly wanted to get away from.

It would have been just as logical as having The Monkey take the tests. He might have done pretty well on the essays; however, multiple-choice tests would have been a problem, as his reference point would have been alien to what the actual designated letters stood for. From his way of viewing the material world for instance, an A grade would have meant Ape, B –Banana, C –Chimp, D- Dung, and E, well there could be no doubt….E- Encouraging me to do drugs and die.

<u>1</u>

<u>Jailbreak</u>

If I had to choose just one song from the thousands stored in my memory that best exemplified my life for the next several months between the years 1988 and 1989, it would probably be 'Jailbreak' by Thin Lizzy. It was a very frenzied period within an already chaotic life and it seemed as if all past misdeeds were finally catching up with me. The shift from bad to worse happened amazingly enough all within a short span of time – six months. People like to say "bad things come in threes", a quip that is profound for those that have never made it past number three on the bad things meter. Bad-Thing Virgins believe there's a universal limit, or ratio, regulating the number of bad things per individual until deception, drugs, and violence take over. When that happens, there is no way to get an accurate count of all the destructive elements in your path. It would be like counting seconds on a clock. I subscribed to a more realistic motto; bad things come in hundreds, often approaching as Brutus did when he greeted Caesar for the last time, smiling ear to ear with a knife in one hand while inviting friendship with the other open palm. The acceptance of drugs is the same as accepting knives, each blade may find different ways of entering flesh, but each still cuts just as deep, tendons are severed, bringing a common reaction—jaw dropping surprise. Numbers remain in red ... streets remain redder.

This is what confronted me after leaving Carbondale and returning to Chicago. Before long, I was right back into the collections/protection game, first-string, all-conference asshole, and last person to observe the toll of playing the game past my prime. A drug addict without restraint and a modicum of class stops being the popular, charismatic guy that has party favors. After a time, he transforms into an object of scorn—nothing but a pathetic junkie.

Over the years, I had accumulated a few warrants for simple assault. Each of the violations had been mostly ignored by the cops as they had bigger fish to fry and my transgressions never cut into the realm of good citizens. I beat up on the same cretins that the cops secretly wished they could get stick-time on.

So, in effect, as long as my altercations were with other felons there were no charges. Occasionally a Sergeant I knew went so far as to indicate the people that needed a beat-down. So some nights I assumed the role of surrogate deputy, punching out any criminals that the cops couldn't arrest due to lack of evidence or offenders that won their court-case on a technicality. In return I was allowed to skate on several complaints. Picture a Rock-Em-Sock-Em Robot, manipulated by a Speed-ball joystick controlled by Dealers, Cops, The Monkey, and to a lesser degree, by me. However, a series of encounters ended all the breaks the cops gave me. My predatorily activities— usually under the radar, were beginning to get noticed, and I was quickly becoming the subject of morning roll call.

My late night safaris were beginning to trample on game trails used by the supposedly innocent humanoid animals living in the brick and glass jungle. I considered the term "Innocent" as a genuinely useless adjective and a dishonest one. My experience had shown that the thin wall separating criminals from upright citizens was flimsy, and certainly not built by stone-masons. Instead, it was built by circumstance and blind luck. Nobody is truly innocent; they just haven't been caught yet. Just ask the cops. They will tell you the same thing.

Any person that claims to be pure, with no hidden vises, obsessions, or sins, is usually a serial felon. A close examination into anybody's most-trusted friend's closet would reveal so many skeletons the room would resemble an Oingo Boingo album cover.

In fact, I'll go a step further "Stare long enough into anyone's closet and bony hooks and skeleton hangers would by far outnumber the dry cleaning and starched shirts." So for me, understanding the human condition was easier, especially after the innocent/guilty way of thinking was forgotten. I'm willing to accept both contempt and shame. But before judging me too harshly, people should first peer into their own closet, better yet, maybe it should remain locked. Otherwise, they might get the idea to write about their personal particular primate or demon, confessing urges to the world to which it clings and whispers terrible things. I prefer they stay with ignorance, stay with bliss, stay within their comfort zone and finally stay out of the role of "Monkey Writing Novelists." There are a limited number of publishers looking for stories about Monkey's, violence, addiction and redemption, so my chances are best if this story is the only one.

Trapped in a downward spiral, I fell, deeper and deeper, swallowed by black and grays, heading to an unseen grave-marker—one that was taking shape somewhere out in the future. Each line or spike of cocaine was slowly forming my final resting place—a place where my prone body already had no discernable heartbeat. The change from 'in-control enforcer' to 'on-the-run drifter' was about to begin.

It seems that such a change should be ushered in the loud report of a gun, not so, instead mine began with a case of the munchies, and not while acting as thug, but while on a date.

The evening was almost at an end. The movie—Naked Gun was over and we were driving to her house, discussing the merits of Leslie Nielsen's low-brow humor. My date was a girl that came from old-money, and therefore she possessed the standard inflated sense of her sophistication. She found the movie's gutter jokes beneath her, commenting with a shrill tone, that she preferred subtle sarcasm to fart jokes.

"My wealthy friends do not go for toilet humor." She scolded.

Don't like toilet humor ... that's probably because growing up they were wimps ... got swirlies as kids ... and are now dramatized by the dirty-dip, I thought to myself.

Rich, poor ... it didn't matter to me. I could fit in anywhere, drink champagne, and swallow caviar, but break out laughing if a buddy 'cut the cheese'. When it comes right down to it; I did not really give a shit if she liked the movie or not and had a different opinion on what's funny. We both agreed on two things: she has a pussy and I should get to know it better. However, before that could happen I first needed to get her home, and do a few railers.

If Naked Gun was a B movie for non-conformist anti-social types, then my life was the same—type of B-movie, with one major difference; the plot of my drama wasn't exactly your run-of-the-mill theatrical story arc. If it were, a hair-raising act of danger and courage would be the thing that finally did me in. But that would be a lie. It was not a drug collection job, hot speedball, stabbing, or another motorcycle wreck which turned my life upside down. It was because, quite simply, I was hungry. There was a McDonalds on the same road as my date's house, so I thought, *What the hell ... might as well get something to eat and kill some time so her parents are asleep when we get there.*

The reason for wanting her parents to be asleep was because they were a couple first-class assholes. Especially her Dad, Jeffrey; a snooty Wall Street bastard who was such an arrogant windbag I wanted to break his nose, or at least steal his Rolex watch, every time we met. On my previous visit, I walked by his Jaguar and gave the polished silver exterior a jagged scratch and the hood a squirt of brake fluid from a tiny canister – stored under my car seat for such occasions.

My abhorrent behavior and angry outbursts, directed at anyone within range, were so out of control, that I wondered if the Taoist in me was gone, reluctantly abandoning the vessel, for the mountains and cherry blossoms. In the absence of the Taoist spirit my frat boy behavior just got worse.

I even went so far as to open the Jag's front door and lob chunks of dog shit into the front seat. I was certain he had his suspicions about who was doing all the vandalism as he was well aware of my hatred, and was close to calling the cops, regardless of the potential reprisals. I guess he'd had enough, but I'd had enough of his daughter, so this was the last date anyway.

McDonald's was the perfect place to stop. I was a fan of the proverbial 'cheap date', only taking woman I loved to expensive restaurants. Since love was the qualifier; there were very few lobster dinners but there was an impressive amount of double cheeseburgers, and when splurging, a small French Fry.

I preferred the kind of generously defined by finding ways to spend less than twenty dollars on a date. My drug use had become so prevalent the days of big-shot wining and dining were over. Lines of coke would have to do what a coat and tie restaurant had done in the past. Yeah ... dates with me were more like 'the date whining and me lining'. If it was going to get me laid then the railers were shared; if sex wasn't on the menu, then they could find their own drugs.

Nothing say's not caring, like not sharing, I thought, while driving into the entrance.

The ordering process only took a couple of minutes. The ordering was fast because the people at the window weren't Mexican so they understood, and spoke English.

"What a pleasant surprise, imagine somebody using the language of an American, while in America." I said to my date in order to make conversation, and to stick it to her mother who spoke very little English. Street talk said that upstanding Jeffery had bought himself a trophy wife from Russia.

We were leaving the McDonald's drive-thru when a boat-sized Buick cut me off. The driver—regardless of the small matter that he was an asshole driver and was the one that had almost caused an accident, gave ME the finger. Not just the finger, he also gifted me with a long chain of obscenities, each phrase centered on his opinion that; I was a jack-off, had a mother that was an Amsterdam whore, and drove like an Asian. Actually, the Asian thing was kind of funny. Since his 'piece of shit' vehicle was blocking my 'piece of crap vehicle', there was really no choice left, except get out of the car and get into 'the role'. Standing my ground was "situation imperative.

What occurred next shocked even me! The asshole behind the wheel was the same asshole from the fight at the bowling alley—a couple years before. I paused to consider the unusual coincidence. In a novel such a fact would certainly be considered creative license or maybe merely an embellishment, and rightly so. But taking into account the amount of fights I had been in, sooner or later, one of the altercations was bound for a repeat performance.

Just my luck that this asshole has to be the toughest of my past opponents! Shit, if karma is going to keep demanding payback, why can't the beating come from the hands of that midget dealer that I'd collected from, or one of the hippies, thumped for Bitsy? I thought.

With a few warrants still outstanding, avoiding another fight was a big priority. To avoid a noisy confrontation, my plan was to talk things down without backing down, as backing down would buck up his resolve to pay me back for the broken nose. It did not go as I planned. He got out of his vehicle and ran to the passenger side of my car, and then flung the door open before I could prevent it

He peered in, and then raised his head back up to glance at me while sneering—undoubtedly ready for revenge.

He began to insult my date, even going so far as to reach in and touch her.

Okay … insulting mothers was bad enough. But, putting hands on a girl was an action that had consequence. Time, place, punishment, forget about those things, Operating rule number five (no time to explain the first four) went something like this; if an asshole takes liberties with a girl, then fighting is the only answer. Rule Five was very clear, it didn't make bit of difference is she was ugly, pretty, fat, skinny; the guy still had a beating coming. My date was beautiful, thus more so the harshness of the beating. Rule five also stated that if the girl was really fat then the guy probably only had a body punch coming. However, there was an addendum attached to rule five that stated: if the guy was with a very fat or ugly date, then maybe he had the body punch coming. All that aside, it was a rule that could never be ignored—man-handle someone's date and the fight is on.

Experience had already taught me that this guy was one tough son of a bitch. Any man that can take five knees to the head is not the kind of fuckhead to be taken lightly. The initial pre-basting banter, between the two of us, went exactly as expected.

"This time things are going to be different, no cops to save you. After I knock you out … you're going to a curbing." He said boldly.

"Curbing!" The word caused a series of thoughts to flow. *Can't let this guy win, or he'll open my mouth, and then arranged my teeth and jaw on the nearest curb. Then stomp back the back of my head, and send teeth and blood everywhere.* The image made me think of a guy I knew that had once hit a car on his bicycle. Teeth and jawbone parts pushed up into his forehead.

I did not reply to his threat of delivering a curbing. *Why bother with formalities?* I thought.

Our previous fight had demonstrated that he had the cranial bone structure of a water buffalo, so I did not go up top. By keeping enough distance between us while dancing as a Savate fighter, I was able to crush his upper thigh with a string of shin kicks. Each low-kick was so brutal it felt like my leg would break before his did. Thankfully, the gods of "Knuckles and Knees" smiled on me, so thankfully, after the seventh shin kick, he finally buckled.

He never landed a punch because after each shin-strike hit his thigh, I leaned back out of range so his counters sailed uselessly past my chin. The shocked expression on his face showed that he'd never been leg-kicked before, and therefore never knew there could be so much pain from bone to thigh contact. *Bet he knows now, should have gone to his leg instead of his head during the first fight,* I thought.

He was winded and only able to maintain a wobbly three-point stance. Finally he gathered enough energy to rise and then stumble around in a dazed half-circle. He fell flat after only a couple steps. His left leg was nothing except a useless mass of purple bruises. There was no way he was getting back to his feet and giving anybody—especially me—a Curbing of any kind.

The temptation to go key-lock one of his arms and dislocate the elbow was hard to resist as years of training had conditioned me to end things with a choke or break. Mercy prevailed, so instead, I waited, legs bent, elbows over ribs, hands prepared to grab, pull, lock, or throw if he made any other threatening moves.

I should have gotten into my car and left; nobody had really noticed the fight, and it quite possibly could have been chalked up to an altercation between two junk-food lovers. But I foolishly overstayed my welcome, thanks to none other than The Monkey.

The coke and hash coursing thru my brain, made The Monkey fade in slower than usual, and with a greater degree of color. He was attired as expected and was dressed for the occasion. I had never done as much hash and coke together before, so this resulted in a more detailed and strangely silly (while managing to be vile and dangerous) vestige of the tempting Primate. He was wearing red suspenders, pancake makeup, and red floppy shoes, morphing into Ronald McMonkey.

Another reason to hate clowns, I thought while waiting for his usual taunts, or stage direction to commit more violence. It was Weird (even for one of my mirages); The Monkey was consuming an Apple Pie. The hash fucked me up so much, that for a second I considered it absurd for a Monkey to be eating anything but a banana pie. Weirder still … the Monkey showed an absurdly clever artistic side I had not seen in the Monkey before.

Really, a clown at McDonalds? Either he is getting smarter or I am getting dumber, I thought. With the amount of drugs I had consumed over time and sent exploding through receptor sites, dumber was the correct answer.

The Monkey was not going to let me leave, not until I satisfied his own primate "fix", by showing more violence. *If you let this guy get back up, he's going to crush your skull on the concrete, better strangle him, only way to be sure. Do another blast of coke first ... get your stamina back up.* He insisted with a tone hard to resist, but I tried to fight him as hard as the human on the ground.

"This is the time to cut him open and cast him back into the void." I heeded my own advice. Since shin kicks worked so well on the Trucker, I sent one flying at the Monkey's head. My earlier attempts at hurting the Monkey should have taught me a lesson. Unfortunately it did not.

The kick passed through empty air and the momentum spun me completely around. I fell.

"What a dolt". The Monkey laughingly said. *"Still think you can hurt me? You just don't get it do you? You can't beat me. Look at you—strange visions and daydreams have become the only reality you know. Do you really believe you can go back to a normal life? There is no place for you left in the real world, so you better get used to this shit, cause it is about to get much worse."* He leaned in, the smell of apple pie, mixed with primate tooth decay, was on his breath. *"Billy, you're on the way to a dimension where "rock-bottom" meets "rock and a hard place. Don't you know that nobody can run from Monkeys or Demons? Hide maybe; never outrun. And Gutting? Really? Come on. If you can't run and can't*

hide and sure as fuck can't land a kick ... how the fuck are you going to Gut anything?"

I was beaten. Hash, coke and Monkey had together won out again. Not beating the Monkey did nothing to diminish the pent-up rage boiling inside me. So I went back to my opponent that was in the midst of regaining his feet. A fast Greco body-lock was applied and secured, paralyzing his torso so that a hip-toss could be utilized and send him crashing to the hard blacktop. I did not make the mistake of trying for a ground and pound knock-out. I took his back by sweeping him on to his stomach, and then laced my forearm around his neck (making sure my wrist bone rubbed the larynx for added discomfort), and put palm to bicep so the python rear choke could be administered. Out he went. No 'Curb Job was given'—from me to him—because some lines should never be crossed, as there is a big difference in being a finisher with a code and an evil piece of shit. He who lives by the Curb dies but the Curb. I was drug addict, but as of yet, not an evil piece of shit.

The Monkey was very displeased by the granting of mercy. *"You idiot ... you just can't walk away ... do you want to fight this guy a third time? Give him a curb job. Billy, if it was you instead of him, laying there on the ground, he sure as shit would smash your teeth out. When did you become a pacifist? Curb him!"*

The drugs wore off and my senses came back.

"I sure as fuck am not going to kill somebody with a Curb Job." Then I told the Monkey to "Fuck Off", and surprisingly he did.

That should have been the end of things except for a minor detail. In between serving up McGrimace Shakes and Hamburgler Unhappy Meals, the drive-thru attendant called the cops. Worse yet, the outdoor video camera caught the whole thing on tape—which made the film potentially "State's evidence B, Your Honor." The first of what was to become months of chases and narrow escapes was on.

The police and sheriffs were not kidding around this time. I was on tape ... I was out of control. There would be no turning a blind eye to my transgressions. To raise the ante on my capture, the cops listed me as armed (not true), dangerous (a little true), and a multiple steroid abuser (true). Putting out a call like that meant; once the cops found me, a bullet, or at the very least a very unhealthy beating was going to be given. Worse yet they added fake charges in order to someday try and turn me into a snitch—which would never happen. I was okay with taking a beating from the cops but turning Rat was only for scumbags. I had to make a hasty exit and get the McFuck out of McDodge. I avoided the rapidly approaching squad cars by making a quick turn onto some backstreets, zigzagging down back-roads, finally getting to a residential district close to where my date's house was located.

After a few nervous minutes, we pulled into a school yard full of swing-sets, volleyball nets, and brightly painted slides. I got out and was in the process of urging her out of the car when a cop flew into the driveway, and cut off the only exit. He flung open the squad car's door open and ran towards me with his gun out. I was fully aware that my chances of escaping the police exponentially increased by not remaining seated in the car. I also knew that no cop was going to risk a board of inquiry by putting a slug into suspect that was calmly getting out of his own car. I made no threatening moves and held my empty hands high in the air. The cop came closer with his weapon aimed at my forehead. He was nervous, shaking, and appeared to be squeezing the trigger a little too hard.

I was sure that this was the first time the cop had pulled his piece and aimed it at a goon. The dark and the unknown conditions were making him even more jumpy and his face could not have been redder and sweatier unless he was a member of the fabled 'dysentery tomato patrol'.

This guy is going to accidentally shoot me. I thought. Then said aloud "Okay ... okay, officer calm down. I'm not going to do anything stupid."

"Your warrant says Armed and Dangerous, so show me the gun, right now!" The cop declared.

"What fucking gun?" I asked him. He ignored me.

"This is the last chance, show me your weapon or else." The cop said almost with a stutter.

Or else ... that's an unusual thing for a cop to say. Wonder what or else means. I did not really want an answer, so I prepared for a fast escape.

The cop took two steps forward. *Good.. I want you close ... keep coming,* I thought to myself.

He took one more step, hands trembling uncontrollably, surely scared, surely a rookie. *He must think that I'm going to be his first big capture, probably already dreaming of the commendation and the promotion."*

As he stepped into the cruiser's headlights, I got a good look at him. Right out of the academy, blond hair, with a physical frame not sculpted from weights, but from Jane Fonda aerobics classes. His slight stature did not hold him back from acting overly aggressive. He waved the barrel of the gun inches from my forehead. Bringing my left hand up, I knocked the weapon away with a hammer-fist, having enough force behind it that it made the cop take a couple steps back.

I turned and sprinted towards the cover of a tall hedgerow.

"Stop or I'll shoot." He said, using a voice that contained the one thing I needed to hear—uncertainty. This guy was much more scared then me. I didn't mind a bullet – as long as it killed me. A bullet was the answer to all my problems, a welcome relief to my growing disappointment in my failure to kick chemicals.

"You're not going to shoot anybody." I whispered under my breath. The next burst of speed took me around the hedgerow. From there it looked as if there was no catching me, but my joy was cut short when a barbed wire fence forced to an abrupt stop. The rusty steel and sharp metal thorns were the only obstacle standing between me and escape. There was no time to slow down, assemble my thoughts, and try to figure a safe way over it. I took a few big strides and leapt into the air.

The height of the leap gave me a greatly improved perspective as to what lay in front of me. All I could see in front of me was open fields, manicured yards, and ... freedom. When I got over the fence, there was no way this cop, already breathing heavy and losing steam, could catch me.

Halfway, through the leap, it seemed like I'd made it.

"Fucking A –right ... no problem," I exhaled with a sigh of relief. That was the thought, right before, a long metal strand of wire went through my thigh, and halted my progress in midair. The fence yanked me back.

Shit! Now what? I was tired and momentarily stalled, but a long way from surrender. Glancing at my leg, it became evident what had prevented me from landing safely on the other side of the fence. A rough, loose, pointed piece of rusty metal had broken off the checked wire grid and stuck about a foot up into the air. The impaling wire went so deep into my leg there was no resisting being pulled back onto a 'straddling the fence' position.

I guess the grass really is greener on the other side.

The cop arrived and tried to assess the situation. I ignored him. He was frozen with indecision, juggling actions, analyzing the merits of re-engaging with an apparent crazy-man. The cop eventually settled on the harmless strategy of yelling "Stop" every second or two. His agitation apparently had caused him to switch to automatic panic response. "Stop ... Stop ... Stop!"

"What do you mean, stop? You idiot! Where do you think I'm going? I have a wire stuck in my leg." I laughed.

While he blurted out commands, I tried to extricate my body off the wire without ripping my leg apart. It was easy to see that a tear like that change me from Biped to Singlet. The cop must have dropped his gun during the chase. So, instead of keeping the promise of shooting me, he could only grab on to my shirt and then blast me with a dose of pepper spray. He was no longer screaming "Stop" instead he went for a new tactic – shrieking girlishly for assistance in a voice filled with panic. It was fairly dark, as only half a moon hung in the sky. The moon was barely producing any light, so I could not see the blood flowing down my leg. However, the wet feeling told me all I needed to know.

"This is an acute wound. I needed to get this fucking wire out of my leg and find somewhere to cauterize it... and fast!" I told myself, not so much because I needed the telling but to reassure my leg that there was a plan. Didn't want my leg worried about getting ripped open. It may sound strange, but as I struggled to free myself, soaked in blood, I couldn't help thinking of the 'Morton Salt Girl' and her slogan. "When it rains it pours"!

You got that right ... pours blood. I laughed as the fantastical hash-thoughts renewed the process of streaming through my brain. This was one of those lucky moment when having a couple grams of coke in my veins, gave me the advantage of numbness. The cop gave me another shot of pepper, directly in the eyes. The coke and my 'set of Spartan Gonads' made the spray bearable *Shit, I've seen much worse,* I thought as the drugs really began to kick in again.

I slapped the canister from the cop's hand and it flew end over end into the bushes.

"What now, dipshit? No gun … no spray, and no brains."

The hash and coke prevented the painful warning signs promising serious injury if I tore my leg off the wire. So … I did just that and it hurt like a son-of -a bitch

Watching the wire slide out of the hole in my thigh, I noticed a whitish vein hanging from the wound. The gaping hole in my thigh caught the glare of a streetlight. The organic tube was not leaking blood....it was leaking a clear liquid. The blood was coming from the puncture, while the white vein was dripping a clear substance thicker, but seemingly like water.

Fuck...that's not good. Probably some kid of vessel that goes to my lymph glan. I'd seen an injury like that before, if not given immediate attention, the eventually dehydration would cause fainting. *Not good!* I thought again.

I ran as fast as I could under the circumstances and paused only once to look back the cop. He wasn't following. Apparently, after seeing all the sharp metal sticking out of the fence, and what the loose wires did to my leg, he decided the chase was over. I picked up my pace, limping, but still doing my best to dart between a series of homes. Then, finally, after several backyards, I got to an open field. It seemed like the pursuit was over, but then I saw the human silhouettes closing in on my location.

The Police back-up units had arrived and were heading right towards me. In the limited visibility, they could not have spotted me from such a distance. But soon they would be right on top of me. I was able to discern—by the different voices, that there had to be at least ten of them. There was no going forward and there was certainly no going back to the fence. That barbed wire had taken enough flesh from me for one evening.

I got low to the ground, real low, and then crawled on my belly to the nearest house. Looking around the perimeter, I saw there was only one place to hide. It was the most secure spot, very little light, hard to get to, not at all obvious, so the cops might not look there.

I belly-crawled and squeezed my way under a wooden patio with only about a foot and a half of clearance above the ground. It was a tight fit. The dirt was wet under the deck, probably from moist leaves, sprinklers, and rainwater.

I immediately noticed the ground under the deck had a very unpleasant odor. It stung my nostrils, much like mixture of dog crap and earthworms. There was definitely something dead under the patio. "Fuck it! Just be glad it isn't you." I grumbled in a voice that was only audible to the vermin that were in hiding. We were cohorts, companions in filth. I hiding from cops and 'the things' hiding from any type of discovery as they probably defied rational explanation.

This is what your life had come to, I thought. It was slightly poetic and ironic at the same time. I was crawling around and hiding amongst creatures resembling my own lowly existence – worms, mites, ticks, and sow bugs, and the unseen. By pushing through the muck, I got far under the patio and into the shadows where frame met foundation. In seconds, some of the cops were literally right on top of me. Four or five were walking the yard, while at least four were standing on the deck directly over my head and chest. I silently gathered muddy leaves over the top of my body.

The cops paced back and forth around the yard, occasionally pausing to talk on top of the deck. At one point, two cops peered through the widest space separating the boards. So close were they—almost face to face—that only planks and narrow strips of dim light separated us. I was able to even see the whites of eyes, which caused me to close my own. It takes an enormous amount of will power to shut your eyes, in order to prevent the reflection from bringing the enemy to your concealment, especially when you know full well the searchers are looking right at you. I kept my eyes sealed, waited with shallow breaths until retreating footsteps told me the cops had moved off the deck. It was at that moment that I noticed something was biting me over and over. Not big chopping bites, more like tiny little piercing bites

The back of my shirt had ripped open and I could feel tiny fangs, maybe stings, maybe something worse, piercing my skin. My first thought was bloodworms or ticks.

It has to be bloodworms. Only those fuckers hurt like this! I thought. Bloodworms were so horrible; they could make a man wish for ticks or leeches. Circumstances were growing ugly. *Well, okay it's bad, but it could get worse, can you imagine a sicker location to have an acid flashback?* That idea was immediately followed by another. *Please no flashbacks ... please no flashbacks ... please no flashbacks.* Then it happened—as it usually does, thinking of the phenomenon most feared, served to aid the act of conjuring it forth. And as if to punish me the flashback was a doozy. I imagined a giant worm with a human face, all except for the mouth that is, the mouth was like something a lamprey would have; thumbtack teeth and multiple sucker lips. That would have been enough to scare the shit out me. However, my mind wasn't quite done with the creation. It had arms and hands, big hands, hands for gripping, tearing, and shoveling flesh into that hideous mouth. It was oozing towards me. Hungry, eager, like a spider clutching a moth. I covered my mouth with both hands, as it was no longer certain that a scream would not burst from my lungs.

I repeated the addict's rosary "It's only the drugs, it's only the drugs, it's only the drugs. Then as if I possessed a magical talisman the human/worm hybrid was gone.

It may have disappeared from my mind, but it still deserved a name, for species identification, so I christened the creature "Horm." Then in the same cerebral breath I mentally implored the spirits to keep the Horm away from me.

After several minutes, I was able to hear the cops moving down the block and into other backyards. "Give it a few minutes.....don't make the mistake of moving too soon." I told myself. It took every fiber in my body to outlast the biting teeth. I remained silent and buried any reaction to the growing pain, and (dare I say).squeamish feeling of disgust. It paid to be careful and not move too soon. Maybe the cops were using the old trick of acting as if they had given up and were leaving, while really just around a corner, or behind some trees.

There was a house about three miles away that I shared—a couple years ago with some party animals. It was a safe haven in order to fix my injuries and formulate my best strategy. My mind mentally counted off ten minutes.

"Long enough ... time to go ... get ready to run while you still have the juice and are only a couple quarts low of body fluids. Take four deep breaths and go"

My pace was severely limited. A straight shot towards my old residence was out of the question. My route was lengthened considerable by an angular running pattern, geometrically necessary if I wanted to stay in the shadows. Crossing streets was exceptionally risky. Experience had taught me that cops always sectioned off observation points, so as to watch in better-lighted and open travel areas. A silhouette in the dark paralleling the uneven terrain is very hard to spot. But a silhouette running through a backlit area with no cover stands out like a sore thumb.

There was no way to completely avoid such dangerous intersections, sooner or later—in the squared off arrangements of yards, a street, highway, or back alley had to be traversed. Add the extra distance required to flank the cops with the broken-triangle running method and the final tally of miles before I reached safely came to an uneasy ten. It was just another mission. I'd made it and still had a quart of blood and lymphoid fluid to spare and maybe could have even gone another ten miles if necessary, but thankfully it did not come to that. All that was left now was to wake up my old roommates at four in the morning.

I laughed while picturing the conversation. "Hi, guys. Remember me ... fugitive gangster, currently being chased by about a dozen cops ... please excuse my blood-soaked attire. So how have you been? How about those Bears ... huh?"

Who Can It Be Now

The moment hovered somewhere between the witching hour and a slow dissolve of the Harvest Moon. My escape; from the things under the patio, pissed-off cops, and treacherous fences was just in time, as the moon had began to surrender space to sunrise. Before knocking on the door, I made an effort to look somewhat presentable, starting with combing hair with dirty fingers and then brushing caked mud, blood, and unknown parasite slime from my shredded clothes, and lastly by coughing up blades of grass and a bug of unknown origin. I could hear people talking inside, so my old roommates had not retired for the evening. By the number of different voices, it appeared they must be entertaining an after-hours group of friends, or tavern closing-time-dregs. I immediately recognized two things, the smell of good Jamaican pot, and music by the Aussie band "Men at Work." The song had progressed to the last chorus, so all the band members were chanting along with lead singer Colin Hay, repeating over and over "Who Can it be now.". How appropriate for my unannounced visit.

Still mindful of staying within the shadows in case any cops drove past, I knocked softly, but insistently, on the ornate oak door. The occupants, although not necessarily singing out loud, had to be asking themselves the same question—"Who Can it be Now?" It was several minutes before the knocking was answered. In the interval, it was obvious by the shuffling sounds, drugs, and god knows what else were being stashed. Every few seconds Vito would say "Relax ... cool it. I'm sure it is only Roger."

I didn't know any Roger, or who else they might be invited to the festivities, but one thing was certain: "They sure as fuck weren't expecting me".

I gave my face a last wipe so as to look as calm and unthreatening as possible; a futile task considering I looked like a fucking lunatic hobo. The music stopped, along with the hushed tones so all that was left was an uncomfortable silence.

At first, it seemed like nobody was going to answer the door. I briefly dwelled on the idea of yelling out to Vito something to the effect of "Open up, chicken-shit. It's Billy... you asshole!" However, drawing attention to the fact that there was a ragged, bloody, scary-looking dude standing on a porch in the middle of the night wasn't a good idea.

I deliberated on the idea of splitting the scene and attempting a mad dash across town to my brother's place. I was just about to give up waiting when, all of a sudden, my old roommate Vito opened the door just a crack. He recognized me and allowed me inside. His initial reaction was one of delight, as it had been awhile since we had hung out. But the expression quickly melted and was replaced by shock, a suitable reaction considering my disheveled appearance and the wild look in my eyes. Part of Vito's nervousness, was most likely due to the fact that: wherever I went trouble was sure to be close behind, and this crowd wanted to avoid trouble as much as me.

"What the fuck happened to you?" He said, while taking a few steps back and looking at my torn pants leg and the glaring wound.

Before answering, I scanned the surprised faces in the room. Some of the people were new to me, and since everyone was on a "Need to Know Basis" no immediate explanation was offered to Vito. I mumbled a polite "how's it going" then motioned Vito to follow me to the kitchen, so our conversation would be private and not cause any panic among the coke-fiends, hash-freaks and pot-heads.

When the two of us were alone in the kitchen, I quickly explained the situation. "Look man; hate to interrupt the party, but there are a shitload of cops after me. Gotta fix up a bad cut, and hide a while. I'll split as soon as my brothers get here to take me somewhere else."

Vito took a good look at the puncture. "What happened somebody stab you again?

"No, man ... nothing like that, I got attacked by a barbed wire fence, but the fence got the worst of it."

"What started it, Billy? Did the fence owe Bitsy money? Vito asked attempting to inject some humor, as he was well aware of my involvement in the collection racket.

Vito's joke made him laugh and calm down, which it turn clamed me down—now that I didn't have to worry about him acting all squeamish and freaking out the other guests. Statistically speaking; in any random group of ten people, one is bound to be a snitch with a big mouth; and as there was at least 15 druggies in Vito's house, the rat-count would be one complete person and a torso-only half person. Statistics don't lie, and the numbers satisfied the 1½ snitches per 15 guests, so discretion was needed.

While standing on the graphite/tan-colored marble tile next to the stove, I pointed to my nose and then taped the adjacent gray metal counter top, signaling for Vito to rail me up. I needed a bump to take away the feeling of nausea and prevent me from fainting. While he laid out a couple of thick lines, I went to the cupboard, grabbed a bottle of Southern Comfort, and tossed back a few shots, so as to "edge off" and dull my pain receptors for the impromptu surgery to come. To me, "Southern Comfort" tasted like bourbon mixed with Robatusen Cough syrup but it was better than nothing. Actually, it tasted so bad that if not for the pain nothing would have been better.

Vito was wearing almost the exact clothes that he wore when we lived together. Not one to stray too far into the world of fashion or good taste, he limited his apparel to blue jeans, a white tee-shirt, and hiking boots—his uniform for every activity. He dressed in the same garb to attend church as he did when doing less formal activates; for instance, rappelling—as he had done with me years ago at Lake Bluff Beach. Vito was five foot tall, skinny, with long reddish hair, and elfin features, a look that always made me think of pixie-lepracon. However, with Vito there was no 'Pot O' Gold'—only Pot—and no rainbows, unless of course, you bought mushrooms from him, then rainbows came in bundles.

Regardless of his trickster appearance, Vito was a stand-up guy, loyal to the core, and could be counted on to help me out. Best of all, he would do so without bitching about the inconvenience or lecturing about my destructive ways. Like most people, he had long given up trying to change me, or warn me about the impending doom.

I was glad there would be no sermon, because now was not the time to hear about my character flaws. A twelve step program wasn't going to shed the cops after me, or stop the bleeding.

"Besides, I'll deal with the doom when it catches me and not a moment before. When that happens doom better bring a parasol and a picnic basket, as taking me down will be an all-day affair." I said to myself while snorting another line. Drugged up, I was brave again ... and equally as stupid.

I looked at Vito, checking for any signs that he might tell the wrong person of my visit and dilemma.

Nah ... Vito has been a proven friend, no matter what. Besides, he owes me for all the times I had to save his bacon from ass-beatings, I thought, while remembering that Vito was famous for letting his mouth get him into trouble, especially after having a few too many cocktails. Which meant every once and awhile, I had to step in and throw a few punches. He was a wiseass but had never been known to tell secrets, just start fights with bigger guys.

The lines of blow, boosted with a few shots, prepared me for the excruciating process of closing the hole in my leg, by cauterizing the wound. It was the kind of chore that required much more privacy then the kitchen offered. So with Vito's permission, I went into his room to play doctor. Not the fun kind of doctor with the opposite sex—as practiced with youthful exuberance; this operation did not promise female companionship, only burned flesh, which was the only option when stitches weren't feasible. It's easier to find a light or match and a metal object to heat, than it is to find a needle and thread. Besides, sewing takes too long. And as I told Vito, "I just can't sew a stitch ... literally."

Vito returned to his guests and (per my instructions) turned up the stereo, in case a muffled scream escaped my lips. As Vito turned up the volume, the music of Cheap Trick reached my ears. "Way of the World" was as good as any other track to provide the cauterization theme. I heated a butter-knife –taken from the kitchen—with a cigarette lighter until it was red hot. This was not the first time I had cauterized a wound. There had been plenty of times for that while in the military, working for Jumbo, or doing Merc deeds. Those were all situations where if an altercation went grim heat-sealing a cut was the only available choice, so I had the experience to perform the surgical work. Walking into a hospital with a knife or gun-shot injury required too many explanations, none of which would prevent the doctor from notifying the police.

Only an idiot would causally stroll into the emergency ward and think they can explain away a gunshot, knife, or baseball bat wound. There just wasn't anything that could justify such a gruesome appearance. For me, there the added incentive not to go, as most times a blood test would register "enough *drugs to make Jim Morrison rise from the grave.*

How would such a conversation sound anyway to describe my current dilemma? "Hi, Nurse. I slipped and fell on a barbed wire fence, and then the strangest thing happened, the fence also ripped off most of my shirt, bit me all over, and then made me do a shitload of drugs."

The knife was hot enough to melt the uppermost layer of epidermal tissue. After manipulating the lymph-gland vessel back in the puncture, I pressed the heated metal directly on the hole. Gritting my teeth, I ignored the pain, along with the unpleasant sight of my liquefied flesh merging together, and making a solid sheath over the once dripping wound. The smell of burnt flesh wafted up into my face and reminded me of a barbeque, except for the fact that it was Human meat on the grill.

It took another burning, in order to completely mend the injury, and kill all the tiny, nasty, critters that were swimming in the festering hole.

"Come on in, Billy. The festering pool of lymphoid fluid is just fine." I imagined a protozoa (with a sense of humor) saying. Then a short spike of acid, stored in by nervous system, provided the picture for the thought. My mind saw a gelatinous single-cell bacteria floating on an inflatable raft in a pool. It wore a straw hat, flowered Hawaiian shirt, and matching shorts. No Speedo, thank god. In one of the bacteria's gooey paws it had a fruity drink with an umbrella in it.

"Fuck … looks like a hell of an infectious party going on in there." I said while staring at the newly sealed (but still oozing pus) wound. It was a funny hallucination, even in pain. Thankfully, I snapped back to reality.

Next, the torn shirt came off so I could rub alcohol over the bites covering my back. There had to be over thirty of the red pustules popping out between my waist and shoulders. Interesting enough, the pinprick bites actually hurt more than the searing of skin, probably because of the elevated creepiness factor, which resulted from not knowing exactly what had been sticking mandibles into my flesh. "Absolutely not from the Horm, that was only an acid flashback." I mumbled—to make it so.

The operation was not over. Blood continued to flow down my pants leg and over my exposed foot. By rolling up my pants leg, another huge gash was revealed on my left calf muscle. Putting another flame to the same knife, I duplicated my medical technique and melted more flesh in order to pull the separated sections of skin together. This time a small gasp got past my clenched teeth. However, I felt no shame for not being able to hold back the pain, as I had probably overloaded my agony receptors, which caused a momentary display of weakness.

The absence of the Monkey during the cauterization process, concerned me. *What better time is there for him to show up and torture me? It makes no sense ... unless he is planning something especially ghastly for me and is only biding his time,* I thought. Not that I missed The Monkey, not at all, but for him not to make his presence known in one of my worst moments was very unusual.

"He must be planning something that will finish me once and for all ... fuck it ... figure it out later." I told myself.

With the medical work done, there was nothing left to do except call my brothers to come get me and take me a suitable place to hide out and get my strength back. The cops were sure as shit going to pay a visit to all my hangouts, including my apartment, the homes of brothers, and closest friends. A hotel was the safest solution until I could get a handle on things and find out how serious the cops were about arresting me this time. Just like Vito, my brothers still refused to give up on me, even though I had long ago even up on myself, and welcomed the finality of Doom. Death is what I had coming, and most people would probably agree that an unpleasant end was deserved anyway.

An Excerpt from The Monkey's Diary

Author's disclaimer: I can neither verify, nor deny, the actuality of the Monkey's diary. He is after all a mere creation of a drug-addled imagination. So, proceeding with that thought variance, his writing might very well be as nonexistent as the Monkey himself. In fact, to go even further to the next logical conclusion this whole novel may be nothing but a twinge of memory from a long forgotten past ... maybe yours or maybe mine. However, in keeping with the musically violent theme of the novel, please read while listening to 'Full Moon Turn my Head Around' by Off Broadway.

4:00 IPT (Imaginary Primate Time)—I'll bet that right about now Billy is wondering why I didn't drop by Vito's house and watch him put hot steel to human epidermal tissue. Much as it would have been nice to observe the wretched act of cauterizing himself, I had other things to occupy my time. Besides if I had been there, it would have been too easy, to convince him to put the knife to his throat instead, bringing an end to his life way too quickly. He has much more drugs and humiliation to consume before I grant him the release of a violent death.

Could he have slit his throat with a dull butter-knife? I have no fucking idea, but it still would have been amusing to watch him trying to saw through an esophagus. It would give new meaning to the phrase 'more gristle for the mill'.

I'm sure he considers it an act of courage to endure the sting of the knife over and over. I'll even bet Billy secretly hopes word gets around about his escape, so the discussion boosts his reputation for danger. Still thinks he's a fucking tough guy. By failing to resist the lure of drugs and destruction, he plays right in my simian hands, confusing courage with folly. Now he is really in deep shit. Sooner or later the time will come when misdeeds would finally catch up and cause him to sink to a new low.

Maybe he'll get lock-jaw, tetanus, or if I'm real lucky, his leg will turn gangrenous and have to be amputated. After all, that fence had to be covered with bacteria. And I don't mean the make-believe kind of germ that float on a raft in a pool. Those only live in Billy's mind. I mean the real kind of bacteria. What do you take me for, a drug addict? Yeah, that would be perfect if Billy lost a peg.

Then he'll be a one-legged fugitive ... friendless, penniless, hopeless. His downfall could be my greatest achievement. There have been countless others brought to the point of suicide by my influence, but a drug-addled wastoid, hopping around on one leg while begging for loose change to get his next fix ... that would really be something to see. I'd like to write more, however somewhere out in the real world a family man tries to push away his tenth beer, a junkie tells himself "one last spike" a teenager logs on to internet porn, a mother trades food stamps for crack, a Wall Street Broker embezzles for his Porsche. I have so much to do and so little time.

Hotel California

It was around 7:00 in the morning when my brothers arrived. We loaded into Tim's Black Expedition, and made a hasty departure from Vito's place, to find a suitable hotel. The goal was to find one within three miles, as there was no point in driving all over town. Before leaving the house, I removed the tattered and bloody clothes, and changed into clean sweatpants, and a polo shirt my brothers brought. The last thing we needed was to attract any unwanted attention, from the hotel staff, be it front desk clerks or security guards.

We stopped along the way so Tim and James could run into Walgreens, get some medical supplies and treat my wounds with something a little better then red-hot butter knives and Band-Aids. They took no chances, buying everything in sight, returning to the car with enough remedies that would have treated an entire Leper colony—a colony not the size of the one in "Ben Hur", but maybe like the one in "Papillion."

We agreed that the Freemont Hotel on 'Old Route 41' was the best place to lay low for a few days. The building was a reputable high class establishment, so it was not subject to random police searches, nor the kind of place a fugitive might hide out. The entrance was also ideal, under a big red canopy, which was at the end of a long service drive, giving us acceptable privacy.

The somber occasion reminded me of the Eagle's song "Hotel California," especially the lyrics near the end ... *stab them with your steely knifes ... but you just can't kill the beast.* "Which of us is really the beast ... me or the Monkey? I asked myself. *It seems as if I am becoming more of a despicable beast then The Monkey.* I thought while Tim parked.

I pushed the deliberations about the nature of beasts and monkeys from my mind. The last thing I needed at this moment was to peer inside my brain and analyze the existence of beasts lurking in the hollow pocket—where my soul should have been. How does the old saying go? Admitting you have a ravenous beast living in your subconscious and an invisible (except to yours truly) Monkey taking over your conscious is the first step to recovery. Not fucking likely. I much prefer a much simpler motto.

"People that live stoned should avoid glass houses inhabited by Mr. Pot, and Mr. Kettle."

After checking in, Tim and James stuck around so we could formulate a plan. A plan that would encompass many elements such as: eluding the police, getting antibiotics without going to a hospital, and leaving the state—at least until things cooled down a bit. It was late in the afternoon when my brothers finally left. The stuff from Walgreens allowed me to change the bandages, pour iodine on the punctures, and then top them off with rubbing alcohol, followed with a layer of Neosporin over all the other ointments—just to be sure. I wasn't taking any chances. After the wounds were attended to; I put some ice to my forehead in the hopes of taking down the fever. It wasn't exactly hospital-grade treatment but it would have to do. Besides, over the years my immune system had become very formidable.

"I need to stop my temperature from getting any higher. Maybe I'll spontaneously combust.....but if that happens, one thing is for sure...... that fucking Monkey is going with me." It really didn't dawn on me that if the infection killed me, then automatically The Monkey will cease to exist—except in another addicts mind. I spoke to an empty room, while considering the conundrums of which came first: the chicken or the egg, and which came first: Billy or the Monkey?

Spontaneous Combustion would be too easy of an end for The Monkey. "He's got a Gutting coming." I told myself again, just as I had every day, and would continue to do until the gutting finally happened. The possibility of revenge pushed me on, and helped get me through the next few days. An oath of revenge would have to be enough, especially since I had begun losing sight of anything else except the primate's death.

I tossed the ice in the sink and got down to business. There was no time to waste, so I proceeded to the survival S.O.P (Standard Operating Procedure) of altering my appearance, so as to make it very difficult to identify who I really was.

"Stay focused....Stay cool... until you make for the hills and disappear." I said to my reflection over the sink, surprised at how pale and feeble my condition was. However, right at this moment how I felt or looked did not matter. I was short on funds, so making a few collections before hitting the road, was going to necessary. I obtained a cheap pair of scissors from a great-looking front-desk girl; so good looking in fact I actually considered hitting on her. However, common sense prevailed, as I reminded myself of a tiny detail.

You're a fucking fugitive with a fever of 104...get over yourself asshole.....go upstairs and put together a disguise...THEN try for the front desk girl. I clipped off my pony tail and trimmed the front and sides. The style was changed drastically; from long, pulled-back, surfer look, to a modified military cut. I played barber with just the right amount of finesse so my topknot avoided resembling a modified mullet, which was only fashionable on top of the Smokey Mountains or in Riverside, CA. Once my remaining locks had the desired shape, I applied hair dye, turning my original color of light brown to an orange punk-rock tint.

Having never dyed hair before, the procedure did not go as described on the instructions, so I ended up with the kind of orange usually reserved for rotten pumpkins and 'Ralph Malph' from Happy Days. All that was needed was to put on a pair of clear, non- prescription eyeglasses, grow on my beard, and nobody would recognize me.

For some reason, playing dress-up caused me to again think back of "The Cure" poster on the stoner's wall. I wondered what advice Robert Smith would dispense regarding this situation. *Would he tell me to apply some eye-shadow? Would he tell me that I wasn't wearing enough black? Would he tell me to forget about Goth and Go Country?*

Of course, it was all nothing but mere speculation resulting from fabrication. But regardless, Smith's wisdom might have been of some help. He (imaginary or not) had already demonstrated his thoughtful approach and logic when viewing the world. His hatred of Mr. Roboto was the sort of sound reasoning and a fugitive could put to use. Unfortunately, there was no poster of 'The Cure' on the hotel wall to help bring him forth, only a generic picture of a Clipper Ship, sailing on an equally generic Ocean. Clipper Ships on posters or in paintings had never given me advice before and so it would be no different now.

I limped to the sofa, collapsed onto the cushions, lit up a Camel Filter and exhaled smoke rings into the stale hotel atmosphere. *Maybe the smoke will eliminate the stench of pine-sol, crappy air freshener, and horror of horrors—the fragrance of a baby having been very recently changed.*

It will take more than smoke; it would take an atomic bomb to neutralize the unpleasant odor floating throughout the room. Fuck it..... I won't be here long enough to let any scents get to me. As soon possible, I'm getting the fuck out of here and going to see Bitsy and get some money.

The last of the misty smoke rings dissipated over a tweed easy chair. The smoke faded out and The Monkey faded in. Unlike most other appearances, The Monkey wore no clothes of any kind, no comically satiric attire at all, only primate hair, primate stink, and a primate craving for face tearing or ball ripping. Seeing him in this state made me wish for everything that I hated – maybe feared less. "Bring on the Clowns, Puppets, Jimmy Buffet, and may god save my soul, Mr. Roboto. I addressed the Monkey."

"What a fine addition you bring to the other aromas. Your smell makes my nostrils want to jump off my face. Now the room smells like diapers, air freshener, cleaning products, and Chimpanzee shit." I told the Monkey, proud of landing the first barb before he began making with the insults. Not the brightest remark ever made, but considering my health it would have to do.

The Monkey responded right away. ***"You look like the junkie I left for dead on the South-Side. He just couldn't lay off the smack. Quite a sight, really, as he lay there; lifeless in his own puke and piss. It was really a nasty overdose."*** The Monkey said while making his intentions evident by twisting his mouth into a contemptuous baboon-like sneer, full of tobacco-stained, sharp canine teeth. He was here to finish me off. People not familiar with The Monkey might not understand why he had tobacco-stained teeth.

However, the primate's enamel wasn't a mystery to me, I knew he secretly smoked like a chimney (despite his denials), using everything from hash to opium—even resorting to lighting up model airplane glue in a pinch. I had suspicions, that my Monkey, had his own demon imaginary Monkey to deal with. Then out of the blue a new idea came to me.

What if the parasitical relationship of Primates went forever, and that Monkey had his own Monkey, and that Monkey had another Monkey, the cycle continuing straight down the line, and on and on and on? Like the optical illusion displaying the picture of a man looking at his reflection in an infinite number of mirrors.

"Look at you! King of the Streets, hiding out in a hotel room, afraid to go out in public, although, I can kind of understand why ... with hair that color. What are you going to do? Sit around here like a pussy, or are you going back out there and collect up some money? This time, don't turn anything over to Bitsy or any of the other assholes you work for ... keep it all, you're gonna need it if the plan is to go across country." The Monkey said.

"Who said anything about going across country? I might just go to Minnesota for awhile." I replied.

"Listen ... if you have to run away, then you might as well head out to the West Coast. Beaches, sunshine and girls. What more does a man need? Besides you and that fucked up hairdo will fit right in with the surfer crowd. I know just the thing needed to clear your head, so you can think straight. A big fat line of blow."

"Yeah.....California....maybe you're right for once, and what could be better than a few lines; might get me back on my feet. Maybe Jed Klampitt had it right all along and California is the place I 'otta be'."

I dumped the rest of a gram seal on the coffee table, and snorted it up with two massive whiffs. Once again—like my stay in the hospital after punching out the Squid—I mixed cocaine, nervous energy and an escalating fever all together.

"Talk about a Speedball." I said to myself. Then out loud, refueled with coke, I told The Monkey to "Go find someone else to torture." There was no argument because he knew I was about to do another strong-arm job, which was what he wanted me to do anyway.

"Okay, but I'll be back. Don't forget who gets you through the rough patches. Without my spurs digging into your backside, you're nothing but a mindless pack-mule carrying out the whims of others. Billy, the time has come to take control of the situation and make a big score. Get out there and get some cash. Fuck the risks!" With this last order, The Monkey faded out, but not before making an obscene gesture crude even by Primate standards.

With my car impounded, I needed new wheels, so a cab was taken to the home of a friend that I'd done many favors for—in return for coke. His name was Joey Erickson. He had become one of my closet friends and went to bars with us almost every weekend. Joey also went to Southern Illinois University, graduating the year Sven and I arrived. My friendship with Joey began in a most unusual way. We had some words outside of a bar and were preparing to kick the shit out of each other in the pouring rain. He had a reputation of being a very good fighter and had beaten up many guys that were said to be known "bad-asses."

We stood outside in the storm for several minutes, moving in a slow circle, feinting takedowns and strikes, each looking for an opening that would allow a finishing move. Knowing that even the winner was going home with a few injuries, we came to our senses, deciding a beer-chugging contest was a far better method to resolve our differences.

Joey's nickname was "The Wrist", as rumor had it that his dick was the size of a grown man's wrist. I was very happy to leave it as a rumor and not ask for proof. Some things were better off accepted as fact.

Joey encouraged the nickname with no small amount of pride. He twisted the famous Ritz cracker commercial so that the phrase became his own, but slightly different and much more vulgar. Joey declared to any girl that would listen, "Everything sits better on a wrist." He was also known for having the best late-night parties with an ample amount of coke and the coke-whores that go with the package.

I took a cab from the hotel to Joey's house and briefly explained the mess, but left the part about "how serious the cops wanted me" out. I convinced Joey to loan me his truck, so some dough could be rounded up. He agreed, with just one stipulation, make a few stops and collect some overdue payments from his customers too.

Before hitting the road, we shot the shit for awhile, listening to the Psychedelic Furs, drinking a couple beers, and ingesting even more coke. I was wired out of my skull. After a couple hours, Joey flipped me the keys to his truck, making me promise to have it back by the next morning.

Lying low would have been the safe thing to do, if I had it within me to do the safest thing. Playing it smart or safe was not something I was accustomed to doing, much preferring to live dangerously. This made my next decision—to take the same girl from the night before to dinner—the second most hazardous choice within in a series of horrible choices. But I had to see her in order to say thanks for not squealing, and to remind her that she must play ignorant if questioned more by the cops about my known acquaintances. She knew some names and addresses that would best be kept from the cops.

We went to a rib joint located in Bridgeport, only a few blocks from Randhurst Mall. We gave our order to the waiter and he went back to the kitchen to pass along our selections to the chef. I let my eyes wander, moving in a complete circle around the room, trying to spot anyone that was staring a little too much in our direction.

Everybody seemed unconcerned with our presence until my gaze got to the busboy station. A busboy has stopped refilling condiments and was looking right at me. There was no mistaking the expression; he recognized me, identifying me immediately as the same person that had slapped him around not too long ago at Boomer's tavern, in downtown Highmore.

He was a barfly-snitch, certainly aware of my warrants, quite possibly even aware of the McDonalds incident. He tried to act casual, folding napkins, sweating, willing himself not to look at our table again. He picked up a basket filled with barbeque sauce, left the bus station and made beeline to the manager stacking glasses behind the bar. The two of them spoke in hushed tones and then walked back to the office area, no doubt to call the cops. For all I knew, cops were already waiting outside, so before bolting out of the restaurant a visit to the restroom was necessary to flush any contraband down the toilet.

By the time I got back to the table two cops were already there. I had a fake I.D and was driving a different vehicle, which meant there was a chance of getting away. All that I needed was to convince them that they had come for the wrong guy. It was a non-starter; before I could say a word, the cops told me to shut up and that they were going to escort me outside. Other officers had already arrived and were waiting at the entrance. Things were happening so fast memorizing individual features for each officer was impossible. The only thing that I recall is it appeared they all shopped for "Village People" mustaches at the same place.

This is going to be a tough one. You're going to have to get past the two cops at the table wait for a chance to plow through the squad blocking the door, and then sprint for the wooded area in back of the mall. I thought, while forcing my mind to come up with a plan ... and quick.

Outrunning the cops won't be easy with a hole in my leg. But breaking free from them once they have me surrounded will be almost impossible. So, bad leg or not, you're gonna have to make your move when you get about ten feet from the door. That will give you three good steps to build up speed and hit them like bowling pins.

"Don't worry, everything will be okay. Call somebody to pick you up. I'll go with these guys and get this all straightened out." I told my date. Turning my attention back to the cops, I again insisted, "I'm not the person you think I am...you guys got the wrong guy. If you let me take out my wallet, I'll prove it to you."

The cops were having none of it and responded by saying, "Yeah sure...you'll get a chance to prove who you are, once you're handcuffed and at the station. If you're not the felon were looking for, then in a few minutes, you'll be free to go." The Sergeant said. However, it was clear (by the sheer number of cops sent on the call), they knew full well that the person in custody was the right guy.

Fifteen feet from the exit the lucky break I was waiting for appeared in the form of an arthritic old lady slowly coming towards us while taking up most of the corridor with her form supported by a four-legged walker.

I waited until the two cops were so close their breath could be felt on my neck. A quick pivot to the left and I was able to put the old lady between me and the two cops following me towards the exit. Gathering some momentum, I turned my 'perp-walk' into a sprint, charging like a bull straight at the larger group of blue uniforms that waited by a hostess stand near the double doors.

I charged forward, hitting the cop's scrum with every ounce of strength, resembling a fullback scrambling for a first down at 3rd and four. Desperate hands reached out for me, clutching, snatching, trying to get a grip on any part of me, or my clothes. The last two or three cops succeeded in grabbing my shirt. It seemed like they had me. Before they were able to haul me in, a tiny amount of coke wrapped in foil dropped from my pockets. *God damn it, I forgot that was in there,* I thought.

Shit! I hope they don't find the blow, I thought, knowing they would search the floor and find another noose to hang around my neck. Part of me wished they caught me and put an end to my addiction by locking me up. However, like most addicts there was a more powerful part insisting I get away so as to find another hit, snort, fusion or spike.

Hopeless and brainless, I sprinted fast, faster than any other time I could remember. In just a few seconds the entire group of cops was left far behind, all except for one. The last cop reused to give up. He had some skills, maybe a track star in high school or a triathlon runner. I could run forever, but this guy stayed with me, stride for stride. I knew that the other cops had to be running for their squad cars, so it was the forests and rough terrain for me.

Meanwhile, the cop chasing me was still on my tail. We had gone about for about two miles and it was beginning to look like the cop was going to outrun me. Then, unexpectedly, he gassed out. Proving once again that track-endurance and submission-grappling-endurance are two completely different levels of stamina.

When thing turn sour, I'll use my wrestler's athletic ability, so as find a way to win over any other kind. But in all modesty, maybe it wasn't my athleticism that won the footrace; it might have the officer's love of donuts. I put a substantial amount of distance between the two of us. In order to make sure the cop gave his partners the wrong direction; I purposely made his last view of my escape a west route through the woods. Then when out of sight, I turned hard east and headed towards the section of the forest where some railroad tracks cut between strands of trees and the highway.

Into the Woods

I ran almost two miles, which created a substantial distance between the cops me, allowing for reprieve in an increasingly bad dilemma. Regardless of the accumulated lead, they stayed on my trail as doggedly as a pack of hyenas smelling fresh-kill. Two miles wasn't enough so I kept up the pace, stopping only when necessary, so as to catch my breath and glance backwards to find out the number of cops still in pursuit. Judging by the different colored uniforms, it was evident that other municipalities had been called and were providing additional assistance in the capture. Surprisingly, ten to twelve officers were matching me stride for stride—must have been track stars in high school—and had not lost sight of me; even closing the gap. Many of the cops no longer posed a threat, having been fooled by my diversion of flanking west or they were so out of shape keeping up was out of the question. They had quit randomly throughout the chase, leaving a succession of cops bent over, gasping with hands on knees. Their bullet-proof vests were no doubt adding to the difficulty of maintaining such a long pursuit. Whether the number of cops had been reduced by diversion or by exhaustion did not matter to me, as the important thing was they were no longer a consequence in the get-away attempt. From my position, away from the business section of town but not quite in the safety of the surrounding woodland, numerous sirens blared, all of which were moving in my direction. Those cars not heading towards me went further east, cordoning off that section and thereby reducing the odds of an easy escape from the county. They did exactly as expected by forming an intersectional picket line. However, operating according to a plan which even I was aware of wasn't going to shift the advantage in my favor, as it was a statically very time-tested plan.

Well, at least you got rid of half of them. Keep moving and find a suitable place to lose the rest of them, somewhere with concealment and plenty of hard- to- get- thru obstacles, I thought, while pondering the pros and cons of climbing a tree to the very top so as to let the cops pass-by, thereby allowing me to reverse course, and to really throw them off. The cons won out because if dogs were brought in I would be certainly fucked, stuck 60 feet in the air with no option but to leap from branch to branch. Doing so would only result in one of two outcomes: a plummeting fall that would break my back or a plummeting fall that would crack open my skull.

"Climbing high atop a tree where the only acceptable eva-sion route, is a limb to limb traverse. There's a situation where the Monkey's advice could be put to good use." I whispered.

Then I came to my senses; being up a tree and having to rely on the Monkey's advice was a horrible idea by any stan-dard. *Shit...don't think about that simian jagoff...just doing so will help him search me out so he can make things a hundred times worse.*

So I kept on running, finding motivation by pretending to be back in the military and going thru Recon Indoctrination School. There, failing was unacceptable if you wanted the co-veted 0321 designation, jump wings and scuba pins. Quitting was not an option; no matter how far the swim, the weight of the gear, or the fast pace of the runs. When that image did not provide the inspiration I needed, I thought about the alley in Africa and the tribal warlords chasing me. That got the legs and blood pumping. Thinking of the old Recon and Merc days helped me stay alert, move in the most clandestine way possi-ble, and keep my eyes peeled for acceptable camouflage to dis-figure my contour. The forest and trees simplified the process of selecting the appropriate music—with the right beat to put my feet to. My brain dropped an imaginary stylus on an imagi-nary vinyl disk. The music of 'The Call' played in my head; and 'Into the Woods' was the song. And so further into the woods I went, on the run, more from myself than anyone or anything else.

"Michael Been, the bass player and singer of The Call had the soaring vocal talent that a pandering asshole, like Bono, only wished he had," I chuckled, letting the thoughts of music once again take the pain away.

I confess that part of me wished The Monkey would to join me, high up in a tree and evading the cops. His ability to release The Beast inside me might prove useful if the cops got within range to apprehend me. The other part of me wanted nothing except to keep the Monkey and Beast both at bay. Letting them join in on the fun would only cause some cops to get hurt, making things much worse for me in court. More importantly, hitting cops with kidney and liver strikes would violate my rule of never hurting innocent people. Once that line was crossed there would be no going back, the Beast and Monkey would own my stupid ass.

There was a series of railroad tracks that went north and intersected the forest. That would be the best bet for leaving the County unseen; either by jumping a slow mover or by simply pushing on and running as if in a marathon. All I had to do was make it unnoticed past a row of houses. The neighborhood was such a perfect example of mundane regimental suburbia, that it reminded me of something from a Tim Burton production.

The cops are still too close to make a break for the tracks. Better hide first and rest. I might be in for a prolonged run if there is no train to jump. Yeah, that's it ... and while hiding, try and pinpoint where most of the cops are searching, I thought. To make the correct course of action easier to enact; I picked out the house that had sufficient shrubbery, woodpiles, and playground structures. A suitable hiding place was found; in a clump of miniature evergreens, growing behind a blue and yellow playhouse with polka dots.

I settled in for what might be an extended wait, and began the process of camouflaging my outline and catching my breath. I pulled off several fan-shaped slender branches, flipped the stems so that each one faced downward, and then tucked the foliage into the waist band of my cargo pants. The decorations were finished by threading a few through my tank top.

The addition of natural concealment gave my clothes a splotchy color pattern that resembled something other than human, a foreign shape very hard to discern in the moonless night. With the camo-ensemble completed, it was time to get moving again. The cop's locations had been triangulated and I'd had more than enough time to rest. My pursuers were really close, but not centered anywhere near the tracks. Good thing.

Interspersed with the sounds of men yelling was the sound of barking dogs, probably German Sheppard police dogs, which meant the police Canine-Unit, had arrived. The barks sounded fainter than the human voices, which was very heartening news. The difference in volume meant that the dogs must be way behind the front line of officers. As I was rose up from my crouching position, several cops appeared out of nowhere. They broke into groups of two, spread out, and methodically began to search the yard for any sign I'd been through there.

Fuck this is not good...the dogs will be here any minute, I thought, knowing full well that no form of concealment would fool the sniffer of a mutt. It was decision time. Jump up, bolt out of the yard and risk being seen or wait it out to see if the cops would lose patience and head off in a different direction. I chose to hang loose and at least give it a minute to see what developed before I made a mad dash across a nearby highway—the last real barrier between me and the tracks.

It would be a big risk—running across a busy expressway. But it was the only way to permanently lose the officers of both dog and human kind. It would make a great video game, 'Fugitive Frogger'.

In order to break up my silhouette as much as possible I threaded my limbs through and around the branches. "You are an evergreen" was the Zen mantra I used to assist the metamorphism into something boreal. I said the words over and over "evergreen, evergreen, evergreen." My mind warped time and space, changed reference points, curved line of sight, made footprints invisible, and dark silhouettes were harmless. I willed the cops to look through me. It was working. When the cops got to the evergreens, they peered into the branches, shone the light around, and moved on. I had become truly an evergreen. *Keep going.... nothing here but pine needles,* I thought, even allowing a sly grin.

Then the German Sheppard arrived; inhaling, snorting, panting, locating and alerting with a resounding string of yelps. The dog raised their hackles, bared sharp teeth, and challenged me to make a move. I accepted the challenge by bursting from the bushes and catching the dog in mid-leap. While the Sheppard squirmed in my hands, I twisted my head away from his teeth, and then tossed him several yards away. While the mutt gathered its wits, I sprinted across the highway. The dog spun around and started to follow me. The animal was brought up short by the handler, who held the eager animal back by the collar. He did not want his canine partner crossing a thorough-fare filled with speeding cars, as a squish might create another possible video game: 'Dogger Frogger'.

The cops didn't even bother to give chase this time. Be-cause, statistically speaking, making it across a highway with a bad leg, in the dark, while trying to dodge two-ton objects going about 60 mph was a long shot. For the cops, arresting human road-kill was just as good as arresting a live fugitive.

Understandably the police waited to see if I got squashed by a Semi, crushed by a Cadi or flattened by a piece of crap Fiat. My capture after such a drawn out chase would be a righ-teous apprehension for them. It was a very scary crossing, just to put it lightly, but I'm telling about it, so I made it. Running across a highway had another consequence, other than injury. The charge of reckless endangerment was added to the growing list of punishable offences because entering the highway put the officers in peril in order to catch me.

After about a mile I got to an open field, flat, very few trees, which presented me with nowhere to hide except for a long double row of hedges paralleling a chain-link fence that spanned about a hundred meters. The cops had gotten back in pursuit by driving over the bridge that spanned the highway. My lead was again cut to almost nothing, maybe a football field at best. Worst yet, the cops had a clear line-of-sight of me crossing the first fifty yards of a forest preserve. I decided to use their uninterrupted visual tracking to my advantage and give the squad a wrong heading.

Once the cops had a clear view of my new heading, I used a tried-and-true double-back maneuver to put me at an area midway along the fence. A headfirst dive took me deep into bushes, where again I became part of the natural landscape. My hurdle, with the subsequent disappearance, made it seem as if I had gone across the whole field. The entire contingent of cops was faked-out. They ran in the wrong direction, leaving only a couple officers behind to stand guard at each end of the fence so as to defend against the chance of me looping back around if the chase continued. Except for the two guys watching false grids, there was finally nothing between me and the railroad tracks. I had to make it to the tracks. Sooner or later a northbound freight train with an open box car would be approaching and I must be on it, as running was no longer doing the trick and I was quickly losing steam.

I only had to be patient for a few more minutes because eventually the cops would grow tired of searching and give up. Then as if I needed more problems, the bandage had been torn off by the bushes and ripped wide open. It dripped blood like a leaky faucet.

"That's fucking great. I can't afford to lose more fluids." I thought while putting pressure on the gash. Ripping some material from to bottom part of my tank-top, a cloth dressing was created and wrapped around the wound. The act of binding the wound was done in slow motion, imitating the speed and rhythm of the evergreen branches blowing in the summer wind. I was back to envisioning myself as part of the foliage again, mentally imploring the cops to overlook me as just another tree or shrub. When I was certain the officers (on each end of the fence) were otherwise occupied with the act of investigating other disturbances, I began the protracted low-crawl through the brush.

Unfortunately, for my flesh, the plants were covered with triangle-shaped thorns, each about a quarter inch long. I slowed down the crawl, so that the plant stalks wouldn't bend or wobble out of sync with the rest of the arboreal wave. The thorns left cuts and scratches over every inch of my body. It made me think of a line from the movie 'Raiders of the Lost Ark', that reflected my current predicament, except in this case, instead of snakes; the dialog became ... *"thorns, why did it have to be thorns?"*

After about forty minutes of creeping like a snail, combined with the additional pleasure of adding forty bloody grooves on arms and legs, I reached a secure position. The tracks were clearly visible, only a few more snail-crawls away. I rested for only about twenty seconds, in order to tap into energy reserves and catch my breath.

The noise of the rapidly approaching cops was much louder. This told me the rest of the cops were returning to the fence to conduct a more thorough search, no doubt because they figured out that was the only place left where I could be hiding. Ready or not, it was time to go before the entire area was surrounded. I eased off the ground into a sprinter's crouch, waited until it was safe, and then galloped out of the thorns and down the tracks. However, even the best-laid plans can go awry. My journey down the tracks was interrupted after only ten or twelve strides by the cop that was on the east side of the fence. Apparently, he had been watching me, amused, the whole time I crawled through the thorn bushes. Now he stood directly in my path, blocking my escape, drawing his gun. The only way past him would require physical violence.

"It will be easier to retreat and make it another foot race." I decided. I'd already out run the cops a couple of time, and could beat them again. 'Chasing and Eluding' was something I was very good at. However, after only a hundred yards I ran right into a group of ten cops on a trail intersecting the tracks. There was no escape this time.

It seemed like all ten of the cops got hold of one limb or another. They dragged me to the ground and piled on. That is when the beating began with nightsticks, fists, and flashlights. One guy even bent my arm so far up my back that my shoulder was partially dislocated. After about a five-minute pounding, they decided I'd had enough, stood back, placed hands on hips, and surveyed the damage. All the cops reacted that way except for a woman officer standing outside of the heap. Up till now, she had only been cowering, afraid to mix it up. As soon as I was a broken mess, she ran in, embracing the flood of courage, and began kicking me in the ribs, breaking one, and without doubt fucking up a few others. *Kicking me, while I'm already in custody—typical of a woman cop,* I thought between gasps and bloody nose bubbles.

When the pummeling session was over, each cop gave me their personal version of, "Had enough, tough guy asshole?"

Truth be told, I had absolutely had enough, but wasn't going to give them the satisfaction of knowing it. So I did the only thing that made sense it that situation.

"You all hit like girls!" Then to the woman officer, "And you sure as shit kick like a girl."

I expected the punches to start raining down again. It did not happen. To their credit the cops did something else, something that showed a great deal of imagination. They grabbed me by the arms and legs and dragged me face first back through to thorn bushes, leaving a network of scars on my face that resembled a picture the canals of Mars. Of course, later they would not only deny the beating, but also explained the scratches as a result of me crawling through the thorns. *Apparently it was the fastest belly-crawl in history,* I would later think to myself.

Doctor—Doctor

Cuffed and subdued, my ride in the back of the police cruiser to the County Jail was uneventful. It seemed that the cops were as tired as me. Even dogs grow weary of foxes, be them treed or run aground, and the call of 'Tally Ho' ceases to be exciting after a punishing, exhausting hunt. While secured in the backseat, I passed the time, by remaining silent, recovering from the beating, and barfing a not-too-modest amount of blood. The cops acted unusually agitated, nervously fidgeting throughout the ride, making it quite evident that each officer knew that procedural boundaries had been overstepped during the arrest. They were responsible for causing serious injury to my head and body, while giving new meaning to the motto 'Serve and protect'.

Blood was slowly oozing from every one of the 30 or 40 gashes. My kidneys felt ready to burst from the numerous shots to my lower back. Each organ hurt like hell, forcing me to expel a half-pint of red cheer via my esophagus and spray the vehicle interior. The fluids exited my mouth and produced a multi-colored pattern. The bile/blood splotch was so impressive it could have been a drip painting by Jackson Pollock. However, in the absence of the renowned artist, my own elegant drip mosaic would have to do. "Now showing; an exciting new Drip and Retch rendering, courtesy of Billy Halverson – a talent new to the art world, but no stranger to crime." Another flashback kicked in and I imagined myself in a new light. A budding artist having eight arms, like the Hindu God Shiva, four of which made flourishing brushstrokes, three held heroin spikes, loaded hot shots ready to go. The last arm punched the wall over and over, until the fist was jelly. Yeah it was surely a flashback, showing all the signs; heart starts pumping, brain starts jumping. I pushed it away, but unlike all the times before, the flashback refused to comply.

In my mind Shiva changed into a Monkey with eight arms. All eight were doing the same thing ... tearing my prone body apart and ... I pushed harder; the vision fell apart. I cringed "That was a bad one," I said to myself in between bouts of traumatic head- and organ-induced nausea. The stomach churning became almost unbearable. Then the LSD residual effects returned in a way not nearly as distressing, producing contrails, plumes in gold and orange, ribbons of vibrations. Then it was all gone; flashback dissipation syndrome enacted and completed. I was back in the car on the way to jail.

Looking back years later, the entire episode made me to feel somewhat grateful the Taser had not yet been invented because, though I possessed no discenable neck-bolts, who in their right mind wants to be Frankensteined? And what would electricity do to the chemicals embedded in my brain?

Eventually, one of the cops craned his head so that he could to view the fluids spurting from my mouth. He was a heavyset-doughy kind of guy that probably couldn't run down a quadriplegic if his life depended on it. He had all the mannerisms of the classic overcompensating blowhard; a personality which complimented his fat frame and 44-inch waist. An hour ago—in the aftermath of the beating—the fat cop had crouched on the ground while trying to stop his heart from exploding. The portly cop had so much butt-crack showing, he would have made a better plumber than an officer of the law. Shit ... better still ... a security guard at the Hostess plant.

The other officer in the car had the ex-military appearance and was an alright guy, probably a good person to have a beer with—when he was off the clock. From what I can remember; the military-looking officer did not hit me and was the only officer that tried to put a stop to the ten against one stomping.

Fatty sure got in some licks before he collapsed with fatigue. Lucky for him he had a badge or dealing with an exploding heart would have been the least of his concerns. Fat cops and women cops – added to the force as a result of politically correct dipshits.

"Do you want to go to the emergency room?" The thin officer asked. He had a very real look of worry on his face, partly due to a legitimate apprehension regarding my health but in all likelihood more so because of the potential law suit.

They'd all be facing some shit if I decided to press charges for police brutality. It would be an easy case to win, since there was no way to explain to a board of inquiry why the entire group of overzealous cops felt the need to punch, club, and kick me.

I almost responded to the stupid question by saying, "No … let's not go to hospital. I'll just puke vodka-blood Seabreeze cocktails all over the imitation-leather seats, and when I'm done redecorating the interior, your pretty little uniforms will be next."

But common sense prevailed and I reminded myself, "You're already in enough trouble, so what use is there in pissing off the cops even more." So, I went with a decidedly less confrontational and more polite answer.

"What the fuck do you think? I have broken ribs, cracked teeth, and crushed kidneys. Yeah, you two better take me to a doctor unless you just want me to croak in the back of this shit-box." By the time the words came out, I wasn't able to correct the tone and message. Once again, and true to form, confrontation won out over politeness.

What the hell? I thought. *What are they going to do, break more ribs, and maybe collapse a lung or two? Fatboy surely doesn't want to go another round"*

I sat back and rubbed some of the pain from my bones. In my mind, a song from the band UFO supplied the appropriate background music for the uncomfortable ride to the emergency room. I mentally selected music from the first album to flow through my brain and ease the discomfort. The song was appropriately titled 'Doctor Doctor'. It had an interesting melody built around sardonic lyrics rising above a churning bass and drum section. The tune fit the occasion like no other. The song was a standout track due to Michael Schenkers jet-engine finger slides traveling down the strings, skating from one fret to the other.

When we arrived at the emergency room, both cops followed me into the examination room. The entire time they never took their eyes off me, never let me to get more than two steps away, or allowed me anywhere near the exits or elevator doors. Since it had been established that I was a proven Runner, the cops knew one thing for sure. That no matter what the circumstances were, if I was given half a chance there was a strong possibility a brand new chase would ensue.

The doctor came in and took a good look at my face and asked "Did this happen before the arrest or after?"

The Physician's disapproving stare at the cops, combined with the way the stern question was phrased, made it abundantly clear that it was not the first time these cops had to take a suspect to the emergency room. Not being quite sure side which the doctor was really on, I decided not to implicate the arresting officers, at least until the rest of the tests were finished. The Doc gave me an entire physical including X-rays. Throughout the process, he kept insisting I make a complaint against the cops as a matter of record. The Doc's repeated attempts for me to nail the cops made me wonder what bad experience caused the Doc to hate cops so much.

I sorted through the possibilities in my head: *Doc's wife cheating with a traffic cop to get out of a ticket; teenage kids spoiled rotten and getting cited with a D.U.I; or maybe the Doc got a speeding citation while racing in the family's cliché-ridden, silver, electronically-deficient, old-school Jaguar, while on the road to a golf outing.* Really no telling what made him so pissed, but he sure wanted me to stick it to the cops. The doctor was the type I despised; rich, pompous, and arrogant. I felt nothing but contempt for his ilk.

The lead detective watched me very closely while I mulled over the issue of whether or not to make a formal complaint. In the end I decided against it. The beating I got was harsh; however, it was one that had been coming my way for a long while. More importantly, I was not a snitch rat bastard — even against cops.

The Doctor was aghast that I was going to allow the cops to slide on getting stick- time on my ribs and head. He read off my injuries: broken teeth, multiple cracked ribs, cuts and scratches covering my face and torso, and what he called a 'lacerated kidney'. Lacerated sounded like too intense of a description. I assumed the term was used to promote his real agenda, the one not involve healing his current patient. No, he only had one major goal—getting the cops suspended. It seemed like it was an obsession with him. I wanted to say to him "Physician heal thyself." However, I kept it as a private joke. During the entire examination process, I kept repeating the same old tired promises, "This is the last time that drugs and stupid mistakes are going to get you into trouble. How much longer are you going to put your family through this shit? After today, no more drugs and no more Monkeys." The attempt at gray matter reprogramming was very sincere. Too bad the habit had become so strong, that it would take much more than fall-back pledges to defeat the legion of demons that tormented me.

However, just because I needed time to heal and would probably have to go in front of a judge soon did not mean the Monkey had won. I was still alive, and at least for now it didn't take the imagination of another for me to walk among the living. My impingement on the material world, wasn't subject to the hallucinations of a Monkey, he was Nothing.... without my 'Something'. Granted, he was becoming more and more powerful and as I appeared to ebb, he seemed to gather substance. But I was a conscience being, breathing, feeling, knowing, whereas he merely a fleeting apparition. I was the twisted embodiment of Rene Descartes, philosophizing, as he had done 500 years ago, but adjusting his assertion of "Cogito Ergo Sum" Latin for *"I Think Therefore I Am"* into my own version. By using a new technique, less cerebral and more ferocious (known henceforth as the *"Halverson Method")* I sought, and found enlightenment of an alternative sort, which in turn answered the Billy/Monkey paradox, creating my own assertion to the universe; "Cogito Ergo Expositus Stomachus Simianus" Latin for *"I Think Therefore I Expose Stomachs of Monkeys."* Strange that clarity would come to me in such an unexpected place; in a hospital while in cuffs. But it did come and I knew the answer. All I needed to do was stay off drugs and think of the Monkey on my terms; as a feeble chimp ready to be Gutted. Under those conditions killing him would not be difficult; the hard part was kicking drugs. The hospital room faded back in as well as the sound of the Doctor and cops shouting at each other, both of which jarred me out of my reverie.

That Doctor really has it in for the cops. His wife must have got baton-fucked by a rookie patrolman. That has to be it. I thought. What else could it be? The Doc finished treating my injuries and also gave me some painkillers to help with the agony every time I breathed. He said the name of the pills but by then I was dizzy, weak and confused.

The medication in all likelihood was "Percocet". However, what my mind translated the name into "Lobotomy-cet", and then "Coma-cet". It didn't matter much, as all I cared about was that the medicine ended the Pain- o- CET.

The drugs did more than just stop the pain, the prescription made me feel so good I actually considered attempting a "Run-o-cet" again. Then I remembered the cuffs and relaxed. The Doctor left the room with my charts and began talking to a nurse down the hall.

The cops waited until we were alone and then asked "Why didn't you tell the doctor about how you got injured?"

"Well … I figured that since I caused you guys to chase me around for five hours, a few kicks and punches seemed like a fair exchange."

That made the cops smile and it was clear that they no longer considered me an asshole, and quite possibly a good guy falling on hard times and bad circumstances.

"What did you do in the Marines?" He asked while pointing at my tattoo.

"Recon Marine, Team Leader." I responded with some pride.

"I was a Marine myself, Infantry, Weapons Platoon. So you were in Recon, huh? That explains why we had such a hard time apprehending you."

"Yeah, maybe, that's not for me to say. Try and remember at my sentencing that we were both once Marines and I didn't squeal on you guys; nor did I hurt any of you. And no offence, but I could have done some damage of my own if I chose to."

His reply was cut off as the doctor came back into the room. He still seemed very disappointed that I refused to indicate that my injuries were caused after the arrest.

"If he is going to be in jail for an extended stay, the infirmary should be the first stop during processing in order to monitor his vitals. Here is the file. My number is on the cover. Please have the prison physician call me immediately."

There was no argument from the arresting officers in regards to that statement. The Fat cop un-cuffed me from the examination table, put both arms behind my back and placed one hand on the metal restraints and the other hand on my closest shoulder. Back in control, he none too gently guided me out the door and into the hallway.

"Oh, by the way, there better not be additional bruises on him when he gets to jail." The doctor said, before leaving for the adjacent examination room.

Shit...Doc....bet the cops would like to give you a few bruises, I thought.

The hallway was empty. At the far end were double sliding Plexiglas doors. To anyone else, the automatic doors meant "hands-free entry" but to me, the opening promised a fresh opportunity to try and win back my freedom—if I could break free and sprint through the exit. The officer guarding me was so out of shape, outrunning him would be nothing, even with my arms secured in such an awkward position.

Unfortunately, the other officer showed up at the end of the hallway, most likely getting there unseen by using another corridor. That eliminated the last chance to get away leaving me with no other option, except to ready myself to be processed into Lake County Jail. A notably horrible shithouse if there ever was one. "Looks like you're going to be in a few more scraps with jailbird assholes before this night is over." I told myself while steeling my nerves, flipping the switch to fight mode, making ready to attitude-adjust anyone trying to punk me out before finding a way to bond out.

Most of my transgressions had been committed against the dirt of society. There was a slim probability that the authorities would release me on my own recognizant – called an IR bond. To be released on IR bond usually required the crime to be a non-violent first offence, the cutting of a deal, or turning a bigger fish in. Due to the false background information, I was listed me as armed and dangerous, some fast talking accompanied by even faster song and dance would be necessary to get an IR. Because one thing certain, there was no way in hell, I going to provide the cops with names and places.

I Wanna be Sedated

The cops brought me into the jail, through several razor-wired barriers and turned me over to the processing deputies to be booked and printed. A thorough search was conducted before being ushered into the herding horseshoe, complete with scalp inspection, and the famous, dehumanizing, glute-spread, an examination routine quite possibly learned from the butt-cheek probing Roswell Alien Invaders. Or maybe it had been learned from a different otherworldly race that had secret Martian technology. A species more advanced than earthlings in every conceivable way except for, apparently, controlling their flying saucers, which, if the scientifically-challenged morons are to be believed, crash in deserts everywhere.

While enduring the embarrassing search, my concern was probably the same as other jailbirds before me: "Spare me the humiliating, bend over look-see; just give me the lethal injection or the voltage." After the search was completed, they took away my shoes and replaced them with cheap paper slippers. With stylish footwear appropriated I was urged through the next sequence of events including fingerprinting and the immortalization of my profile in a mug-shot.

That makes it official ... I'm a mug," I thought, while wiping the ink off fingers and thumbs.

That completed the welcoming process. Next the guards put me into the jail-house community pigpen which was already jammed with alleged criminals. The room was not much different than a warehouse except it lacked shelves and instead had wooden benches taking up available space—benches specially designed to be as uncomfortable as possible. The large room was secured from the rest of the jail by two massive doors with medieval-looking locks.

No suitable adjectives readily sprung to mind as I inspected the facility; grimy—not quite dirty enough, foul – not aromatically unpleasant enough, melancholy –not sad enough. 'Disgusting' will just have to do until a better word is invented.

Each and every seat was filled with every conceivable kind of miscreant; drunks, dealers, violent offenders, gang bangers, and the lowly sex offenders. The sex offenders were separated as much as possible in the tight quarters from the civilized felonious folk. To mix the molesters in with the real criminals would get them beat to shit. There was after all, even in jail, a hierarchy and a code. The arrestees listed on the call sheet numbered well into the hundreds.

The level of anger, body odor, and testosterone in the enclosure was off the scale. Each criminal fed off the mad energy issued from the deviants closest to him. As each inmate got irritated, he in turn elevated the potential for mayhem by passing his negative vibe on to the next row of arrestees. Every criminal was either looking down at the floor—to avoid making eye contact—or was scanning the room trying to locate a weaker jailbird so as to mad-dog the most scared individuals into submission. I did neither, preferring to ignore the entire collection of misfits. The notion that I was somehow better than them keep me aloft, while knowing deep down, we all came from the same mold. Ninety-five percent were probably arrested from some type of altercation having roots in the drug world.

There was one guy that I struck up a conversation with. A giant Samoan dude with an equally giant fro. The guy was so big, a truck scale would have to be used to get a reading, but it had to be at least 450 lbs. He had a long frizzy beard, a full afro, and was also a pit fighter.

It wasn't my way to be chatty, but if you have to make friends in a room full of fuck-heads … might as well be with the 450lb maniac covered in tribal ink and sporting an intimidating black-panther fro. He said his name was Tupu, which was Samoan for "King." After hearing the translation, I thought about how it was interesting that nobody ever said their name meant peasant, worker-drone, or shithead. It was always King, Emperor, or Prince. He was in for D.U.I; blowing FOUR TIMES the legal limit.

"That's fucked. You're four times as big as anyone I know. Doesn't seem fair!" I told him. We spoke for a short time about Samoa. However, after an hour, he got bailed out by his girlfriend, leaving me alone to contemplate the human zoo.

The oppressive atmosphere made everyone overly alert and watchful for any wrong looks or offensive comments which could be taken for an insult. Fighting was both business and hobby for me, so outside of the possibility of getting more time, the idea of potential violence didn't bother me at all, What bothered me was that there was no way of knowing if and when there would be an offer to bond out. Feeling the waves of panic hanging over open pools of Neanderthal hostility caused me to mentally travel back to a place inside my brain where a slice of music was always cued up, making the worst of times bearable. I thought of The Ramones and their song "I Wanna Be Sedated" because at that moment there was nothing I needed more than a Valium or a couple tabs of Amytripileen.

It would be foolish to think that there was any possibility of finding a few downers. Anyone who had managed to get something in the jail was holding for themselves. However, there was some relief to be had if you claimed to be the right kind of addict. A jailhouse physician announced that anyone with a heroin habit could form a line and receive a tiny cup of Methadone to prevent withdrawal agitation and queasiness.

Perfect for me, a good way to past the time, as the syrup was virtually entertainment in a Dixie cup ... much needed sedation. I moved quickly to the front of the line to get my allowance of "synthetic junk". Once the dose was placed into my hands, I tossed the reddish liquid down and got back in line for another shot, figuring that if my stay it this shithole becomes longer than expected I might as well load up on the narcotics. However, this was not the guards' first freak show and they instantly removed me from the jailhouse concession stand. After a few hours a guard called out my name. I raised my hand and he waved me over, taking me into a smaller room adjacent to the processing station.

One of the cops and two detectives were already in the room. The lead detective, obviously in charge, told me to take a seat. Then the threats began.

"If you don't give up some names we are going to hit you with a cocaine charge of "Dealing with Intent to Deliver". That will get you five years." The detective said.

"How do you figure? The only thing you got off me was a quarter of a gram. That amount is legally a "personal use" offence. Come on, any asshole you arrest this weekend will have four times that much in their pocket."

"No you must be mistaken! We got you for sixteen grams." He responded.

"That is a fucking lie and you all know it."

"Yeah, well, who gives a shit what really happened? If we say we caught you with over a half an ounce, then guess what, asshole...we did. Who is going to believe a piece of shit like you anyway?"

"A jury might believe me." I answered.

"Not after we tell them about how you resisted arrest and even hit a couple cops. Yeah ... there's another charge we can add on. How does that sound so far, smart guy?"

"Sure ... I beat up on you guys. That's why I'm the one with all the injuries. My mug shot and the emergency room doctor might tell a different story."

"Okay, genius. You bring in the doctor to verify your account of the arrest, and we'll bring in ten or twenty cops that will tell refute everything that could get you off. You're not going anywhere unless we say so. So do yourself a favor. Give us some solid information, and you'll be out of here today.

"I don't know anything. The only information I have is ... your toupee isn't fooling anybody. Looks like you ripped a patch of hair off your ass and glued it to your head."

He raised his hand to deliver a well-deserved backhand. The blow never landed; the other cop grabbed his arm while whispering, "Calm down."

"We know the truck you were driving is owned by a known dealer. All you got to do is set him up for us and you're out of here."

"First you guys beat the shit out of me, lie about the arrest, now you're asking me to turn in my friend. You have to be fucking kidding me."

"It's your choice; five years for sales and intent to deliver, or help us build a case against somebody else. We got a whole room of assholes in the pig pen just waiting to cut a deal. Might as well be you. Think it over; well be back in a couple minutes." They exited the interview room, the angry one still smarting from the toupee comment.

I knew damn well that turning a dime on my friend was out of the question. But I also knew that I did not want to have to fight false charges, maybe lose, ending up with a five year stint. *What a load of crap. I'm in here for being a lowlife, while the cops are free to frame me with a bunch of lies; just to get credit for an impressive arrest. Fuck, who are the real low-lifes?* I thought silently, while mulling over the options. Finally, I knew that the only thing left to do was 'play along'. With the decision made, there was nothing to do, but wait for the cops to return.

After about five minutes both cops returned. The cop that had the bad rug looked as if he tried to comb the hairpiece, pat it down and straightened it out. But the toupee still looked like it came off his ass. I thought about telling him so but figured I'd wait to see if a deal could be cut. I went into the act.

"Alright, alright, you win. But how do you expect me to help you guys out while I'm stuck in here? I said sheepishly to the lead detective, while doing my best to make it appear that I had given in and was the type of scumbag that would rat out a good friend to get back on the streets.

"Don't worry about that. We'll IR you out today, then all you got to do is make a few buys for us and all your charges will disappear. Except for the assault; you're still going to have to go in front of a judge for the shit that happened at McDonalds."

"Let me get this straight. I score some coke from my friend and give it to you. Then the fake charges along with the fake cocaine will magically disappear. Anyone see the irony here?"

"Jokes aren't going to get you released. Yes or no!"

"Okay. But all the phony drug shit better disappear from my record. I'd like to speak with the D.A and a public defender to make sure you guys don't go back on your word. After all, you can't really expect me to trust a bunch of magicians that are able to make coke appear and disappear anytime they want."

"The D.A will sign off on whatever we do. You want a defense lawyer? That's just fine, but then the deal is off. You'll just have to trust us."

"Yeah, trust you. That's really working out for me so far." I said wanting one more jab at the honesty before cutting the deal. "Okay I'll do it, but I'll need a few days to make some small moves, little buys that won't look suspicious before the big buy." I said agreeably, while mentally mapping out my escape to go out West. It was a journey that would begin the moment the gate opened up to let me out, and without turning snitch.

There was some paperwork and logistical stuff needing to be filed and signed before I would be allowed out of the facilities. By the time my interview was over, most of the other offenders had already been sorted out, either to go home after a bond hearing or to their new home – Marion State Prison. There was nothing to do but wait. I selected a corner bench that was empty of others and listened for my name to be called. The bench was empty, but I was not alone. Within minutes The Monkey materialized, assuming a seat only a few feet away. This time his attire, aside from the usual Monkey stink and Monkey hate, was that of a 1950's chain-gang captive. He had the black and white striped shirt, matching dungarees, leg restraints attached to an iron ball (always thought that was ball and chain was bullshit), and a squared-off work cap.

"Hey, look at me. Save yourself and snitch out your friends. You're way too smart to end up behind bars," he said, emphasizing his command with a dramatic chain rattle, as if he was a primate version of some poor convict, tarring hot pavement, much like Paul Newman in "Cool Hand Luke". Thinking of the movie sent my brain into a cinematic memory syndrome, and from the furthest regions of my mind, a lost mushroom spark ignited, ibotenic acid was decaboxyiated, and introduced to eager serotoneric receptors. Other chemical shit was certainly happening in my brain, but those chemical processes were beyond my capacity of understanding. A mushroom zip/zoom was not the same as a synthetic acid flashback, as residual mushroom trips were less worrisome, more colorful, and rarely became terrifyingly dark. The zip/zoom began …

The Monkey, dressed as a convict, was tied to other monkeys, secured together by a length of chain feed through leg irons. The Walking Boss was none other than yours truly. I had the badge, the Hollywood version of a chain-gang guard uniform, and best of all: mirrored sunglasses. Adhering to the movie theme, I used a cane to walk, and carried a double barrel shotgun in my free hand.

Even in the hallucination, the hot and humid temperature could be felt, and it was hot and humid. The Monkey wiped his brow with his prison cap and looked up at me.

"Take it off, boss?" He asked, while unbuttoning his striped shirt.

I assumed the position of authority by placing my boot on the bumper of the nearest transport truck. The spit some chaw. "Yeah...monkey–boy, take it off."

The Monkey convict indicated the water barrel. *"Get some water, Boss?"*

"Yeah...Monkey-Boy, get you some water." I said to him using a southern drawl.

The Monkey-convict hopped over to the barrel, grabbed the dipper, and scooped up a potion of water. *"Swallow the water, Boss?* He asked. I nodded. As the Monkey-convict brought the cool liquid to parched lips, I raised both barrels of the shotgun and pulled the triggers. The Monkey-convict's head blew apart, filling the air with a cloud of blood and brain bits. I surveyed the rest of the Monkey prisoners. "He didn't say 'please'." Then without any additional gunfire, the entire line of Monkey prisoners, screamed, each individual simian head exploded one by one, like red balloons poked with pins. Then it was over. The mushroom zip/zoom ended, and I was back in my own world of confinement, Lake County Jail, with my imaginary friend.

"Wake up you idiot, what ... dreaming about killing me again? Did you hear what I said ...rat out your friend and get the fuck out of here. You're too smart to take the rap for something like this." The Monkey insisted.

I shook away the mushroom dream. He was only trying to play into my ego, so I had none of it. "If I'm so smart, how come I'm sitting in jail talking to an asshole like you? It is your fucking fault I'm here in the first place. I should have killed you, back in Africa." I said aggressively.

"Sure, blame The Monkey. Isn't that always the way. Listen dickhead you had plenty of opportunities to kick your habit, so don't lay your crap on me." The Monkey said while reaching behind his back.

Please God ... don't let him throw feces again. I prayed. Then out loud said, "Just leave me alone for once, will ya?"

"I'm only here to help. For the last time; rat out a few guys and they'll drop all charges. What do you need, a marching band to wake you up? Eventually all your dealer friends will go to prison anyway."

"Not by my doing." I said this firmly enough that The Monkey was already beginning to fade away. But not before one last degrading insult. *"That's fine, Billy. Have fun dropping soap and getting corn-holed."* The Monkey said and disappeared.

Fuck you! You're the prison bitch." I yelled but he was already gone, which left me once again considering the merits of screaming obscenities at a Monkey only I could see.

Jumping bond would mean no statute of limitations on the charges and they would follow me around for the rest of my life. However, given a choice, I'll take those consequences over rolling over and playing rat any day of the week.

And so I was released under the very specific premise of becoming the cops' own personal Narc. For refusing to cooperate, the future for me promised harsh winds, but wearing a snitch jacket to ward of the karma's chill was never going to happen. Within a couple days, I left the state and began a decades of living and working under assumed names, spending much of the time in Canada.

What lay before me was a life on the run, full of regret, aware of my failings, ashamed for what drugs had warped me into, unafraid but alone. Bad things and worse days were close at hand. However, as bad as my situation was, I was not a rat ... definitely not a rat.

On the Road Again

The recent turn of events accomplished what common sense had failed to do. It finally dawned on me that there was only one acceptable method to get off drugs; leave my dubious existence behind and plot a new course to places unknown and hardships well earned. That was the plan; take to the open road, travel as long as it takes, and never stop until new me was discovered somewhere off the map. My desire to evolve into a better man was not unlike a Christian wanting to be reborn. The difference was my change did not require an anti-science worldview that cast aside knowledge and logic, in favor of fundamentalist ignorance that was retrieved out of embellished folklore but accepted purely as fact. Redemption would be a very disappointing end result if becoming a kook was part of the process.

I served no master or God (unless you count my communion with drugs), and held no faith in religion. Over the years, I grew weary of Nihilism and went back to embracing Existentialism, anchoring it with a twinge of the Humanist ideology. I hoped this transformation was my last, as I had become a Man of the objective world, standing firmly against claims of irrational nonsense, and thereby insisting on empirical evidence for extraordinary boasts. The paradox was that I had no problem accepting The Monkey, mind-reading mutant fish, wood-grain caterpillars, LSD Demons, Horms, and talking Robert Smith Posters when under the influence.

Maybe I was no better than all the fundamentalist dolts that obtained solace in Christian stories that were merely variations of Sumerian and Greece mythology. But at least the drug I worship hasn't ever told me to smite entire cities, stone woman to death, burn witches or kill abortion doctors.

Yeah ... the gospel of cocaine was bad, but nothing compared to the Old Testament. In that book; God tells Abraham to kill his son Isaac, just to test his obedience. Hard to believe—a father is ordered to kill his son by a spoiled, sociopathic God. There's a nice bedtime story for the kiddies. No fucking thanks. I'll solve my drug problem without the help of such an unmerciful, bipolar God.

As my journey to find a new life begins, I will daringly look back on my Sodom of Sins, Gomorra of Greed, but I'll keep on stepping as a Man, not as a Pillar of Salt. That whole Pillar of Salt Story only makes sense if the Virgin Mary was a bag of popcorn. Then again, my refusal to embrace a higher power, long dead in me since Africa, might have been another symptom of my defeat. Anything was possible, but for me illumination existed somewhere down the road.

I hoped when the traveling and self-imposed solitude was done, a new and improved version of my previous incarnation would be born. Regardless of the Monkey's influence, my personal gratification meter was changing, reverting back to the original scale of innocence, a system everyone is blessed with at birth but eventually loses it with age. This manner of counting recognized only virtuous deeds, not the amount of people scared of you. By ignoring ownership of material possessions, nightly female conquests, and other fleeting spoils, a newly defined "Monkey Absent Abacus" was created, and only moved beads to tally good intentions and better acts.

Outrunning myself was going to be the easy part, outrunning the Monkey was going to be a whole different can of "Horms." He always found a way to stay close on my heels, probably by using the same vibrating frequency that all the other jerks used to find me. So I was prepared for a lengthy journey covering unchartered territory.

Throughout the journey, a numbers of cheap vehicles were purchased, ridden hard, then abandoned in favor of another model that did not leak oil, had brakes that worked and tires with tread. The order of cars started with a Chevy Cavalier, switched to a Nissan Pathfinder, then a Honda CRV, next an old Eldorado, and lastly a Buick LeSaber. Whenever possible I played Willie Nelson's song "On the Road Again". I did so for two reasons. The first reason was to inject some good old fashioned country music into my heathen lifestyle, and the second was because Willie was the original Pot Smoking Outlaw, and therefore deserved of some respect. Sometimes even city boys have to pay homage to Honky Tonk Heroes.

In the words of Pete Townsend of The Who, "Going Mobile" had to be done with the barest of necessities, like a rite of manhood as a young warrior cast into the wilderness, experienced alone. The overall idea, called for me to stay far from my gaggle of friends and eventually settle in a variety of remote rural areas (where the availability of drugs and other vices were at a minimum). In the beginning, the mission was simple, assume a new identity, and seek out a job that would help me find peace. No bars, no clubs, no gyms.

That mission would have to suffice until, over time, I had cleaned up enough to give the fucking Monkey a taste of his own medieval medicine; laden with arsenic and mercury. In the meantime, avoidance was best, as he could kick my ass, winning the battle hands (complete with opposable thumbs) down. I would need to in the greatest shape—mentally and physically—to defeat such a crafty and worthy adversary.

"Better men than you have already been destroyed." He said on previous visits and on numerous unexpected meetings. He usually followed up with, *"I've had lots of practice in breaking men. What do you bring into the arena except for arrogance and the ability to hurt everyone that cares about you?"* It was his way of never ending reiteration to reprogram me from "Good Samaritan" to "Good God, What Have I Become"?

It must seem weak to have been continually outsmarted by an imaginary Monkey. But what clever response could I give; that would melt away the fact that he spoke the truth.

To say something like, "You're wrong Monkey," would be a lie ... he knew it, and I knew it. So, I fell back on childish playground insults, relying on verbal barbs that almost always had something to do with gonad scratching, feces throwing, banana stealing, parasite eating, and the ever popular "Chimpanzee Lab Experiment" chortle.

He was a tough bastard and gutting him was taking much longer than expected. But I would not make the same mistake that others (broken by Monkeys) had done. Their destruction was the result of entering into a fight without being in peak form. The Monkey was always in prime condition, I would

bide my time, waiting years if necessary; hiding, healing, issuing the challenge only when there was a good chance of being the victor. In my non-intoxicated visions, the final confrontation was to take place in the Mohave Desert.

Early on, interspersed amid various adventures, the warnings, more so advice, came from an old prospector, appearing
on the ridgeline of the nearest hill. His silhouette was fleeting,
holding no specific cardboard cut-out form, although, it was
funny that along with the tools I recognized against the dawn
backdrop; pick shovel, sledge, he also carried a fly-fishing rod.
His demands that I conquer The Monkey were not the only
thing he foretold. Occasionally he pointed hard-used fingers,
indication spots where fossils lay under several feet of earth.
His predictions of credible finds had a success ratio of 100%, a
divining accuracy usually reserved for ghosts, oracles or dead
ancestors. After each visit, upon on his departure over the
ridgeline, he left me with the same words, "Hurry with what
must be done, you're family is losing faith in you. Your father
does not have long … fulfill the promise while he still lives."
There was something very different about this apparition; fami-
liarity yes, but more than simple memory tricks, He was more
than just a flashback, he was indeed a real punch-me-if-I'm-
lying-Ghost.

I didn't know why he came. However, his weekly visions
of towering inspiration were never wrong. "Could it be God
talking?" I asked during the visions, the only answer was
"You'll find out in the desert."

And so, I ran away. Or to use a less wimpy rationalization,
"I hit the dusty trail". While on the road I took on a variety of
occupations, often living in flop houses, cheap flea-bag hotels,
abandon warehouses, and when things really got bad ... under
bridges. The dingy haunts were so numerous, many merge into
one smelly, roach-ridden shithole. Abodes of peeling paint,
stained carpets, rusty tap water, with sleeping accommodations
containing horrible beds with spotted sheets and blankets—
linen coverings better left unturned. Destinations came and
went and in the filth my resolve was fortified.

The jobs were in some respects as unusual as the locations. I let fate take me where it may, traveling as a tumble
weed, rolling the dice, no real plan in mind, except for staying

one step ahead of The Monkey, and as far away as possible from old acquaintances.

I took on an assortment of strange jobs in exchange of living quarters and meager pay. Many jobs were colorfully weird, and as bizarre as the people I worked for. Throughout this arduous, mind-numbing, humbling experience, solace was found in the knowledge that The Great Spirit was shattering me so as to rebuild me into something worthy of my family's loyalty. Not an empty vessel, just empty.

I milked cows in Janesville, Wisconsin at 3-4 in the morning, at a farm where there was a sneaking suspicion the husband and wife couple that owned the spread were cannibalistic serial killers. After all Wisconsin is the "Serial Killer State," much as Missouri is the "Show me State."

Did this feeling of dread come from an overactive imagination? Or had it been manufactured by viewing too many Ed Gein and Daumer news reports?

To kill (maybe a bad choice or words) time, while completing the unpleasant task of yanking on pinkish utters, or as my brother Sven would say "Jerking off cows," I would think about Ed Gein. Now there was a kook!

Ed was the real life model for Hannibal Lecter, hailing from Plainsville Wisconsin; Gein was a craftsman of "Mengela" proportions, a maker of lampshades and furniture out of human skin. All these thoughts probably influenced my opinion about the farmers. However, the unease came mostly from watching the owners return late at night, immediately digging in the fields while whispering (chanting maybe?) and twitching nervously.

It was the familiar warning vibe we all have felt and never completely understood. It was never wrong in sousing out cretins concealed in citizen form. Whenever the farmers and I got too close, my mind screamed, *Move away! Don't make direct eye contact or it will cause the fiends to become angry.*

It's not that I was afraid of a fair fight with Ma and Pa Pumpkinseed (hell ... they were both senior citizens), but getting a pair of garden sheers in the lungs while sleeping, gave me justifiable pause.

My stay on the farm was not totally absent of levity. After a few months, boredom set in and caution stopped being such a priority. On my way to the milking shed, the farmer passed me on his morning walk to the chicken pen. He moved in an easily recognizable; shuffling-sly gait, insect style; the mode of walking used by old guys having bad knees and a big black secret. Taking care of the poultry was his responsibility, which involved tossing grain to birds, lifting hens to check for eggs, and separating overly aggressive roosters, and quite possibly—praying to Satan.

The last chore—regarding devil worship—was solely of my own speculation while amusing myself by wondering what else he did behind the shed in the locked shack with boarded up windows. The shack was truly a foreboding structure. It was painted brown, had no trespassing signs posted every few feet, and was surrounded by a barbed-wire fence.

"Why?" I asked myself while examining the shacks security. "Exactly!" was the answer.

As I got closer to leaving the farm for "better pastures", there was no resisting the impulse to try and get a reaction from the farmer as our paths crossed each morning.

He gave the usual greeting of, "Mornin', Billy".

I replied with my own greeting designed to get a response. "Morning, Joe ... bury anyone in the garden lately or was that just the roosters screaming?"

The disturbing part of these brief encounters was that Farmer Joe only smiled back, blue eyes sunken into a sea of wrinkles, sparkling with mischief. It was a smile that said, "You're next, if you don't shut your yap." The sensation also told me to get the "fuck out of Wisconsin" before becoming another statistic on the Serial Killer Tourist Information Brochure.

After hastily departing Janesville, the list of trades learned and acquired went on and on.

While navigating the U.S, I went on the assume the roles of: Martial Arts Instructor in Springfield Illinois, Carpenter's Apprentice in Trinidad Colorado, Home Demolisher in Mesa Arizona, Car Salesman in Schaumburg, Screenwriter in Santa Monica, Fishing guide in Canada, Jack of all Trades everywhere and anywhere. The Home Demolisher gig was the least enjoyable of the jobs, as the places we tore down were invariably filled with insects, rats and smelled of piss; likely from the vagrants that slept there. If that wasn't bad enough; the Owner had turrets' syndrome, unable to get through an entire hour without emitting involuntary string of beeps, whistles, and squeals. I quit after several months because the high-pitched noises became unbearable. Everyone on the job worked on the edge, constantly jumpy, as each of us tensely awaiting the next eruption of startling outburst. Earplugs were a non-starter as that would make it impossible to hear instructions or warnings. The Owner was decent guy and it wasn't his fault to be born with the malady, but my eardrums came first.

Whatever the occupation, I strived to adhere to "The Way" of Lao Tzu, avoiding trouble, lying low, one eye open to watch for signs of The Monkey. I kept busy, occupied with the trivial, and thereby morphed into a fluid being, an individual without substance. Living as a gypsy was the only way to stay far away from old friends and prevent making new ones. There were many seasons when the situation or city had become comfortable, making it hard to change locations. When this happened things got dangerous fast. During those worn-out occasions it helped me to remember that it was hard to hit a moving target, harder still to hit an invisible one. Years passed and reformation was not as forthcoming as expected.

Even in the middle of nowhere, at the edge of civilization, sooner or later somebody with drugs would sense my addiction, prey on my weakness; the temptation was difficult to resist.

I would do a little coke, a little became a lot, and crushing disappointment and shame would follow, forcing me to jump in my car and escape. It was a sad dilemma, that driving to another unknown town, alone, in the dark, again was the only safe way to start over.

Square patches of farm ground, industrial parks, forest preserves, and slums all passed in my rearview mirror. The farms had scarecrows, industrial parks had smoke stacks, forest preserves had knurled trees, and slums had winos. I took great care while driving to never look too close at the landscape, especially while weakened, and under the influence of booze or chemicals. I made such a mistake early on in my travels, and the hallucinations made the organic and inorganic twisted into crazy shapes, natural and unnatural congealed, beauty faded, stars spread out leaving behind night skies, then magically on the horizon, a door would fling open, and out would step The Monkey. Hot on my trail again. Assuming various disguises and drifting is the only way to stay ahead of him. Often times, places and circumstances became compromised, and were not able to protect me from The Monkey, stave off dubious acquaintances, provide anonymity, or assist me in adhering to The Way of Lao Tzu. When that happened, I immediately pulled up stakes and returned to the one thing that gave me peace, fossil hunting, in extremely remote areas. During failures of uprightness, safety was always attained by traveling back to inaccessible settings, places only represented as flagged pins on my pale and tattered maps. Further and farther from civilization I journeyed, relying on the lack of irritating people to healing to my mind, and the lack of familiar physic reference points to take me deep into the void. At least by sticking far from cities, it was easy to avoid other criminal elements. In the wilderness, the closest thing to a felon was a Turkey Vulture, and he only wanted to pick your bones, so best to stay alive, or take him with you at last gasp.

Eight Miles High

The last few years of travels generated many questionable encounters. My subconscious was partly to blame, unintentionally sending out random signals across a secret and mysterious mental telegraph, thereby clicking out a message to other nomads that when translated said: "adrenaline, action, drug addict seeks danger." I'd had enough of "Wandering Junkies", "Cow Milking Suspected Killers" and "Slide-Whistle Sounding Superintendents". So I headed back to the secluded deserts, to attain the isolation necessary for self reflection.

There were some things that only the hot sands, black volcanic rocks and shale cliffs could provide. The following months, as "Geologist" took me to digs throughout Utah, northern Arizona, The Lower Rio Grande Valley, The Mohave Desert, and the mountains of west Texas. Acting as a Geologist had many rewards; it was something my brothers occasionally did with me, allowed me to meld with nature, practice oneness with other living creatures, and best of all, rock -hounding kept me far from bad influences, but still within range to incur the occasional sting of angry tarantula wasps, and keep the penance wheel turning. The vast emptiness of the wastelands were the best place to honestly evaluate one's worth.

As Tim and James used to say "there is nothing like looking into the eyes of a million year old arthropod, locked forever in shale, to realize how insignificant we all are."

Sven, Emil, and Mike, usually all had almost the same response for Tim and James. "For you guys, looking into a mirror, will tell you everything there is to know about insignificance." The only variation to the theme was when Mike would ask his usual question "where are all the chicks?"

Whatever the discussion; be it science or chicks, sooner or later (after everyone was thirsty from the digging), one of the brothers would ask the question that all were thinking, "Who has the Grog bottle, how about sharing?"

However, on these last few excursions I was on my own, "lone wolfing it", so to speak.. Legal troubles, compounded by my mental troubles, made functioning—within respectable society, an exhausting chore. The money (from finding and restoring gemstone and fossils) wasn't great, but it put gas in the tank and beef jerky in my belly. Some of the finds were exceptional. I pried a dinosaur footprint out of a hardened mud-hole near St George, cracked open some ammonites outside the Grand Canyon, dove deep into the waters of Lake Texoma for urchins and cone shells, cut out several Trilobite specimens from the hills at Antelope Springs, and chiseled Jade from an abandoned mine outside of Cadiz—which was nothing more than a ghost-town

Because I backpacked without companionship every remote location held the possibility of being waylaid, but the closer you got to the Mexican border, the chance of getting robbed increased dramatically. As I was a fugitive, and carrying a firearm meant certain trouble, a five-cartridge flare-gun was all I brought for protection. Statically speaking, the likelihood of having to fire a cartridge at some asshole was fairly good, due to the inaccessibility of the backcountry hikes. My worst experience with Desert Rats (The human kind) was while digging at a site near the Mexican border, a territory well known for the huge population of Coyotes (the animal and human kind).

The location at the border was to be my final geology excursion. I was tired, needed a break from the fossil digging and was ready go back to Chicago, in order to spend some time with my family. Although the fossil and mineral collecting went well, the spiritual revelation I'd been expecting, never came to fruition.

My car was nearly empty of gas. However, the last mountain was way up north, near the Apache Mountains, and would take about a day to get there. I drove to the nearest little town (trading post would have been a better name) to fill up. I was placing the nozzle back into the plastic holder when a migrant worker approached and offered to sell some peyote buttons.

He had a face that was difficult to forget and painful to remember. All of his exposed flesh was badly burned, melted, possibly the result one of the all-too-common chemical fires at a refinery, or perhaps from a drilling platform. It was a good guess; after all, we were in the vicinity of the petroleum capital of America—southwest Texas. His facial skin had the same consistency of my self-administered cauterization burns, except much more horrible. He told me the quality of the Peyote was unsurpassed, filled with (in his words) "mucho macho mescaline".

The claim sounded like an idle boast. However he went on, in broken English, to prove his point. I was unable to translate everything that he said. But it was evidently clear by his gestures and the few words I was able to understand, what he was trying to tell me—"the plants were harvested from the Chihuahua Desert."

He didn't need to say anymore. I already knew the area he spoke of was a peyote utopia, partially from reading on the subject, and partially from hearing firsthand the stories of experimentation recounted by friends, bizarre tales concerning psychotropic drugs . All Shroomers and Button-Chewers exhorted the spirit-supremacy of the Chihuahua buttons. I foolishly thought that my bargain with Scarface (that is what I secretly called the burned Mexican, but immediately regretted it, as I was certainly no matinee idol) of trading money for peyote was not a violation of the 'No Drugs for Billy' policy.

My belief (or was it wishful thinking) was founded in the knowledge that peyote buttons were highly recommended by those wiser than I. Throughout history, peyote was swallowed by holy seers of all faiths so it was an easy leap of faith to expect button usage would help with the surreal aspect to the writings.

It was promised by sages (of all ages), regardless of their mystic denominations, digesting the buttons would bring forth enlightenment, self-discovery, and transcendence.

I paid the Mexican ten times the price of his wares. The generous payment resulted from the sympathy I felt for the peyote-selling Hombre, and for unkindly naming him Scarface. He probably needed the cash more than me (if such a thing was possible) anyway. Before we went our separate ways, I gave him a box filled with food, thereby keeping only a couple cans of Dinty Moore Stew for later. Supplies weren't a big priority for the next lag of the trip, except for water, and I had plenty of that. Once I shifted into full peyote consumption, hunger would be as forgotten as gravity, tine, distance, and all the other physical restraints. Very soon I would take to the air in wingless flight.

I spent the rest of the day driving north, covering hundreds of miles before arriving at the new collection area located near the Texas/New Mexico border.

I parked my car in a secluded gully, covering it with foliage so that no ranch-hands riding the property could spot my campsite from the herd trails. In a place of geographical, philosophical, and governmental borders, only one thought occurred to me. *I, too, stand at the Crossroads. I am the novelist version of the great Bluesman, Robert Johnson.* Thinking of the Faustian legend, which involved trading talent for damnation, I wondered if Mephistopheles himself would appear out of thin air and offer up a publishing deal for my soul.

My soul is probably worth less than my scribbles. I laughed, while daring the Devil—Ol' Lodger to show his horrid features.

"Fuck it, no Monkeys or Devils, will be found in this "no man's land. I am officially detached from all worldly things"

I chewed the dried buttons, until the plant was nothing but a bitter tasting paste, and then swallowed the mess. Once the peyote hit my digestive tract, the urge to gag was almost impossible to control. There was a slight change in the way my boots sunk into the loose earth as if the ground, under each step, splashed as if in liquid, sending out sand ripples, little undulations that spread out into larger and larger circles. Fluid earth was a signal from my brain that the mescaline was kicking in. So, while mildly floating and enjoying the breeze, I began to scour the area for new or well-defined specimens.

The local Indians had a saying; 'if a man's heart was pure, there wouldn't be any bitterness'. My peyote had the flavor of red ants, which probably said something as to the purity of my heart. In about an hour, the rest of the mescaline took over my sensory system and the surge of chemicals initiated stomach cramps which were so powerful the attacks racked my entire torso. When those subsided, new tremors tensed up my face, and neck regions. It felt as if invisible fingers were pulling on my facial muscles.

A feeling of queasiness became so intense it over-whelmed the desire to explore any further, so I returned to an old cattle road and then took a dry river bed to where my car was parked. I opened the driver's side door and placed the appropriate cassette in the Sony audio deck. "Eight Miles High", by The Byrds began to play.

My legs were like rubber stilts, very unsteady, unable to keep me upright. I found a suitably flat rock, plopped down, and listened to the Woodstock era lyrics, interspersed with Roger Mcquinn's hypnotic jangly guitar.

"Eight miles high – and when you touch down – you'll find that it's – stranger than known."

I flew no higher than eight miles. The way I saw it there was no reason to offend The Byrds, by achieving greater altitude than they dared to climb (but I sure the fuck could have gone higher, stratosphere for me, boys). Touching back down on earth was easy, no landing gear to deploy, just thinking about the ground took me lower, eventually settling down back on the rock. There was none of that Transcendental Meditation or flying lotus position nonsense for me. As I was a Taoist and already one with the earth, water and sky, traveling though other dimensions was no problem. Best of all, my flights did not require a robe-wearing Maharishi with their ZZ Top style beards to be present so as to hand out flowers and chant tantric nonsence.

Happy to be sitting on the rock and once again a terrestrial, I watched for the Spirit Party. Then, right on cue—without fanfare—the curtain rose and revealed the Auras and halos. Swirls of color, rushed in the greet me. Distances and heights became irrelevant, as if peyote created a whole new type of geometry that was spacially absurd. The landscape, including trees, mountains, boulders, and riverbeds flowed towards me and stopped only a few meters from where I sat. The landscape features stayed only a short spell, and then shot back to the horizon line—which was as wavy as an ocean tide. Rocks and boulders ballooned to immense size and then deflated to the size of molecules. The peyote had blessed me with microscope eyes, no better even, electron microscope eyes.

Tiny glowing particles zipped pass my face, trekking upwards, gaining altitude, then converging to form a new

Dwarf Star, which I named Emil, after my father. Finally the balloons, boulders, stars and glowing particles disappeared. The lack of animated scenery was disappointing, so I chewed another handful of buttons and forced my mind to proceed without delay to the next colorful display.

In the absence of atomic particles the red night sky shifted and my human vision became even more powerful. The peyote was turning me into an ocular titan. The shift in hallucinations caused me to believe that I had large compound dragonfly eyes. While seeing as an insect, polarized ultra violet light, filtered into my brain. It was glaring, bright, silver.

Then my vision became that of an Arachnid, my two human eyes multiplied into to a spider's cluster of eight black tiny dots. I saw the desert at ground level, using an altered perception, tiny cacti became spiny mountains, small beetles were as big as Jeeps, and the bats overhead sounded like B-52's with a wing structure of riveted skin flaps.

Then I magically rose and was granted the vision of a red-tailed hawk. While possessing avian sight— many, many times that of my normal senses—I examined the terrain from a sideways horizon line, instantly viewing all angles, all earthly features, and missing not even the smallest detail. In mere seconds, using hawk eyes, I charted and mapped the entire region, vowing to remember the topography for later hikes.

It passed way too quickly and soon the mescaline gift of animal vision ended and was replaced by another chemical mirage.

A new image took shape. Impossible at it might seem, the Prophet—Carlos Castaneda appeared to me from out of nowhere. He spoke to me.

"I am willing to share all the wisdom granted to me by a Yaqui Indian Shaman. I will teach of long lost sorcery and aid in your quest for serenity. All I ask is for three peyote buttons, and one can of Dinty Moore Stew."

I refused to give anything to Carlos, for he was nothing but a mirage made of chemicals acting on my brain. No legitimate shaman would ask for my last cans of Dinty Moore. Such a request would was blasphemy.

"Never ask for another man's last rations." I said to Carlos.

Having a vision of Carlos Castaneda was very weird. His teachings were purely a money con, and presented by a lunatic, obsessed with fame. But, imaging a prophet (good or bad) showed the mescaline was beginning to warp my senses, so even crazier hallucinations were in store.

The dream of Carlos disappeared. The Cholla and Soaptree Yuccas formed and reformed, sometimes remaining simple flora, sometimes shifting into a carefully choreographed dance troupe. There was a tall, spiked, slender tree that preformed a hula. The unknown tree fanned each branch back and forth, while speaking by using subtle flips of narrow leaves—just as Hawaiian girls did with their hands. Whereas, the island dancers waved their arms to say "welcome", the desert tree dancers asked, "How's it going, Billy?

Truth be told; I had anticipated that the visions would have much more meaning. The mescaline was losing strength so I prayed to the gods for one last chemical barb. In no time at all, the sun was gone and only the night sky was above me. I longed to join the "dance of the trees", and mingle under the stars, but the darkness made me uncertain of the terrain, and (even while high) breaking an ankle was never fun. I waited all night for the spirits to reveal their secrets.

There were questions to be answered. "How does a man dispatch an otherworldly Monkey? How do I stay off drugs? Where is inner-peace found? How can I ever obtain forgiveness?" I asked the heavens.

Carlos Castaneda returned from another world. He had probably heard my questions and decided to take shape again. Carlos was the kind of bullshit artist (imaginary of not) that never missed a chance to demonstrate that he, and only he, knew the answers to the most immaterial questions. I sent him away with a subtle flip of my head. As hallucinations go, Carlos was boring, without mystery, a waste of mescaline. The influence the peyote began to fade. A lone Cholla, a final vision, sidled within earshot and whispered a divination; the message was the same one that had been foretold many times. "The Monkey must be fought in the desert, near The Marble Mountains."

Shit, for all the good the buttons did, might have well sewed them on to a fucking coat, I thought.

I gave up on the invisible world. My tent was pitched at the base of a volcanic peak pushed up from a Cambrian sea bed, millions of years ago. Parting the flaps, I crawled into the tent and collapsed on the sleeping bag. I awoke, startled by somebody shaking the tent and yelling in Spanish. I dragged my tired body out of the tent, and was immediately confronted by three Mexicans, each carrying wetback-hand-me-down backpacks. Their ragged clothes and unraveling shoe leather left no doubt they were illegally crossing the desert to hide further north.

There was no mistaking that they meant to rob me and leave my carcass for the cacti-borers—with their saw-toothed mandibles, and brown scorpions. The corroded Steak- knife, held by the tallest of the men, took away any confusion of their intent. Before they could completely encircle me, I pulled out the flare-gun (always kept in my pocket), and shot the guy (holding the knife) square in the chest. It impacted before the sulfur/magnesium chalk could fully blossom. But the cartridge still scared the shit out of him. I ran backwards, while loading another cartridge into the orange barrel, then flipped it closed, ready for more fireworks. It was as if they had never seen a flare-gun before and mistook it for a rocket launcher or something. They ran for the hills or maybe for the Rio Grande. No way to be sure where they were headed, but watching them go, was "Real Grand."

In all the excitement, the Peyote awoke, and gave me another surge. Not willing to waste another "eight mile high", I shot another cartridge into the air, enjoying the orange/red flower of hot power, spreading into a web of blue and green stars. The entire escapade had an intangible broken- film- reel quality to it. By sharpening long sticks, three sturdy throwing spears were made, so in case the amigos returned, I'd catch them off guard, and impale anyone getting too close. I stood guard for about an hour then reentered the tent and tried to sleep. The events of the day left a rather confusing impression, making it uncertain if the flare-gun colors, rainbow stars, floating Prophets, and Mexicans were just another acid trip. If it was it was a good one.

Needing the support of my family again, I traveled back to Chicago, accepting an offer from my brother Tim to work for him as a union Ironworker.

"What could be the harm?" I thought. Little did I know, the harm would be very great, changing me for life.

Head Like a Hole

Back in my old haunts—Chicago—I began work as an ironworker for Local One, without the assistance of attending the apprentice school, so there was much to learn in a very short amount of time. Most of the impromptu instruction was from my brother Tim. There was no better person to "get me up to speed", because Tim had been a foreman for years, knew the trade up and down (literally), and was much respected throughout the union. This made the act of showing up on the jobsite with a greenhorn like me somewhat forgivable. Ironworkers were like the special forces of the construction industry, most ex-military, slightly eccentric, fearless, and fanatically passionate about their trade. To face the daily challenges of an ironworker required each individual to have an exceptional ability to disregard the risks associated with the profession. Some people (outside of the trade) might insist such an assertion is giving them too much praise ... maybe they have a point. After all, an ironworker was only asked to climb hundreds, sometimes thousands of feet into the air, with no safely net, face chilling winds, intense heat, and stinging insects. Performing tasks, such as: climbing a column, or walking the iron, while a crane swung an assortment of beams and columns over their heads. So, in the words of Tim, "maybe people that criticize the heart of ironworkers should Try It."

On the first day on the job, I learned that our notorious acquaintance—Jumbo—had recently also been employed as an ironworker. He served his narcotic trafficking sentence in Joliet, and had been released a couple years ago while I was serving a sentence of my own—traveling coast to coast across America. Jumbo was a perfect example of how some people continue to inexplicably pop in and out of your life.

But it is odd that the good people never reappear, instead it's only the assholes we ran away from in the first place that have the inexplicable ability to return over and over, like a weevil infestation, but worse, as there was no pesticide for the likes of Jumbo.

Tim told me not to worry about Jumbo and drugs. He made sure they were never on the same jobsite together. Surprisingly, the avoidance was not so much because Jumbo was still dealing, instead it was that Jumbo was even more out-of-control, showing up drunk, high on cocaine and morphine, behaving reckless on every erection—the construction kind that is. Truth be told; nobody really wanted to be close to Jumbo, high in the air, when attention to detail and safety was critical to coming down in one piece. We did cross paths a few times, and I was positive that he was being watched, so the conversation was always short and sweet. His appearance had degraded drastically over the years. The previous decades had not been kind to him, no surprise as mixing massive quantities of coke and downers can't be beneficial to anyone's health. When we met—at a union meeting, he was recovering from a bad fall and had one leg shorter than the other. This meant that he had to wear a monster sized elevator-boot on this left foot, having to drag it behind like a movie-fiend from the old T.V series— Creature Features. I guess Jumbo had really become a Zombie. One major difference was that Tim and I were now certain Jumbo dined on human brains. The circle of life is complete.

Having parachuted, negotiated mountain passes, and rappelled from helicopters, I believed that vertical accents and precarious balancing acts were nothing to be concerned about, especially for a man like me. However, a head injury resulting from my last parachute jump proved my assessment of vertical proficiency to be completely wrong. I already had a fear of closed spaces—from the incident in Africa, so I did not need another irrational fear to deal with.

But unexpectedly, from the first day, it became apparent that a fear of heights could be added to the list of mental problems from my years in the military and as a Merc. My health problems had already made me a regular at the Veterans Hospital Mental Health Ward.

The old trauma made ironworking a task of filled with terror. I clung to each beam like a sloth, wobbling nervously atop beams like a hyperactive court jester, finding any excuse to not go higher, without embarrassing my brother. Tim was very patient, a good teacher, but even his impressive skills were not able to undo my trepidation to move high above the ground.

No amount of encouragement and guidance was able to eliminate the phobia of scuttling along the iron connecting beam to column, especially while ignoring hot welding sparks and hotter wasps. I was ashamed of my inability to traverse the simplest of spans, gripping like glue to anything that was within range, moving slowly as a slug. As there was a significant amount of acid and 'shrooms trapped in my receptors, flashbacks and zip-zooms were a weekly occurrence. Wasp faces swelled into bulbous bug-mugs, swinging cables dissolved into slender anacondas, hot breeze took me back to the Saharan Winds making me wish for the Desert, and the last clash with The Monkey. But I was not ready.

Even though I was unskilled, nobody fucked with me. I had a reputation as a very good fighter, not afraid to throw down; maybe the sort of guy frightened by heights but not a bit frightened by a good fistfight. Hell, there was no reason to make fun of my phobias anyway ... I gave myself more than enough shit. There was no doubt in my mind that very soon I was going to "fall into the hole" and break my back. Such thoughts caused my mind to wander, seeking solace in music, as it always did.

Each morning, "Head Like a Hole" by Nine Inch Nails, played thru my imagination, a great song but certainly not the best under the circumstance. Still, I could not get the music out of my mind. Eventually, things got so bad that I started each day with this affirmation. "I guess this is the punishment for being such an asshole. You are going to fucking die today!" To ease my agitation, Tim often pulled me aside, sending me back down to do some ground work such as hooking on iron so as to be lifted aloft by the crane, unloading iron off the flat bed, using the acetylene torch to cut sections to size and the menial task of going to pick up lunch.

The fateful day of my body meeting the unforgiving hard-deck happened while on a hospital job in Park Ridge. It was a plum gig for the crew. Because the urgency of completing the job was paramount, the mission was "to finish fast at all costs." To adhere to such a demand required lots of overtime, at night, in bad lighting, while exhausted.

After only a few weeks on the job we were almost done. The weather was bad, the sky very dark (with no moon), the kind of workday where everything that could go wrong already had, not a good time for a rookie like me to be running around on top of a building. However, just as we were loading up to leave, the butter-bar superintendent strode out to the site, insisting that we put in more overtime and keep working. Adding to the blackness was a strong gale, so nobody really wanted to go back up, but on the other hand nobody wanted to refuse double-time pay of $84 dollars an hour. Credit Card bills won over the argument for "calling it a day" and resting up for what was sure to be a series of long, tough days before the job could be topped off.

We were already an hour into the task of welding trusses about two stories up. My brother sent me down the ladder in order to bring up some more welding rods, and mercifully got me off the iron for a spell, as he could see my condition was approaching freak-out/melt down. I climbed down, went to the truck, filled my pouches with the slender sticks of low-hy rods, and then after smoking a cigarette, began climbing back up the rungs. I was in the midst of stepping off the last rung onto the iron when unexpectedly my tool belt loosened from the weight of the extra rods and bottled water stuffed into pouches for the men. I should have stopped the climb and immediately cinched up the belt and got my bearings. Instead, I began to move from ladder to structure. In the absence of good lighting, it was difficult to find the proper hand and foothold. From that moment, things happened in a blur; my grip on the edge of a beam faltered, then the heavy tool belt shifted my weight, and the ladder vibrated, swayed, and then fell in slow motion.

It must have looked like a cartoon catastrophe; specifically an episode pitting Coyote against Roadrunner. All that was missing was an Acme keg of dynamite and the theme music for Toon-Town.

I decided to leap off the ladder and aim for a pile of loose gravel to break my fall, rather than trying to ride it down on to the hard surface below. So, with a quickly calculated jump, I dropped towards the pile, preparing to break the impact force with a PLF (Parachute Landing Fall). Nothing went as planned and I missed the soft gravel and hit the concrete, landing on my hip and elbow first, then the side of my head. That was all she wrote. This was the second time my gray-matter was jolted inside my skull and resulted in severe brain trauma. Somewhere off in the distance was the sound of a Piper getting Paid, the sound a remnant of a fairy tale or a flashback. I did not know the answer.

By the time I came to, Tim and the guys were already off the building and were peering down at me. Within seconds of regaining consciousness, my entire body began to spasm violently, followed by uncontrollable retching (a sure sign of a concussion or worse). I tried to sit up, so as not to gag on my projectile puke, and was greeted with shooting pain in the lower back, left elbow, and hip. Following the accident, the hospital stay was long enough, with the additional brain trauma treatments lasting another year. During that time, speaking coherently, thinking straight, and being emotionally stable was very difficult. The physical rehabilitation lasted even longer. The funny thing was that during the entire recovery process The Monkey was absent. I thought it was because he preferred not to hit a downed man, but realistically, I knew it was because The Monkey wanted me to be standing up when the last battle began.

After the fall, the vision of the Mohave Desert came more often and the images were distinctly clearer. Added to the visions were words from the Marble Mountains, rising high Joshua Trees, cacti, and ancient trilobite laden shale.

<u>King of Pain</u>

It seemed like it took forever to completely recover from the fall. When my joints finally mended, and the migraines began to subside—although not by much—and with the assistance of prescribed Imetrax and Vicodin, my next occupation was a mixture of part-time writer and part-time MMA coach. Most of the writing was done in the back of the training facility at a cheap desk, certainly designed by some well-intentioned craftsman to be the identical twin of a real mahogany 'Office Pro Work Station'. To save money—and be ready to train fighters at a moments' notice—I lived in the office and even slept there at night so as to make it to the 5 a.m. sessions.

But with use and age comes the inevitable change in appearance. In the same regard that the tabletop was no longer a piece of fine furniture, I too was no longer a perfect specimen, and although in top shape, my exterior also displayed scars, fractures, crooked and bent legs, and a faded finish. I hoped my writing fared better then my body, and the chipped and faded support my laptop rests upon. Maybe the writing would get better with age, unlike the table, and my bones.

I wasn't immune to the scourge of scribes—writer's block—so occasionally it set in, making it necessary to push away from the desk and think back on my life. While considering the past, injuries refused to be ignored, bullet holes, stab wounds, dislocations, concussions, all were remembered and all exacted a heavy toll. In fact, while typing, the nub where the screwdriver entered my scalp and other head collisions often throb, causing pain to squeeze from my eyes, thereby making computer work feel like a 12-round fight.

The old screwdriver puncture is not hard to find as it is only an inch from another prominent slash resulting from a pool cue being busted over my head, north of the smashed nose tissue ridge earned in a pit-fight and northeast of cheekbone tear from a tree branch. The cheekbone scar was a result of the same parachute jump that gave me the first of many concussions. The many injuries, stab wounds, bullet holes, and dislocations push me to write with painful emotion, revisit past adventures with every creak and pop of tortured joints, and prompt for creativity—bordering on the absurd—by piercing a damaged brain.

My first book had been recently acquired by a publisher and we already sent back the first proof. The book is an adventure story involving the real-life exploits of my grandfather. The tale takes place in the early 1900's in the heavily forested area that is now Quetico National Park. The theme concerns his relationship with the Ojibwa people, and how that bond led to the discovery of a lost Annishinabe village in southern Ontario. I chose that subject for two different reasons: love of history and I wanted to pay homage to my father, who never turned his back on me. It is uncertain whether my attempt at writing will gain the salvation I seek, therefore diluting past misdeeds, and purging the ongoing guilt I feel for having let my family down. However, even if the books are not successful, it will not diminish the fact that I at least tried to make up for an intellect used for the wrong purposes.

The easiest way to sum up my reason for writing would be to explain it this way. I'm only trying to make up for decades of ignoring creative leanings in favor of the easy path of violence, and regretful acts done to satisfy the primitive urges of my overactive Raptor Brain.

If success is attained it will be from sacrifice. I am willing to rise above all obstacles; endure starvation, ignore injuries, think past an uncertain of the future, embrace living as tramp, and beat unfavorable odds. It has been correctly stated that most new writers are doomed to fail. Okay, then might as well fail big, and go for a goal of Shackleton proportions (Ernest Shackleton – famous explorer). One of the most difficult aspects of writing pertains to finding funds. My experiment in novel writing, was an out-of-pocket ordeal, often fulfilled by teaching Submission Grappling and Mauy Thai. The physical punishment of rolling in 'The Cage' made my body hurt as much as typing all night caused my head hurt. So, if nothing else, I was balanced detrimentally in both mind and body. Living in the back of the gym wasn't as bad as it sounds. I'd been to worse places—Africa and Jamesville spring to mind. However, there was a situation that defied rational behavior and what an ordinary guy should have to endure. A bathroom was in proximity to the area where I typed. Unfortunately, whenever I was absent from the office, the bathroom was often used by uncivilized assholes that seemed to possess no sense of decorum. The toilet overflowed on a weekly basis, usually after being used by one of the less-thoughtful gym members. The result flooded my typing area and left residue of dirty water uncomfortably close to my feet, regardless of how many times the floor was mopped.

I was always worried that my living space might fall victim to another toilet plugging (being that there is no shortage of dumbasses). So, needless to say, my stay at the Gym was a very humbling experience and served as another reminder to hurry with the whole writing endeavor—before drowning in putrid water. Occasionally I had to sleep in my '93 Buick, and turn in pennies for food. The car was as bent and broken as I was, but the blue-book on the Buick's value was much higher than my own frame would bring.

The damage to my bones and typing on an empty belly was by my own volition. I wanted to test my patience and endure ridicule (never to my face, but nonetheless expressed). It was by choice that appeared to be homeless and suffered. What better way for a fledgling writer to succeed than embracing pain. Doubts, whispered insults, hardships, all drove me forward. If such things are punishment for past actions; then I was glad to collect them, just as a statue of past adventures, still collects pigeon shit. So there were insults behind my back. However, never to my face, everyone knew that saying the wrong thing within earshot, had serious consequences. I had not made the complete transformation to a pacifist, so fists were not out of bounds. However, the Taoist in me managed most times to treat people's bad judgments, as the meanderings of the ignorant, locked into the material world, relishing only greed and consumption.

The only measurement that most people used to form an opinion of my esteem; was by looking at the old jalopy of a car

I drove, and my dressed down and ruffled presence. That was of no real worry, what was of considerable stress was the chance that my writings, published or not, were going to be subject to the same ridicule. Statistical evidence, combined with an industry ripe with predatory practices and scams, directed at inexperienced agent-free writers foretold that ridicule and rejection was going to be faced.

Music got me through the madness as it did in most time. It occupied my mind, and focused thoughts, connected words, untangled unorganized chapters, and therefore eased the senseless churning in my brain. More and more, I suspected the images and ideas that lurked in the deepest recesses of my brain were partly the result of the many tabs of acid taken over too many years. Acid flashbacks, 'shroom zip zooms, or unrealized dreams; it really didn't matter either way it had awakened a spark, and demanded to be released from pen to paper.

"King of Pain" by The Police was one of the songs most often played while working keystrokes for new chapters in methadone precision to Stewart Copeland's snare drum rim-shots. In those days, Sting's lyrics jolted me to the sudden realization that until things were put right, harsh critics of wasted years could not be silenced. I too, would remain just another "King of Pain". Occasionally, while working at the gym, I pondered on what kind of throne The Monkey sat on. Was he "The King of Giving Pain"? Was my brain his castle? And if so was I but a serf tilling away in some forbidden wheat field, seeded with my own use of drugs, and failure to revolt and storm the castle

While traveling, my suitcase of guilt was not beyond easy reach; there to be opened much in the same way a town-skipping carpetbagger might open his when demonstrating his phony wares. Frayed with fruitless indulgence, my suitcase remained heavy, remained cumbersome, and if the Monkey was not soon Gutted, it might pull me to down to the lowest level where blacktop meets hardened earth. More than ever, the desert beckoned and informed me in mystical fashion that only on those sand would my baggage be emptied.

My road seemed never-ending. It was like a highway in Texas I'd been on several years ago. I was driving on Interstate-10 in order to gather ammonites. It was amazing how the stretch of highway seemed to extend hundreds of miles before disappearing at the horizon line. I was convinced the road would never end, and I would never get out of the boring landscape quilted by ranch after ranch. As I drove, the glare of the sun off the windshield was almost as glaring as the fact that I was a blue-state city-boy driving through red-state Hicksville, with towns populated by people that still thought they lived in the Wild West. I passed a myriad of unique towns that were famous for the strangest claims, boasts to attract tourists to places below the Bible- Belt.

Big Springs had the Rattlesnake Roundup, Midland was the home of George W. Bush—a fact only Texans would brag about, Van Horn was the residence of an amazing artist that replicated paintings by Van Gogh to the smallest detail, and El Paso had more chop shops (and crime) than any other U.S city. The only thing good I found in Texas was the Permian Basin, the whole area was rich with fossils (especially ammonites), and so it made for easy collecting.

My brother Tom and I found many outstanding specimens from around the base of the Apache Mountains. While searching the ancient sea floor—exposed by the unrelenting sand storms, we almost got attacked by a Mountain Lion tracking us from an overhead ridge.

The publishing contract was not a big deal in terms of money, but it was still a deal. My brother Jim sent over the photos that go with the novel and we waited for a version of the cover art to approve. Once that last issue is completed the book will be in-play. But until we made it big, I was still a drifter, working on the writings whenever and whatever I was able. The Monkey no longer clings so strongly around my neck. Drugs, booze and violence have long since been replaced by the desire to better myself. But the brain-cell damage had been done and the many hard knocks to my head had slowed the writing to a crawl. The lure of those vices never completely goes away, so I'm wary of being drawn back into that life.

My caution took me to the point in life where (except for a small circle of friends and my family) I was somewhat of a hermit. The amazing thing was that my sister, my five brothers, and I were as close as when we were kids.

In fact, immediately after writing each chapter, I went on "Recon Runs" with my brother Tom. "Recon Run" being what we called a fast paced run mixed with intervals of weights, pull-ups, kettle ball drills, and the occasional tire flips.

The daily regimen of teaching submission grappling allowed me to (believe it or not) be in better shape than when I was eighteen. My students and the serious fighters I trained were always surprised the first time we grappled; after all, who expected that an arthritic guy (up in the years like myself) could tap them out. I guess it was my refusal to accept defeat that had helped me shrug off the pitfalls, slings and arrows, and disappointment, which might be the first act in a future play entitled "The Enormous Failure Looming in the Distance for all Artists."

The stumbling blocks were many in my newly chosen profession as a writer. The margin for error was extremely small and forgiveness for laziness was non-existent if an author wants to be published.

But as mistaken as I might have been on a great number of things, I was sure of one concept: enduring pain and confronting daily obstacles was the only way a voice would be found, the sort of voice that people will listen to. Also .... not enough can be written about the support of my inner-circle, without of which I would have given up long ago. I already mentioned that my father has never lost faith in me and hoped that I might step out from the shadows and do something, if not great, than at least something that could make my family proud. So, in many ways, everything that I have written, or plan on writing, is written for him.

Tied to the Whipping Post

The first book was "in print" and the publisher was living up to all expectations. However, I was still not rich, I was not famous. Fame I cared not for but having a few bucks in my pocket was not a bad thing to wish for. I remain nothing above a beggar. Having a book in stores didn't change the fact that I was still occasionally homeless, unmistakably sightless and blind to the light at the end of the tunnel. My depression and guilt over past deeds worsened every day. I often considered suicide. I thought of death, so many nights, that my research determined the most efficient way to off myself.

If it comes to it, then slitting my wrists will be the way I choose to exit the world. The cut would have to vertical in nature, not horizontal across the wrists. A horizontal slash would sever the tendons attaching hand to arm, and thereby making the cut to the second hand most difficult, leaving the deed undone and rescue possible. Ugly and sad is the result of failed suicide. I repeated the procedure many a sleepless night, so as to not fuck up the suicide and end up in a padded cell wearing diapers. Shit, if that happened, it would be me throwing feces at the Monkey and him tossing it back. That's a fight nobody wants to see. Although I suspected the Monkey would enjoy a turd battle.

I even researched the correct combination of drugs required to achieve the right amount of disorientation and bring forth a mindless stupor, so as to make the act as painless as possible. The drugs alone can't drown out the inner voice that insists I put down the razor. So, a fifth of "Esophageal Rotting" Popov Vodka would have to act as a chaser. It was of poor quality and had a reputation of eating through the stomach walls, but I'd be dead so heartburn wasn't big on my list of concerns.

The writing and other acts of kindness I have done over the last several years win no medals, but hopefully make up for past wrongs. My good deeds don't create false impressions of personal longevity, forgiveness, or redemption, as those things are a long way off, and to think otherwise, would only be another con.

What concerned me the most was not the desire to off myself, for on exceptionally bad days there was a belief that I have it coming—when one lives by the sword, one dies by the razor! So there exited an expectation that, for me, there might not be a happy ending. So, suicidal thoughts were not the feelings that distressed me most, as two other aspects of my condition, were more paramount to full recovery.

The first was that my eagerness to pass on to a better place produced no internal shame, and it should have, at least in regard to my creed, "Never admitting defeat." The second was that the temptation will become so powerful that the siren's song of death will become impossible to resist, and force the act of Seppuku—before the writings were finished. But maybe that might be an appropriate end to a book about a most inappropriate life.

During the worst of these moments, The Monkey called out, as he must have sensed my weakness, and promised deliverance for painful guilt. His guarantee had a major requirement—return to drug use. His voice reached me, even though it had been many years since the last time I even looked at drugs. The primate voice was difficult to resist, it cooed gently to me from far away, imprisoned in the deepest cavern of my mind. But in my weakest moments the voice grew in volume, and when my surroundings were calm, I listened carefully to his words, craving meaning, while paying attention for signs of The Monkey's return.

I felt he was coming back and was only waiting until I had things to lose, such as a new career and self-respect. He never lost his thirst for blood, but there were other poor souls with pumping arteries, to occupy his time, and sate his appetite, while he watched for an opportunity to crush me. He still wants blood … but now only my blood will do!

"Do it … do it … do it! Release your mind from sorrow." He chides, sometimes he threw out the word coward if he believed such language served his intention.

But there was another beast that bit the hardest. Bad judgments in the character of those closest to me, allowing morally corrupt vermin into my inner circle. They lived close enough to threaten blackmail—whenever they wanted something from me. They demanded my dignity be chained in servitude, but all they got was disappointment, as there was not possibility that my dignity was going to be taken by assholes, worthy only of contempt.

So, it wasn't only imaginary Monkeys that tormented me, there were plenty of enemies in human form that wished me harm. They had hearts darker than mine. For decades, they jeopardized my freedom by exposing my old warrants to the local cops, therefore draw attention to what I was ... not what I'm trying to become. None of them knew what their actions could awaken inside me. They felt safe, certain that The Monkey and the Beast that once resided in my brain were dead. The harassment might have stopped, if they had been able to hear the Monkey; when he demanded me to "reach out and snap their necks and then disappear into the wilderness"! Disappearing was something I knew very well, but snapping necks was something I knew better, if the situation required it.

There will be no neck snapping, unless it is my own. Their threats are merely another example of the debt I must pay to some faceless accountant, working in a Dicksonian Christmas play. Here is your lump of coal for your worthless lump of a soul. Those were the words thought in times when losing control seemed possible.

I got through each day by forcing an acceptance of my penance, refusing to give in to anger or fear. I knew there was to be no redemption until I had been tied to the whipping post for a long enough spell. My pride had to be flogged, proud skin, flayed over humbled bones" only then will I be set free. The writing was just a small part of the process that expelled Serpents and Monkeys—Serpents not of the Christian kind, and Monkeys not of the playful kind. My writing continued, brought forth by the pain and regret, and surrendered what was left of my ego, submitting with each new page that waved white flags. While immersed in the creative process, I was reminded of the "Ants and the Grasshopper Story."

The Ants labored feverously on gathering food to be stored, so as to prepare as the punctual, yet very cruel winter approached. The Ants were subject to the same distractions (which I think of the as the insect equivalent as mad, out-of control insect partying) that the Grasshopper was. However, unlike the Grasshopper, they kept their antenna to the grindstone, refusing to cease with the robotic and monotonous task of collecting dead beetles and moths. So, while the social network of Ants set up to survive the fast approaching cold weather, the Grasshopper made merry, doing a jig, playing a fiddle, and acting out in the way that ... someone such as I would. Except, I am unable to bow a fiddle, but I can do one hell of a jig; and with my limited sense of rhythm, hell is where my dance moves belong. Well ... as expected winter came right on schedule, and the Grasshopper had no food.

No heart-wrenching drama, no fancy words—he just quietly died. Each time I recounted the story, an ending of my own was added, so as to fit the theme into my own distorted representation of how the insect-world worked.

"The Grasshoppers brittle husk, dried and preserved, was discovered by the ants after winters snow had melted. As spring had arrived later than usual, all the food-stores were depleted. So the ants dragged the Grasshopper's carcass below ground, through ant tunnels, and into the feeding chamber. The hungry ants shared the meat, and then celebrated the Grasshopper as a hero. Telling future ant generations of how he had supplied his body, thereby saving the entire colony from going hungry." That was my personal ending to the story. Freud would have fun with that one.

I was like the Grasshopper. Wanting salvation, but would settle for celebration. And therein resides the moral "waste your life and winter is going to be very fucking cold".

"As my existence had been lacking, I needed to find a coat, no a parka.....shit....I'd better just put on a suit of armor." It was the same story that used many times (while writing) as a moral compass, but the last self directed phrase served only as a warning that my future was uncertain.

One Thing Leads to Another

Decades came and went since those turbulent days when The Monkey held absolute control over my internal governor switch. He never completely ceased to exist, but the power he once had held over me had become very small. His ability to take advantage of my weakest moments and bring dishonor to my name was growing smaller and smaller. I suspected that as his sway over me faded, he was getting angrier. I feared he was summoning his strength for one final assault on my spirit. The passing of years had dissolved many of my memories, but I was sure, the march of time had also melted away the Monkey' influence over my life. I had kicked drugs, changed my acquaintances, avoided being cut into flank steaks by machete wielding madmen in Africa, survived insane (cannibal?) farmers, lived through 3500 and 30 foot falls, and then beat The Horm (be it real or not, getting away from the Horm's cold embrace and lamprey jaws counts as a win in my book) Much of the success was due to my devotion to The Way of Lao Tzu, and not dwelling on the Monkey's Non-Darwinian extinction. While organizing several notes for another novel, I listened to a song by The Fixx called "One thing Leads to Another." Great tune and invariably correct. "One fucking thing absolutely leads to another fucking thing."

More and more, my goal of becoming a successful writer was finally taking shape. However, much of the advancements resulted from all the assistance my family and friends provided. The writings were as much their achievements as mine. I hoped that someday there would be a steady income from future book sales, then I would be able to retain a smart, if not respected, lawyer to plead my case to a judge.

My thinking at the time was that giving up (to the cops) and getting sentenced could not possibly be worse than the daily flogging endued at my own hand—a flogging that results from the shame of not being strong enough to put up a better fight to vanish the Monkey. In a universe of balanced scales, the progress made thus far should be a time for rejoicing. Up to this point, the good my life has produced, outweighs the deeds of the past. Ten newspaper articles were published about our first novel and the second was almost completed.

There were several Hollywood studios that had read both manuscripts. In addition, there had been good reviews and buzz concerning both projects. It seemed that all the shit accumulated from my previous incarnation was very close to being purged. The initial public offering of "Miscreant Billy Halverson version 001", was slowly and methodically being put to rest, in favor of the new offering – "W.H 002—peaceful Taoist hell-bent on redemption and forgiveness."

However, for every action I'd taken to escape past transgressions, there was an equal amount of actions taken by those unhappy with their own station in life. Welcome to physics 101. Every action resulted in an equal and opposite (and in my case) opposing action. There were still many people that sought to prevent my quest to rise above the chromatic limitations of character. In some respects, I was the rarest of creatures. Not "a good man that strived to not commit bad acts", instead I existed as "a bad man that strived to commit good acts." It is much harder to be a flawed individual that attempts to be something better, despite his shortcomings, than it is to be a natural Dudley-Do-Right. The later never has had to fight a Monkey of his own creation.

Writing has never been about money or notoriety. That way of thinking went against the whole Taoist thing, and in turn made the act of creation merely an act of greed. I intended to give profits from the books to my friends and family as a way of saying thanks. The novels had a deeper mission, to take me from "launching board" to the "cutting board" – where the Gutting of the Monkey (hence this stories title) would one day be surgically appropriated. There was many times throughout the process where good intentions ran afoul of people that wanted to break my spirit and release the beast that desired revenge.

I had no plans to revert back to my old self. That would give the upmost pleasure to those blackmailing lunatics that never wanted me to succeed. They were afraid that I might completely transform from Black-hearted Billy Halverson into Writer Billy Halverson. If that took place, they would lose the illusionary power over my old title of "Desperate Fugitive" and cocaine-hoover.

The constant harassment would have been understandable; if it was done for the right reasons, such as making the streets safe, the result of an overzealous opinion of right and wrong, or if they truly thought it was for the good of all concerned.

However, it wasn't a sense of good citizenship, nor a Bible-Based wish to grant me some sort of absolution for past sins—through punishment. They wanted me picked up as a felon, before I had the chance to do it on my own terms – as a virtuous man that has turned his life around. Then, when I went before the judge I could say to him "your honor I am a reformed man and both The Beast and The Monkey have been silenced forever."

My antagonists, some would use the terms rats or snitches, had a habit of alerting the authorities during the holidays. This caused me to unexpectedly pull up stakes, scramble for money and a place to live. It saddened me that there were people, within my clan, that were still trying to break my spirit, so as to feel good about their own miserable lives.

They would never destroy my will, because little by little, I had been making a paradigm shift, ever changing, ever casting aside demons. I had risen to the challenge, held firm to the ideal of becoming a far better person. When that event transpired, the evolutionary code would be torn apart, thereby dissolving the birth programming that had injected me with limitations. I stood as a stark contrast, to what had been genetically predisposed at inception, and later reinforced, hard-wired in Africa.

It was clear (to all that knew something of my story) the bi-annual act of snitching me out, was done for a purely selfish and opportunist reason. Maybe they had their own Monkey urging them to shatter dreams.

Calling officers to respond to a 30 year old assortment of warrants (that by all accounts have been expunged) was done to make me suffer, and thereby make my family suffer. The pinch came from within my family circle from a sister-in-law or my mother. Both suffered from dementia and took each found pleasure in accusing me made-up criminal activities. Sure....I was a felon, but they tried to convince the authorities that I was Al Capone. They sent letters to the cops stating that I was behind every crime that appeared in the newspaper. The chain of condemnation went something like this: marital troubles—blame Billy, little Bobby not doing well in school—blame Billy, economy downturn—blame Billy, drink too much and have no friends, blame Billy, living an existence devoid of happiness resulting from deep rooted mental disorders –blame Billy. I guess it is human nature to aim at the biggest target.

But, in the course of shameful deeds, I was never of much a target as I was a magnet, the kind that attracts each and every pissed-off particle that gets within range of my nucleus. During the first several years as a fugitive, it was nothing to endure harsh words, unfounded accusations, along with the annual threats to turn me in. I took it all in stride, as just another part of the humbling penance that I was required to pay. However, clearing your name is not an easy task, while relatives continually tell the cops lies, when in reality, all I wanted to do was turn everything around and make up for past transgressions.

However, after fifty-three years on this planet, my vision is poor but my sight has improved remarkably. My previous mode of gauging the consistent barrage of insults and taunts has evolved. Anger would only be wasted on such people, because the sound coming from their lips is only the last gasp from a scornful individual drowning in misery. Finally after years of trying to forgive and forget, the correct frame of mind was taking root.

"Why hate bipolar people, wallowing in self imposed melancholy?" I asked while putting together pages on the subject, so as my personal agenda would not manifest in the novel ... at least not too much.

There was one person of notable insanity that made it almost impossible to look the other way. She had blackmailed me hundreds of times and over the course of two decades. If I was the same man that roamed the streets thirty years ago; a fearful price would have been collected for the attacks. Thankfully, I am not that man ... but I have a pen ... and for my enemies a pen will have to do. By using the instrument of the scribe, with the ink-laded sharpened tip I will open the Harpy's innards as deep as the open cavity that looms in the future of the Monkey. The Horm and other fantastical creatures from my earlier existence get a pass. As they were hallucinations and not real…at least I hoped they were not real, or was going to be in big trouble.

As for the Monkey, I was still not sure what category he would be classified when the story was over. Imaginary freak, demon from hell, LSD flashback, the conjuring of an outrageous mind, or was it possible that he was more authentically alive than I? I was aware that some questions could only be answered when we have our showdown in the desert. But my money was on LSD Induced Imaginary Freak. As was the case with all my writings, there was the temptation to simply call the Monkey an asshole. However, the years had refined my vocabulary, as well as my idea of revenge.

I pictured the movie "Tombstone" while anticipating the showdown. I was Val Kilmer's version of "Doc Holiday", while The Monkey was Stephan Lang's version of "Ike Clanton". The concept worked well, unconsciously giving me an edge, before the fight, due to Lang's excellent interpretation of Clanton. The movie version of Clanton was the kind of portrayal that best suited The Monkey. Thinking of the primate as a sniveling, cowardly, soggy, sloppy, shit-bag prepared me for what could turn out to be a one hell of a fight. Sometimes the stored hallucinogens from ancient massive consumption would kick in. While under the influence of good quality LSD (that had been voluntarily dosed into my system in my wild youth), the "Gunfight at the Windowpane Corral" went slightly different. After killing the Clanton-Monkey, I continued with the rampage, coach-gun in hand, killing other famous outlaws. Billy the Kid, Jesse James, Black Bart, The Rawhide Kid. All were dispatched in a hail of coach-gun pellets, cut to ribbons by own hand. Interestingly enough, in the LSD adaptation, each notorious Badman had bodies of spiders. Which meant each guy had eight arms, eight six guns, and a shitload of tiny little eyes. The arachnid/cowboy image was imposing to say the least. That made their defeat even sweeter.

The visions of what was waiting in the desert prepared me for the inevitable. When the time for the showdown arrives I will have to revert to my former self and again assume the role of a violent man, to win over The Monkey.

In the meantime, it has been a difficult chore to produce the best writings possible, while on the run and/or looking over my shoulder. My deliberations on vengeful relatives and Tombstone were cut short by an unfortunate surprise, while working on this book in early 2011. At the time I was living in Tempe with a couple of friends. I got up to answer a knock at my front door. It was officers claiming to be from the Arizona Highway Patrol and wanted to know the whereabouts of Billy Halverson.

You have to be fucking kidding me, was my first thought. But no, there they stood, faces twisted to an imposing glare, two burly types, in dark colored plain clothes, badges on neck-chains around 19 inch necks.

Highway Patrol .... my ass ... " I thought. These were detectives, big guys, dressed in tee-shirts, ready to wrestle, ready to knock heads, ready take somebody into custody. After the first novel was published, I became careless and relaxed, thinking and seeing myself in a new light. My mirrored image as a changed man worthy of empathy if not respect, was a welcome reflection, but it caused me to forget that until legal representation was obtained, I remained a fugitive. So in my unprepared state, I answered the door in a tank-top, which inconveniently revealed all my accumulated scars, tattoos, and muscles.

Each physical attribute was in plain sight and matched even the sketchiest of roll-call police descriptions. In situations like this, a clean getaway was relative to how good of an actor one can become without the benefit of rehearsals or a stuntman.

There was no net, no safely harness, and no foam mat below. You get one attempt at the double back-flip with a triple twist, so you have to stick the landing, as there were no spotters or second chances. I tried to act calm, talked no more than necessary (nothing says guilt like too much chatter), and demonstrated no signs of resisting. Bolting out the back door was not an option either, because there was sure to be a couple additional officers waiting in the rear of the complex, tasers in hand.

"Hello, we are officers from the Highway Patrol. Were looking for a William Halverson …are you him?" They asked suspiciously.

"No…he is out on a book tour. He probably won't be back for a couple weeks." Neither of the two appeared to be anxious to make an arrest. It was more like they were annoyed to be ordered to follow up on a twenty-five year old warrant.

And then they asked the question all fugitives fear. "Okay, this won't take much time. Who are you and do you have some IDs."

I handed over a fake ID that displayed Ronald Halverson instead of Billy. I explained that I was Billy's brother, Ronald, and was helping with the book orders. Both cops carefully examined the document, appeared satisfied, then handed it back. During the entire time at the front door, they made strong eye contact, sizing me up and down, searching for a sign of abnormal nervous behavior or outright fear. Their body language was tense and coiled, ready to spring if I made any threatening gestures, or did something to tip them off.

At this point in my life, running or putting up a fight was out of the question. The days of hopping fences, sprinting across highways, facing down snarling dogs was far off in the distant past, much beyond arthritic knees, multiple head concussions, and non-aggressive philosophy. The internal truth—of harboring no ill will towards the officers, must have been absorbed subconsciously by their brains. They relaxed and were visibly at ease. I could hear the wheels turning in their heads.

"This guy in front of us is about as dangerous as an eggplant, certainly not the guy were looking for—armed and dangerous. This dude is only another bohemian-artist, latte-drinking, chain-smoking, liberal. He's nothing except another New Age Poet. Guys like him are a dime a dozen nowadays." They did not say it aloud, but their expression, communicated what needed to be heard.

"What is this all about? When Billy gets back, should I have them call you?" I asked the cops.

"Yeah, have Billy call us (handing me their cards), he was a witness in a car accident in Kinston County." The lead defective said. His facial expression hinting that he had no serious commitment to the fabrication, wanting only to mark off this visit on his notepad as completed. It all made sense to me. What cop wanted to waste valuable time doing paperwork concerning an extrication order for non-violent charges that happened twenty-five years ago?

With all the pedophiles, rapists, and murderers still walking the streets, recourses spent on my case were resources taken from much more important investigations.

I knew the traffic story was a lie. However it was not without a creative flourish. I almost was tempted to ask, "You guys ever think of writing fiction?" The traffic story had been concocted so as to not draw suspicion to the act of serving of a warrant. However, as much as I respected the cop's impromptu narrative, there were three problems with the lie.

A: Billy had never been to Kingston **B:** Billy has no license and has not been on the grid for over 30 years. **C:** Billy's last known address was in Illinois. **D:** Nobody, but nobody— except immediate family was aware of where I was actually living. I had purposely given out wrong info—even to my friends, in order to draw the blackmailing asshole into my trap once and for all.

All interruptions aside, I still needed to drive to the Post Office in order to mail out several copies of the novel. So to put the cops off the scent even further, I invited them in while I removed pasta from the stove. Invitations meant legal searches and seizures. No dangerous fugitive would ever do such a stupid thing, such as voluntarily giving up a large portion of their constitutional rights and thereby exponentially increasing the potential for arrest.

The bearded cop said, "Thanks but no thanks," took a final lingering look inside and decided to roll on to more important calls, rather than waste more time trying to track down a reformed felon that was burdened with charges from three decades ago.

They gave me a card, with their police affiliations and phone numbers, printed in bold New Times Roman font, and walked back to their cruiser.

I was certain that this was not the end of the visit. But caution still needed to be exercised. The cops were sure to be waiting around the corner in order to see if anyone ran from the apartment carrying luggage. I figured an hour was a long enough wait to go to the post office.

That is exactly what I did. But not before placing everything that would be needed to continue writing into priority mail boxes. I made two trips to my car, each time waving at the officers that were parked in the space adjacent to my residence.

The visit by the cops changed my mental state in a very dramatic way. The race to finish the second novel was against time instead of against talent. I was no longer a writer struggling to bring honor to my name, striving to redeem myself for the inability to embrace my calling. I was once again a fugitive. Scurrying around like a rat, on the lam, typing in libraries, glancing closely at every face looking for signs of ill-will, formulating escape plans, rushing to complete the last several chapters. Knowing my capture was probably only a matter of days away.

I spent the next two weeks at my sister's place in Tucson. She lived in a secluded neighborhood that was only ten or twelve blocks from some great hiking areas. Her place would provide privacy, while provided ample vistas of palm lined sand to jog on. The new digs were not without a few hurtles that needed to be overcome. Every other day it was necessary to drive my piece-of-shit Buick north to Tempe on the 10 freeway. The amount of traffic during the commute between Tempe and Tucson was substantially more than the three lanes were meant to handle, making the '10' freeway a very treacherous stretch of concrete, much more so than a '93 Buick should be on.

What the '10' lacked in masked highwaymen (that once waylaid unsuspecting travelers on their way west to find gold) it made up for with the sheer volume of motorists driving beyond their reaction time, and even further beyond the engineering restrictions of the rusty hulks of metal they called cars. Tailgating within inches of the motorist ahead was a standard driving technique and overlooked by the police. But I was unable to ignore the invasion into my bumper space, cursing each asshole that filled my mirror. The rudeness and lack of caution demonstrated by other drivers made the ride an infuriating one.

Regardless, the two-hour drive had to be made, so as to handle daily book orders and get to my part-time job in Tempe. Each day I commuted was filled with depression and migraines that lasted for several days. The long drives, lack of sleep, combined with the fear of failure ate away at my state of mind, bringing me very close to admitting defeat. The writing suffered, pages torn up, entire chapters were shit-canned, and creative flourishes were destroyed the same as creative garbage. Morals that should have been stop signs to bad behavior became senseless rants, unworthy of any book.

The bright spot of the entire ordeal was that my sister was always supportive and was also involved in the arts. The decor of her apartment was that of a museum. Old books, older photos of Hollywood from back in the day when Hollywood promised the chance of fame for hopeful starlets instead of rejection. My sister had worked in product placement for the last 20 years and had accumulated countless movie and media artifacts while working on location for one film or another. Original artwork representing theatrical releases adorned every wall ... Robert Smith from the Cure (now apparently stuck forever in the creative region of my brain) was again was conspicuously absent. Being as how I was off drugs, even if there had been a poster of The Cure, would Smith converse with me as he had before.

A full length poster of "The Duke" covered the door to her office. John Wayne in black and white, life-size, full of Wayne's signature swagger, and each of his ivory colt revolvers were ready to blaze western style justice. His expression seemed to imply that any pilgrim entering the room should avoid rustlers and go easy on the whiskey. And who was I to argue with "The Duke." I had always been a fan of John Wayne and kind of regretted that he never appeared in any of my "Tombstone" flashbacks. I could have used him when it came to rounding up and killin' dangerous outlaws. Wayne would have been formidable ally to have, even in acid-dreams; after all, it was "The Duke" that gunned down Liberty Valance.

Paintings, sculptures, rare periodicals, and scripts filled the rooms. Images of movie starts past and present gazed forth from pictures placed strategically in every available space. Bogart, Daniel Day Lewis, Edger G. Katherine Hepburn, James

Dean were all there, each star provided atmosphere, all speaking of ageless beauty and of impending loss. A ridgeline of antique tables from the 30's lined the perimeters of the living area, each a subtle hue of walnut, all with slender tops decorated with animal figures made of glass and aged greenish copper.

Under dim mood lighting, aided by a candle light aura reserved for Muses, I typed furiously, while inspiration came and went, coinciding with the arrival and departure of the creational spark—left behind by the depictions of dead theatrical people, preserved lovingly in picture frames by my sister. In a smaller study, a library of scrapbooks and photo albums chronicled the Halverson heritage, beginning with their arrival on American shores from Denmark.

The Monkey too came and went. He fading in and out, unable to fully take form, only rage and anger a fully realized element, limited by knowing (as he surely must) of his coming defeat and disembowelment.

"Maybe he was scared of me, or maybe scared of the Duke." I thought. While typing at my sister's place, The Monkey pleaded with me to seek retribution on those who cried out for my ruin. My will to ignore him was braced with a steely resolve forged in a furnace absence of drugs. The final curtain was unfurling. He knew it and I knew it. Last act over...Monkey over.

I returned to Tempe after enough time had passed, operating under the premise that it was safe again to work out of my earlier office. I was back in the saddle again. I was John Wayne with quill and storyboard. Riding harder than ever, fast, fortified, renewed, covering so much terrain, that the pony express showed less vigor when compared to the energy I was willing to expend in order to finish the journey.

The lesson of this latest escapade was not lost on me. No longer was I going to take my freedom for granted. Every minute of each day must be spent on the novels. The time had come to produce some respectable material and convince a future judge that I am a reformed man. Hopefully he will come to that conclusion before the next decree of "Bailiff, take him away."

The urgency that drove me to finish "Gutting the Monkey" has now been doubled. There is a lingering certainty that the cops will return and the person making the calls will never stop. This makes me think that the time has come to clear up the past and cleanse the way towards the future.

Shock the Fugitive

The title of this chapter breaks away from the usual method of naming each chapter after a musical theme. A tool used throughout the book to conjure forth old memories, while making unpleasant ones somewhat bearable. This title really holds no resemblance to any song (except for "Shock the Monkey" by Peter Gabriel), a tune used as an opening gambit to an earlier chapter. However, as I write these words, it occurs to me that it makes sense to include a title describing my own introduction to voltage. Seems fair, as I found it so amusing to describe the Monkey's experience with electricity, seems fair to the reader; in that the punishment fits the crime.

The two-week stay at my sister's apartment was over. I would miss the Tucson parks located throughout the desert. It was a great area to run, with an eclectic (and always amusing) population of angry hobos with ZZ Top beards, wanna be models – complete with saggy tits and saggy asses, Tokyo Tourists holding camera ray-guns, and personal trainers that were so numerous, it was as if they grew overnight—out of the sand. Every few meters a spandex-clad (you heard right ... spandex) trainer taught kick-boxing, using a technique that could only have been learned in aerobic classes, but obviously not in a MMA cage. Uppercuts that started well below their knees, maybe in China, mutant fists thrown that were a slow mixture of hooks with straight punches, and kicks that should have been left on the soccer field, along with the 'Soccer Moms'. It was as if the instructor's program was designed for the students to get their asses stomped, or at least ridiculed. Yeah, I was going to miss the free entertainment.

No more fucking around, running and hiding; it was time to finish the novel, it was time to Gut the Monkey ... risks be damned.

When I got back to Tempe, the normal ritual of jogging at "South Mountain Park" and feeding the crows and veracious scrub-birds (before the daily chore of writing) resumed. The crows were pleased at my return, or knowing of the stoic nature of the bird clan (from previous research), maybe it was the bag of bread crumbs they really welcomed. The familiar sand pastures and desert wild flowers were always been inspirational, and many ideas for the first book geminated on the rocky footpaths. Both species—of crow and man—arrived at the park before sunrise, before the sounds of civilization; a lone human in search of his former self, beneath black feathered observers perched high above. Here were my favorite muses; prideful, insightful avian co-authors, giving flight to dreams as well as eager nestlings. The crows proofed all my thoughts, and were unforgiving of whimsical nonsense, always demanding genuine illumination of a black heart, while insisting that I don't hide from the absurdly bizarre parts of my story. So, if you find instances where the narration becomes to surreal, go to the park and blame the fucking crows, but bring bread crumbs, or no audience will be granted.

The park was usually deserted during the hours that I ran. As was the case with most city land—set aside for sports and picnics it rarely hosted events. South Park had no places for troubled youth—obsessed with mayhem, to play video games, and no sections, separated with velvet rope, for Snobs to social network over cocktails. The Crows never vocalized or cawed much, but when they did, it was usually to express mutual distain for all the Rich Fucks.

On the horizon to the north were several homes as big as castles. I had no idea who lived in the expensive dwellings, but was fairly certain they had never seen the inside of a scrub bucket, the business end of a vacuum, or any other household cleaning instrument—unless wielded by an illegal nanny from south of the border. While running, I tried to guess what kind of person lived in each home: Mayor, City Accountant, D.O.M Supervisor, Stockbroker, Banker, Politician. When that got boring, I switched to an easier and more accurate method of tallying the rich folk, naming them for character and not for occupation: Blowhard, Embezzler, Blue-Blooded Bigot, Know-it-all, Old-White-Fat-Guy. Going through the descriptions of the people behind gated communities made the run go by quickly, and before I knew it I was on my way back to the writing desk, and the elite residents near the park went back to planning where to build the next sweat shop.

It was at the park, when the worst possible occurrence transpired, and almost killed me, and the writings as well. I was beginning the routine of warming up both arthritic knees, as each joint had endured extensive injuries from ground fighting, miscalculated parachute jumps, and falls off buildings. Ten minutes into the stretching routine, a motorcycle cop approached me and asked for an I.D. He informed me that the Tempe Police believed the bike (I had ridden to the park) was stolen The motorcycle cop was a walking caricature, wearing leather gloves, a white helmet too big for his melon, shiny black boots, and the aggressive attitude of an authoritarian bully. He even had aviator mirror sunglasses on, as if the stereotype he represented was not quite obvious enough.

I considered asking him "Where Officer Poncharelo was?" then though better of it, because this guy obviously had no sense of humor.

The "stolen bike ruse" was a poor fictional story, inferior to the "Highway Patrol" explanation at my door a few weeks earlier. The stolen bike story was much below the threshold of made-up crap. Nobody with even the minimal amount of brain tissue could possibly swallow that kind of crap. Each of us knew why he was really there, so the only thing left to do was let the game play out and see what happens.

Fuck, not again! I'm so close to finishing the second book...and now this shit. Somebody down there hates me, I thought, while knowing that no help would be forthcoming from *"up there."*

"Okay ... what is your name and date of birth?" The cop asked, while flipping through a notepad.

I was tired of all the running and all the shit that goes with living on the lam, tired of the blackmail, and fuck it all, just tired. The time had come for me to face the music—the kind of music not used in my novels, the kind that involves cuffs and cavity searches. Man ... I was beginning to hate music. "Billy Halverson". I told him. Giving my real name for the first time in years, and it felt good.

The cop ran my background for legitimate warrants and those of the made-up variety. Reactivating, or bringing up old expunged warrants, was an old trick used by the police to arrest suspects. It was a procedure often used in the anticipation of finding recent criminal incidents.

So, while the background check was going on, I worried that fabricated charges might be added. My record should show no criminal activities in over 25 years. I was a truly a reformed man, one wishing to live within the law, far removed from the seedy side of existence. I began to think that the old shit would be overlooked and in only a few minutes I'd be back at the computer. However, things did not go that way. As I indicated before, "somebody down there hates me."

"You have an old warrant for a quarter gram of coke." He said, unable to mask his sadistic pleasure in wrecking a life.

"Come on, you're kidding. That case was expunged 24 years ago. I went to court and completed the sentence."

"No, the record states you're wanted for a probation viola-tion. You left the state without the court permission before pro-bation was over." He said while unhitching the cuffs from his Batman Utility Belt.

It was a bullshit charge but just the excuse he needed to haul me in and look for other potential felonious transgres-sions. Whoever "ratted me out" probably told the cops all kinds of horrible lies. That had to be the reason the cops were willing to take me into custody on such an unwinnable case.

He waited until a couple other cops arrived and then be-gan the cuffing process. My thoughts at that moment were that all the work to become a writer and a productive member of society were over. *Snitches, Rats, and Karma have won out. Now the book will never get finished.* And with my brain condi-tion, certainly another concussion or seizure is what's waiting for me behind bars...not just Bubba.

I was in for a bad time. My arrest would take me away from my medications, thereby risking permanent damage to my mental facilities.

I panicked and did one the thing the cops were secretly hoping for. I ran, or better yet, tried to run, moving on "bone to bone" knees. My escape did not get very far, maybe few steps towards my house, and that was about it. The cops tackled me and Tasered both my legs, hitting me inches above my knees. I felt the current shoot up my hamstrings and collect in my lower back. At first, the sensation felt like a wooden riot ball or a fla-cette-bean-bag struck me, as both were often used to knock down fleeing criminals, without going ballistic.

But, as I lost control of my lower extremities and my bladder, it became evident to me that the damage it had to be from a brief (yet strong), electrical current interrupting my neural functions. I hit the ground hard and the cops hit me harder. If, and when, the book gets finished and a reader questions the validity of some of the more bizarre scenarios, I hope that the reader will remember this: I am the same Billy Halverson that admitted to crapping myself while being electrocuted. Kind of makes this novel rate pretty high on the truth-o-meter?

I was in custody and headed to jail, the perfect environment for The Monkey to regain complete control, and bring about my destruction. Jail—the one place (aside from the jungle) where Monkeys ruled and outnumbered the other occupants by a sizable margin.

As bad as the situation seemed—from the standpoint of injuries and to the writing projects—I had a sneaking suspicion that fate had far worse things in store for me. It would have been easy to attribute "the feeling of doom" to a "bad break" or the spontaneous reaction that follows all misfortune— "expecting the worst is yet to come."

The real truth, the profound inherent knowledge, the real moral to the story, there were greater retaliations that needed to be faced, needed to be endured before forgiveness was ever going to be granted. Facing what was to come was not going to be the problem. Knowing what this would do to my friends and family was.

The ride to the police station house began with uncontrolled shaking and tongue biting; which was the first hint of the impending seizure that was not far behind. Try as I might, nothing was going to prevent the growing mental collapse and blackout steamrolling in my direction.

The height of the seizure hit me just as I was being pulled from the squad car.

"I'm about to blackout, think you guys could support my weight or put me on the ground?" I told the cops to no avail.

Can't blame them, I thought. *They probably hear this kind of shit all the time.*

Then, as expected, darkness came, my legs buckled and my forehead struck the edge a metal box in the garage. A string of thoughts shot thru my brain, fast, much like machine gun orange-colored tracers.

The tracers had words on each metal jacket "Out like a light"... "out at home-plate".... "out of time"...... "out of luck".....".out to lunch". All came and went in "epileptic" flash. But, in reality, I had lost a pint of blood, lost any semblance of consciences, and lost the motor skills required for mobilization of arms and legs. The last thing I remember was a cop (to his credit) stopping the torrent of blood that was spewing from the gash on my scalp. When I came to, it was in the ambulance on the way to Hoag hospital, cuffed to a cushioned table.

Blood in my eyes blocked out my vision. However, being able to see clearly wasn't a necessary requirement for me to notice that my back was on fire and my legs were without feeling.

"It is going to be a long day" I murmured and then passed out.

Death on Two Legs

Popping in and out of consciousness was not helping my attempt to envision what lay in store for me. The ambulance ride was so bumpy; it seemed as if my back was going to snap, and separate vertebrae in two distinct pieces. In such a deranged, confused, certainly painful condition of mind and body, it would be logical to assume the soundtrack to my life had skipped a track, or powered down. Not the case at all, for during the entire ride to the hospital the song by Queen, "Death on Two Legs," played over and over in my head. Lyrics, laced with music, flowed ear to ear, sometimes at the beginning, sometimes at the middle, mostly at the end of the song. However, Brian May's unique fret work remained uninterrupted throughout the peaks and valleys of consciousness ... beginning to end.

I regained consciousness while being wheeled into the emergency room. They had not taken any chances and had me shackled to a hospital gurney. A variety of faces loomed overhead. Every face had a military-style mustache beneath close-cropped hair, making it hard to distinguish the cops from the orderlies. From the adjourning emergency rooms an impressive array of sounds emanated from other patients. The voices were strangled gasps, ranging from low moans to high pitched screams, occasionally interrupted by weeping, and choked-up sobs. Aside from the human voices, I heard the metallic clink and clack of operating tools, spinning swivel chairs and the hydraulic squeeze of large machinery being adjusted.

Doctors ran in and out of the room, asking questions, feigning concern, while never listening to what was said about the pain surging thru my legs and back. The bleeding had stopped thanks to a bandage.

Thankful as I was for having a giant bandage on my head, I knew full well the pressure applied by the arresting officer, did more to prevent a massive hemorrhage than the doctors did.

X-rays were taken and a brain scan ran to determine the extent of my injuries. The brain scan did not reveal any internal head damage, only a lack of common sense, laden with a surreal grasp of reality, emphasized by my abstract view of the world. "Reality-Check Stat." The words echoed in the background, which were surely nothing but my own thoughts, cutting through the actual hospital words of: forceps, sponge, gauze, and the all important insurance questions.

"No bandage or crutches will fix what is wrong with you, Billy" I heard The Monkey exclaim from another dimension, causing me to fear his return.

"I'm not in the Mohave Desert and can't even stand up. This can't be the showdown." I whispered.

Fear turned to panic as I caught a glimpse of The Monkey. He spoke to an imaginary nurse and said, *"Nurse, hand me a scalpel will you? I need to open his cranium."*

In my weakened and mentally injured condition I thought, *Open my cranium? I wonder where The Monkey went to medical school?* Then as an afterthought, I told my furry antagonist "Make sure you scrub up, Primate."

Monkey and Chimpanzee Nurse returned to an immaterial waiting room. Then the real physicians came in to do their work. I was having a maddening time discerning what was real. I thought about falling back on the philosophy of Descartes, but in the hospital, with my sanity collapsing like an old scaffold, I feared that even he would lack the intellect necessary to yank me from the abyss. *Fucking Nietzsche, right again!* I tipped an imaginary fedora to Zarathustra.

Denials by the police of Tasers being used was evident in the swirling conversation taking place between police and hospital staff. The explanation about my leg and back injuries was bought by everyone—except for one doctor. He insisted on knowing how I had sustained Sciatic nerve damage to both legs at the same time without the use of electrical current. It was a good question and everyone seemed to grow silent and anxiously awaited the answer. For me the question remained unanswered as I passed out again, missing out on what had to be a great imagined and fictional account of my capture.

I awoke as my head was being stitched up; no girlish yelps passed my lips, the lack of screams being much to the dismay of some in the room that sought to take pleasure from my pain. As the wound was closed, I could hear the needle and thread passing through my scalp. It was the exact sound that I had heard many times during the numerous sutures previously applied to my head while operating as a Recon Marine and subsequent Merc overseas. I did not know why the sound was so interesting; than again I'm not sure why Brian May's guitar continued to resound in my ears.

After being treated, I was taken to jail where it became clear that I was to be moved to the several other county jails before the ancient warrants were to be taken care of.

I was taken to the interrogation room before being transported to the county jail. There I was met by a Lieutenant whose son played football with my nephew. He was sort of apologetic in having to arrest me and looked to find the whole thing an inconvenience.

"Look ... you don't seem to be a bad guy. But we have been getting phone calls and letters every day for the past month by someone saying you are a dangerous felon wanted in numerous States. It came to a point where we had to pick you up." He said with what appeared to be unmanufactured concern.

"I may have been irresponsible in the past, but I am certainly not the arch criminal that someone wants you to believe. In fact, I am a published writer that has not even had a traffic ticket in 25 years."

I gave him the name of the book and website displaying all the newspaper articles written about the good the aforementioned historical novel had done for the Native American People. He left the room and returned a short while later.

"Well ... it appears that you are not a horrible person that someone wanted us to believe. But now that you are in custody, we can't just let you go. After all there are warrants and you did try to run."

"Yeah ... to get back to my house and grab my medication, so I didn't pass out and crack my head open! Oh yeah ... too late ... about the cracked head thing." I said, while fingering my stitches.

"The officers said that once you went down that there was no further resistance and that from then on it was a peaceable arrest."

"Peaceful for whom?" I said but then changed my tone so as not to be so confrontational. "That's true. I did not resist, because even if I wanted to, I was in the middle of a seizure." I said. He ignored the comment and glanced down at the arrest report.

"Either way the officers have reduced the charge to misdemeanor resistance instead of felony escape. So it will be a matter of clearing up the warrants without having to serve any time. You probably won't even need a lawyer."

The Lieutenant was quite honest and undeniably well-intentioned. However, as it turned out, he was wrong on both counts. While preparing for what was to be a very harsh dilemma, I saw the Monkey again begin to take shape. He faded in, this time without Simian Nurse in tow, emerging completely in the corner of the interrogation room. His grin appeared first, much like the Cheshire Cat; but the smile had a malicious evil, that Alice (caught in a Wonderland of her own), never had to see.

This time The Monkey wore no clothing. Gone were the drug-induced clownish outfits of the past. This was the real Monkey; yellow strangely feline eyes, sharp fangs, heavily muscled sinewy arms, possessing malevolent desires beyond accurate description The only remnant from the old caricature my mind had manufactured, which had given him human attributes and possessions, was wooden club used for beating unruly inmates. He repeatedly smacked the club on his other hand—palm open to receive each blow. He did not need to taunt me this time, as it was clear what he was telling me.

"Now, Billy ... we will see who is to be gutted!"

My only thought upon hearing his threat was, *How will I ever finish the book?*

People are Strange

Two of the arresting officers brought me in to a processing area at the county jail, and placed me on a wooden bench. I was in front of a large Plexiglas security partition, set in place so that the prison medical staff could view the assembled line of miscreants with injuries. The walk from the police cruiser to the imposing sliding admitting doors was a wet one, as a torrential downpour was flooding the usually dry desert. As in my other jailhouse visits, I scrutinized the despondent and wet prisoners. Some were harmless traffic violators, drug felons, violent felons, and the twitchy, wild-eyed Manson disciples. Regardless of their profile, I met each expressionless stare so as to check for signs that one might be a violent sociopath and worthy of being watched. The ragtag assembly of freaks made my thing of the Door's song "People are Strange." I imagined Jim Morrison's singing the lyrics, while riding a snake seven miles long.

"People are strange when you're a stranger –faces look ugly when you're alone –women seem wicked when you're unwanted—streets are uneven when you are down – when you're strange…… faces come out of the rain."

The song fit the circumstances so well, I was certain that Morrison had been in many jails. Each prisoner had to be examined by a series of triage personal that consisted of doctors, pharmacists, and nurses from the mental health department. Nobody was allowed to go anywhere until cleared by the "labcoats," and only on their approval were the rows of felons funneled to the next station. To be slated for general population, an inmate had to prove he was sane and medically fit, but that wasn't decided until after being booked and banded.

I got a good look at some of the so-called rational-well adjusted offenders, and none of them were even remotely sane. The Monkey is much better adjusted and civilized than some of these cretins. I thought while scanning the room of uni-browed, milk-carton-chinned, salamander-eyed, men with fifth grade educations.

Each prisoner was shoved towards the booking area to receive the ever courteous strip search; to be printed, clothed in jailhouse garb and then assigned to your MOD- housing unit. From the second I got there it was obvious that someone had it in for me.

The arresting officers must have called the deputies, and told them that I resisted, and was a wise ass, I thought. My mind prepared for the coming attempts to make me angry. So the chicken-shit deputies could yell out, "Halverson is dangerous. Get the straps and mace."

The deputies that called must have really blown the whole incident out of proportion, I thought. Because while I was occupied trying to endure the incredible pain coursing through my body from head to toe, every deputy glared at me. It was as if I was the only prisoner in the whole jail. I cursed the medical staff under my breath for allowing every other inmate to go ahead of me while I kept being shifted to the end of the line.

I asked for a wheelchair and was refused and told to sit there and shut up until a doctor checked me out. The wait was ten hours. Every hour I tried for the attention of a nurse, indicating with sign language that I was sweating like a pig, nauseous, and trembling. Taken individually, each resulted from suffering a bad concussion, but when the warning signs appeared together, and the same time, it predicted an impending blackout. Finally, after being there for ten hours, they called my name and I limped on one leg into the office.

"What's wrong with you?" she asked. Apparently hopping on one leg and stitches running diagonally from my scalp to just above my eyebrow, wasn't enough to for her to diagnose my injuries. I was glad that the nurse examining me had such towering intellect.

"I got transferred here from the Hospital Emergency room; I suffered a concession, sciatica in both legs, and a blown-out knee. I need my medications and something for the pain." I pleaded.

"Go back and sit down." She said unsympathetically, while continuing to pick at something on her chin.

"Hey, listen. I've got serious brain issues and am hurt real bad. In a few more minutes, I'm going to blackout again." I said, getting mad at her incompetence, not aware that being an idiot helps candidates get hired in the Arizona prison system.

"Go back and sit down and wait for your name to be called. Then the deputies will take you through booking." A nurse with a face like an Emu said. Emu face, scaly neck, stubby beak, Gila Monster Tongue—no hallucination—no shit!

"Hey, listen for a second. I'm real dizzy. I need crutches to move or my head is going to crack the floor again. You don't want my blood pooling all over the floor, it might wash away the diarrhea." That got a laugh from the other miscreants.

She was pissed. I had broken the cardinal rule of bothering a nurse, as well as speaking with sarcasm, and making other inmates laugh. She yelled out, "Deputies."

Great, now I'm tagged as a troublemaker, I thought. The two biggest deputies grabbed me by the shoulders.

"Start walking, you're nothing but a fucking faker." There was no mistaking that the stern tone meant "or else."

"Does that mean I'm fucking other fakers? I just got here, so don't blame me because somebody's fucking the fakers. Do you have an alibi?" I said.

"Say one more thing, inmate". He said while reaching for a canister. I said no more.

In Pima County Jail, the officers beat-down the inmates in a secluded thumping room. But where I was to go next—Kinston County—was different. There, the inmates just "beat the shit" out of other inmates, as the entire jail was a giant thumping facility, and everybody had to fight or be 'punked' and labeled a bitch. Kingston County Jail was going to be my next stop after serving my sentence at Pima. So there was that to look forward to.

From one cesspool to another, I thought. The other inmates were counting time until their release into the outside world, whereas I counted the days remaining in one jail before being sent to another jail for incarceration. The Kingston correctional institution was a facility that was the most crowded, dirty, bacteria infested, violent jail. *That's a hell of a place for anyone to serve time,* I thought.

But there was a good chance the paperwork would get misplaced. So with some luck Pima Jail might be my last stop. It was still something to worry about.

What a fucking drag. It's was like being told 'The Turd dinner is over, and since you were such a good boy, you get to have desert, here is a plate of shit-cookies'. I tried to laugh as I silently considered the dilemma, but it just wasn't funny, not at all.

The deputies dragged me on one leg to the searching area. One guy propped me against the snot-speckled wall, while the other began the pat-down, which was the forerunner to removing all clothing attire—my attire and not the deputies.

At least I hoped it was only my cloths to come off. Otherwise, Pima Jail had a corn-hole station in the processing loop. As expected there were the snide comments and insults so as to force a confrontation and dare any inmates to question the deputies' authority. I was in no condition to question anything, only wanted to get up to the medical housing ward, and get arraigned, and find out how many days this shithole was my home.

Fuck it's like I'm in Lake County Jail in Chicago all over again.

With the pat-down complete, and the all-too-long crouch squeeze over, my bi-curious, handsy, escorts moved me towards the print cubicle. I lost all balance and smacked my head again on the wooden podium. "Fucking idiots, I warned them." I whispered. The glittery tiny lights approached again and then darkness.

I woke up in a dark hallway, in a wheelchair, with a brand new goose-egg to go with the brand new stitches. Still no medicine, and still none of that "good ole compassion" nurses were understood to have. And my luck wasn't changing; directly in front of me, clipboard in hand, white cap clipped onto frizzy hair, stood the most vindictive, hateful, iron-hearted bitch I'd ever met.

"So, welcome back among the living, Mr. Halverson," she said in a prickly voice, as if her mouth was used on too many pricks. The details of her facial features gradually intensified, and there before me was "The Church Lady."

"Is she a flashback or pure natural ugliness?" I questioned my receptors. "It must be real-world ugly, cause I'm too tired to have a flashback."

Then she went through the usual questions to make sure I had knocked retard into my brain and that I was not suicidal.

"What year is it?" I nailed it

"Where are you?" Got that one too'

"Who is the President?" Missed that one, thought it was Clinton. She shook her head (not sadly, but like she was glad I failed a test...bitch)

"Are you thinking of hurting yourself or having suicidal thoughts?" I answered no. Otherwise, I was going to have to get into dignity jammies (fuck...just call them diapers) and have a sleepover in the nuthouse. I'd be put in with all the "I killed my family because god or a beagle told me to" inmates.

"Are you thinking of hurting someone else." I answered no again. But I thought, *Yeah, I'm thinking about killing you, if that condescending attitude doesn't stop.*

"Look, nurse, I just want to sleep. I've been knocked out twice while in police custody. Are you trying for number three?

"You might be faking to get into the medical ward." She said with contempt.

"What is it with you people? Didn't you read the hospital reports? I told the doctors downstairs that I have been under treatment by the Veterans Administration for years," I declared, as I grew tired and more impatient. "Listen, lady, I got over ten years of hospital records that show multiple brain injuries. I'm starting to think that maybe it isn't me with the brain problem." I blurted out, then immediately wished it could be taken back.

"Mr. Halverson, let me tell you something. That is exactly the kind of emotional disruption that is going to make problems for you." She waved The Med Ward Deputy over and wrote on her clipboard. She gripped the clipboard as if it was Moses' tablets. She scribbled with anger, using the kind of wrath only a nurse stuck working in a prison could have. I was not able to see what was written, but it must have been "troublemaker."

While the Deputy approached I thought, *Shit lady, not my fault you're in here with all the cretins, should have studied harder.*

The Deputy grabbed the Wheelchair by the handles and pushed me into the Med Ward C. He watched while I slide from chair to a metal bunk; complete with pre-urinated mattress, no pillow, and a ragged gray blanket that smelled like scrotum sweat. I never personally sniffed balls, but it has to be horrible. There was a label on the side of the bunk, with a number and a few words. My blurry vision prevented a reading, but it too, probably said something like "troublemaker".

Everybody in the ward was injured and in pain. Just as many were murderers and had already been there a few years. They could not be transferred into general population, due to having sleep apnea, diabetes, a bad heart, or some other condition mandating constant observation. I did not sleep the entire first night. The amount of screams was incredible, screams of agony, screams of regret for killing somebody, screams of regret for failing to kill the intended victim; screams for the sake of screaming … fuck it … Screams … screams … screams.

The morning was no better. When I finally found the strength to sit up and look around at the other misfits, I was greeted with a sight that was forever etched in my memory. My bunk was in encircled by a liquid mixture of puke, diarrhea, and urine.

Fuck, somebody really wants me to suffer, I thought, while holding back the bile.

The staff had reserved the best seat in the house for me. My bunk was located in the center of the wards most horrible section of real-estate—"The Detox Neighborhood." The four bunkmates located around me were all kicking some form of substance abuse. Bunk one—a 70 Year Old Wino that crapped himself every hour on the hour. Bunk Two—Meth Head, puking was his thing; that and talking to the invisible man, Bunk Three—Heroin Kick, a Trifecta of puke, piss, and shit. Bunk Four—Painkiller addiction, he could make it to the bathroom, but cried all day and night that something hurt. Everybody in the unit wanted to stuff the old Wino in the Crybaby's mouth to shut him up. On most days, the foul liquids on the floor just stayed there all day. The nurses refused to mop anything up so it was left to another inmate to clean the messes up. Needless to say, there weren't many volunteers.

"Med Call" came and went and there were no meds for me. I wheeled up to the tiny window and asked where my prescriptions were. I was told that none of my records from the V.A or other hospitals arrived in the mail.

"I guess this place doesn't have a phone. Why don't you just call the doctor?" I asked, while fighting a splitting headache that was so painful it crossed my eyes. Then the answer—which I prayed never to hear again—came forth:

"Mr. Halverson, you'll just have to wait. Don't be a..... (At that point it was like slow motion).....t r o u b l e m a k e r!"

I wanted to scream, but wasn't certain I could drown out Mr. Achy Guy, Chatty Meth Head, or Cry Baby Craig.

That is how it went for the next two days. No sleep. I was held (until the Court arraignment appearance) in the filthiest medical ward in the world, given a reputation of an instigator that liked to fight (while in a wheelchair), and was unable to end the incessant garbled voices that droned nonstop in daytime. I thought the first night was bad. Disneyland when compared to the daytime.

We were woken up at 4 a.m. each morning to check for vitals. As it was impossible for me to sleep, I wheeled to an empty corner and tried to find a little solitude. It was impossible. There were about twenty other assholes in the ward. All of whom had some degree of crazy. Throughout the entire day, one inmate after another broke my reverie by attempting to spark up a conversation.

The declarations, excuses, accusations—from lunatic inmates—blurred into one giant meaningless sentence: "I didn't stab my wife on purpose" ... "I didn't kill and bury my mother" ... "my bedsores are bleeding again" ... "is anyone going to clean up the puke?" ... "I hear voices" ... "why are you in here" ... "Kingston County, you never want to go there" ... "which of you assholes stole my biscuit?"

Fuck .... it was mind-numbing. Almost every ridiculous decree issued by another prisoner burst several brain cells in my head.

Finally, it was my time to go in front of the judge. I was taken downstairs to the main courtroom and put into a cage filled shoulder-to-shoulder with other guys waiting to be sentenced or arraigned. I was again one of the last to be called. I was still messed up in the head, barely able to form a cohesive thought; without the proper treatment, and in more pain than could be imagined. I had a migraine on top of a concussion stirred into a cauldron of dangerously low depression and sky-scraping anxiety. My brother Sven watched the whole proceedings from behind a window located in the visitor's area. I looked horrible.

Even the judge was sympathetic and shocked that I was in front of her for a twenty-five year old warrant. The D.A read off the charges, and in my disoriented condition, and without the aid of a lawyer, I agreed to a 30 day sentence, followed by a hold and possible transfer to Kingston County for resentencing.

The 30 days felt like 30 years. On the third day in, a skinny Deputy named Muller begun telling the other staff that I was never a Recon Marine and never in the military, which was why they couldn't get my V.A medical records. It was a lie and an excuse to deny my medications. Finally, the day came when I couldn't take anymore of his shit. I was complaining to a nurse not getting any of the meds for depression and anxiety, and if the situation didn't change something bad might happen,

Muller stepped between us with two more officers to back him up. "Quit crying, Halverson. You were never in the service, much less a Recon Marine. They don't take pussies." He laughed and it took all my control not to sternum punch, which was a spot reachable from the wheelchair.

"You're wrong about me being in the Marines." I said rolling up my sleeve to show the U.S.M.C tattoo.

"And my records, including my DD214, show the Recon Marine M.O.S. My brother got all my medical history from the V.A as proof, he is bringing the entire file to processing, so pretty soon you'll have to give me my medications. And you know an apology might be nice."

"Bullshit. Shut up, Halverson. You're just faking like all the other assholes in here." That comment; got the attention of all injured inmates, especially the ones faking missing arms and legs, faking bullet holes, or faking diabetes. All the inmates were mad.

"No man ... you're out of line, abusing a vet in front of witnesses. That's real smart, Muller. Stopping me from getting pain medicine is one thing, but holding up stuff that has been prescribed by the V.A for my mental problems, everyone here knows that's wrong." I said. Muller stood his ground, but the other deputies backed away, their faces conveying that Muller had gone too far.

"I can tell you from experience, no Recon detachment would ever take a loud-mouth pussy like you, Muller. Is Recon-Envy eating away at your rent-a-cop brain?"

That was it. Two deputies wheeled me back to my bunk and whispered that I'd just made a big mistake. After about an hour Muller rectified my "mistake."

"Halverson, roll it up." Muller said meaning that I was being transferred to another location.

I grabbed my stuff and wheeled into the hallway beyond the thick metal door. There was Muller. "Guess where you're going, Halverson?"

"Am I getting an early release?" I asked, knowing being released had about as much of a chance of happening, as Monkeys flying out of Muller's ass. "Shit...stop thinking about monkeys." I murmured.

"That's real funny. 'Sheltered Living' is going to be your home for the next two weeks." Muller said grinning as a village fool, which he was. The name 'Sheltered Living' was very deceptive.

In prison vernacular, the term Shelter, best described something like a bomb shelter. The cell did not shelter to person sent there; it sheltered everyone else from you. It was where they put medical ward inmates that caused trouble or fought other prisoners.

It was a six by six cell with four bunks. It had one sink, one toilet, no windows, and no phone. Each bunk was only a couple feet away from the toilet and where their fellow residents crapped. The room had nothing to offer except for three other angry guys with mental issues in the tiniest space imaginable.

But not all the news was bad, some was medieval. Out of the entire 24-hour cycle, while being wedged into a concrete hollow, each person got one hour outside alone in the community room to make a call.

I protested the decision, making it clear that my phobias included small spaces, crowded areas, and restricted movement. Muller just laughed.

They forced me into the cell. Within only a few minutes, I began to throw-up, then begun to shake uncontrollably. One of the other inmates hit the emergency button and told the deputy at the other end of the transmitter that it looked like I was having a seizure.

"Too bad," said the voice thru the squawk-box.

I leaned out of the wheelchair to puke for the twentieth time, blacked out, and smashed my head on the toilet bowl rim, hitting the same place that had been stitched up only a few days before. Third concussion while in custody, bringing the grand total since joining the marines to seven, two of which having been previously diagnosed as severe brain trauma.

The deputy came rushing in and shook me awake. (That's right, "shook!"). Then as Muller watched by the door, the deputy lifted me back into the chair by my neck. (That's right "Neck".) While still holding me in a choke (that's right "Choke") hold with one hand, he wheeled me out of the cell and into the emergency section of the Medical floor.

I was "out of my mind" deranged, shocked at the mistreatment. All from a twenty-five year old warrant and because Deputy Muller was a prick, and pissed that I proved him wrong. But, the safe money was on the fact that Muller was a prick of unsurpassed ability.

Who is the criminal now? I thought. The incident was making me loss respect of the law considering my past arrest experiences. While being examined, word of my treatment since my arrival at Pima County Jail got to the Supervisor named Officer Valance. He immediately came to the jail. When he got to the examination room, he told everyone to leave, including the doctors.

"Look, I've seen your military and medical records. Your brother Sven made sure they got to me, and your Sister Ann must have called a hundred times. I was also in the Marines and this shit is not going to happen anymore while you're at my jail. I'm going to move you to Ward D. Nobody on my staff will harass you anymore. But do me a favor, keep your mouth shut about this shit, stay away from Muller, and just do your last couple weeks. Think you can you do that for me?"

"Sure thing, I just want to mind my own business and get back to my life."

"That's good. But, there is something you should be aware of. As much as Muller hates you, it is a sure bet he's already called over to Kingston County jail and reminded them that we have you in custody and there is a hold on the release date. So when your 30 days are over there won't be a release. Kingston jail is going to pick you up on the outstanding warrant. It's a no bail warrant so they'll lock you up till a court day in is assigned."

"Officer, I'm already doing thirty days. And you're saying that I have to be locked up in another jail, until the court consents to see me, and then get sentenced to do more time? This is a nightmare."

He patted my shoulder and smiled, "Don't worry, you were in Recon, you'll get thru this."

He left and I was moved to ward D. I had already lost 22 pounds, while my mental health unraveled, and was on the wrong medications.

Then I found out that nobody had any idea how long my total incarceration was going to be. However the consensus from the jail-house lawyers was that I was looking at about a year.

<u>Kingston</u>

My medical condition prevented me from climbing the steps and taking a seat on the white "convict bus" used to transfer prisoners from Pima to Kingston County Jail. The deputies considered my wheelchair another example of defiance and interpreted it as a refusal to go to the biggest shithole in the universe.

Once again stitches, piles of hospital records, atrophied knees reduced to the size of an anorexic school girl didn't justify my inability to stand, much less climb steps. The pea-brained deputies mouthed something to each other and then called for a special van to drive me to The Towers – the affectionate name for Kingston County jail. I was able to read their lips. It was like a bad dream, or bad acid trip, unbelievably the word *Troublemaker* hovered between the officers and me. It swelled in size, acquired marquee-style colored light bulbs from the void, thereby highlighting the imaginary flashing sign that read…..**TROUBLEMAKER.**

"What is wrong with all you guys. How does Cripple translate into Troublemaker? Have I been sent to a Prison-Planet orbiting an alternate galaxy, a planet that has a fucked up dictionary, which has only one word—Troublemaker—on every page?" These questions exploded in my brain, as it was shocking to me, that all the prison staff were so thick-headed.

Eventually they picked me up in the van. But first they switched me into a dilapidated, ingeniously torturous, wheelchair, missing foot rests, having only elastic cellophane stretched across the frame. The guard-rigged foot rest caused both ankle bones to bang together and rub against each other constantly, further damaging my legs for good.

I arrived at Kingston County and was put through the most arduous treatment imaginable. Muller must have called ahead, and told room service to make me eat the Persecution Platter. I could go on and on about how horribly the guards made my stay. Even going so far as to have fellow gang banger inmates try and fuck me up. That is for a whole other story or better yet Department of Prisons Investigation.

There's a very important detail concerning my time at Kingston County that is worth mentioning. The medical staff skipped the majority examination process and tagged me for immediate entry into the medical ward. But only after the standard ten-hour, ankle-bone crunching wait in a cell so disgusting, that it defies description. Suffice it to state that the toilet had feces stacked up so high, the self-aware (beyond explanation) malevolent mess peered over the rim, as if searching for a new target. A target of what, I was not sure, but I stayed as far away from the bubbling goo as possible, while segregated in the five by five containment (should be contamination) cell.

While waiting for some sort of direction about what the fuck I was supposed to do, I noticed a skinny Mexican Gang Banger staring at me. He glanced around to make sure the coast was clear, and then sprinted across the gap between his holding cell and mine. He got behind me, before I was able to get the broken wheelchair to spin. He reached behind the toilet and retrieved a sharpened object. Crouching behind the doorframe, he tried to strike up a conversation. At first it was just friendly nonsense, feeling me out, which I ignored, except to make it clear with body language and facile expressions that I considered him a skinny punk. His tone became threatening and he made a real pathetic performance to display his gang tattoos.

"Listen, punk. If you think that shit all over your arms scares me then you are mistaken. Here is some ink that should worry your worthless ass!" I rolled up my sleeves and let him take in my Pankration, Muay Thai, Recon Marine, and sword art covering my forearms. He didn't understand, as it there were serious misgivings that he could spell. So as expected he went right to the overt challenge. My worry wasn't about getting stabbed, but more about having to beat the tacos out of this fuzzy-haired weasel, and get even more time. The deputies at both jails already had their sights on me.

Why is it that no matter how hard you try to mind your business in this world, sooner or later, a fuck-head with a knife tries to start some shit? I thought, deliberating how to defuse the situation without having to cripple the gang banger. He wasn't going to leave without making a name for himself.

Wheeling in close I looked him in the eye. "Stab me, motherfucker, I'm having a bad day anyway. So make your move, or get the fuck out of my cell before I strangle you and make you crap all over your clean prison jumpsuit. That will get you a name, but not the one wanted. Once your buddies see you unconscious and covered in shit, you're new tag with be Shit-Weasel. Then nobody will be scared of your stupid ass, and it will be you getting shanked." I wheeled past him and sat in the cell entrance, giving him my back and showing how little impressed I was. He lost his nerve and pushed by me, straight back to his cell. Must have thought I was a crazy old fucker. Nobody likes to fight crazy old fuckers, even other crazy old fuckers.

After the Weasel had gone, I was taken down a long dark never-ending hallway, traveling distance seeming to challenge the physical architecture. My wheelchair, pushed by a Filipino guard, rolled past the Med Ward, the Crazy Ward, The Electrocution Ward, The Water-Boarding Ward, even past the Beat-Up-the-Mouthy-Prisoner Ward. I was shoved into a room that has about as much to do with Medical Observation as Guantanamo Prison. I was back in "The Hole."

Four 300-pound derelicts, sat around a table playing cards, while arguing about the relative merits of settling arguments using sharpened bunk springs. They asked why I had been placed into the disciplinary isolation cell.

"You guys got it wrong, I'm here for a twenty-five year old warrant. I've only just been here a day and haven't caused any problems." I responded.

"You had to do something because you're in The Hole. This is where they put violent prisoners or sexual predators."

Right then my heart melted through the cement, burned through every floor, and dropped into hell. It was going to be long night. I already had a plan to kill myself "death before dishonor." But these assholes are in for the fight of their lives. Wheelchair, busted head and ankles, notwithstanding; somebody in this room is going with me if they come for me when the lights go out. I never slept and kept ready. But nothing happened. The only unusual occurrence, aside from being trapped in a tiny cell with four deviates, was that each inmate took turns morphing into versions of The Monkey. *When are the hallucinogens ever going to leave my system for good?* I wondered. Each deviate said three words while in the form of The Monkey, *"Death in the Desert."*

At four in the morning I was removed to stand trial for my probation violation. When I arrived at the courtroom holding cell there was another long wait before I got my time in front of the judge. My lawyer already warned me that he would ask for a continuance and try for a different venue and maybe we might get a more merciful judge. Everyone that went before me was getting the maximum sentence and the judge was in a very bad mood. I refused the offer of putting things off and told the lawyer that there was no way I was going back to The Hole; I was leaving that night, either dead by my own hand or by being released by the system. But I was leaving. They wheeled me close to the bench so the judge could get a look at me. Once again, my lawyer cautioned me to reconsider and ask for another date. The judge read out loud the arrest reports, while the prosecutor interjected his own criticisms; mostly about how a couple years behind bars would do an asshole like me some good. The Judge was nodding his head and seemed to be agreeing with the D.A. Then the Great Spirit interceded on my behalf. The judge read to the part about why I was at the park every morning – **feeding crows and other birds**. The judge looked into my eyes and said, "Any person that feeds injured animals can't be all bad. Case dismissed." The crows that I fed, every morning for two years had secured my release. The Judge's decision drove home my belief that being kind to animals brings mercy from the heavens. I was out in five hours and after taking a week to recover from the three recent episodes of brain trauma (while in custody), and multiple seizures, I was back to writing and finishing 'Gutting the Monkey'.

The typing was slow going. There were many mistakes to correct and an equal amount of unreadable passages. Trash baskets were filled to capacity with unacceptable proofs and "writer's block" was as common as morning coffee. It seemed that my additional injuries were making it increasingly hard to write. The migraines and seizures came more often and were infuriatingly painful. I eventually left the state and moved to Laguna to live with my bother Sven. He lived closer to the Veterans Hospital so it made getting there much easier.

I needed Sven to watch over me because the seizures were coming much more frequently and added to the "writer's block of pain". Many times I wanted nothing more than to never write again. If it wasn't for my friends and family, especially Sven whom I lived with, there would be no book.

The temptation to return to drugs was strong. The pain, while working the last few chapters was unbearable. But now the novel is done and there is only one thing left to do, in accordance with the title, "**Gut the Monkey**." For there can be no legitimate ending until we (the Monkey and I) square off in the desert. For all the immeasurable discomforts, well-earned punishments, attacks from unexpected people and places, and burnt-out brain cells, it was all worth it. I have written a second book and have done so under almost impossible conditions. Now, there is only thing left to do.

Dirty Creature

According to the governmental propaganda; prisoners of the various United States correctional facilities were fortunate to stay in such a well-supervised system. Of course anyone viewing the jails from the inside probably found the sweeping political changes were really designed to restore Spanish Inquisition-style rehabilitation. So it must have been a sheer stroke of luck that I was able to study the unforgettable points of interest and inhale the flowery aromas of the Arizona jails. Some memories were very revolting and each is probably forever imbedded in my psyche. Whenever I close my eyes the visions return: inmates covered in urine and crap because nurses refused to clean them up, Detox prisoners accidentally shitting in the sink, or just the immense scale of insanity However, upon my release, and while I was occupied in the ever critical task of trying to recover and finish the novel. The Monkey was back in his world preparing to see me for the last time.

As with most epic battles, things had to be prepared before the showdown could begin. The Monkey's pre-fight routine involved rekindling friendships with old acquaintances, all of which were also vacationing from the exhausting responsibility of breaking spirits. The Demon reunion was at a grizzly carnival/funhouse located off old Route 66, a mile behind the Amboy volcano.

Amboy was once a stopover for movie stars traveling from L.A to Vegas. Long ago '66' carried parades of shark-finned convertibles, flame-painted hot rods, and customized limos. Each vehicle was filled to capacity with the same over-indulgent rabble: hollywood starlets (doomed to return to Iowa, after the producer's boner returned to his pants), martini swilling playboys in speckled cardigan sweaters, agnostic guitar strumming pothead/surfers, and the popular ever-generational Jack Kerouac Beat Imitators—longing for poetry, but settling for extravagance. Throwing dust, squealing wheels, the mechanized Jack Rabbits zipped along '66' on their way to the Nevada Casinos, with self-awareness as dim as the distant city-lights.

Decades later, modern interstate highways had replaced route 66. However the parade continued with marchers of a different sort, mostly composed of trash caught in sandstorms, strips of shredded tires sucked briefly into activity by the jet-wash of seldom-cars, and flycatchers winging from fence post to fence post, while taking insects from the air.

Amboy was a decaying ghost-town; with sunken neighborhoods of abandoned schools and forgotten churches, and it was as illusionary as The Monkey. That made it the perfect site for the funhouse. The Monkey arrived and showed his ticket stub to a goat-faced attendant. The Goat-dude had been employed as the mascot for Anton Levay back in the 70's during the heyday of the black arts. It was a good gig for the goat-dude, as Satan worship was all the rage. Levay was the high priest of a sizable coven of black robed goof-balls that wanted more than anything else to meet Beelzebub. Most times, in fact all times, Legion failed to appear, but it was still a great opportunity for an orgy. Anton was a crafty S.O.B.

The Monkey went through a turn-style made of human bones. The turnstile functioned much the same as the token-operated mechanisms located at a New York subway entrance; except at the Funhouse, spinning fibula propellers and tibia supports had been substituted for aluminum. Loudspeakers mounted on rusty poles played "Dirty Creature" by the Split Enz. The song was favorite song among the various Monsters and Monkeys. The tune was at number 30 on the Abomination Top 100, but climbing fast, as the lyrics made the vicious freaks feel all warm and manic inside.

The misshapen crowd loved the musical message. Many of whom halted and listened, while still in the middle of Funhouse events, such as: decapitations, baby fur-seal shucking, pin the battery cable on the donkey, Bobbing for Bobby (Bobby was a dwarf with a bite-sized head), and purchasing cotton candy. Everyone's favorite stanza played:

"Dirty Creature of habit, little horrors here to stay—Anyone in his right mind would tell it to go away – But the riv-

*er of dread runs deep, full of unspeakable things – The Crea-
ture don't mess around, I don't want to mess with him/"*

The song ended and The Monkey immediately searched
among the carnival rides, game booths, and freak show tents
for his old friends. He found them by the Tilt-A-Hurl (a ride
that spun so fast that nothing edible stayed down). Gathered
together were a few of the other Vice-lords; Fats Sugarman
(with the power to make anyone crave sweets), Hookahpus (a
creature resembling an octopus, with a bloated, hookah-pipe
body, filled with crack mist. All eight tentacles were rubber
surgical tubes, attached to a comfortable inhaler), the irrepress-
ible Juggs O' Malley (could make any normal person a porno-
graghy kook), The Pit Boss (a walking slot machine that only
paid off in flattened scabs, but turned people into degenerate
gamblers), and Sticky Fingers McGee (a normal looking dude,
but could make anyone a shoplifter). It was unknown what
made Sticky's hands so gluey. However, many said it was because he was such good friends with Juggs O' Malley.

It was a nasty crew. They might have appeared laughable,
but for the fact, that all were soul ripping, family destroying,
carnivorous fiends. The Funhouse was also "one fucked up"
fantasy park. Rides were also not the kind a tourist would find
at any Earth-bound carnival.

The "Scare-us-wheel" broke off the rusty retraining bolts
and rolled into a pond filled with paranoid Piranha. The Zipper
sewed real zippers, which studded vertically from beltline to
neckline. The Coaster Roller ejected the ticket holders onto the
tracks, at the highest curve, and then rolled over the bodies.
The Monkey conversed with the other Vicelords.

*"I am really getting tired of dealing with Billy. When is
he going to kill himself? I tempt him on a day in and day out
basis. My only real holiday is when he is in jail or running
across country. Shit. All my problems would be over is the
serial killer farmers had planted him in the ground next to
the beets."* The Monkey said with a hint of surrender.

"Listen, Monkey, it is a hard job, ruining hopes and
dreams. You don't think I get tired of watching dolts consumed
with internet porn. We all have our share of burdens." Juggs O'
Malley said, while his hands edged dangerously close, to what
a referee might have flagged as a self-fondle penalty.

"Billy is out of jail and he will want your blood. So meet him in the desert and face up to the possibility of a gutting. A Gutting is an ugly thing to witness, but sometimes finishing off our symbiotic partners must be done to find real happiness." Hookahpus said. He then put one the tentacles to his mouth and smoked some crack, breaking the cardinal rule of: "doing your own stash."

"Yeah, you're both right. That fucker Billy has been a thorn in my furry side for too long. It is time to put "The End" to this chapter in my life. Yes, let it be so; Death in the Desert that is the way of the warrior!" The Monkey said. He walked with the group to the Freak Show tent.

A Circus Barker was outside the tent, attacking a mob of mutant rubes with promises, "Step right up, horrible disfigurements; impossible to look at without cursing your own eyes." He had an alligator snout on top of an eight foot human body, wore red garters on both arms to hold up his striped shirt sleeves, and a straw hat. Every few seconds he swiped at the air with his decorated cane. Many funhouse visitors thought the Barker had all the panache of Professor Harold Hill. In between shifts, he took bites out of the Chickenboy (who by the way wasn't looking all that good). Professor Hill would have never approved of the Barker's appetite of weak mutants. But the Barker was undeniably good at his job and his antics brought The Monkey over to the tent.

"Who doesn't like a good Freak show?" The Monkey asked. Together the group bought a ticket and went inside. The song playing through the speakers changed to "Ballad of a Lonely Man" by Material Issue – most appropriate as it was about revenge, death, loneliness, and deserted highways.

Inside the tent was a collection of freaks unmatched anywhere, except Reality Television. The first display was "Palin Grizzy Mom, " a bear that was considered by the other woodland animals to have brain damage, and had even eaten her own young—to nobody's dismay. There was the Snookie display, Snookie was claimed by some to be the only Palin offspring that got away. However, judging Snookie solely by her looks, it was doubtful she would be eaten—by anything that did not die afterwards.

In the corner display were the Bankers and Investment Brokers—practitioners of an ancient form of magic. They had the powers of Merlin; able to magically take money or homes from poor families, and then—without compassion—toss the broken clan onto the street. But the real magic was in the spells they cast, enabling them to avoid righteous bullets and still fool lower class, time and time again.

The Monkey and his minions were so repulsed by the first three Freak displays they did not proceed to the My Roboto display, which was famous for being equally hated in all dimensions and alternative realties.

Something caught their eye while exiting the tent and they could not tear themselves away. The glass case housed the most repulsive creature the Vice-lords had ever viewed (and Sticky Fingers had really seen some weird shit). The sign simply had two words – "The Horm" and below a warning tag—
Don't feed the Horm or bang on the cage.

The Monkey and his group of deviates prepared to separate, so as to return to the duties; of tempting and torturing their respective wretches. However, a few of the Vice-lords had some advice concerning the best methods for dispensing of Billy.

"Lure him underneath a ledge and drop a Sonora cactus on his head. Leave it to me, ol' Sticky to come up with the best idea. Make him look like "Pinhead." Sticky Fingers intoned to the Monkey. A moment later Sticky heard a commotion near the Freak exhibition. It sounded as if someone or something was getting eaten, curious, he craned his neck to observe the disruption, just in time to see the Alligator-snout Barker take a chunk out of the Chickenboy's thigh.

"No, no! You got it wrong, Sticky. I say dig a pit in the ground and pound stakes, covered with feces, in the center of the hole. Billy falls in, and dies of infectious puncture wounds. Everybody knows you can dig and have plenty of experience using feces." Juggs O' Malley told the Monkey.

"I got it, I got it!" Fats Sugerman yelled excitedly, a little too high from a chocolate fix. "Put a candy bar laced with strychnine on the sand, where the fight is to take place. Billy gets hungry, eats it and dies." Then he too spun around to observe the Barker swallow the rest of the Chickenboy. The Barker belched loudly. "No manners!" Fats said disgustedly, while scratching an itch under the fifth blubber layer. When the scratching was completed, he yanked a package of donuts out from the fourth blubber layer. He offered a donut to each of his friends. Nobody accepted.

"Shut up, all of you. I know Billy better than anyone. It is going to be a stand up fight. His history of addictions will be what defeats him when it is all over. He is no match for me." The Monkey declared. To make his point, he produced a scimitar out of thin air, and then made a few practice thrusts.

"Fun at the Funhouse! Exactly the kind of entertainment I needed before the fight. Billy is about to get ripped to shreds and he's too stupid to realize what's coming. I'm looking forward to the desert," The Monkey told the crew. *"Enough is enough."*

The End

The final excerpt from Billy's diary.

"The End" by the Doors has already been used in the film "Apocalypse Now." I went through my entire memory, front to back and feverishly scanned the entire catalog of music stored in the dominate right side of my brain. However, although I dread using the same Doors song, there is none better. The lyrics are the best preamble to the final curtain call.

"Lost in a Roman wilderness of pain – and all of the children are insane – the killer awoke before dawn, he put his boots on – he took a face from the ancient gallery – and said.....Monkey, I want to kill you! (Monkey is my word not Morrison's)

This chapter will likely conclude with a death of one of the central characters. As I write these words there is no way to determine who will survive. The Monkey has a very good a chance of winning our final showdown. Sure, I've been in many fights and have plenty of experience in giving and receiving injuries, but The Monkey doesn't just hurt a man physically. Hell … he eats his opponent's dreams and has the soul for desert. That kind of attack beats a haymaker or a dislocation anytime. I'm hoping my anger and rage will allow me to "win the day."

His existence turned my life into a terrible experience; an experience about as bad as could be humanly endured. We are both old and have had enough of each other. We are both eager to finish what was started in Africa 30 years ago. Call it a Ho-down, call it a smack-down, call it a showdown, I don't give a shit. The label can change, but the intent stays the same "A fight to the death between two rivals full of hate."

Regardless who will claim victory, it will be a righteous kill, much like the fight in "Thunderdome"—two men enter, one man leaves. In this Gladiatorial Arena, located in the Mohave Desert between several inactive volcanic mountains, one man and one Monkey will enter. Place no bets, because nobody really knows which species will walk out alive. Of course, as with The Beginning, so it will be with The End. Therefore only the perfect song (to be cued later) can provide the necessary inspiration and background for such a bloody and violent confrontation.

When it comes right down to it phrases such as "The End" or "The Beginning" are irrelevant. For me the End is the Beginning. Dead or Alive, I'll be born anew.

This novel is almost at the long awaited conclusion. At times it appeared that the chapters would never be completed and the torture would go on and on. The final chapter can only be written in the most empty, harsh, and desolate of landscapes. For that reason, the Marble Mountains, located deep in the Mohave Desert, off old Route 66 is the perfect place. It has everything; imposing volcanic peaks, rough terrain, extreme temperatures, and a large assortment of creatures that only come out at night (such as I had once been). The dry riverbeds, molten caves, and canyons, each contain invisible "spirits of the earth". Often desert ghosts appear as sand specters disguised as narrow corkscrew twisters, other nights they come to you as a sound – the long lamenting howl of a lonely coyote. Neither version will whisper encouragement or predict defeat. The spirits only had one thing to say to all visitors, "when you're here—in the Mohave, you're as empty inside as the lands outside." It is kind of cool, really.

Long ago, while on the road, I met a wizened Prospector. I stumbled upon him while exploring a cavern engraved into a jagged mountaintop. We continued to encounter each other, during real explorations, and during imagined cross-dimensional acid trips. The Prospector told me the location of valuable fossils. But more importantly, he foretold that I was quickly approaching a very ghastly demise. He told me to change my ways, stop 'about' writing and really begin a novel, so as to keep the promises to my family. He told me to write a book (with James, the rest of my family, and our friend – Philippe. The book was to be about my Grandfather and his journeys with the Ojibwa people.

After the drugs wore off, and I cleaned up, he no longer visited me. I continued to search for him in deserts, forests, and other remote areas. I missed his kind words and guidance. It was only years later, after the mist cleared, that I recognized the Prospector for who he really was—my Grandfather. He had found a way to enter my hallucinations and drag me out of the dark wilderness where I'd been for decades. The Prospector would be sorely missed, especially because I was about to pick a fight with a Monkey/Demon.

But my success or failure does not reside in the voices of remembered and loved ancestors. The future is in my hands and takes shape in the figure of a knife. Hands, knifes, spirits, the recognition of truth, and maybe the desire for forgiveness is that all will be needed for The Gutting.   ***This Concludes Billy's diary.***

The following has been recounted by the Authors

I'm ready for battle, Billy thought. The desert's uneven terrain offers plenty of natural objects that can be forged, whittled, or stretched into weapons. The narrow river banks, old mining tunnels, caves, and sinkholes allow for the creation of excellent booby traps.

"Can the Monkey be Gutted? Can his cadre of demons be cast back into the abyss? Or will I fall victim to weapons used to attack the mind?" Billy asked himself.

It really didn't matter what happens, as the outcome will be the same; sand will turn malevolently dark, wind will moan, blood-red sun will rise.

Dawn came and Sven put another log on the campfire. He and Billy shared a stogie and a shot of brandy. Sven picked a thick branch out of the wood pile and insisted on joining the battle. Billy refused any help.

"The Monkey can only be seen and killed by me. Sven … listen, man, I appreciate the offer. But you fighting an invisible foe would be like a blindfolded kid swinging a stick at a piñata. Shit, with my string of bad luck, you'd probably end up accidentally cracking my skull." Billy reminded his brother.

Billy sharpened his knife several more times on the whetstone, then loosened up stiff muscles by throwing a few punches at the moon, and finally walked away from the fire to meet The Monkey. Billy inherently knew where the primate would be found. He did so by using the same mind-invasion trick The Monkey had used on him so many times.

The Monkey was in the south river-valley, near a deep flood depression, next to a dark-orange rock-colored rock feature. Billy's journey to confront his enemy took him over several ravines. Each depression was separated by long slender mounds resembling earthen roots that spread out from the backdrop of mountains. Along the way, Billy surprised a bloated scaly Chuckwalla lizard. It blinked lizard eyes, flipped his ringed tail a few times, and then ran for a rock crevice. Such a technique was the "tried and true" escape method for the Chuckwalla species. Before disappearing, it regarded Billy with reptilian empathy, showing the kind of sensitivity to the human's plight that one would not expect from a old blooded desert dweller. It was probably only another flashback, but as the lizard exited from sight it said, "Good Luck."

Soon after, a passing Tarantula Wasp, irritable for lack of spiders, added his own opinion, "You'll need luck." That comment ended the internal debate on whether or not Billy suffered from drug-induced delusions. Everyone knew that Chuckwallas and Tarantula Wasps could not speak English. Everyone except those individuals that consumed too much acid that is.

The battleground was ringed with an audience of arachnids, arthropods, insects, and of course ... every conceivable variety of desert cacti.

Thimble Jacks, buzz-beetles, snap-hoppers, scorpions, walking-sticks were all present. The animals that waited to view the battle (between Man and Monkey) lived in the harshest of realms, in an environment that could best be described "everything eats everything", instead of the more common phrase "dog eat dog". But at this moment, the thought of devouring each other wasn't a priority. They were ready for carnage, putting aside their interspecies differences, in favor of a good exhibition. There wasn't any animal on earth that doesn't enjoy a good ol' fashion dust-off.

The battle raged for several hours. Man and Monkey held nothing back and neither granted any quarter to the other. Sven's position at the camp allowed him to view a large dust cloud, which was surely the result of violent activity, swirling up from the riverbed and over the ridgeline. Turkey vultures circling high above had a much better perspective than Sven. The scavenger's viewpoint gave each vulture the ability to watch Billy's knife and spear strikes at The Monkey's abdominal cavity. As impressive as Billy's fighting skills were, he still could not deliver a killing blow. Billy paid a heavy price for every poorly-timed or badly-aimed strike that missed the mark. The Monkey responded with bites that took off fingers and opened wounds that bleed profusely. Finally, the loss of blood caused Billy to collapse and exhale his last breath. The Monkey covered the distance between them with one jump. He stood over Billy for a couple minutes, and then bit off an ear to keep as a souvenir. The Monkey walked out from the riverbed, as he went up the hill, he wiped the blood from his hands, and then stopped and howled, in a way that was more hell-hound than primate.

The Monkey crested the hill and turned to look back at the mangled body of his enemy, Billy Halverson. The Monkey exhaled a sigh of relief. At last, after all these years, the "Billy on the Monkey's back," was finally dead.

Down below in the riverbed a sidewinder rattlesnake slithered among the sand and loose pebbles, traveling over the area where Billy Halverson lay dead. The snake thought nothing of the carcass, as the serpent was no stranger to bad outcomes.

The Monkey's route out of the desert and back to lair, took him directly past the campfire. Sven watched the shape get closer. The Monkey's shape shimmered in the desert heat. The glare of the rising sun made it even more difficult for Sven to determine what approached...man or Monkey. Sven took several steps to the south so that the sun was not directly in his eyes, and then re-focused on the image. As he shifted position he shouted Billy's name over and over. There was no response.

Sven to get a better look at the shape before it finally disappeared behind a ridgeline of boulders. What he saw shocked him. It wasn't his brother Billy fading from view. It was some kind of large, disfigured Monkey. Sven ran towards the boulders. He stopped at the ridgeline, wiped the wind-blown sand from his eyes, and frantically searched for the strange figure. He was too late. Whatever the thing was had completed faded from view. Sven stood there for several minutes, until the rational part of his brain, convinced him that is was all a mirage.

He returned to the campfire and stirred the glowing ambers with a slender branch. Every minute or two he glanced into the gunmetal sky and wondered when his brother—Billy, was ever going to return. Sven finally gave up hope (after waiting for several hours) that Billy was going to return to the camp. He went to the riverbed and carried his dead brother back to the camp. He drove back to L.A and alerted the authorities. The case was determined a suicide. The missing ear and fingers were said to be the result of scavenging coyotes. It was no surprise—considering Billy's past, that the resolution was accepted by everybody. What was not accepted was Sven's declaration that Billy had been killed by a Monkey. But an important lesson was not lost on Billy's family and friends....***The Monkey always wins.*** And if one person took that warning to heart, then maybe Billy's death would have meaning. So perhaps it is safe to say "in the end Billy found redemption after all. Billy's friends and family mourned. But no creature, human or otherwise, mourned as much as the bird and lizard clans.

The Monkey woke, screaming, covered in primate sweat. It was the same, reoccurring horrible, nightmare that seemed to come every few days. In the nightmare, he was tormented by a human named Billy, who kept trying to resist the lure of drugs. It always ended the same way, with a bloody battle in some desert. It was a truly horrible nightmare.

Afterwards – Sympathy for the Devil

A well established destroyer of men—The Monkey—was seated on a wobbly three-legged stool located behind the coat rack inside a Chicago Blues Bar. He patiently watched the opening musical acts, waiting for the headliner to take the stage, and then seize the opportunity to corrupt another life. Pictures of musicians, lined the dirty off-color walls, each displayed an evolution of technique and tradition. All were—in one way or another—influential architects of the distinctive "Chicago Blues Sound. Albert King, Howlin Wolf, Hubert Sumlin, "Magic Sam" Maghett, and Buddy Guy were some of the photographs hanging along the hallway. The old black and white shots gave the place atmosphere.

One picture was tacked high on the wall in a separate section of the bar so as not to be missed by the nightly audience. The frame hung in a place that seemed to imply worship, better yet, wonderment, rather than an ordinary display of performers. The lone portrayal designated a very significant part of a rhythmic history. The person in the picture was the legendary "Delta Blues Man"—Robert Johnson. Folklore claimed Robert traded his soul, at the crossroads, to a simian-looking devil, in exchange for the ability to make a guitar note bend like no other. The talent given to him by the devil was so magnificent; it killed him at the youthful age of 27.

A young guitarist, named Randy Turner, preformed on a splintered, well-seasoned, platform. He slid lightning-fast fingers up and down a Gibson Firebird with amazing dexterity, moving so fast it seemed his hands barely touched the neck. Randy was a Chicago native, born between Clark Street and Wacker Drive, and was somewhat of a local hero. His ferocious, yet fluid style with a slide, had earned him the name "The West Wacker Attacker"

Since he was a big fan of George Thourgood and the Destroyers; the somewhat identical nickname was considered an honor, and a title that gave him much satisfaction.

At the conclusion of the set, the audience rose in unison, cheered enthusiastically, and voiced amazement at the kid's unusual chord progressions.

The guitarist thanked the audience and then went into a room reserved for headlining musicians. The manager flipped a switch, and "Sympathy for the Devil" played through Marshall Amps. To ensure that Satan got his due, the volume control was set to the highest level.

It was past midnight and it had been a long set. There was only one more song list to play, so Randy's string bending had to be flawless, especially since a producer from Southland Records was in the crowd. The big-time record executive was in the house for one reason and one reason only; to hear Randy play, and find out if the kid was as good as everyone said.

Randy rested on the sofa and tried to get some energy back. This night could lead to a contract, so appearing slow and lethargic might ruin all he had worked for.

"I'll close my eyes for only a few minutes. The stagehand will alert me in plenty of time to get ready."

He was jolted awake by the sounds of an animal. The noise wasn't frightening; it reminded him of the zoo animal menagerie, adorning the room where he had slept as a baby. He thought back, decades, remembering the mobile, which hung suspended from the ceiling, and dangled tigers, lions, zebras and monkeys over the crib.

Fully awake, Randy stared in disbelief at the friendly-looking Monkey sitting at the end of the sofa. Funny, the primate reminded Randy of the cardboard chimpanzee that entertained him as a baby. The Monkey held out a closed fist, opened it, displaying a handful of drugs.

"You look tired Randy. Want something to make you feel better?" The Monkey asked,

Cue overture—"I see no Evil" – by Television.

Meet our Authors

John Iverson

Taoist/Warrior
Pankretion

John is a practicing Taoist that values knowledge and ex-perience over anything material. His passion to explore began as a Recon Marine while stationed abroad in Africa, South America and Asia. He is a former bodyguard, no holds barred fighter and currently an expert in the ancient Greek Fighting Art of Pankration. He continually strives to balance his extreme physical nature with a more cultural and spiritual side. By bor-rowing from the philosophy of the samurai warrior – Myamoto Mysashi, he strives to be true to the way of the poet/warrior "pen and sword in accord." He also holds close to the ideals of his ancestors so as to someday become an equally dedicated environmentalist.

James Iverson

James is a father of three and an avid fossil collector who teaches his children the value of staying close to the earth. He is a passionate student of Ojibwa and early European history in North America. Both John and James continue to travel in pursuit of interesting people and places. James was the co-writer of the recently published "Hunters and Hearts" as well as the upcoming "Monster Wall". He is also currently training to compete in his first marathon.

Philippe Farcy

Philippe is the proud father of a son and a business consultant in Chicago. He is an enthusiastic student of history, ancient mysteries and mystical lore. He also enjoys and practices MMA, boxing self defense techniques as well as art research, art forensic sciences and Screenwriting.

Acknowledgements

James and John thank the following individuals for their support and assistance during the development of this novel. Ivey Iverson - former Marine and probably the best father and role model that anyone could ask for. He deserves all the credit for any success that comes our way. The Iverson clan – "Saganawa Emil" (caught the biggest fish this year), "Cold Creek Anne", "Gunny Tom – a dead eye shot and keeping of the flame", "Mohave Steve" who is sworn to the quest. "Drumkeeper James" All of them helped in proofing the story. Special thanks to the other writer – "Guillotine Farcy". Thanks to "Rocket Rochelle" for helping us with the last phase of editing. Tommy (Bodi) Iverson and Danielle, plus their new addition to the family. "Coach Matt" a man with an iron-jaw and steel spine. The fearless cliff divers - Danny, Kevin, Dane, Cameron. Brenda and Kiana - "Rider of the Plains." Colorado Buffs football player and Snake-hunter Ryan Iverson – good ol' no# 69. Carlene and Teresa rest in peace. Zeus – the greatest dog and most laid-back friend a man could ask for. The Norton and Seaquist families for their hospitality. Crazy legs Kirk for believing in the project. Jimmy C. for the all laughs. "Mercurial   Mariel" and "Mayhem Mike" for putting the C in the Crazy and the E in Exaggeration.

Mauro V and former Special Forces operator "No Thumbs M.C" for being good friends throughout the tough times. Pirate Killer- Craig. "Big Earl" from Tempe. "Cement Head" and all the other Greco Roman/Pankration fighters - special thanks to coach Jeff Funichello. All the Arty guys from Camp Zukeran. All the Recon Marines from Camp Lejeune and Onslow Beach (Alpha, Bravo, and Charlie companies). The Amphibious

Recon instructors Little Creek. Our Viking Ancestors. The Scottish Highlanders - Jessie and Frank Lindsey. Our Grandfather and his Ojibwa friend - Two Rivers. Dirty-Water Dick Doggitt and R. Garver for the excellent fishing trips.

Development Director and Producer Dal Walton at Invalesco. William Conner and the staff at **A-Argus Publishing for an excellent job.** All the Gang at Wild Wolf. Erica Burke at "McHenry County Living". Julie Anixter at "Think Remarkable".

The Ely Echo, St Cloud Times, The Mesabi Times, Pioneer Press, Dave Wilsey at 13 Moons, Kathy Gresey Managing Editor Lake County Journal, Helen Wilkie and Rose Berens of The First Nation Ojibwa People. The Great Lakes and Long Beach Veterans Hospitals - for the outstanding treatment and ongoing mental health rehabilitation for patient J.W Iverson. Albert Falcon and all the fighters at Warehouse MMA, The Des Moines Extreme Fight Club, Shoreline Pankration, and American Pankration. ***Brian Hass and the other men at the N.P Department for the fair and just treatment.***

Philippe would like to thanks: his writing partners, "Navigator John" and James for allowing him to join their "fight with the pen" club. Also, all his training partners at the warehouse gym. Last but not least, his friends and family for their support and for not locking him up when his imagination runs amok on the pages.